They're Closing The Lamb and Mus

by Richard Cunliffe

Disclaimer

They're Closing The Lamb and Musket is a work of fiction. All characters and events in this publication, other than those clearly in the public domain, are fictitious, and any resemblance to actual persons (living or dead) is entirely coincidental. The same disclaimer is equally applicable to the various companies and organisations named or described herein.

Dedication

This book is for all my friends in the Wynne household. With special thanks to Chloe, who provided the front-cover artwork.

Author's Foreword

They're Closing The Lamb and Musket is my third book of fiction. Whereas the second book (*Fault on Both Sides)*, was a sequel to the first (*All These Nearly Fights)*, this story is neither a prequel nor a sequel: *They're Closing The Lamb and Musket* is a stand-alone novel in its own right. You're not required to read anything I've previously written in order to enjoy it, and nor will you have to buy a further book to see how the story ends. That's because this story begins and ends with the single volume you're holding in your hands as of now.

That said, readers with a memory for such detail will recall that Jimmy Harris – the lead character in *All These Nearly Fights* – once described the attractive female bartender in a city centre pub as "a welcome upgrade on Derek, the sour and moody and landlord at The Lamb and Musket." As such, there's a small degree of interconnectedness between my first novel and this one. In my mind, The Lamb and Musket sits just down the road from the car dealership where Jimmy used to work. But that's the extent of any crossover – it's a matter of authorial whim, and nothing more.

I have one other point before we get down to the story itself. Actually, it's more of a plea than a point, namely the same plea that I've made in earlier books: once you've read the story, please take a moment to post a review of it on Amazon. Your review doesn't have to be long, and it doesn't have to be kind. The most important thing is that it's ***there***, whatever your opinion. Reviews matter a great deal to indie authors like me, and I'd be seriously grateful if you would take the time to post one.

That's it, then. Thanks for being a reader. See you in The Lamb and Musket.

Richard Cunliffe
November, 2019
(@CunliffeRich on Twitter)

Prologue

1) Four Days in June

    1.1) Thursday

    1.2) Friday

    1.3) Saturday

    1.4) Sunday

2) A Week in July

    2.1) Thursday

    2.2) Thursday Next

3) September Fortnight

    3.1) Closure, Minus 2 Days

    3.2) They're Closing The Lamb and Musket

    3.3) Closure, Plus 3 Days

    3.4) Closure, Plus 5 Days

    3.5) Closure, Plus 7 Days

    3.6) Closure, Plus 13 Days

Prologue

Patrick zips up his jeans and turns away from the urinal. He turns slowly and mindfully, as drunks often will, so as to keep his balance and ensure he remains upright. Then, acting on a post-piss afterthought, he stops, turns carefully back, and spits against the porcelain. His phlegm is tinged with pink. Not the vivid red of earlier this evening, but there's definitely some pinkness there – just enough to let him know that his gums are still bleeding, even if only a little.

When, finally, he gets around to washing his hands, he happens to glance at his reflection in the mirror over the sink. The mirror, which is chipped and old, and flaunts the logo of a long-defunct brewery in one lower corner, has, like most things in the pub, only an hour or so remaining of its serviceable life. Drunk and melancholic, Patrick takes a moment to study his reflection carefully and with intent, as if seeing himself properly for the first time in goodness knows how long. It's a handsome face which stares back at him, dark-eyed and a little bit swarthy – prototypically Irish. Patrick raises a hand to his swollen lip and winces slightly. His mouth will be sore in the morning, an additional discomfort to the storm-force hangover he knows is coming to him – a hangover he could no longer avert even were he to draw an immediate line under the night's drinking and go home right away. Patrick glowers at his reflection and breathes a deep, drunken sigh of regret. He's had his share of hangovers, and this is hardly the first time he's been smacked in the mouth, but tomorrow will be made more difficult by the remembrance that it's Ricky he's been fighting with.

Still moving slowly and deliberately, Patrick turns away from the sink and the mirror and the reflection of his bashed-up face. While he stands swaying at the asthmatic-sounding hand dryer, the door opens from the connecting passageway to the bar, and two more drunks come tottering in. Before the door can swing closed again, Patrick briefly absorbs the hullabaloo of several dozen conversations, a sudden torrent of casual laughter, and the playing on the jukebox of what he thinks is *Back in the USSR,* by the Beatles. Again thinking back to events of earlier this evening, Patrick heaves out another drunken sigh. The last night at The Lamb, and things had to end up like this – scrapping with his best frickin mate in the world. Meantime, that jukebox will soon fall silent for the very final time.

Of the two other men who've come into the washroom, one is bloody Dave Bickerstaff – a harmless enough loon for sure, albeit one who can drive a man to distraction with his ceaseless bullshit about the many racy cars and even racier women which he insists have adorned his life. Bickerstaff hastens into one of the two cubicles against the far wall, where he immediately begins the undignified process of throwing up the excesses of booze which he must have put away tonight. The other newcomer is basically still a kid – he's tall and skinny, without much facial hair, but sporting an egregious outbreak of acne on his chin and forehead.

Although Patrick doesn't know the kid, the kid appears to know him. "Alright, Pat?" the kid slurs, weaving his way to the urinals. Although most certainly drunk, the kid's probably less drunk than Patrick, and clearly in a better state than Dave Bickerstaff, who sounds to be throwing up so violently that Patrick wonders whether the lining of Bickerstaff's stomach will egress along with all that puke.

Patrick isn't in a sociable mood. And he objects to the excessive familiarity shown by the kid, whose casual use of use of '*Alright, Pat?'* has served to wind him up far more than it ever should have done. Briefly, Patrick considers having a harsh word to set the young sprog straight – he tries out several replies in his head, each more belligerent than the last. But in the end, the only harsh word he has is with himself, and before saying anything aloud he resolves not to be quite such a pompous twat. "Sure, what's yer name, kiddo?" he finally asks by way of response.

"Darren," comes the reply, the youngster glancing over his shoulder as he stands at the porcelain. "Or Daz, if you like."

"Well, Darren, I'm alright then. And I hope yer alright too."

Patrick pivots away, puts one foot in front of the other, and aims his drunken self towards the door. He realises that in talking to the kid he still managed to sound up his own arse, but he hopes he spoke in a way which wasn't unfriendly. It seems important, right now, to avoid being unfriendly, for the simple reason that he's had enough trouble for one evening, and surely doesn't want any more. But then, as he reaches out to pull open the door, someone else begins pushing from the other side, and when Patrick takes a step back to see who's coming in, he realises, with a sinking sensation in his stomach, that he will be getting more trouble tonight, whether he happens to want it or not.

In walks the huge, shaven-headed fella who Patrick knew would come for him eventually, but whom he'd largely forgotten about during the drunken travails of the evening so far. The man is again wearing his quilted bomber jacket, with the collar worn low so as to show off the image of the snake tattooed upon his neck. Following him through the door, and then fanning out on either flank, are two of his inhospitable-looking friends. The first, Patrick thinks, is the one they call KGB – the wiry-looking bloke who, ridiculous as it sounds, is alleged to keep a knife in his shoe. The other accomplice is female. It's the same attractive but hard-faced brunette from The Beethoven Lounge, the girl believed to have beaten up Ricky's sister while she was queuing for a nightclub. In addition to a sleeveless leather jacket, the brunette has on a tiny mini-skirt and whale-net tights. Her confident manner suggests she's in no way uneasy about walking into the gents' toilet of a crowded pub while wearing very little, and she smiles almost lewdly at Patrick while her accomplice does the talking.

"My, oh my," says Snake Neck, shaking his head in mock regret and making a show of cracking his knuckles. "Looks like you've been fighting with your silly mates already. But you're in the big boys' playground now, and we hit so much harder than your friends do."

Snake Neck takes a step forward, and Patrick instinctively takes one back. The sudden imminence of danger has taken the edge off his drunkenness, and his mind feels sharp as he frantically considers his options. The hard-faced brunette and KGB have advanced either side of Snake Neck, leaving Patrick no room to try wriggling around the sides. And he also has to rule out any thoughts of locking himself in the second cubicle when the pimply kid, Darren (*'or Daz, if you like'),* chooses that particular sanctuary for himself. It seems, then, that there are no credible means of escape, and Patrick seriously considers shouting for help as the three hard-nuts back him further into the room. But he soon dismisses that idea too. The Lamb is packed out for its final night of trading, and it's way too noisy out there for anyone to hear some hapless dickhead hollering in the shitter.

And so, other than curling up and taking his beating, Patrick considers himself to have only one option left. He can take the fight to these three Brit bastards – yeah, that's what he can frickin well do. His uncle and the others back home would certainly approve of the idea, as would his da, for sure. And even Patrick's ma would have to agree that he was only trying to defend himself.

But if he is going to fight, then he needs to fight soon. He's been backed up to the wall by now, the old wrought-iron radiator pressing into the small of his back. He can feel the radiator's gurgling hotness even through his coat, and despite his precarious circumstances he takes a moment to reflect that the radiator will soon fall cold and silent, its working life over, just like those of the jukebox, the mirror over the sink, and all the other hardware to be found around the pub. It's a big beast, that old radiator, and Patrick knows it will be worth a few quid to whoever weighs it in at the scrapyard.

"Nowhere left to run, asshole," says Snake Neck, less nonchalantly this time, from only three paces away. "You're gonna get such a slapping you'll wish you'd stayed in the old country with the rest of your paddy filth."

Now it's the brunette's turn to make an elaborate display of cracking her knuckles. Then she examines her nails and says to Snake Neck, "Let me have first hit."

Snake Neck glances first at her, and then at KGB. He smiles cruelly, but doesn't immediately reply. In fact, for a brief couple of seconds, no one has anything further to say, neither Patrick nor anyone from among his trio of would-be assailants. The only sound to be heard is the dry retching of Dave Bickerstaff, who has emptied his stomach but seemingly can't abate the need to vomit. Patrick cocks an ear towards Bickerstaff's cubicle, and then summons the courage to take a long hard look at the three people who are here to kick his face in.

"That man being sick," says Patrick to Snake Neck. "The only reason he's so ill is he saw yer fuck-ugly face in town tonight."

Snake Neck, who possibly hadn't expected defiance, looks momentarily taken aback, his mouth falling open just enough for Patrick to imagine the big bastard's teeth clacking together from a good hard smack to the jaw.

"I mean, come on," continues Patrick, by now feeling sharp of mind as the adrenal mechanism of fight-or-flight kicks in. "Ya look hideous enough the way God made ya, but even worse with such a shite tattoo as that." Patrick gauges the distance between himself and Snake Neck, and then shuffles minutely to adjust his footing, getting onto the balls of his feet and bunching his fists. "Seriously," he adds, "just take a look at yerself, will ya? Small frickin wonder yer mates are so gruesome as well."

Now all three of them look momentarily surprised. But Patrick knows that 'momentarily' is the operative word in this instance. They will all tear into him in a minute, unless he can launch his own attack while they're still registering his unexpected insolence. It's now or never for Patrick, and he certainly doesn't want it to be never. And so, with surpluses of adrenalin and whiskey coursing their way through him, Patrick puts a foot on the radiator and pushes off hard, launching himself forward with his fists clenched and ready to swing.

1) Four Days in June

1.1) Thursday

Patrick leans backwards – precariously so, some might say – and hooks his instep beneath the bar's foot rail as a precaution against falling arse over eyebrows. Then, having found his position of comfort and custom – to say nothing of finely balanced equilibrium – he takes his first sip of the lager which Mel has just pulled for him. It tastes good. It's cold and mildly hoppy, and is just about fizzy enough, having enough gas but not too much. Patrick finds himself mulling an already well-mulled thought: that whatever failings Derek may have as a landlord (or licensee, as the man himself prefers to be known), he certainly knows how to keep a decent pint. It's a sentiment which is as true of the cold lager favoured by Patrick on these warm summer evenings as it is of the Guinness he's likelier to drink in the winter months, and also, indeed, of the cask beer which Gareth and his cohorts will occasionally press upon him in an effort to lure him into their circle of real-ale fandom.

Mel walks by on the other side of the bar. She's carrying a small crate of empty bottles, one which Patrick knows she'll be taking to the outside yard. "Back in two," she calls over her shoulder.

"Okay," he replies, lifting his glass for a second sip.

"And don't fall off that bloody stool, at least not until I'm back."

Patrick swallows more lager. Mel is out of sight by now, away down the corridor connecting the back of the bar with both the kitchen and the rear yard. "Sure, I've never fallen yet," he shouts after her.

At least not while sober, Patrick could have added, had it been important to him that he make an entirely accurate claim concerning his talent for balancing halfway to the horizontal on a bar stool. Reminiscing for a moment, Patrick finds himself rubbing the region on the back of his head where he needed five stitches one long-ago Christmas Eve – that being the occasion when he did indeed lean so far backwards on his stool that he overbalanced and caused himself an injury. To say he remembers the episode with genuine clarity would be misleading, given that his fall occurred towards the end of a boozing marathon so heavy as to have tested the capacity of any of the legendary Irish drunkards.

He tries to remember whether Mel was actually working here back then. Sure, she's been a fixture behind the bar a good little while by now, but he's been drinking here for longer. Patrick recently turned thirty-one, and has been a regular at The Lamb and Musket these past fourteen years. Indeed, it was even longer ago when his da first brought him here, back when they weren't long off the boat from Belfast and Patrick had to drink Coke because he was way too young for booze.

After another sip of lager, Patrick glances at his cheap and battered wristwatch. Its strap is mangled, its glass scratched, and its case scuffed, but the watch continues to keep good time. It tells him now that the time remains early. It's barely five o' clock on sunny summer evening, and Patrick is all alone in this big old pub – a pub nowadays looking just as ramshackle as the watch on his wrist, but which has, when he thinks about it, served him equally well. Patrick supposes that another half hour will go by before a few of the familiar faces begin drifting in, and until then the old place will continue to feel just like the ghost pub which it is destined, in any event, to become.

Mel returns from outside. Patrick tilts himself slightly further back, and raises his arms like a man walking a tightrope. "Look, Mel," he boasts. "No hands."

Mel tuts, and when she meets his eye it's with a look on her face best described as a hybrid of smile and grimace. It's as if she's partly amused, yet equally full of contempt. "Yeah, Patrick," she replies. "No hands, and no sense either." But before he can answer back, she heads off outside again, having hefted up another crate of empties to take to the back yard.

Patrick watches Mel as she disappears from view. She has on a pair of jeans which are faded and work-worn. They're also fairly tight, and soon Patrick is mulling another of his already well-mulled thoughts: namely that Mel has a lovely rear end. Come to that, she has a pretty good front end too, and before long Patrick finds his mind circling a well-travelled loop, one where he thinks about asking Mel out on a date, before then listing several reasons not to do so. The most credible of these reasons – or is it merely an excuse? – is that Patrick regards The Lamb and Musket as a sanctuary of sorts, the kind of place to come to and drink with friends, speaking freely with them while putting away his cares for an hour or so. The easy conviviality of that situation would change were he in a relationship with the woman behind the bar, for he surely wouldn't be able to let his guard down quite so far as he does at present. It also bothers Patrick that Mel is a wee bit older than him – she's thirty-six, he thinks – and he wonders (mean-spiritedly, he'll admit) whether she'll look as good as she does now in three or five or ten years' time. Sure, the consideration is a callous one on his part (and absurd, too, given that not many of his relationships make it beyond the six-month mark), but having had the thought, Patrick finds he can neither un-think it nor rationalise it away. But then again, if he's really honest with himself, the real reason why Patrick won't ask Mel out is probably the same reason why his other affairs are so short-lived, and that's that –

"Had your blowtorch on today, Patrick?"

Mel is back again, her question breaking his reverie. Patrick sniffs cautiously at the overalls he's wearing before he finally answers her. "Sure I have," he replies. He takes a second sniff at his work clothes, and then a third. "Why – is the smell really so strong?"

"No," she laughs, shaking her head at him. "It's just that the door's open and there's a little bit of breeze. I think it must be carrying the odour in my direction."

"Odour?" Patrick blanches, his glass halfway to his lips. "Sure, why don't you make it sound really unpleasant?"

Mel laughs at him some more. "What would you have me call it, then? A stench, perhaps?"

"If you must," he replies darkly. "Although I thought 'odour' was bad enough."

"Odour it is, then," she confirms, finding and hefting yet another crate of empty bottles. "Anyway, you can relax. The smell isn't all that bad, whatever we decide to call it."

"Good to know," he says, studying her closely as she carries the crate. Mel's wearing a plain t-shirt, one sufficiently short-sleeved for him to admire the slender muscles of her arms. "But sure, Mel," he adds, "you're finding plenty of empties this evening."

She makes a face at him. "Bloody tell me about it."

"Sorry if I've touched a nerve. So what's the craic?"

Temporarily, Mel sets her crate down atop the bar. "The craic, Patrick, is that I haven't been working here the past couple of shifts, and so standards have slipped a bit."

"Ah. I see."

"Actually, no – correction. Standards have slipped a lot. Which is what tends to happen nowadays, whenever I'm not on shift."

"Is it really that bad?" he asks.

"That bad? You see enough of Derek. You must know he's past caring."

Patrick nods – he knows what Mel means – but then he says, "Sure, his beer's still good though, and that has to count for something."

"His beer is good, but that's about all. He's obsessive, still, about the beer, but everything else has gone to the flamin' dogs."

"What about Yasmin?"

Patrick's question concerns The Lamb's newest employee. Originally from out of town, Yasmin is studying at the local college, and is the latest of many students taken on by Derek during his tenure here. Typically, such recruits will work a few shifts over the summer break, and then quit once the autumn term starts. This year, nobody is certain that The Lamb will remain open come the autumn.

"Yasmin," replies Mel, her eyebrows arching angrily, "is part of the problem. Too busy looking the pretty girl and flirting with the boys. She probably does an hour of real work for every shift she's here." Picking her crate back up off the bar, Mel adds, "I'll be kicking up a stink with Derek if the girl doesn't change her act."

"A stink?" queries Patrick, as Mel once again heads through the doorway to the back yard. "Sure, what about an odour? Or maybe a stench?"

"Do one, Patrick," she calls to him over her shoulder.

Again left briefly alone with his beer, Patrick has time to wonder whether Mel's angst is purely because of an unfair workload, or whether she's a bit wound up – just as the locals all are – by the loss of their latest battle to keep The Lamb and Musket open. After all, while Patrick and the others will be losing a place to meet up and drink, Mel (along with Derek) will be losing a means of livelihood.

On the other hand, Patrick supposes that it's perfectly possible for any woman, Mel included, to get bent out of shape by the super-charged sex appeal of Yasmin. The girl is lithe and slim and leggy; she has inky black hair and big blue eyes, and she has full, luscious lips which Patrick's da reckons would have reduced Marilyn Monroe to fits of insane jealousy. But these are just words, and Patrick knows that words aren't enough to describe the utter sexual magnetism of The Lamb's latest – and probably final – recruit. "She's the full package," is what Ricky said of Yasmin on her first Saturday evening in the job, and Patrick hasn't thought of a better summation, however clichéd and objectifying Ricky's clipped appraisal may have sounded.

Sorry Mel, thinks Patrick. *You may not like Yasmin's work ethic, but the girl's fit as fuck, and that's probably why there are enough punters coming here to leave you with so many crates of empties.*

After a couple of long swigs, Patrick sets down his near-empty glass, and looks up as two fellas walk in through the door. One of them is roughly Patrick's own age; the other is older and grizzled, probably knocking on fifty. Both men are in shorts and vests; both are substantially tattooed; and both have arms reddened by the sun. Patrick knows them, although not well, even though they, like he, come here often. They're the kind of people he's on nodding terms with – the sort with whom he'll exchange an 'Alright mate?' if he happens to pass them in the doorway – but Patrick doesn't know their names and would probably forget them if he were told. The two fellas aren't from Patrick's side of the arterial main road on which The Lamb and Musket sits. They're from the side hosting the flats and the council houses, as opposed to the sprawl of private housing to be found on Patrick's half of the divide. On an evening when he's having several thoughts which he'd admit are uncharitable, Patrick finds himself wondering whether he remembered to lock his van. Now that Mel has returned and is busy serving the new arrivals, Patrick wanders casually to the open front door of The Lamb, and plips the 'lock' button on his remote without removing it from the pocket of his overalls.

Patrick returns to the bar. He stops to swap a couple of words with the two fellas about how warm it is outside, but soon walks back to where he'd left the last knockings of his beer. Sitting down, he once again leans the barstool backwards and hooks a foot under the rail. Then he drains his glass and waits. When Mel finishes serving the two newcomers, she wordlessly asks him whether he'd like another, channelling the question via nothing more than a swift glance. Almost as economically, he replies with a brisk little nod, before reverting to the spoken word when he says, "Have one yourself."

"Thanks," says Mel. Then, maybe because Patrick's little stroll to the door brought more of that *odour* in on the breeze, she asks, "What exactly is it, that blowtorch smell? It's kind of metallic and kind of sulphurous – the sort of thing you might smell if you stood half-a-mile downwind from the gates of hell."

"The gates of hell? Sure, maybe I should bottle it then, and call it Lucifer or something."

"The name sounds a winner," she replies. "Although I'm less sure about the actual scent."

"You asked a good question, though," says Patrick, brandishing a twenty pound note. "About the exact nature of the smell, I mean. See, I mostly use the blowtorch when I want to heat up some piping and bend it into shape. Like today, for instance – when I'm fitting someone a new boiler."

Patrick studies his second lager while it settles in its glass, and then continues his explanation. "The blowtorch is fuelled by a canister of gas – a mixture of butane and propane. Neither gas has a natural smell, but the suppliers deliberately manufacture one, so that you can tell when the stuff is leaking."

"And that's what I can smell on you, then?"

"You know, I've never been sure. What you're smelling may actually be from the copper pipe. That doesn't have a natural smell either, but I've heard that the bacteria on our skin reacts with the copper to create one when we handle the stuff."

Mel hands him his change. "Bacteria – that's nice," she says. "Lovely topic of conversation."

"You're the one who had to ask about work stuff. I can talk about something else if you like."

"Not politics, thanks – especially not the heavy Irish stuff. It's too early in the evening."

"Nor have I had enough to drink."

"There's time enough, Patrick," she murmurs. "There's plenty time enough."

Patrick takes a first sip from his second pint. He jangles his van keys at her. "There may be time," he replies. "But for now at least, I happen to be driving."

While Mel and Patrick have been talking, the two fellas in vests and shorts have produced cigarettes and are making their way to the car park. There, they'll be able to sit at one of the two ageing patio tables which comprise Derek's concept of a beer garden. On their way through the door, they pass Gareth coming in. Gareth is from Patrick's side of the main road, but knows the names of everyone from the other side as well. Patrick isn't certain, but he thinks he hears Gareth greet one of the blokes as Bill, and the other as Ted. Remembering the film, Patrick smirks into his beer no less than if Gareth had called the pair of them Stan and Ollie.

Next second, Gareth has joined Patrick at the bar. Other than a bristly moustache, Gareth is recently clean shaven, and his thick, greying hair looks damp from the shower. "Hello, Melanie," he says brightly. Then, to Patrick – who's five ten, and of average build – he adds, "Good evening, big man." He claps Patrick on the back and shakes his hand at length. Gareth performs both actions with vigour, despite the apparently precarious slant of the stool on which Patrick is sitting. Gareth's learnt over the years that Patrick isn't easily unbalanced.

"Hi, Gareth," replies Patrick, noting the sheaf of printed paper that Gareth's clutching in one hand. Gareth is perhaps ten years older than Patrick, and this evening his clothes do reflect a degree of seniority. Gareth's look is one which might be summarised as 'smart casual' – a style Patrick feels is best epitomised by the way people look at wedding receptions when they haven't been invited to the main ceremony.

Gareth takes a step back and appears to size Patrick up. His eyes are grey and flinty, and he holds Patrick in their gaze for a second or two longer than Patrick feels is necessary. Patrick wonders whether Gareth is about to mention the smell on his overalls, but when Gareth finally does speak all he says is, "You're early tonight."

Making another check of his battle-scarred watch, Patrick sees that it isn't yet half-five. "I've been working locally," he replies. "Fitting a new boiler at one of the neighbour's houses."

"A new boiler?" queries Gareth. "Hell's bells. At this time of year?"

"Sure, it's the best time to get it done. You don't want one fitting on a cold day in January – not when you actually need your central heating."

"I suppose you're right." Gareth looks thoughtful, stroking his moustache – caressing it, really – between finger and thumb. "June is better than January when you put it like that."

"Well anyway, I was finished pretty early, so I thought I'd have a quick couple of pints before heading home."

Gareth's face falls at that remark, which is when Patrick finally makes the connection he should have made after noting Gareth's sheaf of paper and smartness of attire. When Gareth said that Patrick was early, he didn't meant it in general terms; he meant that Patrick was early for something specific. And that something specific will no doubt be the latest of Gareth's formal meetings, one of many convened in the cause of protecting The Lamb and Musket from the pitiless mercies of the bulldozers.

Mel, meanwhile, has pulled Gareth a pint of real ale, and now she comes round from her side of the bar to take the sheaf of paper from his hand. No doubt, Patrick realises, the papers are fliers or posters of some sort, to be pinned up on the walls or distributed among the crowd later on. The thickness of the sheaf suggests to Patrick that the print run was determined by someone with a heady sense of optimism, especially given that this is a Thursday evening and the crowd will be smaller than at weekends. But then Gareth was always like that, and still is, even at his age. The man forever has his head in the frickin clouds.

Mel glares at Patrick from over Gareth's shoulder. The look she gives him isn't sympathetic. *You prat*, Patrick reads into it. *You dozy thick prat. You've gone upsetting Gareth, and now you're going to bugger off home and leave me to deal with him. I'll have him bending my ear all night about how that laddie from Belfast isn't committed to the cause.*

Patrick takes a sip of beer while he works out how to back pedal from the cul-de-sac he has ridden down. "Sure," he says to Gareth. "I'll get myself a shower because Mel's complaining about the odour that's on me. Then I'll grab a quick bit of dinner and come back for your meeting. No good us giving up the fight, is it?"

At that, Gareth smiles almost paternally at Patrick, seemingly thrilled to have won the latest in a million tiny battles comprising a war that's lasted two years and counting. "Good man," he replies, pumping Patrick's hand no less vigorously than before, while lapsing into the faux Irish vernacular which he occasionally adopts when trying to be comradely with The Lamb and Musket's Belfast brethren. "Good man, yourself, Patrick. Good man, yourself." With the handshaking done, Gareth spends a few seconds stroking his moustache, and then asks. "What about your dad? Will he make it along tonight?"

Patrick tells Gareth he's not sure about his da, but reaffirms that he, himself, will be back down shortly. Then he finishes off his pint and heads out to the car park. On the way, he brushes close to Mel, who's pinning one of Gareth's posters to a wall, and murmurs, "Happy now, sweetheart?" She wags a finger at him and tells him to make sure he really does come back. And on time, as well. Also, he should be sure to use plenty of strong gel while in the shower.

Outside, an early-evening sun shines relentlessly on the cracked and dusty macadam of the car park. The shoulders of the two blokes – Bill and Ted? – are red raw and beginning to peel. The pair of them have nearly finished their first pints, and both are smoking greedily, as though they're going head-to-head in a two-man race to the emphysema ward. The main road is looking busy by now – mostly with traffic headed out of town on the journey home from work – and Patrick supposes that to sit out here is to get fumes enough into your lungs, without having to light up any frickin cigarettes.

Patrick gives a nod to Bill and Ted, and then walks to where his van has now been neighboured by Gareth's car. Patrick's latest van is nearly new – he's had it barely a month – and the paint job is bright and shiny. **Patrick Mackey**, it proclaims. **Plumbing and Heating Engineer**. Then, after his phone numbers, email, and social media blurb, it says, **Gas Safe Registered. All Plumbing and Heating Services. Fully Guaranteed. Competitive Prices**.

Gareth's car, in comparison, is fifteen years old. It's a dark blue Ford Fiesta, and its best days are long past. Gareth being Gareth, the car is scrupulously clean, even during a hot and dusty spell like this. But the little car is starting to rust around the arches, and its bonnet is covered in stone chips. Patrick knows that when Gareth leaves the pub tonight, the Fiesta will start up noisily, emitting enough smoke to render the car park redolent of a Napoleonic battlefield.

As Patrick unlocks his van, it's time for another of those well-mulled thoughts, albeit one less well mulled than those concerning the proven quality of Derek's beer or the conjectured pleasure of taking Melanie to bed. This thought concerns Gareth; more specifically it concerns Gareth's sense of priorities. Gareth's an able and intelligent man – at least to Patrick's way of thinking – but he's one who's earning minimum wage in a warehouse job, working alongside people half his age. It seems to Patrick that it's all very well throwing yourself into the service of your community – and, Christ knows, he's had relatives across the water who've died for theirs – but there comes a time when a man has to look after his own interests. By which Patrick means that Gareth, by now in his early forties, ought to be thinking about his future and trying to improve his prospects, rather than coaching kids' football and getting wrapped up in a fight to keep the pub open. It's a fight which Gareth is fighting harder than anyone – Derek the landlord included – and which is sure to end badly in any event.

Patrick hoists himself into the cab of his van for the three-minute drive home. It's frickin hot behind the big glass windscreen, and after starting the engine he cranks the air con' up to the max. Before he sets off he sends a text to Ricky: *Got myself lumbered with one of Gareth's rallies later on. Any chance you can come along with some decent conversation? I'll see if Vince is free as well.*

Text sent, Patrick puts the van into gear and sets off for home. He idly wonders how Gareth would react if he learnt that Patrick has significant shareholdings not only in The Hippy Hops Pub Company – the business looking to sell the piece of land on which The Lamb and Musket sits – but also in Shop City Supermarkets, the retail chain intent on buying up the site. A little less idly, Patrick also wonders whether Ricky, if he turns up tonight, might bring more than decent conversation. He wonders whether Ricky might bring Caroline, his wife these past ten years.

+++++

Although Mel offers to help him move some of the tables around, Gareth won't hear of the idea. The tables are not light, and Gareth – who'll freely admit to some old-fashioned ideas regarding what he calls the propriety of women – insists on doing the grunt work himself. He's more than happy, however, for Mel to put a up a few posters, and he takes a secret, stolen pleasure from watching her move gracefully around the bar in her tight jeans and t-shirt.

It doesn't take Gareth very long to arrange the furniture into his intended layout – he's done the job often enough before. He hauls two tables close to the wall, so that he and his lieutenants can sit behind them while looking out at everyone. He then takes the chairs from some other tables, and arranges them in rows for his audience to face him. Finally, he takes the temporarily redundant, chair-less tables, and moves them away into one corner. Gareth treats the furniture carefully throughout his manoeuvring – handling it as though it were his own – even though everything's a couple of decades old, and is showing such signs of both use and misuse that Derek would struggle to give the stuff away.

By the time Gareth has finished, he has sweat marks on his shirt and The Lamb is divided roughly into two halves – one for the people attending his meeting, the other for those simply out for a drink. He's thirsty after his exertions, and after draping a cloth over the two top tables, Gareth takes a breather to finally drink the pint that Mel pulled for him when he walked in. While he drinks, he ruminates, not for the first time, that it would be better if The Lamb had a raised platform onto which he could have leveraged his table. He isn't a tall man, and he believes that he could command more of his audience's attention if everyone had a better view of him. But there isn't a raised area. The Lamb and Musket is big and flat and rectangular in layout; it's the size of a village hall or an aerobics studio, and is architecturally bland. The bar itself runs along two thirds of one wall, and on one side of it there's a door leading to the toilets. Across on the other side of the room, alongside the main entrance, there's a jukebox, a dartboard, and a community noticeboard. Although the jukebox and dartboard are both somewhat antiquarian, each sees plenty of use. The noticeboard is less well utilised, save for Gareth's bulletins concerning both the anti-closure campaign and the results and league placings of his two junior football teams. These aspects apart, The Lamb is fairly featureless, beyond a ramshackle assortment of furniture and two floor-to-ceiling support pillars standing centrally within the lounge.

Clutching his half-finished ale, Gareth wanders to the jukebox and inserts a pound – sufficient to buy him three plays. He selects music by Blur and Lewis Capaldi; Blur because he thinks Britpop is still cool, and Lewis Capaldi because he hopes Mel will approve. Gareth lingers over his choice of third track, finally choosing The Beatles' *Back in the USSR*. He wonders whether this final choice may be inspired by the ideological consideration that there were no profiteers back in the USSR – no one buying and selling pubs for the sake purely of their balance sheets and shareholders.

Mel has finished putting up the posters. Gareth is happy to acknowledge that their design lacks creativity, but believes they do the essential job of grabbing the attention of anyone who happens to see them. Against a plain white background, there's a simple message in big red capitals.

WE'RE STILL FIGHTING #SAVETHELAMBANDMUSKET

Mel has stuck a couple of posters on each wall, two more low down on the bar surround, one on each face of the supporting pillars, and a succession of them on the wall behind Gareth's table. There remain a good few left over, and these she sets down on the corner of the bar, at the same time catching Gareth's eye, and, by imitating a drinking motion, asking if he wants another pint. "Not yet, thank you," he calls across the room, "but is there any chance of a cup of tea?"

"I'll get the kettle on," she replies, heading out back and leaving Gareth temporarily alone.

He takes a look around. It seems such a big room when it's this empty of customers, so big that his and Mel's best efforts at dressing the walls seem drowned. Gareth preferred The Lamb back in the day, before it was knocked through, when there were three rooms, namely a lounge bar, a tap-room and a snug. But that was then, and this is now. The last refit was more than a decade ago, and although he liked the old Lamb more, the task at hand is to save the newer one. This isn't about the building and the architecture, after all, nor the fads and vogues of interior designers and marketing gurus. It's about people and community, and about avoiding the dispersal of both. Where is everyone going to go if they haven't got The Lamb?

Mel returns from the kitchen. Bill and Ted come in from outside, and Mel begins pulling new pints for them both. Gareth makes a quick check of the table he'll command for the meeting– he absentmindedly smooths out the already smooth cloth – before joining Bill and Ted at the bar. "Kettle's on," says Mel. She's already pulled a pint for Bill – the elder of the two – and has Ted's glass half-filled under the lager tap. "I'll get your tea made in a second, Gareth."

"Thanks, Melanie," he replies. "There's no rush." Then, to Bill and Ted, he says, "Are you here for long, gentlemen? Can I count on your support at our meeting tonight?"

There follows a moment's awkward silence – awkward, at least, for Gareth. He couldn't swear that there's any awkwardness felt by either Bill or Ted because he doesn't know them all that well – this in spite of his making the effort to learn and use their names, having read that doing so is a good way of making friends with people. What he does know about Bill and Ted is that they both live a little way back on the other side of the main road. He also knows that they're in here a great deal (or rather outside of here a great deal, given how much the two of them smoke), spending enough time at The Lamb for Gareth to wonder whether either of them have jobs. Employed or not, they don't appear to lack money either way, and they always look expensively dressed, even when, like today, they're in their vests and shorts. Certainly, they seem to spend fortunes on beer and cigarettes, and the notion of their relative wealth is affirmed to Gareth by the bulkiness of the wad which Ted produces in order to pay for their drinks. "There you go, doll," says Ted to Mel, breaking the silence as he peels off a twenty and flips it across the bar.

Bill, meanwhile, has removed his next cigarette from the packet, and is holding it between two fingers of the same hand with which he's also clutching his pint. He runs his free hand through his close crop of grizzled, greying hair. "Thing about your meeting," he says to Gareth, as he eases from the bar. "You've lost now, haven't you? They're about to grant planning permission, so I hear."

"Trust me, Bill. Nobody's lost yet. There's an appeals process."

"There may be an appeals process, cocker, but can you not hear that noise?" Bill cups his free hand theatrically to one ear. "It's the sound of a chubby wench limbering up her vocal cords."

"Why not come for ten minutes?" asks Mel, handing Ted his change. "When the meeting starts, I mean. Come for ten and just listen to Gareth. At least you'd give your lungs a break from all that smoking."

"I'd spare ten minutes for you," Ted says to Mel, rolling his shoulders and smirking. "What time d'you get off tonight?"

Mel stiffens and gives Ted a cold look. "Originality isn't your forte, is it?" she replies, before turning away and heading out back to make Gareth his cup of tea.

Ted briefly watches Mel from behind, before he turns from the bar and joins Bill for the walk outside. "I'd shag the arse off that," he says to his mate.

"She's a bit old for you," replies Bill, clapping Ted on one shoulder. "What about the other one – the new one."

"Her as well," says Ted with a laugh. "Fuck me, especially her as well. I'd split the both of them clean. Count on it that I would."

Once more alone at the bar, Gareth sighs deeply, and lets his shoulders drop. Saving the pub – *the community* – is all well and good, but there are some people he'd simply rather weren't part of it. Yet he needs such people – he needs the Bills and he needs the Teds. Simply put, Gareth needs numbers on his side. The more people the better. Yet, Hell's bells, his need for numbers will consume his soul the way that things are going.

+++++

Ricky stands at the bar of The Lamb and Musket, and listens in while Patrick takes a phone call. Although he is vaguely interested, Ricky's attention is casual and half-hearted, for this is just another variation on a conversation he's seen and heard Patrick have many times before. In a minute or so, Patrick will hang up and share some banter about what was said – maybe raising a few laughs along the way – and then that will be that. The matter will be forgotten, and the conversation will move along to territories new.

But in contrast to his own relaxed attitude, Ricky can see that Vince is absolutely engrossed by Patrick's carry-on. Vince is sitting on the very edge of his bar stool, upright and stock still, his big brown eyes wide and scarcely blinking as he concentrates hard on what Patrick has to say. Vince, too, has seen and heard all this many times before, yet for him it's always fascinating – forever a big deal.

Ricky knows that Vince is intrigued, in part at least, because Vince himself struggles to use the phone effectively. And Vince is equally mesmerised by what happens to Patrick's accent during calls like this one. Ricky and Vince have known Patrick for twenty years, since the three of them were all aged ten, and Patrick – newly arrived from Belfast – was thrust into their class at school. Patrick's accent back then was so thick that it could have found use as a doorstop, and his new classmates found him almost unintelligible. Two decades of living among the Brits has softened his way of speaking, but when, like now, Patrick gets belligerent or exasperated, or just plain angry, that accent coarsens again – it reverts to type and he starts to sound like his dad, a man whose utterances certainly haven't been moderated by twenty years of English life. Regarding Patrick's old man, Ricky can't imagine that Mr Mackey Senior – currently nursing a pint with his own Brit friends, at a table off to the right – is susceptible to being moderated in any way or by any event. Certainly not by the closure of The Lamb; probably not even the ending of the world.

Customarily tilted on his bar stool, one foot hooked under the rail, Patrick is mostly motionless, save for his free arm, with which he picks up and sets down his pint, and with which, while his pint is set down, he gestures expansively while putting the caller straight on a few things. "Sure, my advert says I'm a plumber," he tells them, slurring ever so slightly after a good few beers, "and that's because I am a frickin plumber. But there's no law of the land which says plumbers have to be on call twenty-four hours, and there's nothing in my advert which says I am." Patrick falls silent and listens for all of five seconds, frustration and disdain writ large on his face. "I'm no different to you," he then resumes. "Yer not open twenty-four hours. If I come to you for food and drink at eight-thirty in the morning, yer doors are closed. Well it's nine-fifteen at night, and my frickin doors are closed for now."

Patrick is a study in contemptuous exasperation; Vince a study in focused concentration. Ricky smirks to himself, and shakes his head while he searches the pockets of his suit for cigarettes and lighter. An hour ago it was so noisy in hear that neither he nor Vince would have been able to listen in on Patrick's call. Most likely Patrick wouldn't have been able to hear himself, and would have had to take his phone outside. That was because there'd been a good crowd in for Gareth's meeting, and the longer it went on – and the more beer that got drank – the noisier proceedings became. 'We're Still Fighting,' proclaim the posters. *Sure we are*, thinks Ricky. *But for how much longer, realistically, for all the drink-fuelled belligerence on show tonight?*

Cigarette in hand, Ricky slides off his stool and gives Vince a quick nudge. It's a bit like nudging the wall of a dam. Like Ricky himself, Vince is a big guy, but whereas Ricky has been neglecting the gym in recent months, Vince is lifting weights five nights a week. "I'm going for a smoke," Ricky says. "Back in five."

"Okay," comes the reply, Vince taking his eyes off Patrick just long enough to flash Ricky one of his smiles. It's a brilliant, humongous smile – big and wide, honest and trusting.

The weather's been warm today, but by now it's cool outside. Ricky is grateful for some respite from the fevered atmosphere indoors, for The Lamb and Musket still feels charged with tension more than half-an-hour after the meeting wound down. Ricky lights a cigarette, and then checks his phone. He exhales a big plume of smoke which meanders away in the glow cast by the lights above the Lamb's front door.

There's a text awaiting him. It's five minutes old. He missed the hum of its arrival while he was still indoors. The message is short and simple. 'When?' it reads.

'Ten or just after,' he texts back.

Ricky slides his phone away and passes a few moments chatting with the other smokers out here. Most have had four or five pints to drink, and that's three or four more than he's put away. Ricky has been on soft drinks and coffee since his one and only lager of the evening, having chosen to exercise caution on account of the driving he still has to do. Accordingly he's considerably less oiled than most, and when a pissed-up Dave Bickerstaff lurches towards him, looking to scrounge a light for his fag, Ricky holds the lighter at arm's length so as to stop Bickerstaff getting too close and spilling beer over his expensively-tailored jacket.

"Whaddaya think, Ricky," asks Bickerstaff, swaying in the night air and dragging on his cigarette. "Good meeting, yeah? We can still stick it to the suits and scumbags, don't you reckon?"

Ricky smooths his lapels, making the point that he himself is wearing a suit – eight-hundred quid's worth, come to that. But the gesture seems lost on Bickerstaff, who continues to stand and sway, and who looks at Ricky through eyes turned squinted and watery by his own cigarette smoke. *Yes Dave*, thinks Ricky. *We'll stick it to them alright. Because piss and vinegar, and speeches and posters, and the drunken proclamations of deluded morons will work absolute fucking wonders against business acumen, legal expertise and downright financial muscle.*

"Totally, Dave," says Ricky, still maintaining a cautious distance from the bloke. "We'll stick it to them alright."

A good few people begin leaving The Lamb. While finishing his cigarette, Ricky chats perfunctorily with several of them, exchanging sentiments similar to those he swapped with Dave Bickerstaff. Those two pricks, Bill and Ted, who live somewhere in the flats, and earn a decent crust fencing stolen goods, head off into the night, moving slowly, as if the beer in their bellies is weighing them down. For all that they've had to drink, though – which must be plenty, given that Patrick said they arrived not long after five, and they're not slow to finish a pint – they go quietly and with less fuss than some, for they're as practised at drinking as they are at petty crime. Then Patrick's dad comes out as well. He's another one who knows how to manage his beer, and he too is less full of bravado than the blokes who clearly lack that particular competence. He doesn't speak of sticking it to anyone, but he does compliment Ricky on his suit – "Bonny tie as well, Richard" – and then tells him he should quit smoking, just as he's been saying since Ricky was twelve or thereabouts. Then, with his piece said, Mackey Senior is away home, and Ricky heads back indoors.

The Lamb and Musket is very quiet now, the remaining customers having broken away into a few small clusters. Gareth, leader of the movement to keep the place open, is talking to the landlord, Derek, in a corner near the door. Gareth's had a good night, his talk of appeals and of fighting on (and on) having gone down well, and his eyes are bright and animated as he chats with their host. Gareth's got one arm folded across his chest while using his opposite hand, typically, to smooth and stroke his Magnum P.I. moustache. Ricky can tell that Gareth gets well and truly off on all of this, but wonders what the man will do when his big crusade is over and the fight is finally lost. For the matter of that, when will the fight ever be lost in Gareth's mind? Ricky suspects not before the bulldozers have done their work.

Derek, the landlord, is a little older than Gareth – he must be mid-forties, Ricky guesses, or fifty even – and he doesn't show quite the same enthusiasm for saving The Lamb from closure. Okay, he may be nodding in agreement while Gareth prattles on, but his eyes show tiredness rather than vigour. His shoulders are drooped, his thinning hair looks lank and unwashed, and his demeanour is that of somebody beaten-down by events. The absence of a tiger from Derek's tank may be due to his hailing from out of town and therefore lacking any real affinity for The Lamb; yet Ricky believes there's more to it than that. Derek's an old hand, one who knows the licensed trade thoroughly, and who understands the lie of the land well enough to realise that when a pub company decides to close and sell up a site, close and sell up is what they do, however long the selling up may take. They're not in the habit of reversing such decisions when confronted by opposition from their tenant, his customers, or the pub's wider community. They don't ever say, 'Tell you what boys, we've had a bit of a rethink. We'll let you keep the doors open awhile longer yet.'

Ricky sees Gareth glancing towards him, as if trying to catch his attention. But Ricky doesn't have time for another of Gareth's sermons, and so he pretends not to notice, turning his back as he moves to re-join his friends at the bar. He walks close by the new barmaid, Yasmin. She's wearing a lilac vest, thin-strapped so as to leave exposed a sunflower tattoo on the creamy skin of her left shoulder. With no one needing serving, Yasmin had been idly examining her fingernails, but she looks up as Ricky draws near, and, unlike Gareth, she manages to catch his eye. But Ricky stays silent, refusing to fawn over her the way so many of the mugs in here do. Instead, he meets her gaze head on, half-smiling at her, before he walks on by without a word. *Yes, I'm going to fuck you*, he thinks. *Not yet, though. Just wait your turn*.

Patrick and Vince are where he left them, at the far corner of the bar. Patrick's giving his leg muscles a rest, having returned his stool to the vertical and unhooked his foot from the rail. His phone call has ended, and so he and Vince are now nattering with the other barmaid, Mel, who has interrupted a glass-collecting expedition to stop by and chat. Mel's another good-looker to Ricky's way of thinking. She must be – what? – thirty-five, maybe going on forty, but she's certainly tidy for her age. And so what if Mel is playing a couple of leagues down from Yasmin? There's no disgrace in that, and Ricky's sure that Mel would make a pretty good *Plan B.* Only thing is, he doesn't need a *Plan B* very often. When Ricky makes a *Plan A* it normally work out fine.

"I'm not putting up with it," Mel is saying to Patrick. She sounds angry – not screamingly hysterical like birds can sometimes get, but most definitely pissed off. "I'm going to have a serious word with her," continues Mel. "And if that doesn't work, I'm going to have one with Derek."

Although Ricky's late to the scene, it's pretty obvious to him what Mel's gripe is about. She's out here, collecting glasses – and there's a fuck-load of them to collect, in fairness – while Yasmin's just preening herself behind the bar. *Why don't you take it outside with her?* Ricky thinks of saying to Mel. *Patrick and I could sell tickets for that one.*

But Patrick, meanwhile, has come up with a less gratuitous reply. He has his phone out again, and is waving it around more expansively than he might have done had he consumed a little less beer. "Sometimes that's just what you have to do," he says to Mel. "You have to give it to people straight. Sure, that's what I just did with those people who rang me up. And once I'd told them straight, we all got along much better than before."

Mel lightens up a little, smirking at Patrick's theatrics and his winning smile, as if indulging a child, or, indeed, a favourite drunk. "Nice one," she says. "So you got them sorted, somehow?"

Vince, whose mouth had been turned down while Mel vented her anger, breaks into a big, child-like smile of his own when he sees her looking happy again. *God bless you, Vince*, thinks Ricky. He knows that Mel is very far from Vince's idea of a Plan B. She's more like a Plan AAA+ to Vince, who dreams the impossible dream whenever he walks in here and sees her working behind the bar. It's this realisation which compels Ricky – who isn't normally introspective – to berate himself slightly for his cynical attitude towards everyone's efforts at keeping The Lamb open. He thinks about Vince not seeing Mel again once the place closes, and wonders how his dear old mate will ever cope.

But for now, it seems, Vince is all set on impressing his poster girl. "Patrick… set them straight," he says, very slowly, and very deliberately, and with great care. "But then he… helped them as well. Gave them… some advice."

After that there's a pause, while Mel, Patrick and Ricky wait to see if Vince has anything further to say. He sits extremely still, his lovely smile now lost to the effort of concentration. There's a faraway look in those wide brown eyes, while his sandy hair, as ever trimmed short, almost seems to bristle from the effort simply of thinking. Just when they all think he's finished for now, he twice runs his left hand – the one with its little finger missing and third finger misshapen – urgently through that short crop of hair. And then, suddenly, Vince's big smile is back in place.

"I… remember now," he says, still taking pains over every word. "Patrick told them to… switch on their taps. And to… turn off their water. At the mains."

"Sure, buddy," says Patrick. "You've got it dead on." It's a simple acknowledgment of the sort that Ricky and Patrick – and Mel to some extent – are in the habit of offering to Vince whenever he manages similar feats of speech and recall. There's a little bit of praise on offer, but certainly not too much, as nobody wants to patronise a good mate.

Vince gives Patrick a little nod, and then picks up his glass of tomato juice. His doing so is usually a sign that he has nothing to add for the moment, and so Patrick takes up the thread when he says, "I told them they'd have to close early, too, because they'll have no water for the bathrooms once the system drains down. But sure, they'd have had to do that anyway – whether I was coming over tonight, or tomorrow morning as I've agreed."

Ricky takes a sip from the glass of Coke left half-finished when he went outside for a smoke. "Who are we talking about?" he asks.

"A place called The Beethoven Lounge," replies Patrick. "It's a new bar in town."

Ricky hasn't seen or heard of it, and his face must show as much because Mel adds, "It's on Honeycomb Street, across from the Turkish barbers."

"Oh yeah," says Ricky, noting again the big boyish smile which Vince finds for Mel when she's talking. "I know where you mean. Where the vegan place closed down."

"You're dead on as well," says Patrick. "Anyway, after all the money they've spent doing up the place, they've now got water coming through the ceiling above the bar. So I told them how to drain down their system 'til I get there. Most likely they've got a leaking tank."

"But surely," asks Ricky, "they'll have an overflow pipe for that?"

"Which is fine when the stopcock fails, causing the tank to overfill. But it doesn't help when the tank itself is leaking, and that's what I'm guessing has happened, probably at the inlet. Sure, it's a five minute job if I'm right. I can probably fix it just by fitting a washer."

"So you won't be needing your blowtorch," says Mel.

Patrick swills down the last of his pint. "I won't," he replies. "Not unless I decide to burn the place down."

"I wouldn't put it past you," says Ricky. "Your lot have got form for that."

It's a quip which raises a small laugh from everyone, Patrick included, although he does flip Ricky the finger. It's a joke that Vince picks up quickly as well, Ricky having ribbed Patrick along similar lines many times over the years.

Ricky also has in mind to ask why anyone would call their bar The Beethoven Lounge, but a glance at his watch tells him that time is tight if he's to make his rendezvous as promised via text. "About time I was off," he says, finishing his coke. "I need to check that I've had enough workers turn up for a shift at Dave Duffy's pie factory."

"Let's hope they're all there," says Mel, moving away with a foot-long stack of empty pint glasses. "Otherwise you'll have to work a nightshift there yourself."

"That's happened in the past" replies Patrick, before Mel disappears entirely from earshot. "Ricky's had to swap his best gangster's suit for some overalls and a hair net."

Ricky grimaces at the memory, but doesn't expand upon it as he readies himself to leave. He enacts with Vince their standard protocol for saying either hello or goodbye, thumping his beefy mate in the upper arm, then steeling himself slightly as Vince returns the punch with just a little interest added. Similarly, he clasps hands with Patrick and they say they'll see each other soon – Saturday for golf if not before. Ricky does his best to pretend that the hint of reproach in Patrick's eye isn't actually there – it's a look that's also becoming standard protocol these days, one reflecting Patrick's clear suspicion that Ricky is off to do more than simply check on his workforce.

His goodbyes said, Ricky makes his way out to the car park. Gareth manages to collar him along the way, breaking off from hectoring of Derek to ask Ricky how he thinks the evening went. Ricky feels that the time is coming to tell Gareth a few home truths on the futility of his campaign, but because time is tight he simply pumps Gareth's hand and tells him more power to his elbow.

Once outside the door, and after quickly checking his watch, Ricky lights a cigarette from which he'll get only two puffs – three at the most – during the brief walk to his car. He does indeed plan to check in briefly at the pie factory – hoping to Christ that he doesn't have to get on the phone and round up any of his staff – before moving swiftly on to an illicit rendezvous with his latest mistress. Yet his mind keeps coming back to the couple of hours just spent at The Lamb, and to Gareth's rallying of the troops for one final showdown.

Little knowing that Patrick thought much the same thoughts earlier, Ricky finds himself reflecting that Gareth is an intelligent man who must know, for all his outward front, that the fight is lost. Yes, okay, the campaign worked well in its early days, and Shop-City's initial application to bulldoze The Lamb and turn the site into one of their many mini-markets was rejected. But now that a newer application – one featuring a smaller building, extra parking, and a few extra trees around the perimeter – has been more favourably received, and has recently been recommended for acceptance at the next council meeting, Ricky feels that sessions like tonight's are simply the death throes of their campaign. Gareth may talk of final appeals to the committee, and of new ideas and tactics, but Ricky, who considers himself a man of the wider world, is sure that the game is up.

Ricky is confident that Patrick feels the same way. He and Patrick have both outgrown the community in which they were raised, and so have wider perspectives than many of the blokes who drink regularly at The Lamb. Ricky's sure that that's why, without even discussing it, he and Patrick didn't sit in the chairs which Gareth had apportioned for the meeting tonight – the seats facing his chairman's table. But nor did they sit so far away that they couldn't hear what was being said. Instead they sat at the bar, specifically at the corner of it closest to the meeting. As such, Ricky supposes, they made themselves and Vince to be semi-detached from the campaign. They put a little bit of distance between their private inner circle and the movement to keep The Lamb alive. But not too much distance – not quite enough to start alienating the people they still like to call friends, however much they may feel they've moved on from the smaller-minded thinking in this little corner of the world.

Ricky drops his half-smoked cigarette, crushes it underfoot, and slides behind the wheel of his six-month-old BMW. It's the third

Beemer he's had in five years, and with this much tech' it's easily the best. But as he closes the door and reaches for his seatbelt, he asks himself whether it was really right for he and Patrick – and, by association, Vince – to estrange themselves from the campaign like they just did, even if only partially. He thinks about the times that the community stood together in the past – most especially when everyone united against Vince being sent to a special school after he suffered brain injuries in the accident which killed his dad. It wouldn't cost anything, thinks Ricky, for he and Patrick to show a bit more solidarity during the end game, rather than being such smartarses. After all, the whole thing will soon be over anyway.

By pushing a dashboard button, Ricky brings the BMW to life. He concludes that a bit of loyalty on his and Patrick's part wouldn't hurt – loyalty to the people who'll have nowhere else to go once the old pub closes down. Ricky knows that Vince will be alright once The Lamb has gone, because he and Patrick will take him to other pubs. But they can't take everyone to other pubs. There's Vince's mum, Yvonne, to name one, and her mate Alice, who's seventy for fuck's sake, and likes to keep score on the dartboard. Then there's old Harry Marshall, who has bad knees, and takes thirty minutes to walk half-a-mile to The Lamb, and does so nearly every night of his life. And there are others, too – people without cars and on low incomes, most likely living in the flats. All people to whom The Lamb and Musket still really matters. And Vince. Even if they do take Vince to other pubs, he won't get to see Mel again, will he?

Before he can finally drive away, a text comes to Ricky's phone. He reads it with his foot on the brake to hold the BMW back. It's from Caroline, his wife and the mother of his son. 'What time are you home?' it asks.

Ricky sighs. For a man who doesn't do introspection, he's had more than enough of it for one night, but somewhere inside of him, on one level or another, he's wondering whether his uneasiness about his and Patrick's detachment is simply a matter of transference, and whether he's really feeling guilty about his ongoing lack of fidelity to the woman he purports to love.

He sighs again. 'After midnight,' he texts back. 'Staff issues at pie factory.' Then Ricky pockets his phone, takes his foot off the brake, and drives purposefully out of the car park.

+++++

Having quit drinking lager once he'd made an early morning appointment at The Beethoven Lounge, Patrick orders his second coffee of the night. He also asks Mel to pour a tomato juice for Vince, who's almost entirely teetotal anyway, partly on the advice of his doctors and partly on the grounds that alcohol would undo some of the hard work he puts in at the gym.

Mel heads out to the kitchen, and flicks on the kettle. While waiting for it to boil, she returns to the bar and gets Vince his tomato juice. She whisks in some tabasco, and leaves the plastic stirrer in his glass when she hands it to him. It's a different coloured stirrer to those used in his earlier drinks – being purple this time, not lime green, and Vince removes it from the glass, cleanses it of tomato sauce by running it between his lips, and then studies the stirrer at some length, as if it were litmus paper extracted from a test tube. Mel finds it endearing that Vince takes pleasure in such childish things. And of course she can't help noticing the way he looks at her, the poor, sweet guy.

As Mel returns to the kitchen, so as to make Patrick's coffee, she reflects that at least Vince has eyes only for her. So many of the regulars have had their heads turned by Yasmin, especially on warm nights like this when the girl wears only a little vest and a pair of Daisy Dukes. Having worked here for five years, and seen any number of younger women – students for the most part – come and go, Mel knows that pretty young things like Yasmin will go down a storm in pubs such as The Lamb, especially when they turn up half-naked for a shift. At the age of thirty-six, Mel is fully aware that she should know better than to let Yasmin's soaring popularity piss her off. Yet somehow it does. Yasmin pisses Mel off like no supposed rival ever has in the past, and she does so by not even considering Mel to be a rival in return. It's clear that Yasmin regards Mel as no more a competitor for the affections of The Lamb's male customers than Anthony Hopkins would regard a stalwart amateur player as worthy competition for the lead role in a major screen production.

Yasmin's attitude to Mel seems best summed up by what happened only ten minutes ago, when Mel invited Yasmin to one side and made a sarcastic comparison between their respective work ethics. "When nobody needs serving at the bar," said Mel, "and I'm collecting empties, then maybe you'd like to help. You know, start doing some of the work you're paid for round here."

Yasmin looked levelly at Mel in return. The younger woman didn't rise to the remark – she didn't respond aggressively, or get in any way prickly about the matter. Her hands didn't go to her hips, nor fold defensively across her chest. But neither did she behave deferentially, like a newbie might when accepting a deserved admonishment from a senior colleague. "Sure, Mel," Yasmin replied, in moderate and reasonable tones, not unlike someone acknowledging the demented claims of an ageing relative that half the population of Nicaragua is living inside the shoe cupboard. "Why don't you go and get the glasses, and I'll load up the dishwasher."

And that had been that. Yasmin had turned, and headed back to centre stage of the bar, Mel's complaint – and Mel herself – dismissed as fripperies.

Mel hands Patrick his coffee, along with the sugar bowl and a spoon so that he can sweeten the drink to his liking. He thanks her, and before paying he asks Mel if she'd like one for herself. After Mel shakes her head and says no thanks, Patrick calls to Yasmin and asks if she'd like anything, putting the question tentatively, no doubt because he's aware of the tension on Mel's part. Yasmin flexes her sex-goddess smile and tells Patrick she'd like a gin – thank-you very much – but she makes no move towards him, leaving Mel to collect the money from Patrick. Patrick proffers Mel a note from his wallet, together with an apologetic look.

"It's no problem," says Mel to Patrick, giving him a little wink. After getting his change for him, she even reaches down the gin bottle and a measurer, setting them both before Yasmin, having decided, for now at least, that she's going to stop letting the younger woman wind her up. After all, when Mel thinks rationally about the situation, she realises that apart from campaign nights like these, she and Yasmin normally only see each other on Saturdays, because that's the only other night Derek believes is busy enough to have them both on.

Cheered by that consideration, Mel smiles and moves away, letting Patrick and Vince talk among themselves for the moment. They intrigue her, this trio of friends: Patrick, Vince and Ricky, who've apparently known each other since school. Vince is sweet and simple, a half-child in an alpha-male's body, and Mel often wonders how he'd have turned out were it not for his accident. Then there's Ricky, who is nearly Vince's size, and is clever and quick-witted. Ricky is a real charmer when he wants to be, but is distant and callous on other occasions, often speaking meanly of the temporary staff supplied by the recruitment company of which he's a director. Of the three mates, however, Mel is most intrigued by Patrick. He has some of Vince's sweetness, and a dash of Ricky's charm, but with seemingly little of Vince's simple-minded gullibility or Ricky's nasty disregard of other people. Patrick has an air of intrigue to him, too, having been born in Belfast to republican parents who moved here to escape the troubles.

But what most appeals to Mel about Patrick is his kindness to his friends. He'll sit for ages with Vince, either in companiable silence or having the kind of simple conversation which becomes drawn out by Vince's slowness. To be fair, Ricky will also sit with Vince in much the same way, but every now and then will leave Vince to his own devices while he nips out for a cigarette and a chat with someone else. It seems to Mel that with mates like Ricky and Patrick, Vince will be fine when The Lamb closes down, but as she looks at him now, sitting quietly with Patrick, she wonders whether he'll ever feel quite so at home in any other pub.

With that last thought comes the realisation to Mel that she's begun thinking of The Lamb's impending closure in terms of 'when' rather than 'if'. And okay, it's a biggish deal to her because she's been working here for nigh on five years, but it's surely a much bigger deal to the many folk who've been drinking here for far longer than that. And from her point of view, losing this gig may just be the impetus she needs to go out and get a proper job again – one with proper hours and proper money. Her daughter Gabby is, after all, nearly fifteen, and has developed a sense of independence to the point where she doesn't need her mum around nearly so much as when her dad walked out on them both.

Derek comes over and thanks Mel for all her hard work tonight. He tells her that Gareth is hoping to get the guy from the local newspaper back in on Sunday night – the night of the weekly quiz – so as to get some renewed publicity for the campaign. "We want to show him that we're still thriving," says Derek, pushing back the straggly remains of his hair with a hand that's prematurely liver spotted. "You know, tell everyone that we haven't given up."

They're the right words from Derek, but he looks tired and sounds even more so, and his tone is of someone chucking in the towel. Mel's sure that just as she's thinking about a new job (a return to estate agency, maybe?), Derek must have one eye on his next tenancy. For now though, Mel too makes all the right noises, and tells Derek it would be great to get a journalist here. She agrees that there's a fight still there to be won. Then Gareth joins her and Derek at the bar. His eyes are alight with the passion he has for their campaign, but Mel wonders how he'll react when the fight is finally done, and most likely lost. How will Gareth fill the hole in his life which is currently occupied by campaigns and publicity, and by meetings and phone calls? And who's going to pick him up and cuddle him when all of this is over? *Not me*, thinks Mel. *At least not in the way he'd like.*

Gareth is telling Derek how he'll bring along a posse of real ale enthusiasts when the reporter comes on Sunday – enough, Gareth claims, to form an extra team for the quiz. Maybe even two teams, he says. While following the conversation, Mel glances up and is thrilled to see Vince doing her a favour by collecting the last of the empty glasses. Then, when she turns swiftly to share her delight with Patrick, she catches him looking skittishly away, and Mel realises she must have caught him eyeing her up.

Mel wonders whether The Lamb will stay open long enough for Patrick to ever ask her out. She suspects not. Although she's noticed how Patrick sometimes looks at her (not so blatantly as Vince, and less obviously even than Gareth, but so covertly that a keen-eyed girl can't actually tell), he's been looking that way at her for a long time, during which he's dated a good few other girls without ever making a serious move in her direction. And anyway, Mel's also noticed the way Patrick happens to look at Ricky's wife during on the rare occasions she comes in here. He'd be playing with fire if he were to ever make his move that way, but who knows the ways of men. Especially the ways of bonkers, boyish, Irish men.

Closing time soon arrives. After picking up the last of the glasses, Vince brings them to where Yasmin is standing behind the bar, languidly sipping the gin which Patrick bought her earlier. Setting the glasses down, Vince looks at Yasmin very deliberately and says, "Make sure you… wash these… please lady."

For once, Yasmin looks perplexed, and doesn't find an answer. That Mel doesn't laugh is only by a supreme effort of will. And Derek breaks off from listening to Gareth for long enough to say, "Thank you Vince. First drinks on the house next time."

"Come on, mate," says Patrick, steering Vince by the elbow, as if Vince had been the one drinking. "Time we were off home."

As Vince and Patrick turn to leave, Yasmin looks at Mel. She shapes up to say something, but then, maybe seeing the look in Mel's eye, seems to think better of it. Yasmin picks up the glasses, and carries them out back. Mel blows a furtive kiss to Vince as he heads out the door. After a second's hesitation, she blows one to Patrick too.

1.2) Friday

Patrick finds the circumstances so whimsical that this ought to be happening in Ireland. His newest customer is Mrs Kristina Cross – one half of the married couple behind The Beethoven Lounge. Her husband, whom Patrick is yet to meet, on account of the gentleman having gone out to the wholesaler's, is apparently called Christopher. So that's Kris Cross and Chris Cross – Patrick thinks this is priceless. He can't stop smiling to himself as he finalises their invoice on his tablet computer.

Fixing the leak above the bar proved a simple enough matter. Its cause had been a leaking washer on the inlet pipe to the tank – just as Patrick had presupposed. Five minutes, and it was sorted. After that, he turned the water back on at the mains, and then stood watch over the tank to make sure it remained leak-tight once full again.

Patrick took an instant liking to Mrs Kris Cross. The trickiest aspect of the whole operation – as often proves the case with town-centre jobs – had been to guard against his van getting a parking ticket while he left it on the kerb outside The Beethoven Lounge. Kris Cross did him proud in that regard, hovering in and around the doorway, keeping a look out for traffic wardens while he went about the task of replacing a washer. She did this in spite of having loads of work to do in order to get the bar ready for opening.

He sits across from her now, at a table near the window, from which they can both keep an eye on his van. Kris Cross is a petite lady – short and slim, with brown shoulder-length hair. She's dressed appropriately for the grunt work involved in readying a bar for opening. A t-shirt, some sweat pants, and a pair of lived-in trainers give her a down to earth look, as does an absence of make-up and nail polish. Her no-nonsense personal appearance contrasts markedly with that of her bar, which has a bohemian feel to it on account of the many drapes and tapestries which are hung about, to say nothing of the mosaic along one wall of a composer – presumably Mr Ludwig van Beethoven himself – hard at work on one of his symphonies. Meanwhile, there's a venerable-looking piano in one corner – roped off, and on a plinth – and light orchestral music plays softly from some speakers in the background.

Patrick asked Kris Cross about the bar's name and all this nomenclature not long after he first arrived. "Everyone asks," she replied delightedly, her smile showing teeth slightly gapped but evidently well cared for. "The Beethoven Lounge – it's such a big, intriguing name, don't you think? The kind of name to get your bar noticed. To get people talking about it."

"Sure, so it's a marketing thing?" he replied. "You're not really into classical music, then?"

"Oh, but we are. It is a marketing thing, as you call it, but it's also the extension of a mutual interest. Chris and I are both musicians, and I could play piano for you if there were enough time this morning. But Chris is good – I mean, really good. He's a violinist, and he could earn his living from it if he had a mind to.

Patrick let her talk on for a minute or two – about classical musical in general, and Beethoven in particular. "His very best work falls short of Mozart's very best," she said, "but he's the better composer overall – at least it is in my opinion, anyway."

"I'm going to have to take your word for that," Patrick replied.

"A bit like George Best and Kevin Keegan," she said. "My father liked his football additionally to his music, and he always said Mozart and Beethoven were like Best and Keegan. Or maybe" – and here she assumed a puzzled air, and literally scratched her head – "it was the other way around."

She looked at Patrick as if he might clarify that one for her, but all he could offer was a polite little shrug. And he made sure it was polite, because at that stage he had yet to do anything for which he could charge her any money. "I'm afraid they're a little before my time," he said. "I can talk van Nistelroy versus Henry if you like. Or Paul Scholes versus Frank Lampard."

At that, it was Kris Cross's turn to shrug. "Perhaps on a different day," she replied, flourishing another smile – a thinner one this time, a little less toothy. Patrick excused himself and got on with the business of fixing her leaking tank.

Less than an hour later, with the job done and dusted, he itemises the charges electronically, and slides his tablet across the table for her attention. "As I told your husband on the phone," he says, "I charge a flat call-out fee of one hundred pounds. And then I charge sixty pounds per hour, plus parts."

Kris Cross produces a pair of spectacles, apparently from thin air. She slips them on to study the invoice, and then peers quizzically at Patrick over the top of the frames.

"And I round my labour charge up to the nearest hour," Patrick adds. "So you pay me for sixty minutes, even if the entire job took forty."

"So what are you saying?" she asks him. "Because this bill only comes to eighty pounds."

"Sure, well there are three reasons why I've discounted my invoice."

She takes off the spectacles and narrows her gaze. "Which are?"

"Well, firstly I like you."

"Hmmm… "

"Seriously – you made me coffee, and you watched my van while I was up in your loft. That has to count for something."

"Something, maybe," she replies putting her spectacles back on and picking up the tablet to study it some more. Patrick's tablet is an industrial grade unit, with a thick rubber protector around the rim. It's surprisingly heavy, which may be why she soon sets it down again.

"But a bit of common courtesy on my part is no reason for you to be halving your bill. Not that I'm complaining, Mr Mackey, but – "

"Patrick. You must please call me Patrick. Mr Mackey – that's my da."

The on and off spectacles are back off again. "Alright, then. Not that I'm complaining, Patrick, but what are your other two reasons."

"Well, you own a bar. You've got customers, and social media accounts. So, sure, I'm hoping you'll tell people what a good service I've given you."

"Chris handles the tweets, and stuff like that. I'm sure he'll say nice things about you if I ask him to. Which I probably will, just so long as I don't dislike the third reason for your discounted bill."

"Well, now," says Patrick, adopting the stereotypically pained expression of a tradesman with bad news to impart. "It's like this – before long you're going to need a new boiler, and I'd like you to think favourably of me when the time comes."

"A new boiler?" she answers sharply. "When? And how do you know?"

"Could be six days, or could be six weeks. Six months, even. I doubt it's more than a year, though."

"But it seems to be working fine. Not that we've really had the heating on, but we've got hot water when we need it."

"Sure, that's great. But it's just so old. It may not go back to the time of Best and Keegan, but it's long before van Nistelroy and Henry." She looks nonplussed at the return to football metaphors, and so Patrick spins a line he's used a few times before. "Look, your boiler's heyday was the nineteen-eighties, just like Maggie Thatcher's, and she's long gone by now."

Kris Cross sighs. "I guess we'd better start saving up," she says, getting to her feet. "Maybe it's a good job you've reduced our bill."

She goes off, then, to get him some money, leaving Patrick to reflect, and not for the first time, that he must be the only member of his family – immediate or extended – who can pronounce the name Maggie Thatcher without preceding it with the word "fookin'". Kris Cross comes back quickly with her credit card, and after Patrick has been paid, and is on his way out, he meets Mr Christopher Cross returning from the wholesaler's. Like his wife, Chris Cross is of smallish height and build, and the box he carries in is more than half his own size.

Kris Cross makes the introductions once Chris Cross has set the box down. "So," says Patrick, "you're Chris Cross the famous musician."

"No," he replies gently, sounding much softer spoken than when arguing on the phone last night. "I am Chris Cross the musician, but there at least two other musicians called Chris Cross, both of whom are much more famous than me."

"Is that so?" says Patrick.

"Although I think," says Chris Cross, "that one of them prefers to be known as Christopher, rather than Chris. And I'm not one-hundred percent sure that that's his real name anyway."

"Yes… Christopher Cross," muses Kris Cross. "He's another one whose heyday was in the eighties. The last I heard, he was still going strong, besides which his music will live on after him, just as Baroness Thatcher's legacy survives her in many ways. So maybe, Patrick, longevity is possible."

"Who knows?" he replies. "Maybe you'll get lucky for a while."

Chris Cross is looking at the two of them blankly. His wife laughs at him. "Patrick wants us to give him the job of changing our boiler," she says. "Whenever the time comes."

"And I want you to promote me on your social media accounts," says Patrick, putting on his best cheeky grin. "That one's a favour for the here and now, please."

"Help me in with the rest of these boxes," says Chris, "and I'll see what I can do."

"You don't mind, do you Patrick," adds Kris. "I'll keep an eye on both your vans."

Patrick's more than happy to help, because he's more than happy to make two new friends. Setting aside the simple consideration that he likes Kris and Chris Cross, he heard the noise their boiler made when, with his work done, he switched it back on to make sure The Beethoven Lounge had some hot water. It was the sound of money coming his way, and doing so fairly soon. Patrick is sure he'll be back here with his blowtorch before many more weeks have passed.

+++++

Having begun work at six in the morning, Gareth gets a break at nine-thirty. Taking his sandwiches from his locker, he heads off to the canteen, where he gets a coffee from the vending machine, and carries it with his food to one of several tables running the width of the dining area. Gareth picks a crowded table – he's always trying to fit in, even though he often feels awkward among his co-workers – sliding in where there's a little room at the end. He nods and smiles at a couple of the younger guys, but gets his head down to eat once the brief civilities are over.

Gareth rarely gets involved in lunch-table chatter, and there are two reasons for his abstinence. The first is that he's a couple of decades older than most of the people here, and although he tries to be one of the boys, he has little in common with many of them. The second reason is that there isn't really any conversation to join in with, at least not to Gareth's way of thinking. What happens in the canteen is that his (mostly male) co-workers eat their food and look at their phones. And although they frequently look up to exchange profanity-littered soundbites, there's no real dialogue as such. No discussion, debate, or legitimate comparison of views. What goes on here is nothing more than coarse banter – the brainless interchange of barbs and banalities. It's all blah-blah-blah in Gareth's opinion. Blah-blah-blah: a random bucket of noise.

It occurs to him, with some sadness, that the Lamb and Musket is similar to this canteen in that regard. Actually, it's a lot like any other place where people gather in numbers nowadays. Folk don't really talk to each other anymore – they exchange content and crudities instead.

There are other similarities between Gareth's local pub and his workplace dining facilities. They both have a careworn, depressingly run-down feel. These cheap, laminate-topped dining tables, for example, are of a similar beaten-up quality to those in The Lamb. And nobody seems to care less when, over in the corner, near the vending machines, one of his co-workers drops a microwaveable lasagne on the floor. A sarcastic cheer emanates from one table, and some idiot, three seats down from Gareth, looks up and shouts "Sack the juggler." Thereafter, the young kid who actually dropped his food runs a gauntlet of jeering while he hurriedly picks up and throws away the lasagne, doing so without making any effort to find a mop or cloth and clean the sticky residue that must have been left on the floor. Nothing at all seems to get said or done about that, and a near silence returns as the guys' collective attention becomes once more absorbed by their phones. And that's not such a bad thing, really, because Gareth needs to do some serious thinking. Tired though he is by an early start following last night's meeting, he tries to organise and make sense of the thoughts racing around his head.

It's taken two years so far – two years to fight twin opponents: George Timkin's Hippy Hops Pub Company, and its partner in crime, Shop City Supermarkets. Two years opposing both George Timkin's plan to sell The Lamb and Musket to the supermarket chain, and also Shop City's' proposal to bulldoze the site and turn it into one of their mini discount stores. Opposing these schemes has been a lot of work – making plans, raising money, spending said money, and then making new plans. There have been raffles and tombolas, press releases and photo-shoots. There have been sponsored cycle rides, and the parading of volunteers in fancy dress outside the homes of both George Timkin and the members of Shop City's executive board. There have been petitions raised, and an organised campaign whereby people in their hundreds have submitted objections to the council's planning department. There has been endless lobbying of town councillors and the local MP, together with session after session of Gareth's action committee, and meeting after meeting among the regulars at The Lamb.

Yet everything has come down to this: the recommendation of a single planning officer to finally allow the proposal. And so all that is left now is to once more lobby the councillors themselves, that they might vote against the recommendation at their next planning session. That's why, during last night's campaign meeting at The Lamb, Gareth suggested the production of what he called 'biography sheets' – single sides of A4 complete with a photo and life story for each the people who'd be hardest hit by the old pub's demise. He wanted to personalise the consequences of the impending closure to the maximum extent – to show the councillors just how much certain individuals would be hurting.

But nobody wants to look like a victim. It's one thing for Geoffrey Norton to raise his hand at a meeting and say he has no one to talk to at home – what with his wife in care and his children moved away – and that he can't afford a car, nor, on account of his gout, walk any further than The Lamb and Musket. But ask the same Geoffrey Norton if you can print an elaborated tale of his woe beneath a photo of him looking down in the mouth and a caption reading, 'Geoffrey's Story' – well, suddenly Geoffrey Norton comes over all reluctant.

Which was why, in order to get the idea carried, Gareth decided to set an example by agreeing to go first – to have the first biography sheet written about him, even though he is gout free and does have a car, venerable and rust-spotched though it may be. In short, he agreed to put himself out there as a victim, even though he doesn't feel that much like one, and even though he does, in point of fact, have himself a life.

But has he really? Has he actually got that much of a life, if he's honest with himself?

Does Gareth's existence on Planet Earth amount to very much more than a minimum-wage job and a lunchtime meal of peanut butter sandwiches in this miserable canteen? Accordingly, has he embraced the fight to save The Lamb merely because he has nothing better to do? And is that why he has prolonged the fight as desperately as he has – because its eventual loss will diminish him so much? Exactly how often, now he comes to think about it, do councillors ever vote against their planning officers' recommendations? These are sobering thoughts for Gareth as he chews slowly and mechanically on his sandwich. He surely will warrant his own miserable biography sheet once the fight is over and The Lamb has closed down.

Two guys, John and Philip, squeeze in close to Gareth at his end of the long table. Both of them have packed lunches bigger than his – they've more or less brought a picnic each. In addition to well-stacked sandwiches, from which meats hang and garnishes drip, the two of them have fruit, crisps, yoghurt, pork pies and sausage rolls. As to John, Gareth genuinely can imagine where he puts it all – the man has a belly so big that he has his chair pushed back a good four inches further than anyone else's. Philip is a different story. He's lean and wiry, like so many of the Polish people working here, but Hell's bells, the man can demolish a rucksack full of food.

For all that they've brought to eat, though, both John and Philip – unusually so for this place of work – will usually find time to talk, albeit it with their mouths full. Often, however, the conversation is about something of little interest to Gareth – John's latest tattoo, for example – and so, after a brief hello and exchange of pleasantries, Gareth usually keeps quiet. Today is no different. John and Philip are discussing the sports headlines, which are playing out, ticker-tape style, on the news channel broadcasting from the TV mounted on the wall over Gareth's shoulder. Gareth looks behind, sees that it's motorsport rather than football under consideration, and so turns away, returning to his inner world of angst.

He wonders, gloomily, what people will think of him when he finally has to concede defeat in his campaign to save The Lamb. They'll think the same thoughts that they've thought for a long time, he supposes – namely that he doesn't amount to very much at all.

And yet it wasn't always like this. Time was when he had a better job and better prospects. And even though back then, just as now, he didn't have a woman in his life, he did have more hope of attracting one. Head of Payroll – that's what Gareth once was. Head of Payroll for Hart-Robinson Hydraulics, a large engineering firm on the edge of town. And he'd still be Head of Payroll, or better, if he hadn't reacted as he had to accusations of impropriety regarding the petty cash. For although cleared of any guilt by an internal enquiry, Gareth took umbrage that his integrity had even been questioned, and resigned his position anyway, acting on a matter of principle. A proud and capable man in his early thirties, he was more than sure that he'd soon find another job.

Ten years on, he looks back with bitterness on how subsequent events failed to turn out as he'd expected. He remembers that it took him three months to secure so much as an interview. And that at that interview, and at the few others which followed, nothing ever went to plan. It was as if he had an enormous sense of grievance in his heart over what had happened at Hart-Robinson, and this feeling of having been done down always surfaced whenever he presented himself before a prospective new employer. Something else began surfacing too, more and more so as time went by, with each successive interview ending in failure. That something else was his ever-mounting desperation at being unemployed.

Eventually, facing burgeoning arrears on the mortgage he'd taken to pay for his modest, two-bedroomed house, he'd been obliged to take an unskilled manual job on wages much lower than he'd previously been earning. Unable, afterwards, to afford the cost of paying off the arrears or resuming his mortgage premiums, he'd struck an agreement with the bank to pay the interest only for a short while, until he could get fully back on his feet.

Gareth has changed job three times more in the intervening decade – once because he got laid off, and twice more in search of longer hours. He's never had another job like Head of Payroll, and hasn't bothered looking for one in more than five years. Meanwhile, he's just about managed to clear the arrears on his mortgage, and is finally, once again, paying more than merely the interest. But he's had to beg his lender for an extended term, and at his current rate of payment he won't clear the mortgage before he's sixty-six. At which point, seriously late in the day, he'll finally be able to think about bolstering his very meagre pension.

Sandwich eaten, Gareth gets another coffee from the machine to go with the individual apple pie he's brought with him for desert. As he returns to the table, he notices that John and Philip are still looking at the TV, and that John is explaining something to his Polish colleague.

Gareth studies the TV more closely. The news channel is still on, and there's some brief footage of a barrister in regulation robes and wig. Then the coverage cuts to a female reporter , microphone in hand , talking to camera outside a court building. The reporter's a photogenic brunette, probably in her early forties – the kind of woman Gareth once foresaw in his life, back when he was Head of Payroll at Hart-Robinson.

"It's the Old Bailey," John is saying to Philip across the table from Gareth.

"Old belly?"

"Old Bailey. The top, top court in this country. It's where you stand trial if you're very important or you've committed some big, fuck-off crime against humanity."

Gareth smiles thinly to himself. It's a reasonable explanation on John's part, albeit one which isn't strictly accurate. Gareth could elucidate further, but what would be the point? And anyway, never mind John and Philip, because he's suddenly had an idea. He's thinking legalities and barristers. He's thinking that with a legal protagonist on board, perhaps the campaign to save The Lamb can be extended for longer. Possibly there are loopholes for the legal protagonist to pick at. And although this may be tiredness talking, maybe there remains a chance, if the legal protagonist is seriously clever, for Gareth's side to prevail against George Timkin's plans to sell their pub.

Except that legal protagonists cost a lot of money – even those who are merely a little bit clever. And there are only sixty-four pounds and fifty-five pence left in the fighting fund. As to the chances of boosting that amount, Gareth doesn't believe that anyone who drinks in The Lamb has any real appetite for further fundraising.

Still, though. Maybe there's a way. And what that way might be preoccupies Gareth's thoughts as he returns his lunchbox to his locker and heads back to the shop-floor for another four hours of packing boxes. He's so exercised by the idea of recruiting legal assistance that he isn't initially listening when his team leader offers him an hour's overtime at the end of his regular shift. When he does switch on to the question, however, he readily agrees to the extra hour, in spite of his tiredness. One extra hour may only amount to five pounds and some pence after tax, but those five pounds will swell The Lamb's fighting fund a little nearer to the point where Gareth can hire the pub a decent legal advocate.

He can still do this, Gareth tells himself. But Hell's bells, it's seriously hard work.

+++

Mel steps briskly off the bus, having come into town for the morning. Mostly she's here because she has a routine appointment with the dentist, but it occurs to her that she might make the most of her trip – and the cost of her bus fare – by investigating the local job market.

Finding a new job is something she thought about again last night, when she got home from her shift at The Lamb, and spent a few quiet moments winding down with a cup of tea before bed. Not only was it the case, Mel reasoned, that her daughter Gabby had reached an age where she could be left alone a great deal more, but it was also true that there were less than three years to go before Ben – Gabby's father and Mel's former husband – was entitled to stop paying maintenance. And so even if The Lamb were to remain open three years down the line, Mel would still need a better paying job in any event.

All of which in mind, Mel got up early this morning in order to prepare a CV. She agonised over it at times, partly because it's difficult to convincingly embellish several years of bar work, and partly because it had been so long since she did anything else that it was difficult to list her earlier achievements. But in the end she was reasonably satisfied with the result, and had several copies printed off long before Gabby was up and dressed.

Then, once her daughter was fed, watered, and sent off to school, Mel's only remaining question was one of what to wear – and there weren't many options for someone who lives mostly in jeans nowadays. It was a choice between two trouser suits, both of which had been languishing in the back of her wardrobe for longer than she cared to admit, and both of which she tried on twice, before eventually plumping for the navy blue one.

And now, fifty minutes later, sitting in the dentist's waiting room, Mel's still feeling self-conscious about the formality of her outfit, and a glance around at the other patients confirms a thought which occurred just before she set out, namely that fewer people dress smartly nowadays, even those in executive jobs. But nevertheless, a girl surely needs to look the part when hunting for work. Doesn't she?

The answer to that question is something she sets out to confirm a little later on. With her dental check-up completed, and a new appointment made for a small filling, Mel sets off for the short walk uptown to where the estate agents' offices are clustered. She does so with a clasp purse in one hand, a little canvass bag holding her CVs in the other, and an added spring in her step from the dentist's nurse having complimented her on that outfit.

Mel knows full well that what she's about to do is unusual, and that the more common approach to job hunting, certainly nowadays, is to search online, but she doesn't really regard herself as 'searching' just yet. It's more the case that she's 'tentatively enquiring', or maybe 'putting out feelers'. Whatever name she gives it, Mel's really trying to find out what her chances would be, in a month or so's time, of returning to a full time job in estate agency five years after leaving her last one. And she has another justification for knocking on doors this morning, namely that the technique has worked for her in the past. She read or heard, many years ago – before Gabby was born, and possibly before she met Ben – that one of the best ways of getting a job was to turn up somewhere and ask for one. Well, she tried door-knocking then and it worked for her – it was how she first landed a position in an estate agent's office. Maybe, she thinks, history can repeat itself.

Yet despite her thinking, Mel grows increasingly nervous as she nears the little enclave of offices and shops where many of the town's estate agencies are grouped together. "You're a bloody barmaid these days," says a shrill, small voice of doubt, nagging away inside her head. "What the bloody hell do you think you're even doing?" And so, procrastinating, she diverts into the sanctuary of a coffee shop, hoping to lay her doubts to rest before proceeding any further.

It's a small shop – busy and bustly; light and clean and airy. The smell of fresh ground beans overlays the hubbub of chatter arising from the eight or ten tables. There's a wall-mounted rack with three of today's newspapers in one corner, and half-a-dozen abstract prints framed up on the walls.

The thing about coffee shops, Mel acknowledges, is that when you go into one you're expected to buy coffee. And so she orders a small Americano at the counter, and then sits down at a corner table just as it becomes unoccupied, chiding herself for having incurred an extravagant expense for the sake of settling down her schoolgirl fit of nerves. She supposes, though, that she can justify the price of her coffee if she can make some real progress towards finding a new and better-paying job. She further supposes that she'd feel better prepared, and therefore less nervous, if she knew exactly what she was going to say upon walking into the offices of any prospective new employer. Therefore, deciding to use her impromptu coffee break productively, she takes a biro from her purse and spends a few minutes composing some introductory remarks on a paper napkin which she takes from a dispenser near the counter.

After a multitude of crossings out and aborted attempts, necessitating a slightly shamefaced trip for another couple of napkins, Mel comes up with:

Good Morning.

I wonder if you can help me. I appreciate you're busy, and so I won't take up too much of your time. It's just that my names Melanie, and I used to work in estate agency, at Minton's, which was just round the corner, back in the day. (Mel especially agonises over 'back in the day', scrubbing it out twice, before eventually opting to include it in the final version.)

I haven't worked full time for several years, but my daughter is nearly grown nowadays, and I'm going to be looking for a new job in a couple of months from now. I wondered if there might be opportunities arising here, or whether you know of anything coming up anywhere else? (And here she adds a note reminding herself to: 'pause, smile, brandish CV, and look hopeful – but without grinning like the village idiot'.)

Mel sits and finishes her coffee, while reading the final draft of her pitch over and over again. She tries, so far as possible, to commit it to memory, aware that she'll create a less than ideal first impression if she waltzes into an estate agency and begins reading from a napkin.

When she eventually lifts her head and looks around, her table is a mini-battlefield of discarded napkins, and there's a middle-aged guy sitting across the way who's looking intently at her. Lustfully, even. His attention doesn't make her feel good, and any attraction is far from mutual. The guy is florid-faced and overweight, in a voluminous and expensive-looking suit. He looks prosperous – a solicitor, maybe, or a high-end accountant – but there's something repellent about him, and although these assumptions are sweeping and unfair, based as they are on a couple of quick glances, Mel imagines him as a man of off-putting habits and unhealthy appetites.

Suppressing a shudder, Mel looks back down and reads twice more through her script. Then, turning the napkin over so that she can no longer see the wording, she recites the whole thing though, under her breath, from memory. When she lifts her head again, she deliberately avoids looking at the repugnant guy in the suit, but she does catch the eye of the barista, who's young and lean, with a rakish goatee. When he offers her a cheeky grin, she blushes a little and smiles tentatively back. But now isn't the time, she tells herself, finishing her now lukewarm coffee and tidying away the napkins. She didn't come here to pick up random men, however welcome some of the attention may be. Telling herself to keep things together this time, she picks up her purse and her little bag of CVs, and heads out onto the street. Then, rather than procrastinate any further, she practically marches the remaining hundred or so yards to the estate agents' quarter, and walks straight through the door of the first offices she comes to.

Inside, the place is airy and modern. These desks and chairs may have been the cheapest in the catalogue, but Mel has no problem with that, reasoning that it's important for a business to control costs. There's also a water cooler and a dehumidifier, and against one wall there's even a small flat-screen TV – it has a news channel playing, but the sound is switched off. Peering briefly at the screen, Mel notices some brief footage of a wigged-up barrister, before the camera cuts to a reporter on the steps outside of court.

Turning her attention from the TV, the next thing Mel notices are the people staffing this office.

There are three of them – two boys and a girl. She thinks in terms of boys and a girl, rather than men and a woman, because none of them look very much older than Gabby. The three of them are in their early twenties at most, but late teens feels more like it. They all have on electric-blue chinos and white polo shirts. One of the boys is laying belly-down on an open section of floor in the middle of the office. He has his legs raised slightly from the ground, and his arms not only raised, but pointing out at ninety degrees from his sides. It's as though he's impersonating an aeroplane, and it's clearly straining him to maintain the posture because his arms and legs are trembling and his face – or such aspect of it that Mel can see – is a very deep red. "Yes!" he's shouting. "Yes, yes, yes! I'm there. I'm there."

"You're nowhere near, you doofus," says the other boy, leaning languidly against a filing cabinet while studying his watch – a watch he's removed from his wrist and is holding in one hand. For whatever reason, he's also red in the face – exertion by association, maybe? – and in his case the colour of his complexion matches that of his thick carroty hair. Thick rimmed glasses, meanwhile, which appear to be too big for his face, complete the impression of someone who might have been bullied relentlessly at school and is now taking revenge upon the world. Certainly, it seems, he's all about taking revenge on his colleague – the one on the floor. "You're absolutely miles away," Carroty Head continues, in a tone of staged nonchalance which doesn't mask his underlying contempt. "Des held it for eighty-three seconds. You're only up to thirty-five."

"Aagghh," hollers the kid on the floor. "Aagghh, aagghh, aagghh."

"Come on Jimmy," laughs the girl. "You've easily got this." Placing a hand on the filing cabinet for balance, she steps on his buttocks with both feet and jiggles up and down.

"Aagghh, aagghh, aagghh. Aagghh, fucking-aagghh."

None of them, so far, have even acknowledged Mel's presence, and in vain she looks around for an adult. The only evidence that any such an individual actually works here can be found in a small cubicle office which is partitioned off in a far corner of the room. Through the office's open door, Mel can see that there's a pair of wire-rimmed glasses on the desk – glasses which somehow seem to belong to an older person – together with a framed photograph of what Mel supposes are the occupant's wife and child.

"Aagghh – can't hold it. Aagghh, aagghh… fuck me, I'm done."

"Fifty-seven, fella. Just like I said, nowhere near Des's time. Des totally rinsed you."

"Aaaagggghhhh," (gasping), "fuck me, what a bastard."

"Never mind, Jimmy," (giggling), "there's always next time."

Mel comes away from the cubicle and looks around the bigger office in more detail. There are some expensive properties advertised for sale in here – their particulars professionally marked out and hung up in frames. The most expensive one she can see costs upwards of a million pounds. Mel thinks about the kind of commission an agency can make selling houses like these, and is calculating the length of time any such commission would cover the costs of opening and running this office, including the payment of salaries to these three numpties, when one of them manages to say, "Can I help you?"

It's the girl who's spoken, and now she takes a step forward. Mel thinks the girl could be pretty if she wanted to be – if she washed her hair, perhaps, and wasn't so industrial in her usage of eyeliner. It would be good, also, were she to stop chewing gum, because then she'd look less like a cow at cud. And if her name badge – the one proclaiming her as 'Gemma' – wasn't worn on such a slant, the girl might look as though she gave a damn.

Mel fleetingly reflects, with no little wonder, that she'd actually been nervous about walking into this place, not knowing it was such a bloody circus. And when framing her answer to this girl, she also realises that her pre-rehearsed script seems scarcely appropriate. *I appreciate you're busy*, for example – what the absolute fuck?

And so Mel regards the girl evenly, and simply says, "Gemma, I'm enquiring whether you've got any jobs coming up here."

It's the carroty headed kid who replies. He too steps forward, an insolent half-smile on his lips, and no name badge on his shirt. "I don't think so," he says. "But it's not for us to say. You'd need to send your CV in, and wait for someone to get back to you."

Meanwhile, the other kid – Jimmy, was it? – is still on the floor, moaning that his back hurts. Gemma smirks, glances round at him, and chews ever harder on her gum.

"I see," says Mel to the carroty head. "For whose attention, please?"

"For Mr Percival. Mark Percival."

"Thanks. Does he have a job title?"

"He does," says the carroty head, without actually volunteering what Mark Percival's job title is. As two seconds of silence then grow to ten, Gemma and Jimmy start sniggering at Carroty Head's impertinence.

"That's good to know," Mel finally replies coolly. "Would you mind, please, telling me what it is."

"Branch manager," Carroty Head replies with a smirk, already turning away and looking at his watch. Jimmy on the floor has announced that he's ready to go again, and that Des is going to get creamed this time.

Seconds later, the three of them are back at the plane game, and have, to all intents and purposes, forgotten that Mel is even in the room. Before she goes, acting partly on a whim and partly on her thesis that calling in person is the best way to make an impression on potential recruiters, she steps inside the cubicle office. She leaves a copy of her CV front and centre on the desk, and attaches a note to it, on which she writes: 'Came to see you today. Would be great to talk.' After all, she reasons, if anywhere needs new recruits, it has to be this place.

Back outside on the street, Mel studies the shopfronts of the other agencies, deliberating which one to call on next. Although this little district has been home to the town's estate agents seemingly since time immemorial, the names above the doors have nearly all changed since she was in the business. After a moment's consideration, she opts to try the offices of Hugo Albrighton, a regional agency which has sprung up in the past two or three years, and whose FOR SALE boards Mel has noticed all over town, their vivid purple and green colours matched by the shop's expansive frontage.

Before heading inside, Mel takes a couple of seconds to look through the window. Prominently displayed, of course, are the framed-up particulars of properties for sale. Beyond this, set further back, are the usual paraphernalia – the desks, the chairs, the phones. At two of the desks, a couple of guys actually appear to be doing some work – and so already this place beats the last one in terms of professionalism – and one of them is talking on the phone. Encouraged by an impression of normality, Mel is about to head on indoors when a third man saunters into view on the other side of the glass. He has his head down and is studying something on his phone, but his expensive suit and expansive girth quickly give him away. He's the florid-faced customer of the coffee shop, the man she intuitively found unattractive. Perhaps aware of Mel's scrutiny, he slowly lifts his head and looks at her. As to whether this portly, well-suited man is Hugo Albrighton himself, Mel can't be sure – although she'd take a guess at yes, because even from this side of the window he exudes an air of being in charge – but what she can be sure about is that there's something about the way he looks at her which makes her feel unclean. It's a hungry, contemplative look which he wears on his face, and seen closer up than in the coffee shop, it makes Mel's skin begin to creep. Deciding, therefore, that she won't, after all, be calling on the offices of Hugo Albrighton, Mel steps back from the window, immediately intent on finding some other office to visit.

But in her haste, she steps back too hurriedly, almost bumping into someone walking briskly down the street.

Even before she has time to take a proper look at his face, Mel knows that it's a man, not a woman, with whom she nearly collides. She's certain of this simply because the man is so big: close up, as they nearly collide, Mel's head isn't much higher than his solar plexus. She's also confident – and she's especially sure of this later on, when she gets round to replaying these events in her head – that a collision could easily have been avoided with a small diversionary sidestep on his part.

But this big, hurrying man isn't interested in small diversionary sidesteps. Instead, he puts a hand on Mel's shoulder and shoves her out of the way. In point of fact, he shoves her hard.

Very hard indeed.

So very hard indeed that she's propelled violently into the large front window of Hugo Albrighton's estate agency. Mel's teeth rattle as her head bangs painfully against the glass, and she drops her purse and CVs before sliding down the window, finally coming to rest on her haunches.

The man isn't in so much of a hurry that he doesn't have time to stop and survey the situation. He stands and glares at Mel as she scrabbles around while trying to orientate herself. For her part, as she looks up at him, she registers closely-cropped hair, a black quilted bomber jacket, and a tattoo on the man's neck of a deadly looking snake – a snake reared up and poised to strike. The man is roughly her own age, give or take. And also, to confirm her previous, fleeting impression, he's a very big man – absolutely huge, actually. Especially from Mel's position sunk down near the floor.

He speaks one sentence. He speaks it vindictively, viciously, and with sneering contempt. "Watch the fuck where you're going, you festering little bitch."

Mel feels an emotional overload of fear, anger, shock, and amazement. Which may be why, when she opens her mouth, what comes out is a discordant jumble of words. "What? You… err, I…"

The man makes a brief movement towards her. Mel flinches fearfully aside, cowering on her haunches with her head tucked down and her arms raised for protection, convinced that the man is about to kick out at her, and certain that one of his kicks will feel like being hit by a car.

Thankfully, no kick actually lands; however she hears him spit at her, and in its own way that feels even worse. By the time Mel dares lift her head, the man has gone. When she looks around, he can be seen heading away down the street, briskly as before, yet with no sense of panic. There's a nasty strutting arrogance to his gait, but no intimation that he feels any need to flee the scene.

Mel gets slowly to her feet, her legs feeling hollowed-out and bloodless, as if they can't be trusted with the job of keeping her upright. She examines both the jacket and trousers of her suit, and then runs her hands gingerly through her hair, searching for where her attacker's phlegm landed. She doesn't manage to find it, but does locate a bump on her head, already swelling up beneath her hairline. She stoops to pick up her purse and her little bag of CVs, and finds herself grateful for small mercies when she notices that the spittle missile appears to have missed her and hit the window.

It's oozing down the pane, thick and gooey and yellow. It doesn't look healthy to her, and she finds herself hoping that the man dies in agony after a lengthy, pain-filled, debilitating illness.

Aware that she's beginning to shake, and that her legs feel wobblier with every passing second, she looks around to see whether anyone is coming to help, or whether there are even any witnesses. A lone woman is walking towards her, maybe forty of fifty yards away. There's no urgency about her, and Mel surmises that the woman turned too late into the street, and probably missed what had happened. Also, if events outside of their window – events *involving* their window, for God's sake – registered with anyone in the Hugo Albrighton estate agency, then it certainly doesn't show. The two guys are still at their desks, seemingly oblivious to the goings-on outside. Maybe, thinks, Mel, their views were so obscured by the display cards in the window that they saw nothing untoward. Or maybe they were too absorbed by their work to notice what just happened, even if what just happened did involve a woman's head crashing into their windowpane. Such ideas are difficult to believe, but they feel less wretched than the thought that the men are behaving normally because they're pretending nothing out of the ordinary just occurred out here.

And the florid guy in the pricey suit? Of him there's no sign at all.

Mel half walks and half staggers away. She's hurt a little and shocked a lot, and isn't at all sure what to do next: whether to report the assault and seek help, or simply head off home. While trying to decide, she returns to the coffee shop and asks to use the bathroom. The goateed barista, remembering her from earlier, says yes, of course she can, and is everything okay, because she's looking very pale? Mel says everything is fine, thanks, before proceeding to the bathroom where she throws up. She then spends a couple of minutes peeing copiously, and then another five simply sitting on the toilet, waiting to stop shaking. Once she has some measure of control and is up off the toilet, she heads for the sink and spends longer than usual washing her hands. Finally, after checking her hair for spittle and the front of her blouse for vomit flecks, she rinses her mouth, fixes her make-up and makes her way outside, thanking the barista for his concern.

Still undecided between reporting an assault or heading for the bus home, Mel walks to the end of the street, her legs still a little shaky. With the sour aftertaste of vomit in her mouth, she heads into a newsagent's on the corner for breath-freshening mints, and is back outside unwrapping them when a white van swings across the street and pulls up nearby. By the time Mel has a mint in her mouth, there's a toot on the van's horn. When she looks closely at the signage, she realises she's seen the van several times before.

"Hey, Mel," says Patrick, lowering the window. "You're looking very smart today. Can I give you a lift anywhere? Sure, if you don't mind a scruffy old tradesman in his overalls."

+++++

Ricky gives his own name and that of his company to the security guard on the gate, and lets it be known that he's here to see Michael Samson, the manager in charge of personnel. (Ricky doesn't mind if people want to call it 'human resources', but wonders why anyone bothers with five syllables when three get the job done.) The guard nods studiously, and writes Ricky's details on a clipboard, before walking round to the front of the BMW and making a note of its registration number.

Once that's done, the guard raises the barrier and waves Ricky through, but not before telling him where to park and which door to walk through, and handing him a DO and DO NOT list of ways in which to behave while on site. (DO wear a high-vis jacket in the factory and the warehouse. DO NOT smoke. Absolutely NO photography of any sort is permitted.)

It's always the same whenever Rick comes here. He always gets told where to park and which door to walk through. And he always gets handed a list of DOs and DO NOTs – he's had enough of the lists by now to paper a wall in Jack's den at home. Also, there's never a flicker of recognition from any of the security guards, each of who, while studiously polite, are unfailingly formal, never quite behaving in way which Ricky would call friendly. Their clip-on ties are always clipped on, and their collars are invariably buttoned up, even on days like this, when it's going to be really hot later and temperatures will skyrocket in their little glass hut.

Not that Ricky would criticise the guards for their curtness and formality – after all, they're only doing what he'd want them to do were he running the company – but he can't help finding their cool efficiency unusual. Not all of his clients are big enough to employ a security detail, but among those that are he can't think of another where the guards would remain so impersonal some eighteen months after he first began calling regularly. At other sites, they'd be a little bit matey with him by now – they'd ask what he was up to at the weekend, who he fancied for the grand prix, and whether he reckoned United were going to make a big signing before the summer was out.

But no, not here. The security guards act in textbook fashion, so much so that an observer might believe Blunco Industries to be a Ministry of Defence installation rather than a factory assembling hydraulic components for cars and trucks. It's just one those companies, Ricky figures, where they like to do things a certain way. To do them *properly*. To do them the way they should be done.

Ricky has long noticed that many things are done properly at Blunco. The space in which he parks his car, for example, is clearly demarcated, and there's a neat little laminate sign – not broken or faded, nor slanted over like that silly arse Patrick on his fucking bar stool – which proclaims 'Visitor Parking Only'.

And when Ricky walks through the door he's been told to walk through, the reception area is a proper reception area. The easy chairs are easy enough – not too plush, but not too spartan either. The magazines on a little side table are all in date, and are arranged in an orderly fashion. The drip tray on the water cooler has been cleaned, and the supply of plastic cups replenished. Meanwhile, the receptionist-cum-telephonist (a middle-aged woman at this hour, who'll be stood down by a middle-aged man after lunch) is always brisk and polite, and is a degree or two friendlier than the security guards, without ever becoming more familiar than is appropriate. Today, as ever, she completes Ricky's visitor pass, asks him to wear it at all times in the lanyard she provides, and then points him to a chair while she telephones to let Michael Samson know he's here.

Ricky checks his watch – it's the Breitling which Caz bought him three Christmases ago, not long after Jack was born. It says he's five minutes early, and Ricky is happy with his timing. He always tries to be at least five minutes early, but not more than seven. While he waits for Michael Samson, he makes sure his phone is on silent and checks it for messages.

There are no new messages, but he rereads the text received earlier this morning from his mistress, Lauren – one of the personal trainers at the gym which he and Vince both go to (Vince more than he just recently). The message, complete with a smiling and winking emoji, thanks him for a 'fucking(!) good time' last night, and asks when he will be up for a repeat.

Ricky is yet to text Lauren back. He plans to do so when he comes out of this meeting, because by then two hours will have passed by then since his receipt of her message, and two hours feels about right. He knows what he'll say as well. He'll tell her that the pleasure was all his, and that he'll see her again very soon.

But he won't make it too soon, however. And actually, reckoning up a few things in his head – dates and timelines and the like – Ricky is nearing the point where he needs to stop seeing Lauren altogether. He needs to start phasing her out before the two of them become over familiar and she tries getting too close. That's because all these short-lived affairs are intended to be just that: short-lived affairs. None of the women involved will ever come close to replacing Caz, with whom Ricky was at school, and who's been his wife for nearly nine years, the two of them having married at the age of twenty-one.

In fact, had it not been for the evaporation of Caz's sex drive in the months after Jack's birth, none of these affairs need ever have occurred. But occur they did. And after Ricky had strayed the once – with the attractive salesgirl who supplied his first BMW – extra-marital sex became something of a drug, even after Caroline rediscovered her urges and desires. Ricky found it especially hard to resist the younger women who became available – those in their early twenties, or even late teens, who were as yet unfamiliar with cellulite and sagging, stretch marks and wrinkles. Ricky's now been 'putting it about' for longer than he's been calling on Blunco Industries, and he occasionally asks himself how long he can go on like this. His usual answer is twofold. One, he can carry on for just as long as he's got a big, swinging dick in his trousers. And two – when he thinks about things more soberly – he concludes that he can continue with these affairs for however long he can sustain the knack of managing them successfully: of initiating his liaisons discreetly, of enjoying them equally so, and of concluding them in such a way that the women involved think it's their idea to bring things to an end, and so aren't minded to go ratting on him to Caz, or even posting a diatribe on the internet about what a piece of shit he is.

Michael Samson's secretary comes downstairs, so as to escort Ricky to her boss's office. To Ricky, this seems another example of the company doing things in a right and proper way. (In other firms he visits, Samson's equivalent would have phoned through and told the receptionist to ask Ricky to make his own way up.) Ricky flashes Samson's secretary his usual smile and exchanges a couple of pleasantries. She's a pretty girl aged somewhere in her thirties, with the misfortune – to Ricky's mind – of being a stone and a half overweight. She's worn an engagement ring whenever he's come here during the past year-and-a-half, and she always has a look on her face which suggests she'd like to mother him. *I don't need mothering*, Ricky thinks, as he follows her up the stairs*, but I'd probably enjoy a ride on your arse if you'd only cut out the cake for a while.*

Samson's office is a good size. A curved desk sits just inside the door, and beyond there's a small conference table near a window, with a view of the road outside. There are four padded chairs on castors around the table, and it's to one of these that Samson points Ricky as he walks through the door. The secretary asks if they'd like coffee, and then goes off to make it when they both say they would.

"Make yourself comfortable," says Samson, taking the chair opposite Ricky's and setting a ring-bound folder down on the table. Blunco Industries' personnel manager is a dapper man, slim, with a neatly trimmed beard. He wears frameless spectacles with narrow, rectangular lenses, and his pale yellow tie is carefully knotted into a compact half Windsor. Today, he also happens to be sporting a very healthy tan.

"Been a few weeks since I enjoyed the luxury of these chairs," says Ricky, swivelling a little from side to side. "Good holiday, then, Michael?"

There follows a short but significant pause. Samson hesitates, his fingers poised over the folder in front of him. Then he says, "It was great, thanks very much."

"Good. Bet it was really nice to get away for a while."

"Definitely."

"And I'm the Ilikay is a fantastic hotel, I'm sure?"

"Best place I've ever stayed," says Samson. "Fiona and the kids loved it."

"Yeah," says Ricky. "They filmed some of Five-O there."

"I remember you saying."

There's another short pause. Samson looks at Ricky as if to ask whether Ricky has any further questions about his holiday in the sun. He appears satisfied when all Ricky says is, "Anyway, Michael, you asked to see me this morning?"

Samson finally opens up the ring binder. "I did," he says. "Some issues have arisen while I've been away – performance issues regarding certain of your staff."

"Is this about a couple of them refusing to do overtime? Julia's been updating me on that."

"It is to do with refused overtime, although it's been more than just a couple of them." Samson looks levelly at Ricky, his eyes appearing not to blink behind those thin little lenses. "There have been six occasions in the past fortnight when your people have refused overtime – overtime which they knew was mandatory, and could be imposed at short notice, back when they signed their contracts."

"Michael," I'm sorry about that, replies Ricky. "But it's going to happen sometimes. I supply you with over a hundred temporary staff – more than twenty percent of your current shop-floor headcount. And while I'm in no way complacent, this is the nature of the beast. Temp's will never be as reliable as your own permanent guys."

"I'm aware of that," says Samson. "I've been doing this job long enough to know the territory. But you're supposed to be flexible and responsive when problems happen. You're supposed to find me new people when existing people fall short, and that's what your organisation hasn't been doing. Julia may well have been updating you, but she hasn't been doing anything to resolve the problems. We've had to pull our own people in, and move them across assembly lines, when Julia hasn't delivered. So now I've got the heads of three different production cells all telling me your agency's as bad as the last one, and asking me if I can find one that actually does what it says it will.

Ricky finds himself wanting a cigarette. He amuses himself with thoughts of how Samson would react were he to simply light up – right here and right now – before proceeding to blow smoke rings at the ceiling while his client stared wide-eyed and aghast. Ricky knows that Samson is exaggerating the magnitude of this problem, and he also knows why. Samson was always going to do this, or something like it, when he returned from holiday, just to demonstrate exactly who's the big dog in this relationship. Ricky, meanwhile, has seen it all before. He's been through similar scenarios, in other offices of other companies, with other pissy executives. And in a moment he's going to make clear to Michael Samson that actually it's he, Ricky, who's the big dog sitting at this particular table, just as he's the big dog at many other tables not even known to Samson.

But before that can happen, there's a knock at the door. The secretary comes back with two cups of coffee on a little metal tray. Like the chairs in reception, the crockery is neither cheap-looking nor ostentatiously expensive. Again, that's Blunco Industries doing things a certain way – a way that's good and right and proper.

After the secretary has gone, Ricky lets Michael Samson prattle on for a couple more minutes. Samson talks in technical terms intended to show off his acumen. He speaks of production efficiency indices, and he emphasises the criticality of flexible labour resource in supporting just-in-time manufacturing. Or some such bollocks.

Finally, as Samson briefly pauses to draw breath, and maybe to unearth a new treasure trove of extra-long words, Ricky interjects. "Look, Michael," he says. "I'll sort things out, okay? I'll knock heads. I'll talk to Julia and make sure she ups her game. And we'll recruit some more operatives – we'll build you a nice little people buffer, and get the factory guys off your case."

Samson looks irritated by the flippancy of Ricky's interruption. "It's fine you saying this, Ricky. But will you deliver on it?"

"I always deliver," he replies, leaning forward in his chair and resting his forearms on Samson's table. "I delivered short term, when your last agency let you down; I delivered again when your bosses said that any permanent transition to our agency had to be seamless. Also, Michael," – and at this point, with a smile on his face, Ricky makes a show of looking around the office, as if seeking out eavesdroppers and snoops – "I delivered once more, when you wanted to take your family on a luxury Hawaiian vacation."

Samson looks uncomfortable again, his face showing the same unease it wore when Ricky first asked how his holiday had gone.

"And now," says Ricky, edging further forward, towards Michael Samson, "I need you to deliver on something for me."

"That's why we're having this conversation," replies Samson tersely. "I told you I'd guarantee your position as our first-line supplier of temporary staff for an entire calendar year. So now I'm trying to make sure you perform well enough that I have no reason not to make good on that promise."

"And we will,' replies Ricky. "Please trust me on that – we will perform. But you misunderstand me, Michael. Because I now need you to deliver on more than just your previous promise."

The look on Michael Samson's face grows yet more anxious. "Like what?" he asks.

"I need another eight pence per hour from you."

Samson may not be the wisest judge of character, but he does know his labour costs, and he's also good at mental arithmetic. It doesn't take him long to tally-up of eight pence per hour multiplied by the hundred-and-fifty-thousand man hours billed by Ricky's company in a year.

"Impossible," he says after scarcely a moment's pause. "We don't have a budget."

"Find one," says Ricky. "It's twelve grand a year – that's all. Find the money somewhere."

His face reddening beneath his tan – possibly due to anger, possibly in shame, probably because of both – Samson says, "It's really not that simple."

"I don't suppose it is. But it can't be impossible, Michael. Like I said: twelve grand – not much more than the cost of your holiday. And you're head of personnel for a business turning over numbers in the tens of millions."

Samson swallows hard before asking his next question – hard enough to make his Adam's apple bobble. "And if I say no?"

Ricky sits back. He lets out a theatrical sigh. "It's a big company, this. A big, listed company – one which likes to avoid scandal. And it seems to me that they like to conduct business in a certain way – a proper way, if you like. I don't think they'd continue to employ you if it came out that you'd accepted an expensive foreign holiday funded by one of your suppliers. They'd call that an abuse of your position, wouldn't they?"

"And you?" asks Samson. He removes his spectacles and closes his eyes while momentarily pinching the bridge of his nose between finger and thumb. "This won't look good on you, either."

Ricky, who knew that Samson been banking on the mutually assured destruction of their respective careers as his safeguard against Ricky spilling any beans – doesn't answer immediately. Instead he turns his attention towards the little tray of coffee. He stirs milk and sugar into one of the cups, before taking a sip and then making a face appreciative of the taste. Only then does he answer Michael Samson's question.

"Thing is, Michael, I deliver a lot of value to my company. I mean, a lot of value. Plus, I answer only to the owner. Things would have to go very, very pear-shaped – I'm talking Charge-of-the-Light-Brigade pear-shaped – before he would ever think of bulleting me. Even so,

I'm not incautious. There's nothing tangible to connect me with your little jaunt to Waikiki beach. Those emails to you with your flight and reservation details? They came from Julia's email address, if you remember. And everything was paid for with a company credit card – not one with my name on it.

Ricky takes another sip of coffee. He gives Samson the chance to reply. But the man only sits and stares, that flush of anger now gone from his cheeks. Indeed, Samson's Hawaiian tan notwithstanding, he now looks so drained that a vampire might have been at large in the offices of Blunco Industries.

"It would be easy for me," continues Ricky, to go to your board of directors with a story. 'One of my people has bought one of yours a holiday,' I could tell them. 'I've fired the miscreant,' I would add, and I would have done, Michael, because Julia's expendable to me. Then I'd ask your board a question: 'What are you fine, upstanding people going to do at your end, given how properly you like to run your company? You surely can't keep a nefarious executive like Michael Samson on your books, can you now?'"

Samson sits very still. His eyes are fixed downwards towards his ring-binder, and his coffee is fast going cold. Without looking up, he makes a plea. "You're going to have to give me time to work on this."

Ricky, whose long-term plans for milking Blunco Industries merely begin with eight more pence per hour, finishes his coffee and sets down his cup. "Sure I will," he says, trying out an empathetic look, although fully aware that it's wasted on Samson's downcast eyes. "Just don't take too long about it, will you, Michael? There is such a thing as taking the piss, and I'll know if you start to take it."

+++++

"So, she's called Kris Cross," says Patrick, chuckling to himself as he stops the van at a red light, "and he's called Chris Cross. And then, when I refer to him as Chris Cross the famous musician, it turns out that there are two musicians of the same name who are more famous than he is anyway."

Sitting in the passenger seat, Mel can't help but smile. Patrick's cheeriness can be addictive when he's telling one of his tales. And his dad – or his da, as Patrick calls him, is pretty much the same. Mackey Senior is maybe more circumspect – more understated, perhaps – but he's basically the same as Patrick once he gets into the swing of a story. It's great when they both go off on one at once, and they're both telling the same story, maybe about something which Patrick's mum (or ma) did, or perhaps some incident or other while they were out playing golf. Mel's smile widens when she recalls the time, one winter's day in The Lamb, when the two of them were talking about getting a –

There!

Mel sees him up ahead, shortly after the lights change and Patrick has the van accelerating smoothly through the town centre. Patrick's in second gear and looking for third when Mel sees the big man – tall and broad-shouldered, shaven-headed and wearing black – as he steps onto the pavement from a shop doorway.

Mel's pulse begins racing the instant she sees him. He's fifty yard away, then only forty, and they're closing fast on him as Patrick moves crisply through the gears. Insane as it will be – *Watch the fuck where you're going, you festering little bitch* – Mel wants to leap out and confront the man. She's angry as hell, and can't let this chance go begging.

Thirty yards, twenty. Patrick, to whom she's said nothing of the incident, will thinks she's bonkers when she demands he stop the van. But still – this has to be done.

Ten yards – they're almost on top of him now, and Mel's starting to see him through the side window rather than the front. She realises her breathing has deepened, and there's a rushing noise in her ears. She opens her mouth to tell Patrick to stop.

Then the big man turns, so as to cross the road. Side on, Mel realises it isn't him. This man has a softer, easier-going face. And there's no snake tattooed on his neck.

Suddenly conscious that she's all tensed up on the edge of her seat, Mel leans back a little and tries to relax. Equally suddenly, she becomes aware of an urgent need to pee again.

"Sure, I understand why you'd choose him," says Patrick, sounding more serious now, clearly having changed the subject. "But it doesn't seem fair on the guy, because I'm not sure he fully understands. You know, making him look a victim like that."

What? Just, what? What the flamin' hell is Patrick on about now?

Mel looks out the side window again, at the cars and the shops and the people passing by. She tries to make sense of what Patrick's is saying, and guesses he's talking about Vince. Gareth will be wanting to feature Vince on one of his profile posters. He'll want Vince to appear as one of life's unfortunates – one of the poor souls who'll be most affected by The Lamb's closure. And Patrick won't be happy about the idea.

"I think I understand," Mel tentatively assures Patrick, aware that she'll sound like a moron if she's got the wrong end of this particular stick. "He's your friend, after all, and so you feel protective of him."

Patrick drives briefly on in uncharacteristic silence. They're at the bottom of town now; they'll soon be leaving the centre behind. *I got it wrong*, thinks Mel. *He was talking about something else, and now I've given him a gibberish answer.*

"Sure, I'm protective of all my friends," says Patrick, before lapsing momentarily back into silence. He sounds wary when next he speaks. "So, do you want to tell me what's wrong with you?"

"Aha," says Mel, feeling tentatively at the ever bigger bump on her head, the one swelling painfully beneath her hairline. "Is it really so obvious that something is wrong?"

"It's pretty clear that you're not quite yourself."

Mel stares out the window some more, watching the shop fronts give way to houses as they head on out of town. On the one hand, she's gagging to tell somebody what happened to her back there; but on the other hand, she doesn't know who the right 'somebody' is. She's fairly sure, though, that that somebody is not Patrick. Like he said, he feels protective of all his friends, and she doesn't think he'll take it lightly if she tells him of events outside Hugo Albrighton's estate agency. Patrick will most likely feel the need to act like a vigilante Superman – to get even on her behalf; to take war to that oversized shitbag and to do something vengeful. And although some of Patrick's people are well known for that kind of thing, it doesn't seem fair to involve him in her fight. After all, his ma and da brought him here to get away from conflict.

But still… if she did tell him, and if he did get involved, wouldn't that bring them closer together? And isn't that what she wants?

Well, maybe she does. But surely not for reasons like this one.

But then again…

"I mean," says Patrick, "it's pretty obvious what's been happening this morning."

She gives a little start. "It has?"

"Come on, Mel," he laughs. "The sassy suit, and the bag of what look like CVs. You've been job hunting, haven't you?"

"Oh yeah," she replies. "I daresay that gives the game away."

"Especially as I picked you up near to where the estate agents are, and that's what you used to do for a living."

"There're no flies on you Sherlock," says Mel, deciding to let Patrick think that what's bothering her is nothing more than a vexing morning's job search. "Do you think it's so wrong of me," she asks, "to be looking for a job before we're even sure that The Lamb will be closing?"

"Sure, the place doesn't own you," he says, giving a very wide berth to a learner driver reversing a hatchback around a corner. "And although you're the best barmaid ever, you might fall short of your potential if you never do anything different with your life."

She offers him a smile. He takes his eyes fleetingly from the road in order to return it. "Thanks, Patrick," she says. "You have a way with words sometimes. I like how you tell me to move on from the job without saying anything to make it sound rubbish."

"You're welcome," he replies. "But sure, you do seem down in the mouth. Has not everything gone to plan?"

"Not quite." Mel thinks of the overweight, leering man who may or may not have been Hugo Albrighton, and of the bunch of kids in the first office she entered – the place which was more kindergarten apocalypse than professional estate agency. Yet these setbacks pale alongside her remembrance of the despicable, unhinged bastard who shoved her hard into a shop window, and then spat vile, threatening abuse even before she could get back to her feet. "It hasn't been a great morning," she adds. "But it's been my first day looking. Things will get better."

"I'm sure they will." says Patrick. "Now, this is your street, yeah?" Then, after he's turned in, he says, "You know you can always talk to Ricky, don't you? I'm absolutely certain he could find you work."

"I know he could. I don't think he handles estate agency jobs, though, and I thought I'd try that first, being as it's what I used to do." Mel leaves unsaid the thought that she's uncomfortable about the idea of being beholden to Ricky. God knows, she's known him long enough, and, yes, he's part of the gang with Patrick and Vince, but there's just something about Ricky which she finds troubling.

She senses there's a dark side to him, a suspicion reinforced by the knowledge that his dad has served time in prison. Mel doesn't want to owe Ricky a favour – not even a small one if she can help it – because she believes he might one day ask for some kind of payback with which she'd feel uncomfortable.

"Sure, I get that," says Patrick. "And I'm sure you'll find something, Mel. But don't forget to ask Ricky, if push comes to shove. He'd definitely help you out if needs be."

"Oh, I won't forget him. If I need a job in a hurry, Ricky's my man."

They're outside Mel's house by now. It's a little two-bed terrace – a council home, on an estate across the main dividing road from where Patrick's house sits in a knot of private housing.

"Thanks for the lift, Patrick."

"You're welcome," he replies. Then, before she can open the door, he adds, "You up to anything for the rest of the day?"

"Oh, you know, this and that." *I desperately need to pee again, and after that I'll be imagining a thousand terrible deaths for a big bastard sporting a snake tattoo.* "I'm not working tonight, so I'll have a quiet one in. I think Gabby is staying at her friend's."

"I see," says Patrick. He doesn't look poised for a fast getaway. Mel can see that he has the handbrake on, and he looks to have the gears in neutral. There's the tiniest of frowns on his face, as if he's silently rehearsing a sentence of some sort, and Mel supposes that he may be about to make a suggestion. Although her bladder is telling her to make haste to the bathroom, she finds herself hoping that Patrick is finally about to ask her out somewhere. Maybe to this place he was telling her about – The Beethoven Lounge.

But a long moment passes wordlessly, and Mel's wondering whether she should be the one to break the silence when Patrick finally goes first. "Well, sure, Mel," he says. "Enjoy the rest of your day. I'll maybe see you over the weekend."

"I expect so," she replies, opening the door and trying not to sound disappointed. "Pub quiz on Sunday?"

"I'll be there," he tells her.

She's out of the van, wondering whether she can make it to the loo before her bladder lets go, when Patrick says, "And Mel?"

"Yes, Patrick?" she says, poised to close the van door behind her.

"Are you sure you're okay?"

"I'm fine," she says, forcing a smile. "Thanks for asking."

Mel closes the door of Patrick's van. She does so with great and deliberate care, because she actually feels like slamming it bloody hard. Then she turns towards home, hurriedly fishing her keys from her purse as she listens to the receding engine as Patrick drives away.

1.3) Saturday

Patrick sits at the breakfast bar in the modern, well-appointed kitchen of Ricky's big executive house. The early morning sunshine streams in through the window, and Patrick luxuriates in its warmth while he sips the coffee Ricky has just made for him. Ricky took pains to grind the beans from fresh, explaining that they were a new blend Caroline had picked up from an emporium in town – "nearly twenty quid a kilo," he claimed, "although they do taste bloody good."

With two mugs brewed up, Ricky then went off to find his golf clubs and shoes, leaving Patrick to ponder a clutch of questions. The first question was double-barrelled: namely what was a coffee emporium exactly, and where was there one in town? The second question, entirely unrelated to the first, and which occurred to Patrick as he ran a hand over the stubble on his chin, was how displeased would his da be when he and Ricky arrived unshaven at the golf course?

The third of his questions came to mind at the sound of footsteps padding the floorboards overhead. Would Patrick get to see Caroline before he and Ricky left for their game of golf?

It's the third question which continues to hold Patrick's attention during Ricky's ongoing absence. He supposes that Caroline will still be in her dressing gown at this hour of the day, and he isn't at all sure whether she'll come down and say hello. It's early for a Saturday, after all, and she'll have Jack to attend to upstairs, doing the things that parents do with toddlers. On the other hand, Caroline does like to see him, Patrick thinks, even if not quite to the extent that he likes to see her, and he believes it's actually a whole six weeks since he and she last set eyes on each other.

"Whaddaya think to the coffee?"

Ricky has returned from wherever he went – to the garage, presumably, or the utility room – and he has his golf bag over one shoulder and his shoes in the opposite hand. He's wearing some dark slacks with a sharp crease, together with an expensive polo shirt in a shade of lime green so vivid that Patrick is minded to put on sunglasses. Ricky's hair remains damp from the shower, and an unlit cigarette projects from a corner of his lips. It bobs up and down as he speaks through the opposite side of his mouth.

"I wasn't sure when Caz first brought those beans home, but I can't get enough of them now."

Patrick takes another sip and nods appreciatively. He gets through more coffee than anyone he knows, drinking two large mugs before leaving the house every day, and never turning down the offer of one from a customer. Also, because not every customer offers to put the kettle on, Patrick brews up a big flask as part of his morning routine, stashing it in the van alongside his sandwiches.

But it's instant coffee that Patrick mostly drinks. He doesn't share the national enthusiasm for coffee-shop culture, and, unlike Ricky, he has steered clear of the middle class imperative to install a shiny chrome coffee maker in his kitchen. So while he enjoys the fresh taste of bean-to-cup coffee, Patrick drinks it rarely, and lacks both the insight and vocabulary of the connoisseur. "Sure, you're right," he tells his friend. "It does taste good. A bit like a caffeinated Guinness."

"And you'd be first in line for one of those," replies Ricky, setting his golf bag down on its stand, "if they ever brought out such a thing."

Ricky rests his golf shoes on top of his bag of clubs. Relieved of both burdens, he picks up his coffee and takes it to the other end of the kitchen. There, he hoists himself into a sitting position atop the draining board, from where he opens the window over the sink. Ricky lights his cigarette and begins to smoke. He does so carefully, with heightened attention to the matter of keeping fumes out of the kitchen. His precautions include holding the smouldering cigarette a long way outside, and leaning out nearly as far whenever he takes in a lungful of smoke.

"A caffeinated Guinness," muses Patrick, idly studying Ricky's golf bag. "Maybe I could patent that idea."

Ricky's golf clubs, like Patrick's, are a high-end set made by Callaway. Although Patrick believes his own are good value, it seems to him that Ricky paid a lot of money for clubs given how little he plays. Nowadays, Ricky gets in a game maybe once a month, whereas Patrick still plays most weeks, sometimes twice weekly during the summer. It's been four Saturdays since the two of them last played together, and Patrick recalls that the weather then, just like today, was warm and fine and dry, and yet Ricky contrived to get his eight-iron muddy after landing his ball in marshy ground bordering the twelfth fairway. A veneer of mud from that day, now dried and cracked, still clings to the eight-iron's clubface, and a thin grimy tidemark, sustained when Ricky strode into the marsh, shows around the perimeter of his golf shoes.

Ricky gulps some coffee, contorts himself halfway through the window for a puff on his cigarette, and then, once back inside, gives every indication of having read Patrick's thoughts. "Yeah," he says. "One of these days I'll get my shit cleaned up."

"Sure you will," says Patrick, reflecting that he's always been better than Ricky at looking after his things, especially the valuable ones. "And one of these days I'll get myself a dinner date with Scarlett Johansson."

Ricky tilts back his head and laughs. "You dickhead," he says. "Although, in fairness, what dazzling, ultra-fit, mega-star actress could possibly resist any man with such a well-stocked tool bench as yours?"

"Exactly," replies Patrick. "Especially one who takes his gas pliers to bed with him."

Ricky laughs some more and takes a further slurp of coffee. He leans sideways through the open window for another inhalation of toxin-riddled fumes, and Patrick can see that although the arm with which Ricky hangs onto the frame is taut with big muscles, he nevertheless has the makings of a beer belly. Come to that, the early morning sun is revealing wisps of grey in Ricky's still damp hair.

Ricky exhales a lungful of smoke and then sits up straight, with only his cigarette arm still outside. He has a thoughtful look on his face, and given that they'd just moved on to discussing fantasy women, Patrick supposes that Ricky may be about to ask him whether he's seeing anyone at the moment. The question, when it comes, may be even more specific than that. Ricky may well ask what happened to that girl, Amber, who Patrick dated a couple of times after meeting her at Micky Ramsden's party?

But Patrick hears footsteps on the stairs before Ricky can ask his questions. "The boss is on her way," says Patrick, with an upward flick of his eyes. Ricky tenses up, as if he too is listening for Caroline's approach. Then, once he's satisfied that her arrival is indeed imminent, Ricky takes immediate action. Still with his arm outside the window, he flicks loose ash off his cigarette, and then takes hold of it as a darts player would his dart, before throwing the cigarette away, into the garden. He slides off the draining board and closes the window, all in one smooth motion. By the time Caroline begins pushing open the door, Ricky is leaning casually against the worktop, coffee in one hand, and poised to ask Patrick a question. Not a question about Patrick's love life; rather a question about their golf game soon to come.

"Are we teeing off ahead of your dad's group," Ricky asks Patrick, "or just after?"

"Just after," says Caroline, stepping nimbly into the room. She's a blue-eyed strawberry blonde, in bright pink carpet slippers and a sunflower-yellow dressing gown. She has her hair in a lilac Alice band, and is carrying a white mug with the red inscription, *#1Mum*. Ostensibly the love of Ricky's life, Caroline is the girl of Patrick's dreams, even in technicolour overload. "Is there any more of that coffee?" she asks. "I've got a mouth like a chargrilled bathmat."

Ricky snaps straight to attention. He puts down his own coffee and gets busy making Caroline's. "I'll grind more beans," he says.

"Thanks, Honey," she replies, passing him her mug. "Make it nice and strong."

"Double shot, coming up," Ricky confirms. "Lots of cream and sugar." Then he asks, "How's Jack?"

"Sleeping like a baby," she replies. "Even if he isn't one anymore." Then she turns to Patrick. "Hi, you," she says, cupping the side of his face with one hand. "Few weeks, no see. How's my Fenian lover been keeping?"

"Much as ever, but the better for seeing you." He steps forward, hugs her chastely. "And sure, teeing off second, just as you said."

Ricky has the beans ground by now, and is pushing buttons on the coffee machine. "Are you going to tell me how you knew that?" he asks his wife.

Caroline thrusts her hands into the pockets of her dressing gown. She gives Ricky her special look, the look that Patrick calls the Caroline Look, finding it just as sexy as any of her curves or contours. It's a look which mixes arch contempt with amused affection. It's part Gallic shrug and part thousand-yard stare. It incorporates a straightening of Caroline's shoulders, an angling of her neck, and a raising of her eyebrows. Her blue eyes turn into big pools, and her mouth assumes a hard, narrow crease of irony which is tantamount to a smile of sorts. *For fuck's sake*, is what Patrick reads into it, suspecting that Ricky's take on it is exactly the same. *I mean, I love you, but really… for fuck's sake.*

"I know you're teeing off behind Mackey Senior," Caroline says, "because that's what you always do. He books the tee times, and his group always tees off ahead of yours."

Ricky's eyes narrow while he computes her reply, revealing crow's feet to go with his greying hair. "That is true," he says, looking puzzled. "But how can you actually know?"

Still with her hands in her pockets, Caroline walks to where Ricky had previously been standing by the sink. She leans backwards against the worktop, crosses one foot in front of the other, and looks at each of Ricky and Patrick in turn. "It isn't difficult, boys," she says. "Whenever you talk about events on the golf course, Mackey Senior is always ahead of you. You might mention how old Billy Spicer, who sometimes plays in his group, tends to hold you up because he doesn't move so fast or hit it too far. And how you, Mr Muscles," – and here she laughs, and points a finger in Ricky's direction – "how you nearly took one of their heads off when you hit the ball further than you expected."

Ricky hands Caroline her refilled mug of coffee. He puts an arm around her waist. "You see what it's like being married to my wife," he says to Patrick. "She notices stuff, you see."

"Sure she does," replies Patrick.

"Sure I do," says Caroline. "Including smoking in the house."

"Ah," says Ricky. Still with his hand round her waist, he pulls her playfully into him. "Let me tell you about that."

"You'll spill my coffee, you fuckwit." She pivots away from his embrace, one hand holding her mug out and away, the other clasping her dressing gown closed over her chest.

"Come on, Caz," Ricky laughs. "Don't be like that."

"To be fair to Ricky," says Patrick, "although a bit of him was in the house at the time, most of him was outside. Including the bit of him that was smoking."

Caroline, having squirmed away from Ricky, sets her mug down on the breakfast bar and retightens the belt of her dressing gown. "Well that's my husband," she says to Patrick. "He spreads himself well, doesn't he?"

Patrick feels the hair on his neck prickling. *She knows*, he thinks. Caroline clearly knows about all these women of Ricky's – the women he won't actually confess to, but is oh-so sloppy about keeping under wraps – Caroline frickin knows about them. Or at least she suspects, certainly enough to drop hints.

And how is Patrick supposed to answer her? He looks to Ricky for help, but Ricky's standing stock still and looking at Caroline, his eyes really narrowed this time, like those of a man stepping into the midday sun from a darkened room. And Patrick can also see that Caroline, in turn, is looking hard back at Ricky.

Then, as quickly as the boat begins to list, it suddenly finds calmer seas again. "I mean," says Caroline, taking one of Ricky's clubs from their bag and casually studying its grip, "look at everything my beloved has on his plate. Husband to me, father to Jack, best buddy to you, Pat, and then working eighty-five minutes in every hour to keep that recruitment business thriving. Small wonder he can still attend meetings to keep that crusty old pub open, and go off playing golf in a hideous snot-green shirt."

"What's wrong with it," asks Ricky, laughing both in mock indignation and, Patrick suspects, considerable relief that the conversation just veered away from what would have been very awkward territory.

"What do you mean, what's wrong with it?" By now, she's taken a cack-handed hold of the club, and is addressing an imaginary ball on the kitchen floor. "It looks like you put on a normal shirt, and then the giant from Jack and the Beanstalk sneezed all over you."

"Well, it's the first fucking time you've said anything."

"I shouldn't fucking need to. Just don't go thinking I bought it for him, will you, Pat."

"Never let it be said," murmurs Patrick, looking on as the two of them continue bickering in a way that's almost good-natured – the way it seems that married couples often do in order to open a release valve on some preceding surge of tension. Patrick watches the interplay, as he has for so long, with affection for the two of them and a pinch of jealousy for Ricky.

Patrick eventually intervenes. He picks up Ricky's golf bag and says they'll have to be going or they'll miss their tee-off time. At the front door, his heart giddy-ups when Caroline says she'll get someone to sit Jack tomorrow, so she can join them at the quiz.

"In our crusty old pub," says Patrick. "Sure, you haven't been for ages."

"Which is why you haven't won for ages," Caroline replies. She kisses Patrick on both cheeks and Ricky on the lips, before adding, "That's the great thing about the two of you playing golf together. One of you silly fuckers actually gets to win."

+++

They're not exactly running late for golf, but they're in a whole other country to running early, and Ricky finds himself taking a firm hold of the grab handle as Patrick corners hard through a twisty series of bends encountered on the country lanes outside town.

Ricky knows that, for Patrick, three in every four Saturdays are not at all like this. Most Saturdays, Patrick arrives early at the course, and joins his dad's group both on the driving range beforehand, and then again in the bar for bacon sandwiches and coffee, all before getting down to the serious business of playing any golf.

The Saturdays when Ricky comes along are different. Patrick picks him up (Ricky living that bit closer to the golf centre since moving three miles out of the old neighbourhood, into an executive home with plunge pool and sauna), and then they make haste to the course, always on time to tee off, but rarely with more than a couple of minutes to spare.

Patrick loses a few precious seconds behind an ageing VW campervan, and once he has overtaken it he seeks to recoup the lost time by accelerating furiously down a short stretch of straight, before taking the next couple of s-bends especially hard. This time, Ricky not only latches onto the grab handle, but looks down to make sure that his seatbelt is fastened. The Killers are singing Mr Brightside on Patrick's car stereo, and it occurs to Ricky that they're an appropriately-named band to find himself listening to as he dies in a car crash. He also considers quipping that their name should be enough to land them on the playlist of anyone hailing from west Belfast. In the end he keeps any dark and predictable humour to himself, trying to relax himself with the thoughts that Patrick's a good driver, and that his big Audi estate has a four-wheel-drive system proven in rallying. As such, the car can corner like fuck, as Patrick seems intent on proving.

What was a twisting country lane eventually straightens, then becomes wider, and ultimately transforms into a sweet, smooth strip of dual carriageway for the last leg of their journey. Patrick soon has the big, four-year-old car cruising at a speed well beyond the legal limit, but Ricky feels it's safe enough to ask him a question now that there are no sharp turns to negotiate.

"Any plans to change the car, mate?"

Patrick laughs. "You think it's too slow?"

"It's obviously fast enough. But it's not new anymore."

"Sure it isn't." Patrick slows minimally for a roundabout, before skooshing through on a tight racing line. "But it wasn't new when I bought it, and I've got an extended warranty on the bits of the car which are expensive to replace. And anyway," he adds, adjusting one hand so that he can point at the odometer, "it's only done twenty-eight thousand, and I'm responsible for just less than half of those, given that I use the van for work every day."

"Fair one," replies Ricky. "I just wondered, mate."

"Different story when you have a company car," says Patrick. "How're you getting on with the Beemer?"

Ricky says his new car is terrific, and spends a short while exalting its smooth power and sleek looks. All the while, Patrick nods in acknowledgment, never quite taking his eyes off the road.

There was a time, Ricky remembers, when Patrick wouldn't have been so relaxed about the comparative ages of their cars. Not many years ago, soon after they began making proper money, they would compete with each other – although without ever admitting as much – to see who could have the newest and best of everything. Clothes, houses, cars, TVs, golf clubs – they had themselves quite a spending war, always trying to outdo each other, but with Ricky usually a little ahead.

In recent years, however, Patrick has ceased to compete, even though Ricky's the one who's become a parent. Patrick nowadays seems entirely comfortable owning a car older than Ricky's, just so long as it's a good car. Nor has Patrick ever spoken about moving out the old neighbourhood, preferring to modernise the house he scrimped and saved to buy back when they were barely old enough to get mortgages. Also, when Caroline bought Ricky his Breitling watch, Patrick never did anything to replace the battered old Seiko residing on his own wrist. Admittedly, Patrick did get himself a new van just recently, but then again his old van was so fucking ancient it probably saw wartime service. And anyway, the new van was a business expense, and business expenses are another thing entirely.

Ricky's unsure whether Patrick no longer takes arms in their spending war because he's concluded he can't hope to win, or whether he's simply become a man of altered priorities nowadays. Patrick still spends money when he really wants to, and he's never shy of getting in his round at the bar, but for the most part he seems careful with cash nowadays. Occasionally, he'll speak quietly and soberly of his share portfolio – the one he manages online, by himself, without recourse to brokers or middlemen – and he seems quite pleased with the way it's developing. Ricky wonders just how much money the fucking thing is worth.

But it's not a subject Ricky gets time to ponder this morning. For one thing, Patrick has just pinged the Audi through golf club entrance, and is zooming up the driveway to the car park. For another, Ricky's phone is humming with an incoming text. It turns out to be the latest instalment from Lauren, his bit on the side from the gym. It's a picture message this time – a selfie – and it has to be said that Lauren looks seriously fit. She's facing what he recognises to be the full length mirror in her bedroom, camera-phone in one hand and a feather duster in the other. She's pouting at the camera, and all she's wearing is some wine-red lingerie. 'Am doing the housework,' the picture is captioned, 'but no cobwebs in the bedroom.'

Ricky affords himself a wry little smile, angling the phone away from Patrick for reasons of privacy. "Good news," says Ricky, brightly. "I've had a full quota of staff turn up for a weekend shift at Blunco. I always worry about absenteeism on Saturdays."

Patrick swings the Audi into a parking space. He kills the engine, unfastens his seatbelt, and throws Ricky the kind of glance which says he thinks Ricky is shitting him. But his only verbal reply is less confrontational. "What I worry about on a Saturday is my da having palpitations when we cut it so fine getting here."

Ricky, who likes to be early for business appointments, but cuts himself some slack in the running of his personal life, takes a glance at his Breitling. "We've got a few minutes," he says. "But I do need to buy some balls."

"Thought you would," says Patrick, opening his door. "That's why I brought some along for you."

They change into their golf shoes in the car park, and then, despite Patrick's prescience regarding Ricky's requirement for a pack of new balls, they end up in the pro shop anyway, after Ricky decides they'll need more cold drinks than they've actually brought with them. Still, though, by moving at military speed, they arrive at the tee with a minute to spare. Cutting it fine, but without being late. No, not late at all.

And it wouldn't have mattered too much, anyway, had they taken another couple of minutes. That's because, just as Ricky suspected, everything is running behind, and there's a queue at the first tee. This is simply how things are most Saturdays, with players beginning their rounds feeling tense and with their golf muscles not properly warmed up. Accordingly, they'll hit poor tee shots, their balls finishing either short of the mark, or wildly off target in the rough. As a result, play is held up and the group behind are delayed, causing the players in that group to become tense and frustrated, which results in equally poor play on their part, creating a further hold-up in play, and so on and so on…

None of which prevents Patrick's dad from looking pointedly at his watch as they arrive behind his group in the queue. The brief glare he gives each of them in turn – his scowl lingering longest on Patrick – will, Ricky knows, be in consideration not only of their seat-of-the-pants timekeeping, but also of their not having shaved.

When greetings are exchanged, though, the sharp edge of Mackey Senior's tongue zeroes in on an entirely different target. "Good morning to you, Richard. As a proud Irishman, I ought to applaud the colour of your shirt, but I'm afraid I can't help finding it quite hideous. It's altogether too lurid, I'm sorry to say, especially on a wonderfully sunny morning like today's. Where on Earth did you get it from? That gorgeous wife of yours surely won't have bought it for you."

"We had the conversation before setting out," says Patrick. "That gorgeous wife of his has already admonished him somewhat for daring to wear the thing. She shares your opinion that it's a lump of snot with two sleeves stitched on."

"I should think she does," replies his dad. "Tell me, Richard, maybe you're wearing it to put my Patrick off? You're looking for an advantage, perhaps, in your big money game?"

Ricky has lit a cigarette by now. "Not as such," he says, declining to bite back. "But on the subject of advantages" – and now he's addressing Patrick directly – "we do need to talk about handicaps."

Patrick and his dad, and the other guys in Mackey Senior's group, all start laughing. "I'll give you ten shots, sure" says Patrick. "Just the same as I usually do."

"You've won the past two games," replies Ricky. "It's got to be time for an adjustment in the handicaps."

"No chance. I only won them narrowly. And you won the two before. I'd say the handicap's set about right."

"You saying that it's set right has to mean it isn't. You should be giving me a twelve shot start."

"Twelve shots! You can't decide you're getting twelve just because – "

"Gentlemen, gentlemen," interrupts Mackey Senior. Like the rest of his playing group, he's been watching the exchange with a degree of amusement. "I'll do a little arbitrating now. Patrick – you want to stick at ten; Ricky – you're looking for twelve. So, Patrick, you'll give him eleven shots. That'll be fair. I'm sure it'll make for a good, close game."

Patrick looks set to argue some more, but then Roy Beresford, his dad's longest-serving golf buddy, gets in on the debate when he says, "Eleven's probably fair, Pat. You have been hitting it really well the past couple of weeks."

"Is that so?" muses Ricky, taking a drag on his cigarette. "Maybe it should be twelve, then."

"Sure, you'll have eleven," says Patrick, giving Ricky a steely look as the others begin laughing again. "And you should never have had that, you chiselling bastard."

Ricky's about to tease Patrick some more when his phone hums with another message. Mackey Senior, who had stepped away to make a few practice swings, immediately stops what he's doing and stalks back towards them. He points the butt end of his driver at Ricky and says, "I do hope you're going to switch that fucking thing off before you commence play."

Ricky's aware that Patrick's dad takes his on-course etiquette very seriously indeed, and knows not to mess with him when he starts talking like this. It's one thing Mackey Senior being mildly vexed about Ricky and Patrick arriving unshaven and scarcely on time, but when he points his driver at people, and invokes such expletives as 'fucking', then he really does mean business. So although Ricky has a five inch height advantage over the Ulsterman, and also an easy four stone in weight, he finds himself taking a step back. "No problem, Mr M," he replies. "I'll sort it straight away."

"Make sure you do," Mackey Senior replies. He turns away and trundles his golf trolley forward as his group nears their turn to tee off. Then, when he looks back again, he forms his first and second finger into a make-believe pistol and mimics firing it at Ricky. He also hams up his native Belfast accent. "Next time, Richard, I'll shoot yer fuckin' kneecaps."

+++++

Patrick stands on the first tee, watching and waiting for his da's group up ahead to get out of range. His da hit a decent tee shot –

pretty straight and pretty long – and Roy Beresford managed something similar. But Harry Culshaw, when it was his turn, topped his ball badly, sending it scudding a meagre eighty yards along the ground, thereby not reaching the fairway proper. To compound the error, Culshaw then got over-ambitious with his second shot. The smart play, from a poor lie, would have been to take a relatively lofted club, and give the ball a modest clip down the fairway. But in an effort to make up lost distance, Harry Culshaw made a full swing with a relatively straight-faced three-iron, resulting in another poor outcome. Culshaw's club snagged up club in the long grass, and his ball, when it came to rest, remained sixty yards behind those of his playing partners.

Back in the tee box, Patrick watches as the hapless Harry Culshaw plays his third shot. It proves to be Culshaw's best effort so far, but Patrick still needs his da and Roy Beresford to both play again before they'll be far enough out of range for Patrick to tee off. Ricky, meanwhile, lurks in the bushes adjacent to the tee, smoking another cigarette and texting from his phone. In that he hasn't yet struck a ball, he isn't, technically speaking, ignoring Mackey Senior's instruction – one handed down in accordance with the club's book of rules – to switch off his phone before he begins playing. Nevertheless, Patrick certainly feels his buddy is infringing the spirit of the rule, if not the letter.

After making a couple of practice swings, Patrick addresses his ball as the group ahead finally move out of range. He's about to begin his backswing for real when he realises that this simply won't do. He feeling uppity and on edge, and if he swung right now he'd most likely produce a poor shot.

It's Ricky who's put him in this mood. Trying to haggle an extended handicap of two extra shots – and managing to get away with one – wasn't just about the extra shots in and of themselves. It was a little act of gamesmanship, Patrick realises – one of Ricky's stratagems for getting under his skin. And he ought to have expected it, really, or something similar, because he's known Ricky long enough to know that whenever and wherever Ricky plays games, he always plays to win.

And so Patrick steps away from the tee, and makes another couple of practice swings – slower swings this time, intended to help him relax. There's a murmur of impatience from the group of four behind, and so he turns towards them and offers a smile. "Sorry gents," he says, "only I wasn't quite ready."

One of the guys says something back – something sarcastic probably, but Patrick doesn't really hear the fella because he's trying to refocus on the task at hand. Once more addressing his ball, he looks at a spot two-hundred-and-thirty yards down the fairway – the intended landing area for his shot. Then he looks at the back of his ball, sitting on its tee, and begins to draw the head of his club backwards.

Two seconds later, he's completed his through-swing, and is watching – with his club held high in a classic finishing position – as his ball sails through the air, hard and fast and long. It lands almost exactly where he'd visualised, and then kicks on, getting a good run on the dry, springy turf. By the time it comes to rest, it's almost up with his da's group after all.

Ricky has stepped out of the bushes, and is standing a couple of yards behind him in the tee box. "Fuck me," he says. "Great first shot, mate."

"Thanks," says Patrick, with a smile. "Let's see what you can do."

Patrick knows that Ricky can play bloody good golf on his day. When the two of them first took up the game – in their late teens, more than a decade ago – Ricky was the better golfer. He had more natural ability, and being bigger, he hit the ball further. Over time, though, that balance of power has changed. Patrick's in the ascendancy now, having played and practised far more often. But Patrick knows that Ricky's a 'streaky' golfer – the kind who can produce great golf when his mind's really on it. If Ricky can play the entire round at the top of his game, he'll more than hold his own in this contest.

Patrick watches quietly as Ricky steps up to his ball, that lurid green shirt of his billowing gently in a placid breeze. Ricky looks a little bit awkward and ungainly, exactly like a man who has some talent for the game but doesn't play often enough to feel wholly comfortable on the first tee, especially with play backed up behind. But he looks comfortable enough when he begins his swing, rocking his hips slightly to commence a forward press, and then bringing the club back in a slow, wide arc. Then he triggers his hips again at the commencement of the downswing, his arms just a fraction behind and moving fast through impact.

Boom!

Ricky smashes it.

And he'd probably have driven the ball even further than Patrick did had he not turned his wrists a fraction at the critical moment, causing a slight left pull. Rather than finding the fairway, Ricky's ball finishes snagged up in the rough, approximately a couple of hundred yards from the tee.

"Fucking fuckety-fuck," he hisses to himself, stepping away from the tee box and swiping his driver viciously at the bushes where he'd previously been lurking with his phone. "Fucking fuckety mother-fucking bastard."

"Bad luck, mate," says Patrick, shouldering his golf bag for their walk down the fairway. "Great contact on the ball." He's grateful that Ricky picked this hole to find the rough. As stroke index nine on their card (statistically, therefore, the ninth hardest hole on the course), the first hole is one of the eleven where Patrick gives Ricky a free shot.

It takes them a couple of minutes to find Ricky's ball. It's snarled up in some fairly long grass, with a little knot of saplings standing in its flight path to the green. Still swearing under his breath, Ricky is obliged to play a short, simple chip to the fairway, from where he has hundred-and-thirty yards remaining to the green. He takes an eight-iron for his third shot, but catches the turf before impact, causing a high, 'fat' trajectory, which leaves his ball fifty yards short of its target. He then finds the green with a pitching wedge, before taking a respectable two putts from fifteen feet. A six for Ricky on the par-four first.

Briefly, Patrick struggles to capitalise. He too leaves his approach shot some way short, but then chips to five feet and holes his putt for a four. Ricky having scored six, net five, Patrick wins the hole, going one ahead in their favoured match-play format. With another cigarette lit, Ricky takes out his phone as soon as they're clear of the green. "Mate, I know," he says, catching Patrick looking at him askance. "I'm sorry – I just need to deal with this, and then it's switched off for the rest of the round."

Patrick doesn't reply, allowing an uneasy silence to settle during their short walk to the second tee. He's feeling edgy once more, fully expecting Ricky to offer up some glib new comment intended to convey that this latest texting chicanery is once again work related. 'Lazy fuckers,' Ricky might say in a moment, supposedly of an imaginary group of itinerant workers who haven't turned up for a make-believe shift at some hypothetical factory or other.

But Ricky stays silent for once, maybe because he can sense the irritation bristling within Patrick, but also perhaps because Patrick has forged a little ahead of him on the path to the second tee. *Caroline has to know something*, Patrick is thinking to himself, *or at least have a few frickin suspicions*. For all that Caroline qualified her comment about Ricky spreading himself thin, Patrick's sure that she must have sussed her husband out by now. She's perceptive, after all, as proved by her observations about who tees off first at golf, even though Patrick doubts Caroline has set foot on a course in her life. He wonders how he'll reply to her if Caroline ever comes straight out and asks him if Ricky has been seeing other women. Sure, Ricky is his mate, but then so is Caroline as well. What the frickin hell is he supposed to say, if ever she asks?

And as for Ricky… why? Just, why? Why would anyone lucky enough to be married to Caroline ever have just cause to go putting himself about? Fuck's sake.

The tee box for the short, par three, second hole sits on top of a high grassy mound. Patrick breaks into a trot at the end of the path from the first green, running up the side of the mound, and then resting his bag next to the tee markers themselves. He looks towards the green, where he sees his da's group holing out their putts and replacing the flagstick. Patrick can see that the flag, today, is set towards the right, on the narrowest strip of green, guarded by bunkers front and rear. Registering, also, that the tees are set a further back than usual, Patrick takes out his seven-iron, when on another day his eight might have done. Then he tees up his ball. By the time Ricky makes it up the slope, Patrick is ready to play.

Ricky, to give him his due, looks a little sheepish as he shows Patrick his phone. "Here, mate," he says. "You can see I've switched the fucker off, finally."

Again, Patrick waits to see whether Ricky will spin him a yarn about the nature and origin of the messages. But all Ricky says, after a puff on his cigarette, is, "Going with your seven? I'd have thought the eight."

Patrick's not sure whether Ricky's genuinely surprised, or whether this is simply more gamesmanship. Maybe Ricky's intending to plant seeds of doubt as to Patrick's choice of club. "The tees are quite far back," says Patrick. "I don't reckon the eight's quite enough club."

"You're the boss," says Ricky, unshouldering his bag, and then, thankfully, stashing the phone away in one of the bag's many zip-up pockets.

In truth, the shot feels to Patrick as though it falls between the two irons. He doesn't think he can reach the green with his eight, but also feels that the seven may be too long. That's why he chokes down an inch on the grip, and makes a slow, easy swing – one well within himself. Aiming left of the flag, at the safer part of the green, he makes good contact with the ball, and consequently finds the centre of the putting surface. Two putts will get him his par, and he doesn't have to give Ricky a shot on this hole.

"Nice safe shot," says Ricky, presumably by way of riling Patrick with faint praise. He steps up to the tee, eight-iron in one hand, golf ball and cigarette in the other. He tees up his ball, takes a last draw on his fag, and after chucking it down he gets ready to play. Ricky looks to be aiming straight at the flag.

Again, the forward press; again, the wide-arced swing. Again, he smashes the ball. And this time its flight is straight.

Ricky's boldness nearly pays off. His shot does actually carry the front bunker – but not by enough. His ball pitches on the up slope, just beyond the bunker, and then rolls slowly back into the sand.

Patrick looks at Ricky, and tries hard not to laugh. "Mate," he says, "that's so unlucky. If only you'd gone safe, like me."

In the absence of any bushes to thrash at, Ricky whacks his eight-iron into the side of his golf bag. "Fuck!" he says, limiting himself to a single expletive this time, albeit no longer under his breath. He re-shoulders the bag and grins ruefully at Patrick. "S'pose that'll teach me not to go winding you up."

"Sure it will," says Patrick, knowing there'll be plenty more winding up before the round is complete.

Ricky turns out not to have too bad a lie in the sand. He splashes out onto the green, and then takes two putts for a four – a respectable enough bogey. But Patrick takes only two putts himself, thereby making his par and opening up a two hole lead.

Ricky finds rough again from the third tee, and ends up making another six. But because it's a hole on which Patrick gives him a shot, and because Patrick only makes five himself, the hole is halved, leaving Patrick still two up. The fourth is halved also, but only after Patrick misses a three footer which would have won it.

Patrick carries his frustration over to the fifth tee, where he carves a drive left, towards the main road and out of bounds. Ricky takes advantage to win his first hole of the morning, leaving Patrick only one up as they approach the par-five sixth.

Having won the previous hole, Ricky is now first to tee off. He splits the fairway with a good, lengthy drive, and as he leaves the tee box he renews his campaign of gamesmanship, making the observation that Patrick should be further ahead given how well he's been hitting the ball, and that Patrick will regret not having a bigger lead now that he (Ricky) is beginning to play well.

"Oh, you fucking think so?" says Patrick, teeing up his ball, gritting his teeth, and then hitting an even longer drive, one that runs maybe twenty yards beyond Ricky's. "Take that, you Brit bastard," he says, stepping away from the tee and flipping Ricky the finger.

"You got lucky, you paddy fuck-face," laughs Ricky. "We'll see who wins the fucking hole."

"Oh, we'll see, alright," replies Patrick, also laughing. "Sure, we'll fucking see."

Heading after their balls, they walk a couple of hundred yards in comfortably companionable silence. Patrick looks on as Ricky first lights another cigarette – maybe his third or fourth in only five or six holes – and then takes a glance at his fancy, expensive watch. Patrick also checks the time. It's quarter-to-ten, which means two things. One, they're making reasonable time, especially for a Saturday, when the course is so busy and crowded. Two, Vince should have arrived at the gym by this time, and be beginning his Saturday workout."

"The big man'll be in his natural habitat," says Patrick. "Pumping iron and kicking ass."

"Count on it," says Ricky. "And he'll be wanting me to kick your ass, too."

"Away with you, you frickin balloon. Vince is on my side today."

"Is he fuck," snorts Ricky, coming to a halt as he arrives at his ball. Patrick notes that they're level with the third fairway bunker, meaning that Ricky has driven fully two-hundred-and-sixty yards – this is pro-level golf, near as damn it. Ricky hasn't got a free shot on this hole, the first of the three par fives, but if he can launch his ball somewhere up near the green, he's going to be well in contention anyway. He's got his three-wood out, which Patrick thinks is probably the right club for the job.

Ricky makes another good swing, connecting solidly with the ball. He isn't dead straight, but nor is he too far off line, and it looks from here as though he has the distance spot on, his ball coming to rest maybe ten or fifteen yards to the left of the green. He'll have a good birdie chance if he can chip close from there.

Patrick makes a point of applauding the shot. "Well done, Brit fucker," he says.

"Thanks," says Ricky, as they advance towards Patrick's ball. "Vince would be happy for me, I'm sure."

"He ain't seen nothing yet," says Patrick, as he begins to size up his own shot.

"Fighting talk," murmurs Ricky, but Patrick zones out of whatever his opponent says next, just as he zoned out of comments made by the fellas behind them, way back on the first tee. Patrick has a five-wood in his hands, and is focusing intently on his next shot. He's planning a big, high, left-to-right fade, intending that the ball should land softly on the edge of the green, check slightly, and run gently on towards the flag. There are many things that might go wrong, yet such a shot simply feels right to him. The ball is sitting up nicely on the turf, and his instinct is that the high, soft fade is exactly the correct play.

Patrick takes aim. He waggles the club a couple of times to loosen up his muscles. Then he fires.

Ten seconds or so later, it's Ricky's turn to applaud. Patrick's shot has worked out exactly as visualised, finishing nicely on the green, pretty damn' close to the hole. It's hard to be certain from this far back on the fairway, but Patrick reckons he'll face a putt of no more than eight feet. Sure, Ricky may have opportunity to make birdie, but Patrick appears to have a very decent chance of an eagle three.

As things turn out, Patrick doesn't need to make his eagle. That's because Ricky's chip to the green finishes fifteen feet from the flag and he needs a couple of putts to get down, thereby recording a five. Having two putts to win the hole, Patrick does his level best to take only one: eagles are scores which come to him maybe three or four times a year, and he can't remember the last time he had one while playing with Ricky. After lining up his putt, he gives the ball a good firm tap – he won't mind being off line, but he'll be angry if he comes up short. For a good while, the ball looks to be missing well to the left. But then it breaks right and begins to threaten the edge of the cup, before bobbling on a spike mark and jolting left again. From six inches out, it looks as if the putt will slink just past the cup, but then it breaks right just a fraction more…

… before finally dropping into the hole.

Before Patrick can even punch the air, Ricky has him in a bear hug from behind, and lifts him easily up off the floor. "Bloody well played, mate," Ricky says, pogoing around the green with Patrick in his arms. "Best hole I've ever seen you play."

"Thanks," says Patrick, grinning as Ricky eventually puts him down, and acceding when his mate beckons for a high five. "I thought I did alright."

"I thought you did more than alright. Vince will say you were fucking fluky, though."

Patrick's pretty happy for a while after that. The banter between himself and Ricky remains good natured, and he's able to set aside, for a short time at least, both his disappointment with Ricky for cheating on Caroline, and also his simmering resentment of him for not having the wherewithal to come out and actually admit it. The match itself swings one way and then the other for the next few holes. Sometimes Patrick's one hole up, sometimes three, but mostly two, and that's how things stand when they arrive on the fourteenth – the third and final of the par three holes. It's also the longest of them, at one-hundred-and-ninety yards, requiring a wood off the tee – or maybe a long iron – and as such it's ranked stroke index number eight, meaning Patrick has to give Ricky a shot.

Also, because it's a tough par three, play has slowed down, and a queue has formed on the tee, meaning they get to chat to Patrick's da and his mates for the first time since the opening hole. It was a gorgeous sunny morning back then; now it's a gorgeous hot day, although one becoming a little too sticky and uncomfortable to be traipsing around a golf course while carrying a heavy bag.

"Well then, lads?" says Mackey Senior. There are sweat marks emerging on the chest of his pale blue polo shirt. "How're you playing? I'd have expected you to catch us up before now, what with you having youth on your side and there being only the two of you."

Patrick sets down his clubs. He doesn't feel as though youth is very much on his side these days, and he supposes it's about time he bought himself a trolley so that he can pull his bag around on wheels. "We lost a bit of time looking for a ball or two," he replies. "But mostly we've been doing alright."

"Especially Tiger Woods, here," says Ricky to Patrick's da. "He only went and eagled the sixth."

"I wondered about all that cavorting on the green," says Mackey Senior. "But sure, well done, son. Damn' well played. What's the score now?"

"I'm two up," says Patrick.

"The joys of matchplay," says his da. He reaches for a club as his turn to play draws near. "You'll struggle, Richard, to beat him from there."

"Maybe," replies Ricky. "Patrick's playing well, but it ain't over 'til it's over."

"Sure it isn't," agrees Patrick. "Especially when you've been hitting it well, yourself."

Yet despite the generosity of his words, Patrick's feeling confident about the match. Sure, Ricky's in decent form, and he'll have a free shot at three of the last five holes, but Patrick knows his own game is good today – good enough for him to put this match to bed. It's a confidence which is borne out when his da's group clears the fourteenth green and he finally gets to tee off at this long par three. He takes his five-wood again – the club with which he performed his earlier heroics – but he doesn't play a soft fade this time, given that the distance is somewhat greater. Instead he truly smashes his ball, hard and high, straight and true, directly at the flag. It pitches short of the green, but gets a good run, and just as at the sixth hole, it finishes roughly eight feet from the flag – ten feet at most.

Patrick turns to Ricky, unable to keep a smile off his face. "I'm happy with that," he says. "My five-wood is working well today."

Standing, waiting to play, with his own five-wood tucked under one arm, Ricky lights a cigarette. He looks as weary as Patrick feels – there are no bear hugs or high-fives this time – and he seems a bit punch drunk by now. "Nice one, mate," he replies, exhaling a big cloud of smoke. "Another great shot. You're just a fucking show off, sometimes."

+++++

Lauren's text to Ricky – the one captioning her in that red lingerie – had read: 'Am doing the housework.'

'Hope the blinds are drawn,' he texted back, 'or the neighbours will have heat attacks.'

'Like I care,' she then replied.

'You look so hot.'

'So when you here next?'

'Bit difficult.'

'Why? Wtf? Thought I looked so hot!'

'Its Saturday. I have golf and some work. And stuff I have to do at home. You know its hard for me.'

'I want you hard for me.'

'Lol.'

'Fuck lol. When you here?'

'Really difficult to talk or text now.'

'So when?'

'This afternoon.'

'Here then?'

'No. I mean I get back to you then. Best I can do. Not trying to be difficult. Bear with me yeah? Babe you look so hot.'

When she didn't immediately reply, Ricky then sent: 'Definitely will get back to you this p.m. Be sure of it. And will see you soon. Promise that as well.' That was while he was standing on the second tee with Patrick. After that, he switched off his phone and put it in his bag. The time then was roughly half-past eight.

Now he and Patrick are standing on the seventeenth tee, and the sun is at its height. Patrick is two holes up, with only two more to play, and Ricky, who can now do no better than win both holes and so tie the match, finds his attention wandering. He's wondering what messages, if any, will await his attention when he switches the phone back on.

It's Patrick to tee off first on the twisty, narrow, par four seventeenth. Ricky hasn't had that honour since the twelfth tee, the eleventh hole being the last he actually won. Since then, Patrick has won the thirteenth, to restore his two-hole lead, and thereafter it's been all that Ricky can do to cling on to Patrick's coattails, fighting and scrambling to halve the past three holes. Ricky's especially pleased that he managed a net half at the fourteenth after Patrick's brilliant tee shot, but the time has come where halves will no longer do. Ricky needs to win the seventeenth, and then he needs to win the eighteenth, and the chances of him doing so look slim, especially given that he hasn't won two consecutive holes all day. It's not that he's been playing badly, especially for a man who doesn't play that often. It's that Patrick's been on tip-top form – that's all.

But then, golf being a game of vagaries, full of ups and downs, Patrick makes a rare mistake from the seventeenth tee. He pulls his tee shot a fraction, finding the trees to the left of the fairway.

Ricky's feeling hot and weary in the mid-day heat. He drains a bottle of water, putting the empty into a wooden bin beside the tee box. "That wasn't your best," he says to Patrick while lighting a fresh cigarette.

"Sure, it wasn't" says Patrick. He too sounds tired, and he's moving less quickly than earlier. His face and arms have browned up in the sun, and with him not having shaved today he has a vaguely piratical look to him. "Go on, mate," he says to Ricky. "See what you can do."

Ricky considers his choice of club. The fairway is tight and narrow, but this isn't a long hole, and so he selects his three-wood, sacrificing a little bit of distance for the sake of accuracy. After teeing up a ball, he takes a deep drag on his cigarette before resting it next to the tee markers. Then he addresses the ball and makes his forward press; he attempts a smooth backswing and then an easy follow through.

His caution pays off. Ricky finds the middle of the fairway. It's not his longest shot ever, but as he and Patrick head out after their balls, Ricky calculates that he'll have no more than a five-iron to the green – probably only a six, come to that – and his position is surely better than Patrick's, whose shot will be encumbered by those trees. If Ricky can only win this hole, then the eighteenth is one where Patrick gives him a shot. He'll surely have a chance.

Ricky walks the fairway to where his tee shot came to rest, and puts his bag down on its stand. Then he sets off to help find Patrick's ball in the rough, but Patrick waves him away when he soon locates it. Returning to his own ball, Ricky watches and smokes while Patrick deliberates at length over how to play his second shot. For a good while, Patrick simply stands in the rough and stares at the trees that lie between his ball and the green, as if trying to see a line through. He eventually comes back to the fairway and looks intently down it, towards the flag, his face a mask of concentration. While Patrick makes up his mind, Ricky takes a new bottle of water from his bag. He returns it after one single swig, and while he's about it he decides it's time to catch up on his messages. He therefore reaches for his phone and switches it back on. Patrick, meanwhile, has selected a club, and is staring at the flag again. Then he puts the club back, and selects another.

Ricky realises that rather than play safe, Patrick is about to try something ambitious. He must be able to envisage some sort of shot over or through the trees, and thence onto the green. As Ricky looks on, his cigarette spent, but the butt still held between two fingers, Patrick makes a couple of lazy practice swings before addressing the patch of grass where his ball must be nestled down. He waggles the club a little, before looking up at the trees and then waggling the club again. He swings back slowly, so slowly it's as if he's still deliberating the merits of this particular shot, but then his downswing really ignites: Patrick smashes the club-head hard and fast into the thick, clingy grass, almost as though trying to kill a venomous snake he might have found lying there.

It was a bloody risky shot – one which risked Patrick burying his ball even deeper in the long stuff. But it seems to be Patrick's day today, and his ball duly spurts free. Even then, it might have ricocheted off some trees and dropped back into trouble. But no. Ricky watches as Patrick's ball torpedoes cleanly through the air, Patrick scampering eagerly from the rough to follow its flight. It soars and soars and soars, and Ricky is certain, for a moment, that it's about to punch a hole in the cloudless blue sky.

Patrick's ball eventually lands on or near the front of the green. Coming out of the long grass, there's no way he could have imparted any backspin on it, and so, having pitched and bounced, the ball scurries on, like a tiny little mouse hastening away from a cat. The lack of backspin works out well for Patrick. The hole is cut towards a back corner of the green, and his ball finishes only a few feet from the flag by the time it comes to rest.

Finally discarding his cigarette end, Ricky applauds generously. "Well done, mate," he calls. "You're a complete fucker, but well done anyway."

Patrick's wiping long grass off his club-head with a towel. "Thanks," he says, grinning like a big kid who's just been laid for the first time. "I was a bit lucky, sure. That ball could have gone anywhere, you know."

A few minutes later, the match is over. Ricky puts his second shot into the bunker, and although he plays a great shot out, Patrick lags a putt up to less than six inches. Realising he can't do better than halve a hole he needed to win, Ricky offers Patrick his hand and tells his friend well played.

"We both played some good stuff," Patrick replies. "I guess I just found the right shots at the right times."

Although the game is decided, they choose to play the eighteenth anyway. While Patrick makes practice swings on the tee, Ricky takes out his phone to check what messages have come in. From Lauren, in response to his promise to get back to her this afternoon, there's a two word reply: *You'd better.* By way of emphasis, there's another photo of her, still in her lingerie, but her pout to the camera is harder faced this time. Worryingly, instead of the feather duster, she's now got some kind of sports bat cocked over her shoulder. It's too small to be a baseball bat – rounders, maybe? – but it certainly looks hard enough to cause some pain, and the image gives Ricky pause for thought.

It gives him less pause, though, than the other photo message which has come in while he's been out hitting golf balls. This message is from Caroline. It says: 'In the park. xx' There's an accompanying photo – one of Jack strapped into a kiddie swing. The sun is shining in the park, just as it is here on the golf course. Jack's looking directly at the camera while sporting a thrilled little smile. Maybe there was more breeze there than here, or maybe Caz had been pushing the swing vigorously – either way, Jack's fair looks tossed and wavy. His joyous smile and air of minor dishevelment make him look even more adorable than usual, and Ricky suddenly feels a lump rising in his throat.

He begins to compose a reply.

"Sure, you didn't see that, did you, Ricky?"

Ricky looks up from his phone. He's failed to notice Patrick's shot, and now all he can do is gawp stupidly down the fairway as he tries to seek out the ball.

"Right down the middle," says Patrick. "Best drive I've hit all day. And it got a great kick off the turf. It must have gone three hundred yards."

"And I missed it, mate. Shit, I'm sorry."

"You'll be frickin sorry if my da sees you with your phone out again."

"I know, I know," Ricky replies. ""I'm sorry about that as well. But you know I have to check in sometimes."

Patrick gives him a look. Ricky can read in Patrick's face the question on Patrick's mind. *Check in with who?* That's what Patrick's thinking.

With a little shrug, Patrick steps away from the tee. "You'd best play your shot," he says wearily. "It's too nice a day to be falling out over phones and texts."

As things turn out, Ricky actually plays three shots, and smokes an entire cigarette, before Patrick next picks up a club. That's because Ricky gets underneath his drive, sending the ball way too high, advancing it only a hundred-and-fifty yards down the fairway. Then, playing his second shot, he catches the ball too thin, with the result that it bumps and scuttles along the ground, and when it comes to rest it's still some forty yards short of Patrick's gargantuan effort from the tee. Finally, Ricky's third shot is good – a solid seven-iron which finds the heart of the green. It's only then, as Patrick lines up his approach, that Ricky gets his opportunity to send Caroline a reply: "Never seen Jack so happy. He will break a million hearts when older. Miss u both. Couple of pints and back soon. xxxxx"

Patrick's second shot is good, but it doesn't match the quality of his drive. Yes, he finds the green, but his ball finishes more than thirty feet from the flag – slightly further away than Ricky's. After Patrick's first putt drifts wide, Ricky finishes with a flourish by holing a long one. He records an unlikely four, net three, which is good enough to win the hole, albeit too late to alter the outcome of the match.

Patrick pats Ricky on the back as they walk off the green. "Sure," he says, "whichever one of us Vince did want to win – and fair enough, it was probably you – he'd be happy enough with the way we both played."

"He would," replies Ricky. "But you're right – he would want me to win. We Brit bastards have to stick together."

The two of them head to the car park. Ricky's still thinking about Vince as they stash their bags in the Audi and change out of their golf shoes. Vince will be home from the gym by now, and most likely eating the lunch his mum will have made. It will be a huge plate of lasagne or meatballs, and she'll have served it up on a tray while he sits and watches the sports channels. Vince will be listening to the TV through one ear, and his mum through the other. She'll be telling him all about her morning – who she bumped into in town, for instance, or how hard it was to park her little car. Maybe she'll have news for Vince regarding the fall out between the Ashwells and the Cuthbertsons over the Cuthbertsons parking their motorhome outside the Ashwells' house. Vince's mum – God love the dear woman – is rightly keen to keep Vince engaged with the world around him, but Ricky believes a man can have too much engagement when he's trying to concentrate on the lunchtime kick-off between Spurs and fucking Chelsea.

Just like a man can have too many women, come to that.

And Vince remains on Ricky's mind when he and Patrick, with their bags stashed and their shoes changed, walk towards the shade and sanctuary of the clubhouse, the sun hot on their necks, their shadows short and stunted. Ricky has his phone out again, and is composing a message to Lauren.

It's partly because he's texting Lauren that he's still thinking about Vince.

One thing Ricky has never yet done, while riding this long and shameful cavalcade of infidelity, excuses, deceit and evasion, is invoke the name of Vince as his reason for not being somewhere when required. He has never yet told Caroline, or any of his other women, a lie to the effect of: "Hey, I can't be at such-and-such a place at such-and-such a time because I need to be with my disabled buddy, Vince." Much as his love for Vince, and his loyalty to the big guy, offer great scope for an alibi, Ricky will only ever claim to be spending time with him if that's what he's actually doing.

To incorporate Vince in his web of lies would be stooping too low. Unacceptably low. The karma would feel so bad.

Still, however. It's fucking tempting sometimes.

'Weekend is a write off,' Ricky messages Lauren, as he and Patrick near the clubhouse doors. 'Just loads to do at home and at work. Really sorry. Monday night though?'

He doesn't have to wait very many minutes before a reply comes back. Patrick and his dad are queueing at the bar, and Ricky is sitting with Mackey Senior's playing partners, Roy and Harry. The three of them are sweaty and dishevelled. Harry and Roy are looking crisped-up by the sun, and Ricky knows they'll be as keen as he is to get some cold beer down the hatch. He's listening idly to the pair of them, joining in only intermittently, as the two older guys have the kind of conversation beloved of many golfers following their weekend rounds – the one where they talk the arse out of the game they've just played, always analysing it from the perspective of a golfer whose capabilities are far greater than their own.

"If I made the eighth in two," says Harry, "I'd have fancied myself for the points. I always putt well on that particular green."

Ricky looks at the man coolly. *If Hitler had won the war*, he thinks, *we'd all be either dead or sporting moustaches.*

"I was through the back," says Roy. "But if I'd played a decent chip I'd have had a good chance as well."

It's then that Ricky's phone hums with Lauren's incoming reply. Briefly, Roy and Harry glance at him – from the looks on their faces, you'd think never heard a cell phone before – and then the two of them go back to debating which of them is the better golfer on Planet Make-Believe.

'You cant just pick and choose,' reads the message on Ricky's phone. There's no photo this time.

Ricky decides that if Lauren wants be awkward about this, he'll simply let her get on with it. And so, setting down his phone, he avoids replying immediately, but is mentally toying with a few different responses when Patrick and Malachy arrive with the beers. "You gentlemen all have sunny faces," says Patrick's dad. "But sure, you're looking knackered as well. That's your just deserts for presuming to take on the pride of Ireland in this grand old game of golf."

Cue a round of banter, with good natured insults zinging to and fro across the table. Ricky remains partially apart from it all, his mind debating the pros and cons of playing quite so fast and loose with that half of the human race possessed of two X chromosomes per cell. He is, though, dimly aware that the English are getting the worst of the verbals, much as they got the worst on the golf course.

Suddenly it falls quite around the table, and when Ricky breaks away from his inner dialogue he realises they're all looking at him. "Sure," says Patrick, "I think he's back with us."

"I'd like to know where he's been, and how he got there," says his dad.

Ricky stretches in his seat and stifles a yawn. His bones ache, and he suddenly feels properly tired. "Sorry, gentlemen," he says. "I'd just left the room for a moment. What is it I can do for you?"

"Well, while you were daydreaming, a good chunk of cash changed hands over here," says Mackey Senior, with a nod at Harry and Roy. "We were wondering whether you'd like to pay what you owe before we're all away home." He casts Ricky a flinty smile, and rubs fingers against thumb, making the universal sign for money.

Ricky grins back at him. "Is that a republican threat?" he asks. Mackey Senior promptly reverts to an earlier hand gesture – the one from hours ago, back on the first tee, making pistol fingers at Ricky and pretending to fire them.

"Or, sure, you can settle later if you like," says Patrick, affecting that payment isn't essential right now, even though neither of them have ever been late squaring up after the monthly golf game.

"Not, it's fine," says Ricky, reaching for his phone and checking the strength of signal. "Of course I'll pay it now. Especially with the IRA on my case." He opens up his banking app and begins the process of transferring a hundred pounds.

Harry Culshaw, who plays golf with Patrick's dad less regularly than Roy Beresford does, looks on with an expression of scornful amusement. "Everything's on phones with this generation," he says, either not having seen this particular ritual before, or not having had it explained to him, or possibly not having bothered to listen when it was explained. "What's so wrong with paying good old-fashioned cash."

Ricky, who has enough cash on him to settle this bet twice over, considers proving as much by taking out his wallet and waving a good old-fashioned wad under Harry's nose. He also thinks of acknowledging the bloke's point about everything being on phones by showing him the photos of Lauren in her underwear and then watching while a cardiac arrest ensues. But in reality, Ricky would never be that rude to one of Patrick's dad's friends, and so he smiles politely at Harry while completing his transaction, waiting for someone else to explain why he and Patrick always settle their golf bet electronically, via internet transfer, rather than in hard readies.

It's Roy Beresford who's sitting closest to Harry. He leans in close and says, "Ricky and Patrick never pay each other when one of them wins at golf. The loser pays into an account they've set up for their disabled pal – the one who was in a car accident."

Harry looks confused. Mackey Senior expounds upon the subject. "The money goes into a fund for a young fella called Vincent, who's been friends with the boys since they were all at school together. Vincent has also been handicapped for more than ten years, sure he has, in consequence of a car crash which killed his father. Ricky and Patrick set up a fund for Vincent quite a while back, and one source of its income is the money paid by whoever loses at golf. An internet transfer saves either Richard or Patrick – usually Richard, the sorry British loser – from having to go to the bank."

"I didn't know that," says Harry. "I'm sorry if I sounded rude."

"Sure, it's no problem," says Patrick.

"You maybe weren't to know," says Mackey Senior.

"We're cool," adds Ricky, setting down his phone and picking up his pint. To Patrick, he adds, "That's three on the bounce you've won. I want twelve fucking shots next time. Thirteen, even, if you're going to play like you did today."

Patrick grins at him. "Talk to the handicap committee," he says, gesturing at his dad.

"Sure, Ricky", responds Malachy, between sips of cold lager. "Thirteen's a big number, but I'll have a wee think about twelve for you."

"Think on that you do," replies Ricky, mimicking the Ulsterman's pistol fingers as well as his accent. Ricky then drains half his pint at once, and then leaves the other four bantering while he heads outside for a smoke. The bright sun is hard on his eyes after only a few minutes indoors, and the glare makes it hard to see the screen of his phone properly. Still, though, he composes a reply to Lauren's message. He decides to be placatory for now.

'Look am sorry about this weekend. Truly I am but you know how things are. Monday evening though? Will make everything up to you.'

Back in the clubhouse, Ricky finds the guys finishing their beers and debating whether to have another. The consensus is that they'd rather head off, and so Ricky downs the remaining half of his pint and follows them all outside. Another debate ensues in the car park, this time over the logistics of everyone getting home. Seemingly, it makes most sense for Patrick's dad to travel back with Patrick and Ricky, and so there's a brief delay while his clubs are moved out of Roy's people carrier and into Patrick's Audi. While this is happening, Lauren's reply comes in. It's just a terse: 'Who knows? Ask me Monday afternoon.' Ricky slides away his phone without troubling to reply.

Minutes later, he's in the back seat of the Audi, alone with his thoughts while Patrick and his dad yammer at each other. Although still making good time, Patrick drives more circumspectly with his old man in the car and without a tee time to meet, and so Ricky doesn't feel any need to reach for a grab handle. He settles into his seat, grateful that the air conditioning quickly gets a grip, and wonders how big a problem Lauren will prove to be.

He doesn't think the woman will go quietly. She will cause problems, he reckons, if he tries to phase her out. That in mind, maybe he could engineer matters so that she's the one who ends their affair. Perhaps he could introduce her to someone else. But then again, who exactly?

"Sure, it's wrong that we pay for TV licenses," Ricky hears Patrick saying to his dad. "The frickin BBC should have to compete with everyone else – it should have to stand on its two feet, or fall over and die if it can't attract the revenue."

Patrick? thinks Ricky abruptly. Could he actually introduce Lauren to Patrick? But Ricky quickly dismisses the idea. If Patrick got close to Lauren, he'd quickly learn that he (Ricky) had been cheating on Caroline. And while Ricky can live with Patrick having his suspicions, for Patrick to have Ricky's philandering confirmed would be an entirely different matter – an awkward one given Patrick's affection for Caz. Certainly a matter Ricky doesn't want to entertain.

"I get your point," Mackey Senior replies to Patrick. "But by direct debit, my monthly payment for a TV licence is less than half the cost of a single round of golf. Apart from all the television, I'm happy paying that just for advert-free radio."

How the fuck did these two get on to talking about this old malarkey? Ricky pushes their conversation out of mind while he thinks further about the Lauren situation. It occurs to him that she might put an end to their affair if he were to become less the alpha male – if his vitality in bed were to deteriorate, for instance. A follow-up thought then occurs: maybe, to such purpose, he could get some bromide for his coffee. The absurdity of that idea brings him out in a fit of giggles, which, so as not to appear the village idiot, he hides behind a staged attack of coughing. This, in turn, prompts Patrick to glance concernedly in the mirror, and Mackey Senior to deliver a new missive on the folly of smoking.

Then, once he has his giggles under control, and the two up front have returned to debating the rights and wrongs of state-funded TV, Ricky develops his ideas a little further. Another way of making Lauren dissatisfied with him would be to wear himself out on a new mistress. Even if the plan failed, it would be fun trying to make it work. More fucking than taking bromide. Lots more fucking fun. Ricky begins to consider what women he has lined up. Who are the candidates waiting in the wings?

In the front seats, Patrick is asking his dad if it's true that nobody back in Belfast bothered with television licenses in the old days. Mackey Senior replies in the affirmative, but before he can elaborate, Ricky leans quickly forward and asks, "Quick question, gents. Is Mel working at The Lamb today?"

There's a moment of quiet in the car. Then Patrick's dad says, "Don't think so. I had a pint or two last night, and I seem to remember Derek saying the young girl Yasmin was on."

"Thanks," says Ricky, reclining in his seat again. Though pleased, he tries to keep a neutral look on his face. He has an inconsequential answer prepared should either Patrick or Malachy enquire why he's asking about Mel – something about getting back a leant-out CD – but they never ask the question, so engrossed are they in nostalgic reflection of an unofficial licence embargo during the days of the troubles.

"I remember they sent a detector van into Turf Lodge," Mackey Senior is saying. "Well, the van went in alright, but the crew came out on foot. The locals set fire to the van and then pelted the crew with eggs."

"Bloody hell," says Patrick, laughing.

Ricky spends a couple of minutes listening as Mackey Senior, encouraged by Patrick, talks further about Irish republican life during the seventies and eighties. Ricky even does some prompting of his own, wanting to put a respectable distance between the question he asked about Mel (which was really a question about Yasmin) and the request he'll be making next. As such, he leaves that request right until the last minute, to the point where Patrick is about to turn onto the road leading to Ricky's executive neighbourhood in order to deliver him home.

"You know, I've still got a thirst on me," says Ricky, leaning forward again. "And I think Caroline's taken Jack out for the afternoon. Would you mind dropping me at The Lamb, Patrick? I'm in the chair if either of you have time for a pint.

+++++

Unlike Ricky and Patrick, Gareth has no game of golf to play, but on that same Saturday morning he's out of bed even earlier than they are. Waking at five is ingrained into him by virtue – if it may be called a virtue – of his shift pattern at work, and he finds there's little hardship, anyway, to get up before six on such a beautiful summer morning, one on which the sun is already shining through his bedroom window from a cloudless blue sky.

After heading downstairs and boiling the kettle, he drinks a mug of tea outside the back door, shivering slightly in a thin dressing gown, while restlessly pacing the six paving flags which comprise his extremely modest patio. The neighbours' ginger cat peers down haughtily at him from the dividing fence, but his efforts at outstaring it come to nothing when his attention is caught by an aeroplane high in the sky. It's the plane's vapour trail he really notices, it being vividly white against an otherwise unbroken pale blue vista. Gareth aims a half-hearted kick at one of his rickety old garden chairs, and tries to recall the last occasion when he actually sat in a plane, or, indeed, took a proper holiday of any description. He tries, also, to imagine when he'll next go abroad again, and because his doing so doesn't appear likely over any foreseeable period, he returns gloomily indoors, his mind enveloped in a melancholic fog. Beautiful summer mornings are good for a man's spirits, but they have their limitations when he has no more money than a refugee just off the boat.

Indoors, Gareth breakfasts on cereal and toast, before making a second cup of tea and drinking it while watching the news. He learns that one of the tech' giants has just acquired a gaming business called Skeleton Homestead, paying its twenty-year-old founder a hundred million dollars for the privilege. Gareth has only the dimmest of ideas as to what Skeleton Homestead does, and doesn't particularly wish to learn any more, but as he looks at his television screen – specifically studying the bespectacled face of a geeky youth who's just earned five million dollars for every year he's been alive – Gareth wonders how the world can dispense its available fortune in ways quite so disproportionate.

With his second mug of tea finished, he picks up a pen and makes himself a To Do list for the day. He writes it on the back of an envelope which carried an appeal from a charity doing famine-relief work in Africa. *If I had a hundred million*, he thinks, *I'd give ninety-five of it to people without food, water, housing, and sanitation. With the rest I'd buy The Lamb and Musket, put Melanie in charge, and purchase another pub for Derek somewhere else.*

His To Do list reads:

1) Shower

2) Housework / Washing

3) Shopping

4) Eat

5) Legal Stuff / Solicitor Research

6) Review draft ideas for Profile Sheets

7) Show Profile Sheets to Derek

8) More food

9) Cut grass (if time)

10) Ironing (watch TV)

Gareth draws a big circle around the list, and then an arrow leading off the circle. At the end of the arrow, he writes: "Money Making Ideas?"

He then draws another arrow off the same circle, at the end of which he writes: "Melanie." But before he goes upstairs for his shower, he crosses "Melanie" out, using aggressive, thick, repeated strokes. He's embarrassed by the thought of someone discovering his having written it, either later today, or maybe tomorrow, were he to die of a heart attack, or in a car crash or something.

Once he's had his shower, Gareth gets dressed, and then goes methodically about the housework. He does the dusting, and he disinfects the kitchen surfaces. He cleans the bathroom, and loads the washing machine with laundry. The washer, when he switches it on, kicks unsteadily into life – it sounds grumbling and cranky and horrible – and he knows the day is fast approaching when he'll have to find enough money to replace the thing.

Gareth makes his third mug of tea, and has another round of toast. The carpets still need vacuuming, but he figures it's too early for that particular task given that the noise would wake the Harrisons next door, who happen to own the ginger cat to which Gareth lost his earlier staring contest. And so, leaving his plate and mug to soak in the sink, he writes out a shopping list – he writes it on the back of an envelope which carried an exclusive offer for him to buy a cable subscription at half price – and heads off to the supermarket. At least he'll beat the crowds at this hour of the day.

He shops carefully and frugally at the supermarket – comparing prices between brands, looking out for bargains, and taking pains not to buy anything which isn't on his list. He comes straight home afterwards, unpacks the shopping, and washes up his breakfast things in the sink. The washing machine has finished its cycle, and so he takes his clothes outside and hangs them on the line to dry. While he's about it, he glimpses movement in the Harrisons' upstairs window, and concludes that it will therefore be okay to do the vacuuming. He completes that particular job in roughly twenty minutes, and with his carpets cleaned he then sets up his laptop on an occasional table in the front room. He could have used the desk upstairs, but Gareth likes to look out at the passers-by. While he's waiting for the laptop to boot up, he boils the kettle again.

With a fresh mug of tea made, he sits at the laptop and finds it still to be booting, pretty much as he expected. The computer's desktop display is visible by now, but the cursor remains in egg-timer mode, and the machine is making the crinkly, gravelly, scrunchy noise which says it's still coming to terms with his having switched it on. Like his patio chairs and his washing machine, Gareth's laptop has seen better days. It's old now, old and slow, its processing capacity almost overwhelmed by the ever-burgeoning volume of data the internet sends its way. While he waits for it to get its act together, he gets up out of his chair and switches the stereo on, tuning in to local radio and humming along absentmindedly to an eighties tune he vaguely recalls but would struggle to name. He also casts around for the To Do list he wrote earlier, and having found it he crosses off 1) Shower, 2) Housework / Washing, 3) Shopping, and 4) Eat. He also over-scores the circle he drew around "Money Making Ideas?", and when he looks up again he can see through the window that the Harrisons emerging from their house. Somewhere in their thirties, they're an intense looking couple whom he wouldn't have marked down as pet lovers. Wearing track suits and carrying gym bags, they climb into their SUV and hustle away down the road.

Finally, the laptop is as ready as it's going to be. Item five on Gareth's To Do list is 'Legal Stuff / Solicitor Research', and so he opens up a browser and begins typing in what seem the likeliest search terms for the task he has in mind. Only halfway confident of what he's looking for, Gareth is searching in the hope that there may be a legal procedure available to help him subvert, or at least delay, the council meeting set for three weeks hence – a meeting at which The Lamb's future (or lack thereof) is set to be decided. He's also hoping to find a solicitor who'll be available to help implement said legal procedure. Gareth figures that if he can only buy some time, then that time can be used for more lobbying, more persuasion and the generation of new tactics and ideas – namely all of the stuff that gives his existence any purpose nowadays.

The early stages of his search don't go well. There clearly aren't any pre-packaged, off-the-shelf legal mechanisms available which might alter the timing or the outcome of the council meeting. And there are few – very few – instances of council planning committees ever voting against the recommendations of their officers in applications similar to the one with which Gareth is concerned. Worse still – and this was something Gareth already knew, but found himself researching again, just in case he'd missed something previously – there are scarcely any occasions of supermarket groups failing to take over pub sites once they've made their intentions known. Sometimes there is no opposition at all, sometimes the opposition is easily quelled, and sometimes the determined efforts of local patrons can drag the fight out a little longer. However, once a brewery and a supermarket have an agreement in principle, it seems that nothing and nobody gets in their way for very long.

Eventually, his neck cricked and head aching, Gareth closes down the browser and slumps back in his chair. Closing his eyes and holding his hands to his temples, he remains there, unmoving, for a couple of minutes, conscious that he's been sitting at his computer for ages, but that progress against '5) Legal Stuff / Solicitor Research' amounts to barely more than zero.

A flurry of adverts play on the radio station he tuned into. One of them invites him to de-stress in comfort with a luxurious spa weekend.

Gareth finally sits up again and opens his eyes. Before he can reconvene his internet search, his eyes are once again drawn to movement outside the window. He sees that it's Katie Yeomans, the daughter of a couple living a few doors down. Having reached that seemingly amorphous age between adolescence and womanhood, Katie looks alluring in denim shorts and a snug little t-shirt. Gareth watches her go by, and then eases out of his chair. He walks to the window, where, for the benefit of anyone watching him, he makes a show of allowing in some air, while at the same time (and not too obviously, he hopes) getting to study Katie from behind as she strolls away down the street.

A few seconds later, Gareth returns to his chair. He has a stirring in his trousers, but in his head he's hot with shame. The girl has to be – what? – fifteen, maybe. Or sixteen by now. Possibly she's old enough in the eyes of the law, but it's equally possible that she's not, and either way – Hell's flaming bells – she's far too young for him when he's getting on for three times her age.

Gareth reopens the internet and returns to his research. He's afforded a moment of hope, and even excitement, when he reads that a pub's patrons can apply for it to be listed as an asset of community value, and that this will help protect it against the predatory instincts of those who would turn it into an oversized convenience store. But Gareth's spirits sink again, no sooner had they soared. When he reads on, the finds that he'd have needed to apply before now, were he to have any hope of fending off Shop City Supermarkets, and he chides himself for not having unearthed this idea many months ago…

… (*if only*, he thinks, *he didn't spend his time perving after schoolgirls and barmaids*) …

… besides which, when he reads on some more, he finds that listing The Lamb as an asset of community value would have afforded only minimal protection anyway. The act would have done nothing to block planning permission, but would simply have given the 'community' first option on buying The Lamb and Musket from George Timkin's Hippy Hops Pub company. As if those kinds of funds could ever have been found!

Frustrated, Gareth again slumps back into his chair. Minutes later, his ever-encircling bitterness about money bites him that little bit harder when the local radio station includes the sale of Skeleton Homestead in its top-of-the-hour news broadcast. And that's not the only news story featuring big bucks changing hands: apparently the British actress and prominent socialite, Andrea Campion, is to receive a twenty-million-pound divorce settlement from her film-producer husband.

By way of easing his agitation, and also, perhaps, his guilt at leering after girls of school-going age, Gareth straightens back up and searches his laptop for pictures of Andrea Campion, whom he knows to be somewhere in her thirties. The internet certainly isn't short of images. She can be seen in any number of evening dresses, bestriding one red carpet after the other. She's also pictured bikini-clad on some of the world's most glamorous beaches, and, additionally, topless on a yacht – the picture taken, Gareth imagines, with a long-distance lens. And then there are some screen-shots of her in scanty underwear, from the Hollywood blockbuster which made her name – a film in which she played a secret agent doubling as a high-end call girl, but turned out to have been an alien cyborg all along.

Abruptly, Gareth closes down the screen. Although this brief frisson of sexual excitement is a welcome relief from the fruitlessness and frustration of his morning's research, he can't help feeling disappointed with himself. Shaking his head, he gets up from his chair, goes to the kitchen, switches on the kettle (again), and then heads out back for a quick walk around his little garden. He's hoping the outdoors will cool him off somewhat, but it's hot in the garden by now, and he finds it hard to believe that only a few hours have passed since he stood shivering out here while drinking the morning's first mug of tea. Gareth spends a few minutes in quiet contemplation of his lawn – which needs weeding – and his fence – which needs staining – before coming back inside, making more tea, and then settling back at his computer, intent on resuming his research without further carnal distraction.

Having failed to find any obvious legal remedy, he begins an online search for solicitors who may know a less obvious one. At first he searches for a specialist in the field – he hopes that there's a legal eagle out there who has made a name for them self specifically by defending pubs from closure.

However there is not, so far as he can see.

And so next he looks to see if there are solicitors locally who'll work free of charge, or maybe very cheaply, if the cause is seen to be just. Is there someone out there who'll embrace a David versus Goliath story?

But that comes up fruitless as well. Yes, there are solicitors who do legal aid work, but it seems that getting access to legal aid is like getting access to the quarterdeck of the Titanic. The available budget for legal aid is continually shrinking, and in any event the facility is for people in dire personal circumstances, not those fighting to save their local pub from closure.

In the end, it all comes back to this: if Gareth wants to enlist a legal expert then he's going to have to pay for one. And there's little point researching exactly which solicitor to use unless he can first find enough money to purchase a few hours of their time. It's surely also the case that a good solicitor won't come cheap – Gareth holds with the maxim that the payment of peanuts procures the services of monkeys.

He reaches for his To Do list. Regretfully, because he knows he's achieved nothing of note, he ticks off: 5) Legal Stuff / Solicitor Research. His eyes linger once more on "Money Making Ideas?", to which he now adds a second question mark, before over-scoring the surrounding circle again. "There," he murmurs under his breath, "that will really help, won't it – making the bloody circle thicker?"

Gareth finally closes down his laptop, and after putting it away he re-reads items six and seven on his list.

6) Review Draft Ideas for Profile Sheets

7) Show Profile Sheets to Derek.

Gareth lets out a little sigh. The profile sheets were his idea. And he still thinks they're a good one: he believes that highlighting the real, personal and negative effects that The Lamb's closure will have on certain of its patrons is the best chance he has of emotionally leveraging the council. If there's any way that the committee can be persuaded away from their planning officer's recommendations then this has to be it.

And yet.

It feels cruel to go into print with the news that Geoffrey Norton has bad gout and no car. It feels crueller still to point out that Vince Broderick is mentally impaired after the accident which took his father's life, that his greatest pleasure is seeing his friends at the pub, and that The Lamb and Musket is the only pub local enough to where he lives that he can be reasonably trusted to find his own way there and back. In similar vein, the profile sheets for Elaine McThomas and Robbie Arrowsmith seem like unkindness too. Gareth feels bad about zeroing in on people like that, making their vulnerabilities a matter of written record.

But then again, he has precious few chances of saving the pub – *their* pub – and these profile sheets might just do the trick. Nobody would think them a bad idea if they actually kept The Lamb open, would they now?

And Gareth has, after all, drafted a fifth profile sheet – one that puts him in the spotlight and lists his own deficiencies. He reads through it now. Of course, his sheet is less compelling than those of the others – it talks of a man merely fallen into straitened circumstances and lacking a social life outside of the pub's environs. But people would expect his sheet to read that way, he thinks. They know he's not really a victim. They understand, surely, that he's putting himself in the mix in the name of the greater good, that he's simply showing some camaraderie with the four others profiled this way.

The next item on his To Do list is to show the sheets to Derek at The Lamb. Until he can get down there, he folds the profile sheets in half and slides them into an envelope which once carried a reminder that time is running out to claim back his mis-sold Payment Protection Insurance. As he does so, it does occur to him that there are ways in which his own profile sheet could be re-written so that he really does look like an unfortunate. He thinks:

Gareth Rogers. Infatuated with barmaid, Melanie Jones. Dreams of making her Mrs Melanie Rogers, but still lacking the courage to tell her as much. Unlikely to find said courage given that he hasn't been intimate with a woman in more than twenty years, and is worried that if The Lamb closes he won't actually see Melanie again. Either that, or he'll resort to hanging around outside her house, inventing arcane reasons for his being "in the area", for use as explanations when she happens to walk out the door.

Hell's bells. Could it ever really come to that?

Gareth checks the time by an old desk clock which he keeps on the mantelpiece over the gas fire. The morning has raced away from him, and now it's nearly one o' clock. Having risen early, he's feeling tired, and he decides on a nap before heading off down the pub. Moving from his chair to the small sofa in the corner, he kicks back, resting his head on one arm and his feet on another. He dozes off, thinking of Katie Yeomans strutting past in her short shorts, and of Andrea Campion, as depicted in the seedier images of her which are rattling around the internet. He thinks of Melanie working behind the bar in a tight-fitting pair of jeans. Urges stir restlessly within Gareth, but they don't prevent him from falling asleep.

He sleeps for nearly an hour, and then wakes with a dry mouth. He makes yet another mug of tea, and while waiting for it to cool he goes upstairs for a wash and a change of shirt. Once his ablutions are completed, Gareth studies his moustache thoughtfully in the bathroom mirror. He likes the moustache, and has had it so long that he can't imagine his face shorn of it. And yet he wonders whether it doesn't make him look dowdy – conformist and dull, maybe. It's a thought to pursue further on another day, and meanwhile he undoes two buttons of the shirt he's just put on. After studying his reflection some more, he does one of them back up, before finally nodding an approval at his appearance.

Back downstairs, he drinks his tea, and then heads off to The Lamb, clutching the five draft profile sheets in their envelope. He leaves his car at home, partly because it's a nice afternoon for a walk, and partly because he may have three or four beers – that's assuming said beers are on the house, as they often are when he's there to discuss some aspect of the anti-closure campaign with Derek.

Gareth finds the old place far from full – it rarely is of an afternoon, even on a Saturday – but there's a reasonable crowd gathered both inside the pub and at the smokers' tables just outside the door. Inevitably, Bill and Ted number among the latter; both are again wearing shorts and vests, and they look more and more browned (or even reddened) with every passing day of a hot, dry summer. Inside, there are maybe a dozen folk, including Patrick and his dad at one end of the bar. As might be expected, Patrick has his foot slung under the rail while he balances, as per usual, at a precarious angle on his stool. Ricky's there also – in in a shirt so vividly green that to look at it feels like an assault on the senses – but he's propping up a piece of bar a good distance away from the two Mackeys, and appears to be deep in conversation with the newer barmaid, Yasmin.

Yasmin's presence behind the bar is a disappointment to Gareth, in that her being here suggests Melanie isn't working this afternoon. There's no immediate sign of Derek either, and so, as he approaches the bar, Gareth rummages through the change in his pocket, wanting to make sure he has the means to buy a drink before he sets about ordering one.

He stands adjacent to Ricky, so as to be noticed by Yasmin. "The entire band," Ricky is saying to her, "plus their PR people, and assorted hangers-on – they were all staying in the same hotel as me."

"That's pretty cool," she replies, a tight little smile playing on her lips. "I'll bet you were following them round all weekend."

"Nah," replies Ricky. "Those dudes were following me." It's a cheesy line, but Gareth notices it's enough to yield a quick laugh from Yasmin, plus a swift appraising glance for Ricky as she tosses her hair.

Conscious that neither of them has so much as acknowledged him, Gareth clacks a few coins down on the surface of the bar. "Hey, Gareth," says Ricky, turning halfway towards him and clapping him on the shoulder. "How's it going, buddy?"

Yasmin, though, is much cooler towards him. That seems to be the way with her. "What can I get you?" she asks.

Gareth smiles, doing his best to be friendly. "A half of IPA, please, Yasmin."

"Let me get it," says Ricky, sliding off his stool in order to retrieve his wallet from a trouser pocket. "And make it a pint, would you, Yasmin."

Yasmin, who'd already reached down a small glass, flashes Ricky an impatient look as she puts it back and selects a larger one. In turn, Ricky treats Gareth to an amused, man-of-the-world wink. Gareth feels embarrassed about Ricky buying him a pint when he hasn't come out with sufficient funds to reciprocate, but chooses not to countermand the upgrade in case he causes further irritation on Yasmin's part. Instead, he thanks Ricky warmly, and watches Yasmin as she moves to the IPA pump and pulls him his pint.

It feels obscene to watch her for very long, however. In a cropped top and an eye-wateringly short skirt, Yasmin has so much flesh showing that Gareth feels obliged to turn away. Gorgeous though she looks – and it does occur to Gareth that she could pass for a younger version of the recently-divorced actress, Andrea Campion – Yasmin's appearance is simply too indecent that a man can feast his eyes for very long. Turning deliberately towards Ricky, and stroking his moustache as if preoccupied with deeper thoughts, Gareth asks, "Do you happen to know whether Derek's about?"

He isn't sure that Ricky even hears him. The IPA pump being a hand-pull, Yasmin has to arch her spine and extend one foot backwards in order to exert enough force to get the beer flowing. The action accentuates her cleavage and causes muscles to tighten in the back of her thigh. And, unlike Gareth, Ricky doesn't appear to have any qualms about watching her while she works. He has the look on his face of a hungry man studying a gourmet menu.

It's Yasmin who finally answers Gareth's question. "He's out in the yard," she says. "Counting empty barrels."

"Thanks," says Gareth. "Thanks," he then repeats when his beer arrives foaming on the bar. Yasmin wordlessly takes a twenty from Ricky and gets him his change from the till.

Gareth gives his beer a moment to settle and tries to think of something to say.

"You're not buying one for me, then?" Yasmin asks of Ricky.

He laughs. "You're not supposed to ask."

"There are lots of things I'm not supposed to do."

"And yet I bet you're good at them all. What is it that you'd like to drink?"

Gareth finally moves away, pint in one hand, envelope stashed with profile sheets in the other. While waiting for Derek to come in from the yard, he gravitates towards the jukebox. As his beer is yet to fully settle, he puts it down while studying the playlist. Although he hadn't been intending to put money in the slot, he's drawn, just as he was two nights previously, to *Back in the USSR*. He grubs around in his pocket to find the fifty pence necessary for one play.

With his selection made, Gareth turns away from the jukebox as the first chords strike up. He notes that Bill and Ted have come indoors for a refill, and that Patrick has moved across to talk to Ricky while Yasmin is preoccupied pulling Bill and Ted's beer. With Patrick's dad left temporarily alone, perched on a stool at one corner of the bar, Gareth approaches him to exchange a few words.

"Well, Malachy," he says, "from the look of you all, you and the boys have been playing golf."

"Aye," he replies. "I daresay the shirts are an easy enough giveaway?"

"That, and the suntans."

Mackey Senior idly examines his own tanned forearm. It's sinewy and freckled, and has a livid, two-inch scar running diagonally below the elbow, which Malachy will, when pushed, explain was caused by a rubber bullet while he was on a protest march, three decades back. "You should take up golf yourself, Gareth," he finally says. "It's a fine sport, and you'd get yourself plenty of sun – in the summer, at least."

"It's a great idea, Malachy. But I'm far too busy for that."

At first Mackey Senior merely nods, as if in agreement. But then he looks Gareth very directly in the eye, and asks, "With what, exactly?"

Gareth, who had just begun sipping his pint, nearly splutters it back into the glass. Then, once he finally has some beer swallowed, he makes a point of casting his eyes around the pub and gesturing accordingly with one hand. "Well, with The Lamb of course. With the campaign to stop it closing."

"But seriously?" says Malachy. "Gareth, let it go. You've done all that you can, and you're not going to go changing any outcomes now. That fella there will be alright if it closes," – and here Mackey Senior points at Derek, who has come in from the backyard and appears to be working out how many bottles he has in the fridge – "because he'll get another pub, sure he will, and meantime Patrick says Mel is already looking for a job. I know the closure will be harder for some people than others – and I gather from Derek you're here to show him those sheets you've been working up – but if The Lamb does shut down, we'll all find a way of moving on. Just some of us a bit faster than the rest."

Like many of The Lamb's regulars, Gareth has been lectured by Mackey Senior before now, though rarely so vehemently as this. He takes a few seconds to let it all sink in, especially the news – Hell's bells! – that Melanie is already looking for work, and he takes a big sip of beer before delivering his reply.

Even then, it's a reply which, when it finally comes, doesn't really amount to much. Gareth doesn't embellish it with a great deal of defiance, simply trotting out, "It isn't over yet, Malachy," and letting that simple statement stand as the limit of today's fighting talk. Then, given the implacable look on Malachy's face, and also because Gareth is feeling far from bullish following his fruitless morning on the internet, he tries to sidestep any further argument. With a little nod towards Bill and Ted, he ponders a question aloud. "I wonder where those two will end up if the place does close down. They seem to be here every day."

Mackey Senior eyes up Bill and Ted like a wild-west sheriff might eye up some cattle rustlers. "Those two?" he sniffs. "They'll end up somewhere. They'll be alright. I've seen plenty just like 'em."

Bill has produced a customarily thick wad of cash from the back pocket of his shorts. He peels off a note, ready to pay Yasmin.

"But where on Earth do the two of them get their money?" asks Gareth. "Where does it come from when they're drinking in here all the time."

Malachy lets out a wistful sigh. "From places and schemes and people that you don't want to know about, Gareth." An absent look comes over the Ulsterman, one which makes Gareth wonder whether he's thinking of places and schemes and people back in Belfast. "As I very recently said, I've seen plenty just like 'em."

Mackey Senior might have let it rest at that, but for whatever reason – maybe, for instance, because Gareth's eyes have lingered for too long on that big wad of notes – he offers up another observation. "One thing's for sure, Gareth. Those two don't have money and free time to spare by punching in at a warehouse. And if you don't mind my saying so, you ought to be thinking about your own career. A capable man like you should be doing more than he is. Again, maybe you're too long on this campaign of yours."

Gareth feels stung by the observation, and this time he's minded to bite back – it's not as if he hasn't tried to do better for himself. But before he can say a word, they're joined at their corner of the bar by Patrick. "Hi Gareth," he says, clapping him on the shoulder just as Ricky did earlier. "How's it going with you?"

"Alright, thanks. I seem to be receiving plenty of advice."

"All good, though, I hope?"

"Certainly, it's all good," says Malachy, looking evenly at Gareth. "Be sure to think on about what I've just said."

A moment passes during which Gareth remains mute with annoyance while, at the same time racking his brain for a polite way of telling Malachy to mind his own business. Then Patrick says to

Malachy, "Ricky's going to stay here a bit. He'll get a taxi back, so you and I can go, if you like."

"You've got his golf clubs, haven't you?" replies Mackey Senior. "They're still in your car."

"Sure, I can store them at my place until we play next. He won't need them for another month at least."

Mackey Senior nods his understanding, and Gareth glances across the bar. Bill and Ted have been served by now, but are taking a moment to leer at Yasmin as she resumes her conversation with Ricky. "I wonder if Ricky's going to have competition," says Gareth, "if he's staying here for the purpose of sweet-talking Yasmin."

"Richard will be just fine," says Mackey Senior, finishing off his beer and easing down from his stool. "His is another type that I happen to know well."

"What type is that?" asks Derek, arriving at the back end of Malachy's observation. He's sporting his usual hairstyle – a Bobby Charlton comb-over, falling lankly to disarray – and he has on a frayed white shirt gone grey in the wash. "What gossip have I missed out on now?"

"Ricky's type," replies Patrick. "I think my da's suggesting he's the wrong man to mess with."

"That's exactly what I'm suggesting," confirms the older Mackey. "I'm entirely sure that Richard's a complete fucker if you choose to cross him."

"Except at golf," retorts Patrick, smiling. "He's a complete fuckee on the golf course."

Patrick's quip gets everyone laughing, but once the hilarity abates Gareth waves the envelope holding the profile sheets at Derek. "I need to show you these," he says.

"That's fine," says Derek, brandishing some stationery of his own – a notepad and pen that he whips from a back pocket. "But give me ten minutes, would you? I just need to work out an order for the brewery."

"No problem," says Gareth.

"And if you've written one of those sheets about Vince," interjects Patrick to Gareth, "you'll run it by Ricky and me as well, yeah? Before you go publishing it?"

"I promise," says Gareth. "And his mum, too."

"Well, we have to be off," says Malachy. "I've promised my good lady wife that come sunset the lawn will be considerably shorter than at daybreak."

"Sure," says Patrick. "And his good lady wife is someone else not to fuck with."

"But if I hadn't," replies his dad, "you wouldn't even be here to beat the English at golf."

More laughter all round. Then Derek goes off to complete his order, while Patrick and his dad make ready to leave. Gareth can see that Yasmin is deep in conversation with Ricky, and is sipping something exotic-looking from a tall glass – most likely it's the drink she was trying to coax from him earlier. Bill and Ted, meanwhile, drinks in one hand, unlit cigarettes in another, have made it to the exit. Any minute now, they'll be topping up on nicotine.

Brushing past, on his way to the door, Mackey Senior pauses, and takes a firm hold of Gareth's bicep with one hand. Whatever other damage that rubber bullet did, it clearly didn't affect the man's grip. "That pair, again," Malachy says, with a nod towards Bill and Ted as they both head outside.

"Bill and Ted?" replies Gareth. "What about them?"

"Sure, it seems to me that you're looking in their direction a very great deal. Well I'm having a think to myself, and I reckon you're still wondering where all their money comes from."

"Okay, well yes I am. Maybe, in an idle sort of way, I am wondering."

"Sure, well you've a few minutes while Derek finishes his order. So why don't you go outside and ask them?"

"Ask them?" queries Gareth.

"Ask them," says Mackey Senior. "Just go over and say, 'Fellas, I was wondering how you come by your money when you're in here all the time with big bundles of cash but don't appear to have jobs to go to.'" Then Malachy gives Gareth a little wink, and squeezes his arm even harder for a second. "Who knows what answer you'll get," he adds, before finally releasing his grip and following Patrick to the car park.

+++++

Mel's back garden isn't, in truth, so much a garden as a fenced-in rear yard with a few plants in some pots and a timbered outhouse. Like the rest of her home it's of a compact size – compact, that is, when she's inclined to speak favourably of it, whilst cramped is more the operative word when she's minded to be frank.

Compact or cramped, in the afternoons the rear yard makes a nice sun trap either way. And having high fences, it's overlooked only from the upstairs windows of the houses adjacent on either side. Trusting both sets of neighbours as she does, the rear yard is one of Mel's favourite places during the summer, and it's where she can be found now, where, with her day's chores done, she's lolling in her bikini on a sun-lounger, sometimes reading a page or two of her book, other times simply lying back and soaking up the sun.

Up above her, the window to Gabby's room is open, and Mel can hear music playing at a volume just shy of too loud while her daughter readies herself for a sleepover at the home of a long-time school friend. Putting her book to one side, Mel sets the lounger to a more reclined position, and then settles back with her eyes closed. The late afternoon sun feels pleasantly warm on her face, and she remembers for a while what it was like to be Gabby's age, and how much promise the world seemed to hold when she stood just a little way back from the edge of womanhood.

And it's not as if the world feels short of promise now. Okay, the last few years haven't been easy, what with raising Gabby as a single parent, and it's true that Mel would like to have more money behind her, and to be buying a home rather than renting from the council. But on the plus side, she has her health, she has Gabby, and she has the prospect of searching, once again, for full time work. The more she thinks about it, the more excited she is about resuming a career.

Also, she still has her looks. Mel knows that there are women ten years younger who'd like to look this good in a bikini. And she still *feels* young – she still believes that the world is alive with potential. Including the potential to find love again.

Although perhaps not with Patrick. Not when he dithers so much about a simple thing like asking her out for a drink. Quite frankly, Mel doesn't have time for ditherers. She may be looking good and feeling young, but her birth certificates doesn't lie. And in her head she can hear a clock ticking, nearly as clearly as she can hear the music emanating from Gabby's room.

The afternoon may be late, but the sun feels oppressively hot against her closed eyelids, and so, without opening them, she reaches down and runs her fingers over the paving, seeking out her sunglasses. She finds them and slips them on, instantly feeling the respite.

Mel suspects she needs to be more decisive about finding a man. Perhaps she ought to go proactively looking for one, in the same way that she went looking for a job yesterday. There are internet sites and all sorts these days. Or maybe, if she actually made the first move, she would still have a chance with Patrick, who's handsome and funny and kind. She thinks about the way he was in the van yesterday, when he picked her up just after… just after… just after…

And now the events of Friday morning come rushing back in a flood of panicked thoughts. Mel remembers looking in through the window of Hugo Albrighton's estate agency, and also recollects the moment when she stepped away, nearly colliding with the big man. She recalls him pushing her hard into the window, and vividly remembers her head bouncing painfully off the glass, before she then slid down the pane, all the way to the floor. Finally the big man's grinning, savage face, and that awful snake tattoo. "Watch the fuck where you're going, you festering little bitch."

Abruptly, Mel sits up, feeling suddenly cold, conscious that her breathing has quickened and that her arms have developed goose bumps. She whips off her sunglasses and peers at the tops of the surrounding fences, briefly persuaded that someone was spying on her.

But of course there's no one there. And when she cranes her neck, there's no one in the upstairs windows of the adjacent houses either. Everything is normal, except in her mind. Pivoting on the lounger, she plants her feet firmly on the floor and then stands slowly up. Her heart feels fast and her legs not quite steady. She can hear the lazy drone of an unseen insect passing somewhere close by, alongside the remorselessly kitsch rhythm of a boyband playing through the speakers upstairs.

Mel goes inside and gets a glass of water from the tap. She drinks it while standing with one hand holding to the edge of the sink. When she begins to feel normal again, she goes upstairs and pulls some shorts and a t-shirt over her bikini. She also fishes a pair of sandals from the wardrobe and finds a band for her hair. Then she goes back downstairs and makes herself a coffee, which she's nursing at the small table in the kitchen when Gabby finally comes down.

Gabby's wearing ripped jeans, white sneakers and a summery top. She's clearly been straightening her hair. Her face is made up to an extent which, just like the volume of her music, pushes the limit of what is permitted without quite amounting to a transgression. Still just about a schoolgirl, she's trying hard to look like a young woman, and succeeding to a frightening degree. Additionally, she has a small, pink overnight bag which she sets on the floor while she pours juice from the fridge. "Hey," she says, by way of a greeting, having last set eyes on her mother a couple of hours ago.

"Hey yourself," replies Mel. "Are you all ready to go?"

"As soon as I've drunk this."

"Well, I've got my coffee to finish," says Mel, briefly raising her coffee cup, "and then I'll walk you round to Sally's"

Gabby, who'd been returning the juice carton to the fridge, pivots swiftly around, the soles of her sneakers squeaking on the floor. "You'll walk me?" she blurts, with a swift look at the oven's in-built clock. "Mother, it's just gone four-thirty in the afternoon."

"I'm still going to walk you round there."

"Are you for real?"

"I am. Call it an intuition."

Gabby closes the fridge door. "I can't believe you, sometimes," she says. "This is just so overprotective."

"Gabby," says Mel, "I'll make a deal with you. I'll walk you as far as Sally's house. And then, rather, than turn around, I'll keep on walking, as if I'm going to the shops. That way it looks as if we kept each other company while we were both going the same way. Nothing overprotective about that, is there?"

"You went to the shops earlier."

Mel lets out a long, loud sigh. "Don't fight me, sweetheart. Not over this – not today. Either I'm walking with you or we're both staying here."

For an instant, Gabby looks set to argue. But then, maybe sensing Mel's steadfastness, she confines herself to a big sigh of her own, and lets that stand as her protest. "Well okay," she says, after a perfunctory sip of orange juice. "You'd better finish your coffee, then."

Thankfully, the walk to Sally's goes okay, though both mother and daughter are uncommunicative to begin with. Mel figures that Gabby must be pretty put out at being accompanied on a walk she's previously made many times by herself. But then, after a while, Mel finds herself rubbing the bump on the side of her head, and decides to give herself an easier time over having made this call. *Better safe than sorry*, she thinks.

It's as they're passing The Lamb and Musket that Gabby breaks the ice, asking her mother whether she'll working later.

"Not tonight," replies Mel. "I'm back in tomorrow."

They walk on in renewed silence for a short while. Then, once they've turned a corner, leaving the old pub behind, Gabby asks, "Is The Lamb really going to close, then? What will you do for money if it does?"

"It probably will," Mel replies. "Which will be a shame. But we'll be okay, sweetheart – you and I. I'll find work. In fact, I've already started to look."

"Is that why you had the computer out yesterday morning?"

"I thought you were too sleepy to notice, but yes, that's the reason why."

"And you'll find a job? Just like that?"

"It's a bit more than 'just like that,'" says Mel. "But I will find a job. And anyway, if I don't, I'll just have to rent you out as child labour. You're not yet so big that you won't fit up a chimney."

The line earns Mel a laugh, and normal relations are fully restored thereafter. They're both in good spirits by the time they reach Sally's house, and Gabby doesn't seem to mind that her Mel's presence is noticed by Sally and her folks, although she is quick to trot out the line that 'mum's just on her way to the shops'. Having suggested it in the first place, Mel's happy to go along with the ruse, claiming that they're out of milk at home, and after leaving Gabby at Sally's house she even completes the charade by heading to the grocery up the road, and buying a two-pint carton of semi-skimmed. It does seem an excessive length to go to, but hey, you can never have too much milk. Besides which, she remembers that Sally's dad does own a drone and – creepy and absurd as the thought may seem – it does occur to Mel that he may actually be tracking her progress. After the events of yesterday, she feels entitled to a little paranoia at least.

Her journey home is pretty uneventful until she once again passes The Lamb and Musket. Her path crosses those of Bill and Ted as they come barrelling first through the front doors, then across the car park, and eventually onto the pavement. Although wobbling a little, theirs is the deliberate gait of men who've had lots to drink and are therefore having to concentrate on walking straight, and who are, by and large, managing to carry it off. Gareth is with them too, and at first Mel assumes it to be a coincidence that he's leaving at the same time as this pair of chancers. But then, from the way they're talking among themselves, Mel suddenly arrives at the idea that the three of them have been drinking together. Also, from the way that Gareth is trying, but failing, to walk straight, Mel intuits that he's been trying to keep pace with Bill and Ted in the boozing stakes. What a bloody dickhead.

"You won't forget, will you," says Bill – the older of the two – to Gareth. He reaches out with both hands and mimics someone turning a steering wheel. "We get you a motor; you turn up and deliver for us."

"You can… totally… be sure… totally be sure…" replies Gareth, working hard to enunciate, and slurring his words when he does.

My God, thinks Mel, as she draws ever closer. *Gareth's pissed completely off his face.*

"Totally be sure… totally be sure…" He's swaying and staggering, and his eyes are wide and wild. Totally rely… rely on me. Me."

Bill and Ted notice that Mel has arrived on the scene. "Hi, Mel," says Bill. Lovely to see you out."

Ted looks her up and down, his eyes lingering on her legs to the extent that she wishes she'd put on some longer trousers. "Lovely," he echoes.

"Lovely jubbly," laughs Bill, lighting a cigarette. They all stink of booze.

Gareth is last to notice her, but when he does it's as if he's been poked with a cattle prod. "Mel," he blurts, lurching towards her, but not quite making it, bouncing first off Bill and then off Ted, before having to stoop and then steady himself by resting a hand on the low wall running the perimeter of The Lamb's car park. "Melanie… Hell's Mels… Mel's hells… I mean… Mel… maybe I…"

By now, Bill and Ted each have cigarettes on the go, and both are bent double with laughter.

"Bloody hell, Gareth," howls Bill. "'Hell's Mels' – you silly fucker. Is it the drink that's got to you, or the fucking sun?"

It's quite obviously the drink, but Mel can see from the redness around Gareth's neck that he'll also have sunburn to go with his hangover. Angrily, she rounds on Bill and Ted. "What the bloody hell have you done to him?"

"You what?" asks Bill, wobbling a little as he spreads his arms wide in a posture of innocence. "Fella comes and joins us for a drink –

and at our expense, I'll mention – not our fault if he can't handle his beer."

"Yeah," adds Ted, again looking Mel up and down. "You want to watch what you're saying, you know. You could land yourself in some serious trouble."

Ted's scarcely disguised threat sends a shiver of fear through her. But because familiarity breeds at least a degree of contempt, Mel feels anger as well. Cold, vengeful anger, which, though suppressed since yesterday's attack, now comes surging to the surface. "What do you mean by that?" she demands, finding the courage to take a step forward, getting right in Ted's face. She's only dimly aware that her hand not carrying milk is clenched into a fist – clenched to the degree that she's digging her nails into the heel of her palm. "Just what the hell do you think you're saying, you jumped piece of mouthy little shite?"

Mel's so close she can smell the sourness of lager and cigarettes on Ted's breath. At first he look surprised, but then his eyes harden, and Mel's sure he's about to raise a hand to her. Maybe Bill thinks the same, because he lunges forward, wraps his arms around his drinking partner, and hauls him back a yard or two. "Come on, Ted," he says. "Time we were away."

"No fucking way," says Ted, his face contorted as he strains against Bill's grip. "She shouldn't have said her shit. I can't just let this go."

"You need to just let this go," replies Bill. "You shouldn't have said your shit, either." With his arms wrapped firmly around Ted, he cranes his neck to look at Mel. "We're sorry about this," he says to her. "No harm meant. It's the beer talking." Then he whispers in Ted's ear, and manages to manoeuvre him another couple of paces away from Mel. "I'll get this one home," he calls to her. "You do the same for Gareth, if you can."

Mel stands rooted to the spot, her heart hammering like she's just put in a sprint finish at the end of a marathon. Her fingers gripping the milk are white at the knuckles, while the nails of her opposite hand are digging harder and harder into her palm. For a long moment, she watches Bill and Ted's slow, tortuous retreat, the two of them continuing to grapple as they meander awkwardly down the road. When she finally turns away and tries to move, her legs feel wobbly, just as they did after yesterday's assault and also after her flashback of earlier this afternoon.

But her unsteadiness is as nothing when compared to Gareth's. He now has two hands on the low wall, and is leaning over it while throwing up into The Lamb's car park.

"Bloody hell, Gareth," Mel sighs. She eases down next to him, one hand on the wall, the other on his shoulder. "What have you been up to, mate? Are you alright?"

He angles his head to look at her. Liquid vomit drips from a corner of his mouth, while the remnants of some solids linger in his moustache. His eyes, meanwhile, are all over the place – they're zipping around manically, like two wartime searchlights whose operator has lost track of incoming bombers. They finally focus, after a fashion at least, on her. "Melanie," he blurts as before, and then his brow creases, as if he's trying to remember. "You were… here… earlier… Bill, Ted… you… OhmyGod!" He leans abruptly forward and throws up some more. When he eventually turns back to her, he's red in the face from the exertion of convulsing, and a long twine of spittle hangs from his lips. Seemingly aware of this, he runs a forearm across his mouth, but the act of removing his hand from the wall leaves him struggling to stay balanced, and he nearly falls over. "Hell's bells," he moans. "You should never ever, ever. Ever see me like this."

Mel's experience informs her that drunkenness has several stages. There's tipsy; there's drunk; there's very drunk. Then there's absolutely wankered – and this is the first time she's seen Gareth in such a desperate state as this. She pats his shoulder in an effort to console him. "Don't worry," she says. "You're not the first and I'm sure you're not the last. Now stay here, because I've come out with no phone, so I'm going into The Lamb to call you a taxi."

She straightens up to go inside, but her suggestion seems to have spooked Gareth. "No, no, no," he says, somehow getting up too. "Taxi… no need." Then he manages to walk two paces away, before falling down hard on his hands and knees.

Mel goes to him again. "Come on, Gareth. Be bloody sensible, mate."

He manages to get up once more. "It's okay – can manage." He raises an arm and points waveringly down the road, in the direction of his house. "It's three minute walk… taxi not necess…" Abandoning any attempt at speech, Gareth lurches broadly in the direction he'd been pointing, actually managing a succession of steps without falling again, but in a line no more linear than the ECG printout out of someone suffering heart palpitations.

Mel is uncertain what to do for the best. At times like these, what she'd really like is a less sympathetic personality – one that would allow her to head off home without worrying about Gareth or letting the uncertainty of his fate trouble her conscience. But on the basis that she simply isn't that kind of girl, she supposes that she should head on into The Lamb and get him a taxi, or at least some other form of help. But if she leaves him alone, if only for a minute, then he could end up anywhere – in the road, for instance, with a juggernaut bearing down on him. And it is only a few minutes' walk to his house, albeit in the wrong direction for her. Besides which, the diversion might actually be a good thing, in that it would save her from catching back up with Bill and Ted, and from having to deal with any further unpleasantness on Ted's part.

Decision made, then. Still clutching her two-pinter of milk, Mel quickly catches up with Gareth, and takes hold of his arm as he stumbles along the pavement. "Come on, you big wazzock," she says. "Let's bloody get you home."

Gareth gives her another nonplussed look, his brow creasing up again as he once more goes about the process of remembering that she's actually there. Then he tilts back his head and laughs, the action rendering him even unsteadier on his feet as he lopes along. "Won't… always… not like this," he mumbles nonsensically. "Not when Bill… gets me a car."

"Gareth? You've got a car."

"No… 'nother car. Hell's bells… a money car."

"Okay," she says, taking a firmer grip of his arm as he diverts violently towards the kerb's edge. "Whatever you say."

He looks directly at her, and for the tiniest instance there's a look of coherent sobriety in his eyes. Then he laughs and looks away. "Sorry Melanie… makes no sense, I know… I was dreaming you see."

"I'm sure you were."

"'bout Andrea Campion."

"Yeah? Well I'm sure many men do."

"She looks… like Yasmin. Yasmin at… The Lamb."

Mel thinks about that one for a couple of seconds. Then she says, "Fair point, Gareth – she does a bit."

"But neither of them… is you."

"That's true as well, mate. Neither Yasmin nor Andrea Campion is me."

"With your shorts. And your legs."

"Err, I'm fairly sure they both have shorts and legs of their own."

"I know… that," he replies. "I know that… Melanie. But… your shorts… and… your legs… are the best… And they are… coming back… to my place. With me… And with you… of course… Your legs stay with you… all the time."

"Gareth," begins Mel, with an inner little sigh. She might have foreseen this.

"Not sure… about… your shorts… though… You take them off… sometimes… I'm sure."

"Gareth, I'm walking you to your front door," she says. "Think of it as a dazzling example of outstanding customer service, especially as I'm not even on shift. But that's all it is, Gareth. Don't go getting any ideas."

He hangs his head, so losing what little concept of direction he had, necessitating Mel to steady him as he once again veers towards the road. "I had lots… of ideas… today."

"It sounds like it. Don't go getting too many more."

"Money car… was best idea… Bill's idea."

"Whatever," she says. Against her better judgement, she finds herself halfway interested in this utter nonsense. What the hell is a money car, exactly? Mel doesn't like the idea of Gareth getting mixed up with anything concerning Bill and Ted. But she doubts she'd get much sense out of him were she to ask about it now.

Gareth falls quieter after that, and his pace picks up a little. It's as if he's realised what an idiot he's been, and simply wants to get home. The two of them nearly collide with an elderly woman pulling a shopping cart, and they receive their share of scornful looks from other pedestrians, but eventually Mel has Gareth standing on his doorstep with his keys in his hand. She's in no mood for taking further shit from anyone, and has readied herself to speak firmly with him should he try anything on with her, and to knee him hard in the balls if speaking firmly doesn't work.

In the end, no such response is necessary. Maybe the walk has finally sobered Gareth a little, because he looks at her sheepishly and says, "You're not coming in… are you?"

"No further than your front room," she replies. "I'd like to see you sitting down, in a chair, so that you can get some rest before you need to stand up again."

Gareth doesn't actually make it to a chair. Once indoors, deciding he needs the toilet, he goes upstairs on his hands and knees. Mel waits in the narrow hallway, and remains there for a couple of minutes after hearing the toilet flush. When the cistern has refilled and the house has fallen silent, she calls Gareth's name, but gets no reply. Tentatively, she heads up the stairs, still calling out to him, only to find him sprawled, face down and fast asleep on the bed. She goes back downstairs and gets the washing-up bowl from the kitchen, before leaving it by his head in case he needs to be sick again when he finally awakes. After that, she takes his keys, lets herself out, and posts the keys back through the letterbox once she's locked the door behind her.

As Mel's walking home, she realises she's locked her two pints of milk inside Gareth's house. But that simple error doesn't feel like her biggest mistake of the afternoon. What on Earth was she thinking of earlier, she now wonders, when she was planning to get a man back into her life? Why on Earth would she ever need the aggravation? Hell's bloody bells, as a certain numpty might well say.

1.4) Sunday

I'm absolutely saying no," says Patrick to Gareth. For emphasis, he slaps a hand down on top of the bar. "It's definitely not for the papers. I'm not even sure about your council meeting. But definitely not the papers."

It's Sunday night at The Lamb and Musket. As such, it's quiz night, although this one, so far, feels different to many that have gone before. For one thing it's busier than usual, with more people and more teams involved, and that's partly because Gareth did manage to persuade a journalist here, together with an attendant crowd of real ale enthusiasts. A further reason why this Sunday feels atypical to Patrick is that Caroline, Ricky's wife, has promised to be here, although she and Ricky are yet to arrive. It's three months or more since Caroline last came to the quiz, and Patrick's happy to admit – to himself, at least – that her imminent appearance has left him excited, just like some love-struck young kid.

And then there's this, the third thing that Patrick finds different about this particular Sunday: him standing at the bar with Gareth and Derek, arguing the toss about the personal profile sheets which Gareth has mocked up, each sheet featuring the difficult life circumstances of someone who drinks here at The Lamb. Patrick's arguing, in particular, about the sheet in which Gareth has profiled Vince. *Vince's Victim Sheet* is the name that Patrick gives to it, and the portrayal of Vince as a victim is what troubles Patrick most about the whole idea. He doesn't think of Vince as a victim. He thinks of him as someone who's been dealt a truly lousy hand but is playing his cards brilliantly well.

"I do understand what you're saying," says Gareth. "I too am reluctant to put this in the papers."

"Then don't," says Patrick. "Don't put it in the frickin papers. It's horrible, Gareth. It's horrible, and it's cruel. Sure, I know what you're trying to do with this; I know that you're trying to tug some heartstrings. And reluctantly I'll go along with it, so far as circulating this stuff among council members is concerned. But putting it in the press for everyone to read? That's got to be a no."

Gareth shrugs and sighs, and massages his moustache between finger and thumb. He also raises a hand as if to give his neck a rub, but then flinches, and quickly lowers his hand back down. Gareth's neck must be hurting him – it looks red raw from the sun. "But Patrick," he says, "Mike Gibney the journalist is here tonight. I've got to give him something."

"Sure then, Gareth. Give him this." Patrick opens his arms expansively, and casts a glance around The Lamb and Musket. "Give him the whole pub. Give him the community. Tell him it's a crying shame that a place pulling in this many people is destined for the axe. But don't go serving up my mate – disabled, half orphaned and partially brain damaged – for everyone to read about."

"Oh, Patrick, Hell's bells," murmurs Gareth. He folds his arms, in what may be the beginning of a sulk. "What do you think, Derek?"

"What I think," replies Derek, "is that…"

But Derek doesn't seem to have a firm opinion on the matter. He leaves uncompleted whatever it was he was about to say, and in the meantime he breaks off for another look at the five sheets – *five sheets for five victims*, thinks Patrick – which Gareth has set out tidily and discreetly, in one little corner of the bar. "What I think…" Derek repeats, but then runs out of steam again, without actually telling anyone what thoughts, if any, are running through his head.

"Well, what I think," ventures Mel, interceding as she pulls some lager, "is that Patrick is right. This stuff doesn't belong in the papers. And, anyway, I don't think they'd publish it if you gave to them."

"You really think that?" Gareth looks downcast. He has, Patrick notices, been especially sheepish around Mel this evening, and even more deferential to her than usual.

"Yes, I do really think that," says Mel emphatically. "Your man Patrick here is dead on," she adds, adopting a comedy Irish accent, "as they like to say in Andersontown, or wherever it is."

"Nice try, Mel," says Patrick. "But it's Andersonstown – with an S. Andersons, not Anderson. But sure, it's just as often called Andy Town. Or Angry Town, even."

"Sure, I'll be remembering that, so I shall."

Gareth, meanwhile, has gathered up his profile sheets and put them back in their envelope. Patrick tries to say something consolatory to him – something to let Gareth know that everyone appreciates his efforts – but such words that Patrick can bring to mind are lame and perfunctory, and that may be because his attention has been distracted by the presence of a stranger. Hovering close by, having just gotten served, aged somewhere in his forties, the man sports a crewcut, and has sly, watchful eyes. He appeared to pay particular attention to Patrick and Mel's conversation about the geography of west Belfast, and Patrick, who hasn't noticed the fella drinking here before, supposes that he may well be British military, or ex-military, and could have seen service across the water. If that supposition is correct, then it's quite likely that the man won't care very much for Irish republicans, and nor will his two mates to whom the stranger now returns while carrying three pints.

Making a mental note to keep an eye on the three blokes, especially later in the evening, when lots of beer will have been consumed, Patrick picks up his own round of drinks and returns to the table he's currently sharing only with Vince.

Vince puts a thumb up to thank him for the tomato juice, before returning his attention to the picture-round opening section of the quiz. "I've only... got four... so far," he says to Patrick, speaking very slowly and with great care, sliding the sheet with ten pictures across the table.

It's been another hot day, and it feels close and sticky inside The Lamb and Musket, what with it being so crowded in here. Patrick is feeling sweaty following his argumentative exertions at the bar, and he wipes a forearm across his brow as he studies the photos. The picture round is often Vince's best round, and to know four of the ten is pretty good, especially as Patrick is struggling to name that many himself.

"Cheryl Cole," says Vince, pointing at one of the photos.

"I don't think she's been called Cole for a while," replies Patrick, "but that's certainly who she is." He writes down 'Cheryl', and the puts 'Cole' in brackets, and then Vince points out Michael Macintyre, who Patrick also recognises, together with George Foreman, whom he doesn't, but whose name he happily writes down because he's aware that Vince knows his boxing, if not his fat-free grills.

Vince then points to a man in racing overalls – possibly a Formula One driver or a motorcyclist. The man has a chiselled jaw and a little spike of hair. Again slowly, but with great certainty, Vince offers the name of Robert Kubica.

Patrick wouldn't have recognised the face if Kubica had knocked his door and asked him to fix a burst pipe. But he's heard enough of Kubica's remarkable back story to know that the driver made a comeback to Formula One several years after losing most of the use of one arm in a horrible racing accident. It's a heroic story, Patrick thinks, and one with which Vince will feel a degree of empathy. Patrick writes down 'Robert', and then, hovering his pen over the page, asks Vince, more in hope than expectation, whether he know how to spell Kubica.

Vince's reply, in his faltering, grasping style, leaves them both chuckling quietly. "These days.. Patrick… I'm struggling… to spell… fucking Vince."

Patrick writes Kubica down phonetically and in brackets – ("Cube-It-Za") – trusting that others in his team will know the correct spelling once they arrive. Then he swivels the photo sheet back around, and points out the one face he can name which Vince so far hasn't.

"Sure," says Patrick, tapping his forefinger down on the paper, just above the face concerned. "It's Tom Hardy."

Vince looks at him blankly.

"Tom Hardy," Patrick repeats. "The actor."

Another blank look, and a long, slow shake of the head.

"Bane in The Dark Knight Rises? Alfie Solomons in Peaky Blinders?" Patrick mimics the removal of a flat cap and subsequent slashing at an opponent with the razors stitched into its peak. "You like Peaky Blinders, mate."

Vince just shrugs, as if to indicate he hasn't a clue.

"Fair enough," says Patrick, with a shrug of his own. "Well sure, it's Tom Hardy anyway."

Patrick writes down Tom Hardy's name, simultaneously marvelling and despairing that Vince can be so sharp at times, and so off-the-pace at others. It's as though, somewhere inside his head, there's a munitions box of stun grenades, one of which might go off at any moment, randomly incapacitating certain of Vince's faculties, while leaving others intact. And there's an irony that Vince doesn't recognise Tom Hardy, because now that Patrick thinks about it, there's actually a passing resemblance between the two of them.

It's a thought which must absorb much of Patrick's attention, because he fails to notice the new arrivals until the very last minute.

They're some good looking new arrivals – all three of them. Patrick looks up from his answer sheet to see Ricky standing there. Ricky is clean-shaven, with a good shirt on his back and Caroline on his arm. Caroline is a vision. A different vision to yesterday's multi-coloured one, because today she has on some black jeans and a white, short-sleeved blouse in which she looks, of course, utterly gorgeous.

That Caroline looks so good is hardly shock news, but what does come as a surprise is that Ricky has a different woman on his other arm. She's another good looker, one whom Patrick doesn't even recognise at first, although it's clear from the look of delight on his face that Vince is quicker off the mark.

"Hi guys," chorus Caroline and Ricky.

"Well, hello strangers," chips in Ricky's younger sister, Esme.

Vince is up off his feet with a hug for them all, and Patrick stands too, waiting his turn and trying to figure out how long it is since he last clapped eyes on Esme. Ten years ago, when he was twenty and she fifteen, she had a crush on him which he tolerated with generous good humour. Later, by the time he and Ricky were twenty-six and Esme twenty-one, she was a petite and sexy business graduate, her infatuation with him a mere footnote by then, as she readied herself for a move to Frankfurt with her German boyfriend. Then, two years afterwards, she was back in the UK, the German boyfriend also a footnote by that stage in her life. Patrick remembers seeing her at Ricky's house at the time – she'd had her hair cut short and he hadn't particularly liked it that way. That was just before she departed again, this time to Scotland, when a new career opportunity opened up in Edinburgh.

Patrick also remembers Ricky very recently telling him that the firm she'd joined in Edinburgh was moving her south once more, and that she'd therefore be based back in town. Patrick had looked forward to meeting Esme again, maybe even to seeing whether any of that adolescent crush might be rekindled. But he'd soon forgotten the conversation with Ricky. Forgotten it until just now, when the gang all walked into the pub.

Esme's grown her hair again. Patrick likes it. And who cares if she's wearing a smidge too much makeup for such a pretty face. He can live with that for now.

Taking his turn after Vince, Patrick kisses Caroline first, then Esme. Greetings are exchanged, although he's not sure exactly what he says or what gets said to him. He's intoxicated, he realises, by their very presence. Sure, he's in love with Caroline – he knows that. He's been in love with her for two-thirds of his life. But to look at Esme, all sexy and grown up, and very possibly single, is a treat for Patrick's eyes.

Ricky says he's going to the bar. Patrick says Ricky can stay put, sure he can, because he, Patrick, is going to get the drinks in. Ricky says no, because he'll get them in instead, and that Patrick and Vince should remain at the table because the girls will want to have a catch up with them both. At that, Ricky heads off, everyone else sits down, and Esme, with a bright smile, albeit one which betrays a touch of nerves, asks, "So, Patrick, how've you been? And you, Vince? How's it going?"

"I'm the one who should be asking," Caroline says to Esme. "I don't see them very much more often than you do."

"Sure, I'm just grand," says Patrick, conscious that he's sweating again, and running a forearm across his brow while trying to look casual about it.

They all then look to Vince, who initially answers with a thumbs-up, a polite nod, and a widening of the smile he's been wearing ever since Ricky and the ladies walked in. When he does speak, it's to slowly articulate that he, like Patrick, is just grand, and thanks very much for asking. Finally, as the conversation seems set to move on, Vince flourishes the picture-round images and instructs Patrick to complete the answers before trying to persuade either of the women home with him.

"He knows you too well," says Caroline, shuffling next to Patrick and sticking a friendly elbow into his ribs.

"That's Kirsty Young," says Esme, when she stops giggling for long enough to look at the photos. "You know, the broadcaster. I met her once, at a conference."

"And that one there," adds Caroline, "is the one-time peanut farmer, Jimmy Carter."

"Sure," says Patrick. "Of course. Wasn't he also a one-time US President."

"Yeah – literally a one-timer. He only served a single term, before losing the next presidential election to Ronald Reagan. He never recovered, politically, from the Iran hostage crisis."

"There you go," says Esme. "That's my sister-in-law and her amazing brain for you."

"And this hostage crisis?" queries Patrick with Caroline. "It took place how many years before we were born? I'll never get over how you know so much stuff."

"And that's why you love me," she answers, sticking another elbow into his ribs, and leaving him wondering whether she knows just how close to the truth her reply truly is.

Esme and Caroline move on to agree that the only black-and-white photo among the group is of old-time movie legend, Ingrid Bergman, which leaves the group with two photos left to guess. One of them isn't of a person: it's the 'mystery object' photo – an image of an everyday item photographed from a puzzling angle, requiring them to work out what it is. On the basis that none of them have any ideas, and that Ricky has a decent track record with mystery objects, they defer the question until he is back from the bar.

This leaves one photo. It's of a young woman in what looks like an England football shirt. "So who's this?" Patrick asks of Caroline and Esme.

"Well, she's a footballer," replies Caroline. "So you guys should know. It's one of the sports you're into."

"She represents neither our gender nor my country," replies Patrick. "But you two, on the other hand…"

Before anyone can reply, Ricky, who's back from the bar just in time to hear those last two comments, sets down Caroline and Esme's drinks, before picking up the sheet of images and holding them to the light. "Gah – women's football," he says, throwing the sheet down with disdain. "What a pile of pish that is."

"A pile of pish," echoes Caroline sarcastically, shaking her head as Ricky returns to the bar for the remaining drinks. "Another top-ranking contribution from my liberally-minded husband."

"But he does have a point," replies Patrick. "Especially when it comes to goalkeepers. Sure, it'd be generous to say the standard of women's goalkeeping is pish."

"Oh, Pat," admonishes Caroline. "You're just one Neanderthal defending another." Then, because Vince has his index finger raised at them – his way of telling them he's got something to say if they'll all just slow down a minute – she adds, "Yes, Vince? Go ahead and chip in as well. Are you going to defend your best buddies this time around? Or do you have a more enlightened view?"

"Women are getting.. better at football," Vince manages to say. "But not at goalkeeping. They should... be allowed to play… with a man keeping goal."

"And there you have it," says Patrick, laughing, once he's sure that Vince has nothing left to add. "And this from a man who watches more sport than any of us."

"You're cavemen and misogynists, all three of you," says Caroline, but by now she's laughing, and part of the reason, Patrick supposes, is that Vince can get away with saying things which he and Ricky can't. But it will also be because Caroline has never embraced the feminist cause in a truly fundamental way, and therefore her earlier irritation with Ricky may really have been, in part at least, about something else altogether. Based on the hints she was dropping yesterday, Patrick thinks he can guess what that something else may be.

Meanwhile, Ricky himself is back, now with drinks for himself, Vince and Patrick. "Have you got the mystery object?" he asks.

"We were waiting for you," replies Patrick.

Ricky picks up the sheet and peers at it, before casting it aside just as disdainfully as before. "It's a mouth organ," he says.

Patrick writes down 'mouth organ'. Caroline inches ever closer to him, looks at the other answers, and laughs at his phonetic rendering of Kubica before spelling it properly for him.

Ricky asks, "Who else haven't we got?" When Vince then points at the women in the football top, Ricky says, "Still not? Didn't the girls get it?"

"No," says Caroline. "The girls, as you call us, did not."

"Why do you and Patrick both think we should?" asks Esme of her brother. "Do you think we're lesbians or something? If I'm going to watch people getting muddy in shorts, I want it to be men."

Patrick nudges Caroline, and then, more to humour her as anything else, for he can see her getting riled with Ricky again, he says, "You see – it's not just blokes with old-fashioned attitudes."

Patrick meant it as a harmless joke, and sure it enough, it draws a little smile from Caroline. But the effect of his supposedly light-hearted observation on Esme is startling. Her mouth turns down at the corners, and a miserable look comes to her eyes. "I'm sorry, Patrick," she says, seeming to draw in on herself. "Did I say something wrong?"

"Bloody hell, no," he replies, alarmed that his throwaway comment could have such a dramatic effect. "If anything, Esme, I'm the one who's sorry."

"Chill out, Missus," says Caroline, kindly, turning to face the younger woman. "We're all cool here."

"Everything's fine," adds Ricky, laying a hand on his sister's arm. "Patrick meant nothing by it."

"Sure I didn't," says Patrick. "I wouldn't upset you for all the world."

Esme blinks away a couple of tears, causing Patrick to worry that she'll break into a flood. Vince labours halfway to his feet, reaches across, and like Ricky, places a hand on Esme's arm. "Hey," he says softly. "Pretty girl."

Caroline hands Esme a tissue. Wriggling free of everyone who's trying to console her, Esme dabs the corners of her eyes and manages a nervous, embarrassed laugh. "I'm sorry, Patrick," she says. "I'm being silly, I know. I've had a lot on my mind, and I know I'm overreacting to things."

"You're certain it's not my fault?" he asks. "I wouldn't upset you Esme – not for a gold watch."

She manages another little laugh. "A minute ago, you wouldn't upset me for all the world. Now it's just a watch."

"Sure, but gold though, don't forget."

"It's fine," she replies, getting to her feet. She reaches for his hand and gives it a little squeeze. "Not your fault at all. I'm just going to the loo. I'll be fine in a minute."

Esme leaves the table. After swapping glances with Ricky, Caroline gets up and follows her. Patrick, Ricky and Vince all look at each other. Patrick opens his mouth, but Ricky speaks first. "Don't worry, mate," he says. "Nothing to do with you." Although he was solicitous to his sister while she was at the table, Ricky sounds offhand now, as if his sympathies have their limits. "She's a bit all over the place at the minute. I'll tell you both the story later, but not right now. If we talk about it while they're gone, they'll know what we've been saying once they're back. Fucking women and their antennas."

Patrick idly wonders whether 'antennas' is the correct word, or whether Ricky should have said 'antennae'. Caroline would know, but then they'd either have to explain the context of the question to her, or invent a made-up one which she'd probably see through anyway. Patrick decides he doesn't need his query answering anytime soon, not if by articulating it he runs the risk of upsetting Esme all over again. "Fair enough," he says to Ricky, noting that Derek is at the bar with his microphone in hand, and is about to begin the main part of the quiz. "Let's make the most of Caroline being here, and get this thing won."

Vince responds to that by lifting his glass for both his mates to chink against. He does so with his worst hand, and therefore Ricky and Patrick chink their glasses with the utmost care, so as not to knock Vince's from his grasp. "You're right – let's do this," says Ricky. "There's plenty of competition tonight, though, and Caz will win us nothing if the two of them don't get back from the bog."

Patrick can see that Ricky is correct about the extent of competition. Looking around, there are maybe ten teams taking part tonight, which is three or four more than usual. In addition to their own team of five – which must have a good chance with Caroline in its ranks – Gareth has a team of real-ale enthusiasts and a journalist, and they seem the kind of high-brow gang likely to know plenty of stuff. Additionally, Patrick's da has good levels of general knowledge, and he appears to have as many as seven quizzers on his team – probably making them favourites for the prize. But there are others here who could win this. Rudi and his guys from the nearby car dealership, for example, have proved themselves capable in the past, and then there's that pair of scrotes, Bill and Ted – if Patrick's remembering their names correctly – who appear to be unscrupulous about summoning help from Google when they think no one is looking. Then there are two other teams made up of people Patrick hasn't seen here before. For one, there are the three guys with crewcuts who he earlier thought might be military men. The other is a small team comprised by two people in late middle age, who may possibly be man and wife. Patrick thinks the pair of them look like university lecturers, although he'd struggle to explain why he thinks as much, other than that they're wearing what he calls clever-people spectacles.

Patrick thins that's it in terms of favourites, dark horses, and totally unknown quantities. Otherwise, there are another three teams of locals, which, though large in number, will probably prove also rans. But then again, Patrick supposes, you never can know.

Derek clears his throat with the microphone switched on and held close to his mouth. He sounds phlegmy and wheezy, even at the height of summer, as if he swallowed a pint of wet cement a few minutes back. He bids everyone a good evening, recaps the rules, and reminds team captains that they should have their picture rounds completed by now. He then extends "an especially warm welcome to Mike Gibney, from the paper," before getting the quiz's next phase underway. It's the Read-All-About-It round, featuring ten questions concerning the news and current affairs of the preceding seven days. Patrick, Vince and Ricky manage to answer three of the first five, and when the women return to their table, Caroline answers a fourth, additionally correcting one of their three, pointing out that it was France, not Iceland, with whom the UK had been contending fishing rights that week.

Esme, who has reapplied her makeup, has a big smile for everyone, and apologises for "making such a scene." She nods as though somebody's put fifty pence in her slot when Ricky puts his hand on hers and asks if she's okay, seeming especially keen to reassure him that she's fine.

Otherwise, Esme remains quiet for most of the Read-All-About-It round, before contributing an answer to the very last question, when Derek asks: "What is the name of the "British actress who got divorced this week, receiving a substantial settlement from her husband's movie-making fortune."

"Andrea Campion," says Esme. "It was on the radio yesterday."

"It was," agrees Patrick.

"Well done," says Caroline to Esme.

Ricky has a smirk on his face. "I'd give her a substantial settlement if she came round our house," he says.

Caroline flashes him another irritated glance. It's the second time tonight he's managed to get substantially under her skin in less than half an hour. "Fuck's sake," she snaps at him, shaking her head.

Ricky raises his arms in mock surrender. "It was a joke, my darling. A bloody joke."

"A bloody shit one, Ricky. And not at all funny."

Esme, at this, is looking perturbed again. Patrick, attempting an abrupt change of subject, says, "We made some good answers there, and we did okay at the pictures too. Sure, we've got to be in the running at this stage."

But Ricky and Caroline simply glower at each other.

"Come on, you guys," says Esme. "I don't need this."

"Nor do me and Vince," says Patrick. "If we can't keep the team together, I'll have to lead a breakaway faction. Like they do in the republican army."

Caroline gives him a wan little smile. "I'm sorry, Pat," she says. "And I'm sorry, Esme, too. And you, Vince. I'm just a moody cow tonight. I should have stayed home."

"Me too," says Esme.

"You shouldn't say things like that," replies Patrick, straight-faced. "We wouldn't have got Ingrid Bergman without the two of you."

His quip raises smiles, if not laughs, and everyone just about manages to refocus as Derek comes back on the microphone to introduce the Top Five round. He asks the teams to write down the names of the current top five global car manufacturers, by volume, and the five all-time highest point scorers from the European side in golf's Ryder Cup competition.

After some discussion, the team comes up with Ford, GM, Toyota and VW as four of the five top manufacturers, and leave the fifth still to be determined. When it comes to the golfing question, all eyes turn to Patrick.

"I'll make a shortlist," he says, turning over the answer sheet so as to scribble some possible answers on the back. "I've got Garcia, Poulter, Westwood and Montgomerie. Thinking further back, I've got Faldo, Ballesteros and Olazabal."

"What about Justin Rose?" suggests Ricky.

"Or Bernhard Langer?" adds Caroline.

Patrick writes down Rose and Langer. "That's nine names," he says. "And we have to choose five. Sure, I play a bit of golf, but I'm no more a fan of the professional game than the next fella."

"You're still best placed to choose," says Ricky.

"Yeah – go ahead," says Esme.

"And we won't hold it against you if you're wrong," says Caroline. "Just bloody be right, that's all."

But Vince has his finger raised. "Patrick," he says, indicating that he wants the answer sheet.

Patrick slides the sheet towards him. Vince takes a pen with his good hand and carefully scores out four of the names. Then he slides it back to Patrick, with Garcia, Westwood, Montgomerie, Faldo and Langer all still intact.

"No Seve?" Patrick asks Vince, receiving a short shake of the head in reply. Patrick then addresses the others. "Vince watches more sport than any of us," he says.

"Go with his answers, then" says Caroline, with a thumbs-up for Vince, and so Patrick transfers the five remaining names to the proper side of the sheet. Derek thereafter calls an interval to the quiz, in order for people to smoke outside or buy beer at the bar. Ricky accordingly takes his sister for a cigarette, and Patrick finishes his pint before getting up to get another round of drinks in. At the bar, Mel, like Caroline and Esme, is looking lovely, and appears to be working very hard given that there's a bigger crowd than usual for a quiz night. She's serving several people at once, and doing so with great aplomb, all the while keeping a smile on her face, even though Derek is of little help to her, prattling away as he is with the real-ale crowd at one corner of the bar.

Patrick has no one to help him carry the glasses, and so it takes a second trip to the bar before he has everyone's drinks ferried back to the table. Ricky and Esme are still outside, and Caroline has moved into Patrick's seat so she can better talk to Vince.

"Vince has been telling me about his victim sheet," says Caroline, as Patrick sits down in what was previously her chair.

Patrick nearly spills beer. "Jesus – is that what he actually called it?" Then he realises that Vince and Caroline are laughing at him.

"That is what he called it," replies Caroline. "He thinks it's funny. He also says that you and Ricky are overprotective of him – that you try too hard to spare his feelings. Isn't that right, my sweet?"

Vince nods, smiles, puts both thumbs up.

"I'm sorry, mate," says Patrick. "I guess we should have asked you."

Vince digests this. Thinks about it. Then he shrugs and slowly shakes his head. "It doesn't matter," he finally enunciates.

"Glad we got that sorted, anyway," says Patrick. Then, to Caroline, "Good job you came along."

"Yep. We know that Vince is alright, at least." She lets the sentence hang a little, and then says, "I think you are, too."

Patrick replies, "I'm fine." He too leaves a pregnant pause. He says, "I'm not so sure about Esme."

"Ricky will tell you about his sister. She's sustained a touch of damage, poor kid. But I'm sure she'll repair, given some time and a little TLC."

"What about you and Ricky?" queries Patrick, after a moment spent summoning sufficient courage to ask – a moment during which the tension feels to rise quite palpably. "Tell me to mind my own business, but is anyone else feeling damaged nowadays?"

Caroline runs a hand through her strawberry blonde hair. "Mmmm," is all she replies, at the same time sliding her eyes almost imperceptibly sideways, towards Vince, and then back again.

It's that Vince thing, thinks Patrick. That thing when Vince is sometimes switched on and sometimes switched off, and nobody can't be sure whether he's on or off at that precise moment. But if he is switched on, then he's sharp enough to pick up on this conversation, and there's no guarantee that he'll keep it to himself – there's certainly no surety that he won't tell Ricky about it. He was, after all, best mates with Ricky for a little while before they knew Caroline, and that was several years before Patrick even set foot in the country.

"Caroline, sure, would you excuse me just a moment?" Patrick says. "Back in a minute," he adds to Vince.

He gets up and hurries to the gents', where he fishes around in his pockets for a piece of paper. He's wearing the trousers he wore for golf yesterday, and he soon finds the scorecard from his round. On the reverse of it, leaning against the edge of one of the sinks, he writes:

'If you want to talk about anything (I mean anything at all) you have my number. We can talk in total confidence. It's okay.'

As Patrick finishes up writing, he hears the cistern flushing inside one of the toilet cubicles. Still adjusting his belt, out walks the military-looking man with the crewcut, the one who Patrick noticed earlier at the bar. The man smirks as he eyes Patrick over. He says, "Writing down the answers you've Googled?"

Patrick feels an anger rising. "This has nothing to do with the quiz," he replies, returning eye contact long enough to show that he's not intimidated. Then, from the other side of the door, and down the short length of corridor to the bar, Patrick hears Derek doing the same thing he did earlier – namely clearing his throat noisily with the microphone switched on – before announcing a recommencement to the quiz. Patrick smiles grimly at the man with the crewcut. "Don't forget to wash your hands, soldier," he says, before turning and heading through the door.

Back in the bar, he finds that Ricky and Esme have returned, and so he slides into his pocket the note he wrote to Caroline, before sitting back down, between the two women. Caroline briefly casts him a look. It could be he's reading far too much into a half-raised eyebrow, but he supposes she's asking, *What the fuck were you doing, you silly arse, running off like that? Did I freak you out or something?* As the quiz gets back underway, Patrick ponders how he can best pass her the note without any of the others spotting him.

+++++

Maybe it was because she knew there'd be a journalist in attendance, and with the journalist, a photographer. Or maybe it was simply down to her knowing that The Lamb would draw a bigger crowd tonight than it usually does. Providence was another possible explanation – it could have been the gods intervening to prepare Mel for the unexpected encounter coming her way at the very moment when the interval ended and the quiz's second half began.

Whatever the reason for her decision, Mel had chosen to dress more smartly than she usually did for a shift behind the bar. She had forsaken her regular jeans and t-shirt for some smart slacks and a blouse. And although her open-toed sandals were entirely impractical for bar work – and most likely contravened a raft of health and safety regulations – that didn't matter a jot to her. She felt good in them – that was the important thing. By feeling good she'd been able to get her job done well. She'd provided speedy service with a dogged smile, and this during a busy interval when everyone wanted a drink and Derek was less use than a leaf-blower in the Arctic. Eventually, with the drinks served, and following Derek's announcement that the quiz was restarting, everyone had drifted away from the bar and back to their seats.

Everyone, that was, except one man.

This one particular guy had remained standing at the bar, even though she'd already served him a pint of Old Chancer and a tonic water with ice. And although the other customers are now re-seated, he remains standing there as of now, as Derek kicks off the A to Z round with the question: "Which historical figure gave rise to the expression, 'Crossing the Rubicon?'"

Mel's quite sure that she hasn't seen this man before. Lean and slim, he's also scrupulously clean-shaven, which is unusual for a Sunday evening in these parts. He has on a plain, white, long-sleeved shirt, with the cuffs neatly folded halfway back to the elbows, revealing, on his left wrist, a dress watch which is slim and discreet, but also, Mel suspects, pretty bloody expensive. The man's hair is grey, going on white, and his spectacle lenses are small and circular and frameless. He has a reassuring, well-to-do air, and to look at him somehow inspires the thought that everything's going to be alright.

Trying to sound merely curious, neither commanding nor rude, Mel asks him, "Aren't you going to fill out the rest of your answer sheet?"

"My wife will cope admirably for a few minutes," he replies. It's an answer which should sound pompous, and yet it doesn't. "She knows close to everything there is to know about virtually every recognised subject on Planet Earth."

"Good for her," replies Mel.

"Tell me," the man says, "are you Melanie Jones?"

Mel must have looked surprised, because he quickly adds, "I'm sorry – I didn't mean to startle you. It's just that," – and now he lowers his voice, so as not to be overheard – "you left your CV with us on Friday morning. My name's Robert Hopwood, of Hopwood and Partners, estate agents."

"My goodness," says Mel. "Did I do something wrong?"

"Wrong?" He laughs. His laugh is a low, throaty chuckle which really ought to emit from someone rounder and bulkier than he. "I'd say you did something right."

"I'm sorry," she replies. "It's just that… well, you turning up here. In person, I mean. It's a bit of a surprise."

"It was my wife's idea, Melanie." He takes a couple of seconds to fiddle with those folded-back cuffs. "May I call you Melanie – is that okay with you?"

"I prefer Mel. But yes, of course."

"Thanks. Well, as I say… Mel, it was Alison's idea. Alison likes a pub quiz, and so, when I told her I'd received, by hand no less, the CV of someone working here, she suggested we come to the quiz and – hoping you don't mind – check you out, as it were. Do you mind that, by the way?"

"No, I don't," replies Mel. She like the guileless way Robert Hopwood smiles at her, and she finds herself smiling back. "I came unannounced to your place of work. It has to be okay that you come to mine."

"Excellent. In which case, indulge me a moment while I just take Alison her tonic." He walks briskly to his table, sets down both drinks, whispers briefly in his wife's ear, and then comes back to the bar. "I won't take up too much of your time when you're working," he says. "But, look, it so happens that I am about to recruit. I need a manager at the branch where you called in the other day."

"A manager?"

"Correct."

"Forgive me," says Mel, "but I thought you had a manager there already. When I left my CV the other day, I was told to leave it for Mark Percival."

"I'm impressed that you remember his name. But as of Friday afternoon, Mark doesn't work for us anymore. I'm personally running the branch now, and will be doing so until I can find a replacement."

From Robert Hopwood's sudden coolness of tone, Mel concludes that Mark Percival's departure wasn't an amicable one. She thinks about the wire-rimmed spectacles and the family photograph sitting on the desk in that little cubicle office, and feels sad that their owner may now be out of work. Still, though, the man was running a bloody unruly branch.

"So, are you interested?" asks Robert Hopwood.

"Of course. I'd have to be. But Mr Hopwood, I've been out of estate agency for several years. And I was a negotiator before – I've never actually managed a branch."

"I know," he says. "I've read your CV, remember? But I admire the initiative of anyone who goes door-to-door looking for work, and as for management skills, you're the one running this bar, at least so far as I can see."

Mel finds herself blushing. "Derek does do a bit more than compere the quiz, you know."

"Hah – I'm sure he does. Now look, if this job doesn't sound right for you – if you don't want to be a manager – then that's fine. But if you are interested, why don't you come and talk to me about it during the week. No promises, Melanie – or Mel, as you prefer – but I do see potential in you."

Mel thinks back to Friday morning, and to the trio of clowning kids front and centre of that chaotic outfit. The thought of kicking them into shape does hold some appeal for her. And she already has a great many ideas about the things she could do with a manager's salary. "I'm definitely interested," she says. "I'd be very happy to come and talk to you."

"That's super." Robert Hopwood slides a business card across the bar. "Give me a call tomorrow morning. We'll fix up a date and time."

Mel says she'll do that, and then, with a polite cheerio and a valedictory smile, her potential future employer re-joins his wife at their table. Rather guiltily, Mel looks across to see if her current employer has noticed any of what's just gone on, but Derek seems preoccupied with asking the quiz questions, the latest of them being: "Which author received a fatwa in nineteen-eighty-nine, following publication of his book, The Satanic Verses?"

+++++

"A fat what?" asks Ricky.

"Fatwa," replies his wife. "It's a death sentence handed down by fundamentalist Islamic clerics to people they believe have blasphemed their religion." Almost as an aside, she says to Patrick, "The answer's Salman Rushdie, by the way."

After querying the spelling, Patrick writes down Salman Rushdie. He reckons the team has correctly answered seven, maybe eight, of the ten questions asked in this round. That's pretty good, but he isn't sure they're doing well enough to win. The big group of people on his da's team are all looking confident. Then there's that couple who are new to The Lamb, the pair who might be university professors, and who intrigue him all the more after the bloke spent ages talking to Mel at the bar. They're dangerous contenders, Patrick thinks. The woman appears to write down an answer to every single question, usually after conferring very little, if at all, with the man who Patrick surmises is her husband.

"And so," says Derek, over the microphone, "onto the Connections Round. Answer all four questions for a point each, and then correctly identify the common factor connecting the four answers in order to win an extra point. Question one, the Plymouth Voyager minivan was the first mass-market vehicle to have what kind of accessory fitted?"

Patrick looks at his team members in turn. They look back at him, and also at each other. None of them seem to know the answer. "Anyone know when the Plymouth Voyager dates to?" asks Caroline. "It would help if we knew the period. Sat' nav's are from a different era to sunroofs, aren't they?"

"Well, I've never even heard of a Plymouth Voyager," replies Esme.

"It'll be American," says Ricky. "But I haven't a Scooby what the answer is. Nor the year when they brought them out"

Vince pulls a face and exhales through gritted teeth.

Patrick checks out the other teams. The car salesmen seemingly don't know their Yank Tanks all that well, because they too appear at a loss. His da's team are debating frenziedly among themselves, whereas Gareth's real ale fanboys are looking maddeningly smug –

then again, they always frickin do. The academic-looking couple, meanwhile, have already written an answer.

"Question two," says Derek. "What river rises slightly north of Luton, and has a confluence with the Thames in the borough of Tower Hamlets."

"These questions are bastards," says Patrick.

"It's the Lea," says Caroline. "The River Lea."

"Yeah – that'll be the one," says Ricky.

Patrick writes down their answer.

"Question three," says Derek. "Which Peter Gabriel hit song includes the line, 'Watched by empty silhouettes, who close their eyes but still can see?'"

"Don't know," says Ricky.

"Nor me," says Caroline.

"I'm not great on this round," says Esme. "I couldn't name you a Peter Gabriel song."

"Jesus," says Patrick. "It's a fiendish connections round, for sure."

Esme gives him a smirk. "Are you Catholic boys supposed to say 'Jesus' like that?"

"Only when our mothers aren't present," he replies, pleased that Esme's got enough wits back to banter with him. "And when the pub quiz is a Christ-Almighty bastard like this."

Question four, says Derek, "Who was the first Jamaican American to serve on The Joint Chiefs of Staff, and was its chairman during the ninety-one Gulf War? And then, question five, of course, what connects the previous four answers?"

"The Chiefs of Staff is easy enough," says Caroline. "It must be Colin Powell."

"Okay," says Patrick. "We've got the River Lea and we've got Colin Powell. So we need a Pater Gabriel song and a car accessory which somehow connect with them both."

"Games Without Frontiers?" muses Ricky. "That was Peter Gabriel, wasn't it?"

"You're right," says Caroline, "it was. And Sledgehammer. But I don't know if either of them fit the lyric, or what the connection could be."

"I won't bring you again," says Ricky, "if you can't help us win this. You're normally good at connections."

"Let's brainstorm some lists," says Patrick. He turns again to the reverse of the sheet, where he writes down the two Peter Gabriel songs they have, and also begins making a list of car accessories.

But they don't make much progress before Derek moves onto the final round – the wipe-out round – with ten further rapid-fire questions. Shortly afterwards, the quiz is over, and they're required to write a team name on the top of their sheet before swapping sheets with another team for the purposes of marking. They've done pretty well in the wipe-out round, Patrick thinks, just as they've probably done pretty well in the quiz overall. But he's not sure that pretty well is good enough to win.

"We need a team name," says Caroline.

Patrick writes down, 'The Birds are Back in Town', and she smiles when he shows it to her. Then he gets up and goes to his da's table to swap answers for marking.

"There you go, son," says Malachy as they exchange sheets. "I think you'll find you're marking the winners' paper tonight.

"I'd be watching out for the couple over there," replies Patrick. "Sure, they look a couple of brainboxes."

Roy Culshaw, Malachy's golfing opponent yesterday, and pub-quiz team mate tonight, gives Patrick a knowing smile. "Tell me," Patrick, he asks, "did you get Slade on the connections round?"

"We got slayed alright. We only knew two of the answers."

"Ah, that isn't quite what I meant. Slade, the band? Noddy Holder? We only got two to start with, but then I reverse-engineered the others. Oh, never mind – you are all a bit young. You'll see when you start marking."

Patrick takes his da's team's sheet back to his own table. Ricky and Esme have headed out for a smoke. Vince has gone to the gents. Patrick shows the sheet to Caroline. His da's team have called themselves, 'As Good as it Gets', and they've answered every question in the connections round. They too have come up with the River Lea and Colin Powell. Then, for the car accessory they've answered: cup holder. Followed by Solsbury Hill for the Peter Gabriel song. As to what connects the preceding four answers, they've written down: 'surnames of the original band members of Slade'.

"Holder, Lea, Hill, Powell," says Caroline. "I think they're right, the clever fuckers."

"Clever, arrogant fuckers," replies Patrick, "with a team name like that – 'As good as it Gets'. Probably my da's idea once he's had a couple of beers in him."

"Oh dear, Pat. I think we might not win, and after I said the team needed me. Sorry about that."

"Doesn't matter," he replies. "It's great just to see you, sure."

"And it's great just to see you, too." Her mouth forms a smile which, though lovely, doesn't hide the sadness in her eyes.

"Earlier on," he says, "I sensed you wanted to say something to me. But we weren't alone then, and we won't be for long now. So, I wrote you this." He hands over the message written on the back of his scorecard. "You know you can talk to me, don't you? Anytime you like."

She reads the note, and then tucks it into her bag.

"Anytime you like," he repeats.

Caroline gives him a long look – a searching look. As if weighing up his loyalties. As if weighing up his motives, too.

"Jesus, Pat. I wouldn't know where to start."

"The beginning's a good place."

Her eyes continue to hold him. "Now, don't be a twat."

"I'm sorry," he says. "I didn't mean –"

"No," she interrupts. "It's me who's sorry. You're trying to help, I know. I didn't mean to jump down your throat."

"Look," he says, "there's no need for either of us to be sorry. I'm just saying I'm here if you want to talk, and I thought you might want to do that because… because of, well, stuff."

"Stuff?"

"Sure, stuff." Patrick searches for a clarifying phrase less explicit and less socially awkward than 'Stuff like Ricky seeing other women,' but can't think of one right now. "Just stuff," he finally concludes, feeling mentally lame.

Then Vince comes back. He has a big smile on his face which goes some way to banishing the creeping sense of melancholy felt by Patrick, and which Patrick suspects Caroline's feeling as well. "Good quiz," Vince says, after sitting back down. "And," he adds, haltingly to Caroline, "brilliant… to see you."

Caroline reaches over and squeezes Vince's knee. "You too, Vince. Brilliant to see you, my sweet." She leans back again and looks at Patrick from the corner of one eye. "We'll talk soon," she says quietly to him. "Sometime very soon."

+++++

Derek announces that the lowest score in the quiz has been recorded by the team calling itself, 'Rod Stewart's Trousers'. It's no great surprise that this particular team finished last, consisting as it does of a handful of locals who take part most weeks without ever winning. The team members, though they're honest triers, are narrowly focused and lack real star quality. They tend to know many of the answers contained in the gossip columns, but very few to be found in the broadsheets.

Second last is 'Butch and Sundance' – the name taken this week by Bill and Ted. Their lowly placing leaves Ricky suspecting that the two arseholes couldn't be bothered with Google on this occasion, or maybe, with the pub more crowded than usual, they were unable to use their phones without getting caught.

Derek continues to announce the results in reverse order. In the end, 'The Birds are Back in Town' finish fourth. They have a point more than the car salespeople and one less than the real-ale aficionados. The battle for top spot proves to be closely contended between the heavily-manned team headed by Mackey Senior and the middle-aged couple who Ricky hasn't seen before, but who look to him like winners of the world librarian championships. And as things turn out, 'As Good as it Gets' prove not quite good enough, losing out by two points to the librarian pair who, for whatever reason, have called themselves, 'A Promising Candidate'.

Everyone applauds the winners warmly, even though nobody seems to know who they are. The guy then goes on to win an even bigger round of applause when he goes up to collect the cash prize. After conferring briefly with Derek, the latter announces that, "Mr Hopwood would like to donate his and his wife's winnings to the campaign to keep The Lamb and Musket open, and he wishes us every success in our fight."

Every success? muses Ricky, as he takes his sister outside for a cigarette. It seems that any kind of success would be a fucking start. He checks the time showing on his Breitling. It won't be long before the countdown to closure is measured in hours, never mind days or weeks.

While they're outside smoking, Esme gets talking to the younger sister of a one-time school friend. The woman had been quizzing for 'Rod Stewart's Trousers', and when everyone finishes their cigarettes, Esme adjourns to the table of tonight's gallant losers in order to continue their chat.

"Where's Esme?" asks Caroline when Ricky returns alone. "Is she okay?"

"She's fine," he replies. "She bumped into Lizzy Kent, from back in the day. They're having a bit of a catch up."

"Don't think I know a Lizzy Kent," says Patrick.

"You do," says Ricky. "From when we were still at school."

"Michael and Becky Kent's sister," adds Caroline. Hung around with the Dobson twins."

"Year below us." This contribution from Vince. Patrick, meanwhile, sits and frowns, his face scrunched up by the effort of recollection.

"Come on, Mr Memory," says Ricky, growing exasperated, and gesturing in the direction of Lizzy Kent's table. "You must remember. Frizzy blonde hair. Big tits."

"And a fanny like a horse trough," adds Caroline. "I think, Pat, you were the only boy who never went with her."

"Although there's still time to remedy that," says Ricky.

Patrick appears to take the teasing in good spirits. "Sure," he says. "I never went with anyone."

"Poor boy," replies Caroline. "That's because no one could understand your accent. The girls didn't know whether you were asking them to put out or to let you copy their homework."

"Good point," says Ricky. "Maybe that's why he's still on his own."

Caroline looks at Ricky, the amusement on her face a welcome change from the irritation she's shown him for much of the night. "Could be," she agrees. "Come on, Pat, spill the beans. You've been single – yet again – for a few months now, haven't you? What's going on in the life of Patrick Mackey? Haven't you got anything to tell us?"

Patrick bats the question casually away – too casually, it appears to Ricky – much as he's batted it casually away for most of the past decade or so. "I'm still waiting for the right woman."

"Yeah, yeah, yeah," sighs Caroline.

"Heard it all before," says Ricky.

They all look to Vince, to see if he wants to join in with the ribbing of Patrick. Maybe he hasn't followed this particular discourse, because all he offers is a shy smile and a shake of the head.

"But anyway," Patrick adds, abruptly sitting forward – it's as if he's trying to alter the subject as much by change of tempo as choice of question – "what's the matter with Esme, now that she can't hear us talking about her? Sure, that wasn't like her earlier – not how I remember, anyway."

Ricky exchanges a look with Caroline, trying to work out how much he should say. Then he glances over his shoulder, in order to make sure his sister remains out of earshot. "Esme's had a few issues," he says.

"But is she okay?"

"She will be. It's just she's had a few hard knocks, one after another."

"Is this anything to do with her breaking up with that German guy?"

"Mattheus," says Caroline. "Maybe it does, in part. Although that was a while ago, now. Then she moved to Scotland, where she met someone else. But when her firm moved her south, the new man decided to stay put."

"He was a penis, anyway," says Ricky, recalling a man he didn't meet many times, but invariably found himself wanting to punch.

"Ricky," protests Caroline, "we hardly knew the bloke."

"I knew him well enough. Hamish McPenis – that was his name, or should've been, anyway."

"So what's the story?" asks Patrick. "She's struggling to get over these fellas?"

"Well, Mattheus she is," replies Ricky. "Hamish McPenis not so much. But something else has happened. After moving back down here, she went out with a few of her new colleagues a week or so ago, and some other girl beat her up outside a nightclub."

"Fuck's sake, mate. You're joking."

"Wish I was." Ricky catches himself gritting his teeth. He feels pissed off and vengeful. He doesn't really want to talk about this, but it is Patrick asking, and Patrick is more-or-less family. "Apparently they had some sort of argument, and then this girl dragged her out of the queue and pretty much punched her lights out."

"Jesus," says Patrick. "And you say this was a week ago?"

"A week ago last night."

"And the poor kid's been twitchy ever since," adds Caroline. Scared of her own shadow, almost, and understandably so."

"Sure, but that doesn't sound like the Esme I remember," says Patrick. "She was always so feisty – so full of sass."

"I'm sure she'll get that back," says Caroline. "But it will take time. This wasn't just some hissy catfight – Esme took a pretty good beating. It would have been worse but for bouncers."

"And this is the first time she's been out since," says Ricky. He turns and again looks across to where his sister is chatting with Lizzy Kent. "I reckon she's doing pretty bloody well under the circumstances."

"She is," agrees Patrick. "And there was me poking fun at her. I feel really bad about it now."

"Mate, it's fine," says Ricky.

"Not your fault," adds Caroline.

Vince, who's been listening with an expression of dark solemnity, gives his head a long, slow shake.

"Still, though…" says Patrick, letting the sentence tail away, before suddenly asking, "But what's happened since? Are the coppers involved?"

Ricky shakes his head. "No more than they had to be. Esme wants it kept as quiet as possible. She's just trying to put it all behind her."

"Not that Ricky and I will be leaving it there," says Caroline. "That bitch won't get away with it. There'll be a reckoning."

"What are you going to do?"

Ricky lets out a sigh. Although he recently smoked a cigarette, he opens his packet and takes out a new one. "I'm not sure yet," he finally answers. And if Ricky's honest with himself, what he really means is that he hasn't the first clue how to proceed. "I mean," he continues, "if it's a bloke who hits your sister, well that's straightforward enough. 'You just go round his place and bury him in the yard. But another woman – well, that's different, and I haven't worked out how to settle the score. But I will be settling it, Patrick. You know me well enough."

"You know who this girl is?"

"Only vaguely. But I will find out more. Including where she lives. There are coppers who owe me favours."

"There are people everywhere who owe Ricky favours," says Caroline. Ricky gives her a wink. She smiles thinly back. Ricky's glad that normal relations appear to have been restored – whatever normal is at the moment.

"Let me know if I can help," says Patrick.

Vince is nodding. "Me too," he says.

"But be careful as well," says Patrick. "I come from a land where lots of score settling has gone on. That's why so many people there have more than their share of scars. Sure, those of them still breathing, anyway."

"Yeah, I know," says Ricky, digging his lighter from his pocket and standing up to head outdoors. "But there are some things you can't let go, you know?"

Patrick says he knows, and Ricky makes his way to the door, exchanging a look with Esme on his way, gesturing to make sure that she's alright and is aware of where he's going. Outside, he smokes his cigarette quickly, while checking his phone for texts and voicemail. Tonight, the only messages really are work related. There's nothing from Lauren, which is no surprise as he doesn't expect parlay with her before tomorrow. But he's disappointed not to hear from Yasmin after they got on well yesterday, when he called in here after the golf. With his cigarette smoked, he's soon back inside, idly nattering with Lizzy Kent and Esme – telling his sister to be ready to leave soon – when he quickly becomes aware that there's a bad vibe coming from the far corner of The Lamb. It looks and sounds like an argument of some sort.

The dispute begins with raised voices – Patrick's dad's is one of them – and at first Ricky is unfazed by it all. It's far from unusual for Mackey Senior to wind someone up late into the evening, nor for both parties to end up getting belligerent with each other.

Normally, however, someone will intervene to calm things down – Derek or Mel, or one of the regulars – and everyone will be friends again very soon after. But this time, matters are escalating – the raised voices are quickly joined by others, and all of them are growing louder still. Ricky sees Patrick get up and go hurtling into the melee which is forming around the bar. In Patrick's wake, Vince gets ungainly to his feet and lumbers after Patrick as quickly as he can.

From across the bar, Caroline meets his eye and gives him a *do something* look. He's about to go and join his friends when he feels Esme's hand holding his wrist. She looks frightened. "Don't, Ricky," she says.

Urgently, he beckons for Caroline to come over, and then he reaches down to release his sister's hand from his own. "It'll be fine," he says. "Now sit with Caroline a minute."

By the time Ricky joins the commotion, he finds Patrick and his dad squared off against three mean-looking guys, all with crewcuts. Mackey Senior has his teeth bared, and looks ready to bite off someone's head. Patrick's face, too, is flushed with anger. Meanwhile, the three crewcuts, though not young, look lean and fit. Their eyes are cold, hard, untroubled. And they look contemptuous of this challenge. A half dozen other blokes, including Derek, Gareth, the journalist Mike Gibney, the golfer Roy Culshaw, and the speccy bloke who's just won the quiz are all gathered close by, trying to get among the opposing parties in an effort if not to keep the peace, then at least to constrain the war. Mel's in among it, too –

respect to her – whereas several of the locals are clustered around the periphery, part fascinated and part horrified, seemingly frozen in place by the turn of events.

"That's quite enough, gentlemen," Ricky hears Derek saying in his gruffest, sternest voice. "This is unacceptable on my premises, and has gone far enough already."

"What's unacceptable," says one of the crewcuts, is Irish terrorists murdering my mates and then complaining of oppression."

"You'd know all about it," replies Malachy, "when you're staring at women and children down the barrel of your gun. You think you're such big men, but you're actually really small. Small men with small brains. Small dicks as well, I'm sure."

"You fucking scumbag." One of the crewcuts hustles a pace closer to Mackey Senior, which in turn prompts Patrick to step protectively in front of his dad. "And what are you going to do?" demands the crewcut. "Cheating in the quiz won't get you far in a fight."

"Nobody was cheating," replies Patrick. "Except maybe the British army – as per usual. As for the fight, just come and have a fucking go."

The crewcut takes another pace forward, his eyes shining in bloodlust. Derek, Mel, and the quiz winner all try to get between him and Patrick. "Seriously?" the bloke scoffs. "I mean, it's three against two for starters."

"Three against three," says Ricky, stepping alongside Patrick and his dad. With a glance across the pub, towards Caroline and Esme, he removes both his wedding ring and the Breitling watch. "Look after these, would you?" he says to Mel. She looks annoyed with him at first, but then slips both the ring and watch into the pocket of her slacks. In spite of the circumstances, Ricky can't help noticing that Mel looks glamorous tonight. She clearly scrubs up well, and it seems high time to him that Patrick made a move on the woman, just so long as Patrick can first emerge from this altercation with a head still on his shoulders.

Then Vince squeezes in alongside them both. "Make that four against three," says Ricky to the crewcut, hoping that the combined bulk of both he and Vince will sew a seed of doubt in the minds of these guys.

But the looks on their faces remain implacable. "The more the merrier," says the lead crewcut – the one fronting up Patrick. "Bring it on, boys."

Then one of the other crewcuts steps out from behind his buddy. He narrows his eyes and stares curiously at Vince, maybe realising that Vince's cogs aren't all in sync'. "Yeah," he echoes, "bring it on. There might be four of you, but one's an old man and another's some sort of retard."

That does it for Ricky. He surges forward, and senses Vince trying to keep pace with him. He has fists clenched. He's ready to do this. But suddenly Mel's there, in the tiny bit of space still remaining between him and the crewcut at whom he was about to launch himself. Clearly, the crewcut is also ready to fight, and the fact that it's a woman who's standing in their mutual no man's land is surely all that's keeping either of them from getting stuck in.

"Here," says Mel, digging into her pocket for Ricky's watch and ring, "have these back." She hands him both items, and then turns her attention to the crewcut. When she speaks to him she's absolutely seething. "I've had an entire weekend of assholes pissing me off, but you're just about the biggest asshole of the bunch. If you want a fight then you can have one with me, because let me tell you, dick-face, there's no way you can speak to my friends like that and expect to get away with it."

Ricky hadn't noticed Caroline getting up from her seat, but she suddenly emerges from the crowd with Esme close behind, and both move to centre stage. "And for the avoidance of doubt," she says, standing shoulder-to-shoulder with Mel, you'd have to fight me into the bargain. My friend Vince is worth a million-and-one shitheads like you."

"Two-million-and-one," says Esme. Her voice falters a little, but the look on her face is more angry than frightened. "You lot won't know what's bloody hit you."

For the first time, a couple of the crewcuts actually look alarmed. Ricky knows it's because they're uncertain how to deal with a female threat. But he also knows that if panicked, these guys may simply lash out. He's moving forward again, trying to get between the crewcuts and the women, recognising that matters are becoming seriously crowded and out of hand, when one of the crewcuts raises his arms and shouts, "Enough!"

He shouts loudly, with enough sense of authority that everyone suddenly stops jostling. They stop yelling, too. And they turn towards him.

"Look," he says, "his head moving slowly from side to side as he speaks, trying to command the attention of all parties. "We don't mean to insult people, and we have no argument with most of you. But we've fought for our country – we've fought for all of you gathered here – and I can tell you that these two men," – he gestures dismissively towards Patrick and his dad – "these two men are IRA sympathisers. Our quarrel is with them, and them alone."

"Which is fine," says Mackey Senior, his tone icily cold as he steps back in front of Patrick. "Only you can leave my son out of it too."

"No they can't," says Patrick.

"Nor me," says Vince, who has the meanest look that Ricky's seen on his face since before the big accident.

"Yeah," someone yells from the edge of the crowd. "You don't get to speak like that to Vince."

More raised voices. More jostling. Ricky sees Esme losing her balance, and he reaches out to grab hold of her arm. Then…

"That's enough!"

This time, the call for abatement doesn't come from Derek or any of the crewcuts. It comes from Gareth. And rather than yell from the middle of the crowd, he has moved to a position behind the bar, and then made his plea using the microphone with which Derek had compered the quiz. The aggro subsides slightly but not wholly – there's still some pushing and arguing going on – and so Gareth, having apparently turned up the mike, shouts, "Enough! I said enough!" Finally, thankfully, within a few seconds, some sense of order prevails. Ricky can see the quiz-winning librarian bloke whispering into the ear of one of the crewcuts – as if to placate the man – and Derek attempting something similar with Mackey Senior.

"Thank you," says Gareth, still over the microphone. Presumably so that he can be seen better by everybody, he hoists himself up onto the bar, his sunburnt neck looking like a slice of raw meat under the glare of the above-bar lights.

"We've had a great night up to this point," continues Gareth, "and we surely don't want it ending in violence and acrimony. To that end I'd like to address you three gentlemen who've fought for this country. I think I speak for us all when I say thank you for the sacrifices you've made."

"Well said," says someone from the crowd.

Pompous prick, thinks Ricky.

"But I'd also like to say this," adds Gareth. "We're a close knit group of people in The Lamb, and yes, the men you're quarrelling with are IRA sympathisers, but they also happen to be our friends."

"That's right," calls another voice.

"Hear, hear" says a third.

"One thing I've learned from Malachy," continues Gareth, "ever since he moved here with his family, is that there are two sides to every story – especially stories of conflict – and that it's a mistake to demonise an entire community based on only one perspective."

More assenting voices from the locals. The crewcuts, in comparison, are looking guarded and wary, but at least they're not punching anyone or arguing back at Gareth. "Malachy's our man," calls someone, and this time Ricky thinks the voice belongs to Michael Kent – Lizzy Kent's slightly older brother, who, back in his schooldays, was as spectacularly unsuccessful with the opposite sex as his sister was prodigious.

"That's right," says Gareth. "Malachy is our man." Smiling wryly and caressing his moustache, Gareth seems to enjoy being the centre of attention just as much now as when the anti-closure group meets and he makes one of his speeches. "But, Hell's bells, I am going to counsel our Ulster friends from winding us Brits up when everyone's had a couple of beers. Things will turn ugly that way, as everyone here can see, and that's the last thing we want tonight. Not when there's a gentleman of the press among us."

This time there's a little bit of laughter, and a smattering of applause. "Well said, Gareth," someone calls.

"So, how about it, everyone?" says Gareth. "Can we possibly put our differences aside? Maybe have a final beer together, and go peaceably on our way?"

More people are applauding now, and louder than before. Looking around, Ricky can see that Gareth has greater command of the room than he ever manages on those campaign nights. Mike Gibney, the journalist, has moved away from the throng, to a corner of the bar, where he's scribbling frantically in a notebook.

Ricky swaps a glance with Caroline, and then moves to where Malachy is still faced off against the meanest-looking of the crewcuts, with Patrick and another of the one-time soldiers in very close surround. "Right then," says Ricky, trying to sound open, easy, and cordial – the way he does when pitching potential new clients –

"it seems to me that Gareth's talking good sense for once. How about I get everyone a beer?"

The two key protagonists confront each other for a moment longer. Then Mackey Senior looks at Ricky, the makings of a smile on his lips. He turns back to the crewcut. "My friend Richard is right, you know," he says to the man. "Gareth is talking sense, and he does that so infrequently it would be wrong not to drink to it. What do you say?"

The crewcut looks to his mates. "Come on then," he finally replies. "We'll have that drink if you're mate here is going to pay."

And so the whole group of would-be brawlers shuffles its way to the bar. Mel and Derek duck under the serving hatch so as to pull the pints. Gareth slides down from his lofty perch, in order to take the plaudits and the back slaps. The man from the paper continues to scribble in his notebook. And Ricky reflects that things don't always end quite so peacefully. On occasion, when these Anglo-Irish arguments break out, his friends from Belfast do end up fighting against the English.

+++++

In 2002, the 21st of June was a Friday. For Ricky, it would prove the longest day of the year in more ways than one. The fun began early, with Brazil the opponents on a warm Friday morning. Later in the afternoon, a more localised form of opposition would materialise in the guise of Simon Evans's gang – a mean and nasty crew made up of Russell Smith, Pete Fenton, and, of course, Simon Evans himself.

But for now, it was only seven-fifteen in the morning. An hour of the day which was, by miles, the earliest that Ricky and his friends had ever arrived at school. Or, indeed, ever would. Such was the consequence of England playing football against Brazil in the World Cup quarter finals, a tournament being played in Japan and South Korea, with this particular game kicking off at the local time of three-thirty p.m.

Three-thirty p.m. in Japan's Ecopa Stadium was seven-thirty a.m. at home in Britain, which was why many heads of schools and businesses had invited their pupils and employees to turn up early and watch the game in assembly halls and meeting rooms, rather than risk them arriving late, or maybe not at all, were they to view proceedings at home.

Accordingly, Ricky and most of his schoolmates assembled in the main hall just prior to kick off. It had to be said, though, that the TV which had been wheeled out for the occasion, although big by 2002 standards, was far too small for some three-hundred kids and a handful of teachers all to get a good view. Which was why, with Caroline between them, Ricky and Vince muscled their way towards the front. Despite there being older kids present, the three of them forged a path through the assembled ranks, and ended up with just the hardest fuckers from the higher years standing closer to the TV. Of their own age-group, only the trio of Evans, Smith and Fenton had a vantage point anywhere near as good as theirs – a state of affairs reflecting Vince and Ricky's ongoing struggle against Evans's gang for top-dog status within their year.

Ricky was surprised to see that Patrick Mackey – the skinny Irish kid – had also turned up for the game. Mackey had, over the course of the tournament so far, shown time and again that he wasn't an England fan. In years to come, Patrick would tell Ricky that he turned up that morning because his dad (or his "da", in Patrick's own parlance) had said that it would be a good idea to try and fit in a bit more with the other kids, but when Michael Owen opened England's account midway through the first half, fitting in didn't look to be high on Patrick's list of priorities. From the corner of his eye, Ricky saw Patrick standing scowling and immobile, his arms folded across his chest, while the other kids all danced and cheered in celebration of England having taken the lead.

It was probably Patrick's downbeat reaction to England's goal that saw him land in such trouble later that day. But then again, he'd been in trouble for much of the tournament, particularly for supporting the Republic of Ireland when he was actually Northern Irish – a subtlety which had been lost on many of the kids until Pete Fenton, most likely egged on by his old man, had made a big deal of the discrepancy. Patrick received no end of ridicule after Fenton's intervention – "the mick's so thick he doesn't even know which country he's from" – most especially when the Irish captain, Roy Keane, invited scorn upon himself and his country by walking out and flying home after a bust-up with team coach, Mick McCarthy.

Ricky and Vince had been left puzzled by Patrick's strange allegiance to what they called the southern Irish team – so much so that they asked Vince's dad about it. Vince's dad was a big bear of a man with a surprisingly dexterous touch, one who earned a living selling wood carvings he made in a workshop at the bottom of his garden. He had a dexterous mind, too, allied to a patient manner, and always found time to answer the boys when they troubled to ask him a serious question. Vince and Ricky sought him out on a warm summer evening in the few days between Ireland's loss to Spain and England's game against Brazil. This was ten months before the big accident which would leave Vince's dad dead and Vince himself changed forever.

"The northern Irish are a divided population," he replied, in answer to Vince and Ricky's enquiry. "In football, some of them support the country of Northern Ireland; others support The Republic." He looked into their still-puzzled faces, set down a figurine he'd been smoothing off, and seated himself on his workbench from where he began to explain matters further.

"You see, we, the British, occupied the country of Ireland for hundreds of years, and when we finally withdrew from the larger part of the island we negotiated an agreement to border off six counties in the north-east corner and call it Northern Ireland. It would remain in the UK, rather than be part of the new Irish Republic."

"Why was that?" asked Vince.

"Because that was the preference of the majority of the people living there. They were what we call loyalists, or unionists – people who were loyal to the crown, and who wish to remain in union with the rest of the UK. They outnumbered, and still do, the republicans and the nationalists in that particular part of the island, though not on the island of Ireland as a whole. And that, essentially, is what the republicans fought the loyalists over for so many years. People say it was about religion – Catholics versus Protestants – but really that was just because most republicans were Catholics and most lost loyalists were Protestants. What they were really fighting about was whether the people of the six counties wanted to be part of a United Kingdom or a United Ireland.

Ricky nodded slowly, taking it all in. "So people like Patrick," Vince said, "support the southern Irish team because that's the country they really want to be part of. That's what you're saying, yeah?"

"Pretty much," replied his dad. "Republicans don't recognise Northern Ireland as a country, or if they do, then they do so begrudgingly. As such, they can hardly support its football team, can they?"

"I suppose not." It was Ricky who answered this time. "But haven't they stopped fighting each other now? Since they signed that agreement a few years ago?"

"The Good Friday Agreement," said Vince's dad. "Well done for remembering, because it was four years ago, when you two were ten."

"Thanks," said Ricky, blushing at the compliment. In that his own dad was in and out of jail for a miscellany of petty crime, Vince's old man was the closest thing he had to a credible father figure, and Ricky always felt a small swell of pride whenever the big guy said something nice about him.

"And you're right," continued Vince's dad. "The republicans and loyalists have mostly stopped fighting each other – apart from a hard-core handful on either side – and they are trying to resolve their differences by peaceful politics."

"So, what do you suppose is the story with this kid, Patrick?" asked Vince. "If it's that important for his family to consider themselves Irish, why are they living here in England? I could understand them getting away to avoid the violence, but if they're not fighting anymore then what's the point?"

"Good question," replied his dad, who always tried to share the compliments around. "I don't know the answer, and there could be lots of reasons; but if I had to guess, then I'd imagine it's a question of economic opportunity. I've never been to Belfast, but I do know that big business steered well clear of the area when people were shooting and bombing each other, and prosperity isn't something that comes back overnight. Patrick's dad may have thought he could do a better job of providing for his family by bringing them to England."

"You're saying he couldn't get a job over there?" asked Ricky.

Vince's dad flashed him a conspiratorial smile which made Ricky feel indulged, while at the same time narrowing his eyes in a way which conveyed mild reproach. "Don't go putting words in my mouth," he said. "I have no idea whether your schoolmate's father had a job back in Belfast. I'm simply saying that he may – and I do emphasise the word 'may' – he may have thought he had better prospects over here."

"Or he could be a supergrass," said Vince, his eyes lighting up excitedly. "He could, couldn't he? Like you hear about on the news? He could have grassed on some heavy dudes, and be living here under a new identity."

"Hah!" replied his dad. "I think my explanation is likelier, don't you? But once again, well done for knowing about such things." He slid down from his bench, picking up the figurine and some sandpaper.

"Of course," he added, "if you really want to know why Patrick and his family are over here, you could try asking him."

"I suppose," said Vince.

"If we could understand his paddy accent," replied Ricky.

"But ask him with some tact and good manners," continued Vince's dad, ignoring Ricky's little barb. "I know what you two can be like at times. And Vince, I suggest you keep your supergrass idea out of the conversation. Imagine if Patrick's dad really were one. You'd probably get reported to Special Branch, and then they'd have you shot for blowing his cover."

"Not at my age. I'd just get a slap on the wrist."

"Do you want to take that chance?"

"Can I have his PlayStation when they shoot him?" asked Ricky, punching Vince in the arm.

"Nah. You'd get shot too, as an accessory to it all."

Ricky and Vince exchanged mock rueful looks. "Another thing," said Vince's dad, using the figurine to point at both of them in turn. "I know I told you to try asking Patrick why his family are here, but don't necessarily expect him to know all the answers. You're dad doesn't tell you everything when you're fourteen."

"Yeah?" queried Vince. "What haven't you told us?"

"The meaning of the word diaspora. The Irish diaspora is very large, you'll find."

Vince and Ricky swapped another look, but by the time Vince opened his mouth to reply, his dad had turned away to resume sanding the figurine, refocusing himself on the business of turning timber into cash. It was a regular gambit of his to leave an issue or a question hanging and unanswered, something for the boys to find out from another source.

"What was the word again?" asked Ricky.

"Diaspora," replied Vince.

"Caroline will know," said Ricky.

"So will the internet," said Vince.

It went without saying that the internet would know, but asking the internet was less fun than asking Caroline, to whom Ricky would happily listen for hours. One question which Caroline had never, however, answered to Ricky's satisfaction was why was it that she actually had a soft spot for the silly Irish kid, Patrick. That said, Ricky had only himself to blame for Caroline not having answered the question, because he had not yet got around to asking it. He supposed, really, that he already knew the answer: it was that Patrick had something about him which the girls all liked. Okay, so they mocked his accent and his attitudes and his awkwardness – and they laughed at him for saying 'sure' so much, and for calling his mum and dad his ma and da. Yet it was clear that they still found the lad to be attractive. He had a darkly handsome face and a winning smile; plus, the things which were awkward about him also made him vulnerable. And Ricky was just starting to comprehend that a little bit of vulnerability wasn't necessarily unattractive.

Ricky had deliberately had precious little to do with Patrick since introducing himself, a year or more ago, by butting the Irish kid firmly in the face, thereby splitting open his top lip. Satisfied that he'd laid down a marker of sufficient gravity, Ricky left Patrick alone after that, letting some of the other kids – Simon Evans and his gang, principally – do what bullying of Patrick there was to be done. Ricky's reasons for leniency were twofold. Firstly, so as to appear the true alpha male, Ricky was happy for it to be thought that there were fish in the sea too small for him to be bothered with, especially if the likes of Simon Evans thought such fish worth frying. The bigger reason, though, concerned Caroline: because Caroline liked Patrick, she'd have given Ricky hell had he caused Patrick too hard a time. And so, just as long as Patrick did nothing to cross him,

Ricky was happy to leave the weird Irish kid alone – to not mock his accent, and to leave his handsome face intact.

Accordingly, when Michael Owen scored England's first (and only) goal against Brazil, sending three-hundred schoolkids and a wider nation into a joyful dance of mass delirium, and while Patrick, in comparison, stood stony-faced and scowling, and Ricky, as a consequence, then found himself wanting to head-butt Patrick again, he actually held back from doing so. He knew he'd only get grief from Caroline for taking aggressive action. He also knew that while his old man, were he to be watching, would most likely approve of such behaviour, Vince's dad certainly wouldn't, given the sympathy he'd shown for Patrick's family while they were talking in the workshop. Besides all of which, Ricky could see that the Evans-Smith-Fenton axis had also taken note of Patrick's sour demeanour, and he knew they'd be going after the moody little fucker before the day was out.

In any event, the national mood of celebration inspired by Michael Owen's goal didn't last very long. Rivaldo equalised some twenty minutes later, before Ronaldinho went on to score the Brazilians'' winner from a free kick – the goal being a fluke if Ronaldinho intended to cross the ball, and act of genius if he intended a shot. Either way, England's keeper, David Seaman, appeared to be at fault with his positioning, and as such the goal proved a big, controversial talking point, one which would crop up often when football was discussed in the nation's diminishing number of pubs, The Lamb and Musket included, more than a decade-and-a-half later.

Masterpiece or fluke, a goal was a goal, and England were out of the tournament. A dispirited and mournful populace returned to its offices and classrooms for a long day of work, drudgery, and bitter recriminations – recriminations against both the Brazilian team for winning the game, and their English counterparts for losing it.

But for Ricky at least, things weren't all that bad. Okay, he had wanted England to win, but hadn't been too bothered when they'd lost, not if he was honest about it. Ricky could take football or he could leave it – unlike Vince, who remained sour and grouchy until the time came to go home. And anyway, the result notwithstanding, the game had heralded an exciting new development for Ricky. While standing watching the match, he'd had a feel of Caroline's arse and she had neither moved away, complained, nor otherwise resisted. Other kids would have noticed what was going on, and Caroline, in turn, would certainly have noticed their reaction. And yet she was cool about such a public display of intimacy on Ricky's part. What Ricky hadn't been sure of was whether the episode marked a permanent recalibration of the physical boundaries governing their relationship, or whether Caroline's indulgence of his touching her up before a large audience was merely a one-off, rather like the school choosing to screen football at half-past-seven in the morning.

Ricky planned on having the matter clarified later that day, at Caroline's parents' house, once school was over, and before her mum and dad were home from work. But as things turned out, he and Caroline would get back there a good way behind schedule. The delay, when it came to pass, occurred at school's final bell, as the two of them – together with Vince – made it downstairs from the science block, from where they would head outside and then onwards for home.

It was the sound of someone hollering which held them back – hollering from the last classroom on the left, where old Mr Padbury held his art classes. Given the other priorities he had in mind, Ricky wouldn't have bothered to investigate, but Caroline took his hand and led him towards the commotion, with Vince also following along. Gathering round the small window in the classroom door, they looked inside to see the culmination of an event envisaged by Ricky early that morning. Russell Smith and Pete Fenton each held Patrick by an arm, whereas Simon Evans, having one hand at the Irish kid's throat, had pushed the scrawny fucker up against the whiteboard on the front wall. Wriggling and yelling, Patrick wasn't short of spirit, or at least he was until such time as Simon Evans punched him hard in the guts, whereupon he went limp, his face contorting as he gasped for air.

Ricky was pretty indifferent to the goings on behind old Padbury's classroom door. Okay, Simon Evans was Ricky's enemy, but Patrick Mackey – with his stupid fucking surname, and his stupid fucking accent, and his scornful indifference to Michael Owen's goal – was hardly Ricky's friend. Ricky simply didn't have a dog in this particular fight.

Or at least he didn't until Caroline let go his hand and nudged him with an elbow. Turning towards her, Ricky found Caroline's gaze to be urgent and imploring. It combined the command that he go in and do something with weary exasperation that he hadn't already done so. When he thinks back now, it's his earliest recollection of her giving him what Patrick would come to call The Caroline Look.

"Bloody hell, Ricky," Caroline finally seethed, after he responded with little more than a shrug. "Help him out, will you? I thought you were better than this."

Her comment stung him, and it occurred to Ricky that he'd have to get his own arse into gear if he wanted to continue getting touchy-feely with Caroline's. Whatever new privileges she may have ushered into their relationship could equally get withdrawn if he were to walk away from Patrick's plight. But despite this realisation, Ricky still held back a moment longer. He and Vince were outnumbered by Evans, Smith and Fenton, and it didn't cross his mind that Caroline would want to help out, or that Patrick might have more of a role to play than that of the victim. He certainly didn't imagine that either Caroline or Patrick would prove any more competitive in a fight than a Morris Minor in a drag race, and so far as Ricky was concerned, therefore, it was two versus three, and he felt bad about involving Vince in a scrap where the odds weren't favourable.

But while Ricky cogitated, Vince took matters into his own hands nevertheless. Nudging Ricky from his other side, Vince pushed open the classroom door and barrelled ahead, seemingly unconcerned about the number or quality of their opponents. "Let's go," he said. "We've been wanting these fuckers, haven't we?"

When he heard the door opening, Simon Evans took his hand off Patrick's throat, stepped back half a yard, and whirled round to see who was coming in. He had an alarmed look about him, and was probably thinking old man Padbury had just arrived, or, worse, that it was one of the younger male teachers – someone faster and fitter than Mr Padbury, and less inclined to put up with this kind of malarkey.

But Evans's expression swiftly changed when he saw the three of them standing there. The panic disappeared from his face, and although his look remained guarded – out of respect to the calibre of his opponents – he knew what Ricky knew: that the numbers were in his favour. Patrick and Caroline didn't really count.

"The fuck d'you want?" Evans asked, before turning back to face Patrick with a fist raised, ready to throw a big right cross.

But Patrick, despite his arms being pinioned by Smith and Fenton, was ready to fight back. The interruption had afforded him a moment to both catch his breath and conceive a counter attack. As Simon Evans turned back towards him, he lashed out with his foot, catching Evans firmly in the balls. Evans immediately squealed and doubled over, frantically clutching at himself.

"Not bad," said Ricky from just inside the room, wincing in mock sympathy. "That's got to hurt, I reckon."

From the noise Evans made, it did indeed hurt, and worse was to come for him. As he stood there, stooped forward, hands grasping his manhood, he was slow to step out of danger as Vince advanced with both fists raised. And although Evans did manage to turn partially away from the big, arcing haymaker which Vince aimed at his jaw, it still caught him a juddering blow to the ear, sending him pivoting into a desk, from where he crashed to the floor, one hand holding his head and the other still clutched hard between his legs.

Of Russell Smith and Pete Fenton, Fenton's nerve broke first. He let go of Patrick and tried to run around the outside of Ricky, towards the door. But Ricky, conscious that he'd let others do the fighting so far, wasn't in the mood to let him get away. Pete Fenton was a hard kid and big-built, but he didn't have sufficient bulk to remain on his feet when Ricky stepped across the room, put his shoulder to work, and checked Fenton into the wall. Fenton followed Evans's example in falling to the floor, in his case groping and tearing at some still-life artwork which had been tacked to a cork board. Then, as Fenton scrambled up again, onto all fours, Ricky got behind him and got ready to launch a big kick.

"This is how it's really done," said Ricky, with a glance at Patrick. Then, standing to the rear of Pete Fenton, he swiftly swung his leg, toe-ending Fenton viciously between the legs. Fenton let out a desperate, agonised wail, and convulsed on the floor, holding himself with both hands.

All of which left Russell Smith as the only member of Simon Evans's gang still standing – indeed, the only one without his balls kicked in. With his two buddies writhing on the floor, he made his own dash for the exit. Ricky, having moved to intercept Fenton, was too far away to stop him. Vince made a grab for the kid, but Russell Smith, as the smallest and nimblest of the trio, managed to swerve desperately from Vince's grasp. Suddenly, only Caroline stood between Smith and the door, and while Smith was smaller than Evans and Fenton, he was certainly bigger than Caroline. As Smith bore down on her, Ricky could only look on, frozen in horror, willing Caroline to get out of the way.

Which she did – coolly and calmly. But rather than give Smith a clear run for the door, Caroline not only stepped aside, but pushed a chair into the would-be escapee's path. Russell Smith clattered into it at speed, and lost his footing entirely. Although he grabbed at a desk in an effort to remain upright, he fell especially heavily, most of his weight bearing down on one hand as his palm hit the floor. Caroline, standing closest to the action, would later tell Ricky she was sure she heard the crack of bone. Everyone heard Smith's howl of agony, just a split second after he landed.

Rolling his shoulders, as if to loosen up after being pinioned, Patrick stalked after Russell Smith. Smith was on his knees, holding his wrist and weeping in pain. Patrick threw Ricky a steely glance as he limbered up to boot Russell Smith from behind. Even from halfway across the classroom, Ricky could see Patrick's eyes burning bright with cold and vengeful malice. "Sure," said Patrick to Ricky, "this time I'll show you how it's done."

But then Caroline stepped between Patrick and the stricken kid on his knees. "Don't," she said gently. "He's had enough already."

"It's my wrist," wailed Russell Smith, who would indeed turn up in plaster the following Monday morning – albeit walking more easily than Simon Evans or Pete Fenton. "You've gone and broken my fucking wrist."

If Caroline felt any remorse, she wasn't showing it. "Shut your whingeing," she snapped. "Or else I'll kick your bollocks in myself." Then, to Patrick, who still looked scarily mean, even to Ricky, she added, "But as for you, Pat – you can stay out of this now." It was, Ricky thinks, the first time he'd heard anyone refer to Patrick as 'Pat'.

Vince, who'd hauled Simon Evans up off the floor, and had been throttling him with his own tie, materialised at Patrick's side and laid a hand upon his shoulder. "Careful, Paddy," he said, laughing. "Once you start obeying her orders, there's never an end to it." He stuck out a thumb so as to gesture at Ricky. "You only need to look at this one over here."

Moving between rows of desks, Ricky zigzagged his way in from the perimeter. He raised his voice to address Evans, Smith and Fenton, all of whom, with Evans gagging for breath and Smith howling like a baby, had made it very unsteadily to their feet. "You three twats," he said, "can all fuck off home. But you're never going to live this down – not in a million, trillion years." Then he turned to Caroline. "Are you happy, Caz?" he asked his fourteen-year-old girlfriend. "Did we do okay?"

Caroline smiled at him. "Yes, I am. And yes, you did."

Vince still had a big hand laid on Patrick's skinny shoulder, and now Caroline took hold of Patrick's opposite arm. "You did okay as well," she said. "All you needed was some help from your friends."

"Whoa," said Ricky in immediate response. He looked hard at Patrick, whose vengeful blood lust finally looked to be abating. "What – we're the paddy's friends now, all of a sudden?"

"Why not?" replied Caroline. "It's about time he had some."

"And respect to him," said Vince, "for catching Evans in the nuts like that."

"Just listen to the two of you," replied Ricky desultorily. "The kid's a fucking weirdo. He doesn't cheer for England, and I can't understand half of what he says."

"He does happen to have a name, you know," retorted Patrick, stepping back and slightly aside, so that neither Caroline nor Vince had hands on him anymore.

"Yeah, and it's a weirdo name," laughed Ricky. "I mean, Patrick Mackey – what the fuck?"

A flash of fire in Patrick's eyes. Then he made for the door, which was still open following the shambling retreat of Simon Evans's gang. "Thanks for helping me," he called over his shoulder. "Whatever your frickin reasons were."

As Patrick walked away, Ricky caught a furious stare from Caroline, causing him to once more imagine the withdrawal of new privileges, only hours after they were first granted. "Hang on, Paddy – Patrick," he called. "Just hang on a minute, would you?"

Patrick stopped in the doorway, and turned to face them all.

"Vince was right," Ricky said to him. "It was a decent kick you landed on that spack-head, Evans. Fair play to you for that." Then, to a still stern-faced Caroline, Ricky raised his palms in implied surrender. "Tell you what, Caz," he said, "me and Vince will be mates with Patrick if you'll explain to us what a diaspora is."

2) A Week in July

2.1) Thursday

It's just after half-past eleven in the morning, and Patrick has a job booked for half twelve. As such, it's high time he logged off, made a quick coffee, and got ready for work – high time he suspended his online share-trading activities, and became Patrick the plumber again, if only for a couple of hours.

He closes the computer, tidies his desk, and heads downstairs from the poky spare bedroom which he long ago made into an office. But Patrick finds himself reluctant to put on his overalls and head out from the house. He's made a profit of two grand trading shares this week, whereas, in comparison, he's about to go and fit someone an outside tap for the sake of a hundred-and-fifty quid. Patrick doesn't deny that he's made a good living from plumbing, and acknowledges that without it he wouldn't have had the funds to begin building his share portfolio in the first place, but three years after opening an online trading account, things are certainly going well for him. Well enough for him to be questioning how long he'll remain in the plumbing business, in answer to which his current thinking is two years, perhaps, or maybe only twelve months. It certainly does seem reasonable on his part to ask whether he needs the aggravation – the dirty, messy jobs, and the sometimes awkward customers – when he can, in a good week like this, make two grand sitting at a computer in his spare room.

It's a cultural thing, he reflects, as he stands in his kitchen, waiting for the kettle to boil. Patrick is conditioned to think of plumbing as a proper trade – a respectable line of work for a respectable working man – whereas the buying and selling of shares feels a far shadier venture. And there's certainly more risk attached to online trading. Patrick supposes that one of the reasons he's still a plumber is that whilst his share portfolio could be decimated within minutes of the markets opening, there'll always be someone wanting a sink unblocked or a bathroom suite installed.

Also – and this is quite a big also – he doesn't think he's ready for the reaction of other people to the news of him hanging up his overalls in order to play the markets in his dressing gown. His ma and da, for instance, would be perturbed by the idea, as would many of the other people who live around here. Most of them know that he 'dabbles' in shares, but it would be a different matter if they knew he did it well enough to pack in the day job. His 'retirement' would appear flash, and he'd become that little bit further estranged from the community than he already has. Things would feel awkward for a while, and although he knows a time of such awkwardness will, in the end, prove inevitable anyway, Patrick hasn't quite reached the point where he's ready to precipitate it.

One man who doesn't seem embarrassed at causing his friends awkwardness is Ricky, not given the way he's been carrying on with Yasmin – the barmaid from The Lamb. Sure, it was one thing when Ricky was sneaking off to commit his infidelities a little more discreetly – at places Patrick didn't go to and with women Patrick hadn't met. But this is different. This is with the hired help at The Lamb and Musket. The way that Ricky and Yasmin are over-friendly across the bar is embarrassing, as is the way they go outside for cigarettes together when she has no customers to serve. Then there are the lingering looks they exchange when one of them is headed home. The furtive, flirty smiles and winks. The touching of each other's hands and faces. Even, on occasion, his giving her a lift back to her place – as if things couldn't be any more obvious.

It's an awkward situation, indeed. Awkward enough to make Patrick angry, putting him, as it does, in a difficult spot where he has to choose which is his greater loyalty – the one he owes to Ricky or the one he owes to Caroline. And it makes Patrick even angrier that Ricky seems to blithely assume that it's upon him who Patrick's favour will fall. But this isn't the limit of Patrick's anger. He's angrier all the more that Vince, also, has to witness these shenanigans of Ricky's.

Previously, Patrick had lacked surety as to what extent, if any, Vince knew of Ricky's womanising. Patrick hadn't been certain of Vince's capacity to make the right connections and draw the necessary inferences when Ricky's phone hummed with messages while the three of them were having a pint, and shortly afterwards Ricky made his excuses and headed off to sort out some alleged work problem. But if Vince hadn't worked it out before, Patrick's fairly sure he's got it sussed now. Vince watches Ricky and Yasmin, and the look on his face becomes bleak and helpless. At times, it seems he wants to say something, but can't quite work out what. His being lost for words may not necessarily be due to his disability, given that Patrick regularly feels much the same way.

With his overalls finally on, Patrick completes his preparations for going out to work, flitting to and fro between his kitchen and the small utility room extending off the back of his house. Having built the extension himself, the utility room serves as both a mini workshop and a place to keep tools, although it also fulfils other bespoke requirements as and when required. For the past three weeks, for example, dating back to when Patrick and Ricky last played golf, Ricky's clubs have been taking up space in one corner of the workshop. Their being here came about because Patrick was driving that day, and kept hold of the clubs in order that Ricky, who was without his car, could remain at The Lamb and thereby begin what was, with the benefit of hindsight on Patrick's part, a pre-planned campaign of seduction vis-à-vis Yasmin.

Patrick eyes up Ricky's clubs, and gives further consideration to a course of action he's already thought about a very great deal. It's been on Patrick's mind for a couple of days that the customer for whom he's about to install an outside tap lives not very far from Ricky and Caroline. It's been equally on Patrick's mind that he could, once the job is done, call in and return Ricky's clubs, on the legitimate pretext of his being in the locale. Ricky, most likely, won't be home. Caroline probably will.

+++++

Having arrived well ahead of everyone else, Gareth surveys the scene for about the hundredth time, and laughs nervously at precisely how fitting a venue this is for the commencement of a crime. This patch of dirty, gravelled wasteland – one on which some derelict old buildings have long since been levelled, but the much-promised new investment continues not to materialise – is such a hackneyed setting for a bunch of crooks to gather that the entire scenario feels like a dodgy cops-'n'-robbers film from the seventies.

A bunch of crooks. That is what they are, Gareth realises: a bunch of bloody crooks. Hell's bells.

Five minutes have passed since Gareth parked up. His accomplices aren't due for ten minutes more. Gareth always arrives early – for absolutely everything in life – but he was especially prompt today. His being over-punctual came about in part because he felt nervous, and equally because the pragmatist in him allowed an extra chunk of time in order to accommodate the vagaries of his allocated car. This little old Renault is inclined to stall at low revs, and he wanted to make sure he got it here without a hitch.

Actually, the Renault which Gareth thinks of as both little and old is, he knows, slightly bigger and three years newer than his own car. It has lower mileage too, and although the interior has the scuffs, smells and embedded hairs to indicate that at a large dog has run riot in here, a good valet would surely prove an adequate remedy. If something could be done about that low-rev cut-out, then this would hardly be a bad car – certainly a better one than Gareth's own – yet it's deemed of such little worth that he's supposed to deliberately crash it into another vehicle sometime in the next half hour or so. He feels somewhat affronted that a car potentially superior to his ageing Fiesta is considered all but scrap by the people putting this operation together, but then Gareth has gotten used to standing on the lower rungs of society's infernally unjust ladder.

Cash for Crash. That's what Bill called this scheme during that warm, drunken afternoon at The Lamb and Musket, Ted looking on with a big smirk on his face. The plan as hatched was that Bill and Ted would provide Gareth with a car, a 'money car', as Bill had called it – "an old knacker, Gareth, which will earn you a fortune" – and would also pay for an insurance policy in Gareth's name. Gareth would then drive the car, at relatively low speeds, into the back of another vehicle, one containing further associates of Bill and Ted. The occupants of said vehicle would then proceed to claim on Gareth's insurance for whiplash, mental trauma and loss of earnings – to say nothing of the actual damage to their vehicle. The proceeds of the claim would subsequently be divided up among Bill, Ted, Gareth, and the four occupants of the other car.

"We'll do it in the town centre," Bill said at the time. "In the middle of the day."

"That way," added Ted, "we should end up with some genuinely independent witnesses. It all helps authenticate the claim."

"You'll clear three grand at least," affirmed Bill to Gareth, while crushing out one cigarette and immediately lighting another. "Maybe nearer five."

And to Gareth, who was enjoying the sunshine outside The Lamb, and whose head that afternoon was pickled in beer, Cash for Crash sounded like a pretty good idea.

It seemed a lot less like a good idea subsequently. The next day, when he woke up sober, but with a head pounding as if he'd fought ten boxers, and with his neck so red and raw that he may as well have slept restlessly with a cheese grater on his pillow, Gareth had to confront the unpleasant reality that he'd signed up to do something very dubious indeed.

He meant to have it out with Bill and Ted the very next day, during quiz night at The Lamb. He planned on telling them that after sober reflection he wanted no part of this. But what with his apologising to Melanie for getting so drunk, and looking after Mike Gibney, the journalist, and then, near closing time, making a decisive intervention in the Anglo-Irish rumpus, he simply never got round to making his excuses. And then, a day or so later, when he finally did speak to Bill and Ted, again at the picnic table outside The Lamb, the conversation hardly went to plan. When Gareth explained that he'd been having a rethink about the whole idea, and had decided that Cash for Crash really wasn't for him, Bill lit a cigarette and simply stared him down for a good five seconds.

"That's unfortunate, Gareth," Bill eventually said. "You see, I've made commitments now. Plans have been laid; wheels are in motion. If you pull out now, you'll owe me a few quid in recompense."

"But Bill, I have a problem with the legality of this."

"No need for a problem, cocker. Because there is no legality to this." Bill looked at Ted and they both laughed, but the harshness in their eyes remained.

"But... it's just that... well, you see... I've been thinking about the no-claims bonus on my own car. This will affect that, won't it?"

"You haven't got it protected?"

"No. It costs extra."

At which point Bill rolled his eyes, and Ted began laughing as though this were the funniest thing he'd ever heard.

"Alright, then," said Bill. "The way to look at it is like this: you'll still be in profit, even if your premium does go up. But look, as it's your first time I'll be gentle with you. I'll try to find you a few extra quid to cover the increase in cost. Now Gareth, take a look at this." Bill produced his phone, and began scrolling through some photos of cars. "I've picked you this nice cute Renault here. We'll all be in the money. You wait and see."

First time? Thought Gareth, feeling like a man on the edge of a precipice. *Hell's bloody bells.*

No longer feeling brave enough to try backing out, he then attempted to act cool about still being in. He made a couple of clumsy jokes about how 'gangsta' the Renault looked, and breezily attempted a mock negotiation of the extra cut required to cover his increased insurance premiums.

But deeper down, Gareth felt ashamed. And he felt like an idiot, too.

He still felt the same way a couple of days later. Which was why, in an effort to justify his decision to recommit to himself to the scam, he began making spending commitments with regards to the money he'd be making. He phoned a local solicitors' office, and made an appointment to discuss legal strategies for preventing, or at least delaying, the sale of The Lamb and Musket.

Rather than feeling better after putting down the phone, he merely felt like an even bigger idiot than before. And his sense of idiocy only ballooned when he met said solicitor a couple of days later, and discovered that there was, from a legal point of view, very little to be done about Shop City Supermarkets purchasing The Lamb and Musket from George Timkin's Hippy Hops Pub Company.

Gareth sits in his allocated Renault in this far-flung corner of a derelict industrial site. The other parties to the forthcoming craziness will be here in just a few short minutes. ("A quick talk through," Bill has promised, "and then off to the High Street.") Gareth's nervousness, along with his sense of idiocy, has risen to critical levels while he's been sitting here fretting. In that he now has a solicitor's bill to pay, he feels more than ever that he has to go through with the scheme. And yet – Hell's bells – the whole thing is just so bloody crazy. Remembering that his long-ago resignation from a good job proved to be such a serious mistake – one from which he has never fully recovered – Gareth sinks further into anxious misery. He grips the steering wheel with clammy hands, and wonders whether this latest decision will prove equally bad.

+++++

With the outside tap fitted to his new customer's house, Patrick takes payment, says his thanks, and drives his van half-a-mile down the road. He then parks up near the kerb, switches off the engine, and thinks hard about what to do next.

One option is to go back home and make himself busy, maybe immersing himself once more in the trading of shares. Or, keeping his overalls on – metaphorically speaking, at any rate – he could get on the phone and chase down some of the work he's recently quoted for. Afterwards he might head to the golf course, and hit some balls on the driving range. Maybe even play nine holes.

Alternatively, though, he could do what he clearly had in mind when he stashed Ricky's golf clubs in the back of his van. He could take them round to Ricky and Caroline's house in the hope of finding Caroline home. Their place is less than a mile away – he could be there in under a minute from now.

Patrick is surprised and pretty disappointed not to have heard from Caroline since that Sunday evening in The Lamb, precisely two weeks and four days ago, when the two of them connected strongly – at least so he thought – and Caroline said she'd phone him soon. Still sitting is his van, Patrick runs through some of the reasons why she may not have called. One such possibility is that she concluded Patrick would always side with Ricky in any dispute between her and her husband. Alternatively, given how the night nearly ended up, Caroline may equally have decided not to become further embroiled with a lunatic Irish family who still got into fights on quiz nights in pubs. And a third potential reason, Patrick supposes, is that Caroline may have sensed a spark between he and Esme that evening, and unselfishly wanted to give the two of them some time and space uncomplicated by her troubled relationship with the man who's both Esme's brother and Patrick's best mate.

But he knows that there is, of course, a further possible explanation as to why Caroline hasn't phoned him. She's a woman, ultimately, and as such she'll do simply as she wants, whether her actions – or lack of them – make any sense to him or not.

Patrick finds himself in a wary frame of mind. Whatever reasons Caroline had for not phoning him, it seems likely that those reasons will remain in force. Accordingly, were he to phone her now, and ask whether this is a good time to call round, there's a decent chance her reply would be negative. Therefore, having finally decided that he will indeed drop by, Patrick also determines that he will do so unannounced. With his decision made, he puts the van in gear and heads off quickly, before he has time for a change of mind. He's deeply conscious that this is no innocent social call he's about to make. He's either trying to heal a marital rift between two of his oldest friends, or exploit that rift to his own selfish advantage. Patrick simply isn't sure which of his two motives happens to pertain the strongest.

Ricky and Caroline's house is one of half-a-dozen four-bedroom detached properties in a secluded cul-de-sac. Their lawn is neatly trimmed, courtesy of a man they pay to do the mowing, and there are some plants in pots and a couple of hanging baskets, all of which Caroline keeps looking nice. The block-paved driveway has more than enough space for both cars – unlike their previous house just around the corner from Patrick's – and although Ricky's big BMW isn't on the drive, Caroline's smaller one certainly is. Everything is pretty much as expected – and, indeed, hoped.

Patrick parks his van immediately outside. As his mouth is feeling dry, he drinks the cold dregs of the coffee remaining in his travel mug. Then, conscious that his hands are sweaty and his heart rate up, he slides out of his van and climbs down to the pavement. He feels exposed, out-of-place, and almost like a trespasser once he's at the kerbside, and he tries hard to appear relaxed as he walks to the back of the van and takes out Ricky's golf bag. Turning to face the house, he shoulders the bag, and, still striving to give off a casual air, ambles down the driveway towards the front door. It being another day of fine weather, the sun's glare is reflecting off the windows of the house, and so he can't see whether or not

Caroline is looking out at him. But in the event that she is, Patrick tries to fix on his face an easy-going look – that of a man without too many cares in the world – as opposed to the expression of someone shitting himself as he calls unannounced on a woman he's fancied ever since he's been old enough to fancy anyone.

He reaches the front door. He rings the bell, and waits.

It takes quite a while for the door to be answered – long enough for him to stage a further, agonised dissection of his motives for being here – and he's about to ring the bell for a second time when he glimpses blurry movement behind one of the adjacent windows. Then there's a further delay, during which he wonders whether Caroline, too, is wondering what the hell his game is. Then the door is finally opened.

Caroline's wearing some cut-off denim shorts, a raggedy white blouse, and a seductively impudent smile. Her hair is piled up in an anarchic thatch-work of tresses, and there's a slim, sleek pair of sunglasses pushed high up on her forehead. Her arms and face and legs all look nicely tanned, and Patrick is struck with the impression that he interrupted something she was doing in the back garden.

She looks appraisingly at Patrick, and then eyes up Ricky's clubs. "Oh, goodness," she says, after a theatrical gasp of breath. "Did we arrange to play a game? I'll have to fire my social secretary, I'm afraid. And I haven't ironed my plus fours."

"Let's see now – I'm not sure anyone with a social secretary would do their own ironing."

"Yeah," she replies, wrinkling her nose at him. "Maybe you've got me there." Then she leans out through the door, and kisses him on the cheek. "You'd best come in, then, lover boy."

"Sure, though, but am I interrupting anything?"

"Sure, though, but no you're not." Caroline has stepped backwards and aside, allowing him entry to the house. "Nothing important, anyway."

"It's just I've had Ricky's clubs about my workshop for a while," Patrick says, not immediately moving from his spot outside the door. "And then I was due to be just around the corner from here, fitting these newlyweds an outside tap…"

But Caroline is giving him a look – a Caroline Look, no less. A look which riles against his verbiage, and appears to question why the fuck he needs explain himself for calling at their house.

"Whatever, Pat," she says, waving a dismissive hand as his little speech turns to dust. "Just come on in, and bring those bloody things with you."

"Yes, Ma'am," Patrick murmurs, stepping inside.

"Would you mind putting them in the garage?" Caroline asks as she leads Patrick through the hallway.

"No problem." He puts the clubs down at the far end of the hall. But before he can open the door to the garage, he senses movement at waist level or thereabouts, and when he glances down he can see, sure enough, that Jack has emerged from the little den he has downstairs – the one running just off the hall.

The kid has his mum's hair – strawberry blonde and inclined to chaos – alongside his dad's John Wayne swagger. "Uncle Pat," he says happily. "What are you doing here?"

"I've got your da's clubs, Jack. Sure, he left them in my car."

"And your Uncle Patrick was in the area," adds Caroline. "Fitting some newlyweds an outside tap." She looks at Patrick, and they both laugh.

Jack looks from one to the other or them. "What are new-lee-weds?" he asks.

"They're two people," says Patrick, "who are married to each other, but haven't been married for very long."

"Your dad and I used to be newlyweds, Jack, back when dinosaurs walked the earth."

The kid casts his mum a wide-eyed look, which she immediately mirrors back, accompanied by a big, beaming smile. "What big eyes you have, Grandma," she says to him.

Jack turns his attention back to Patrick. "I'm watching Horrible Histories," he says. "Do you want to watch it with me?"

Patrick shoots an enquiring glance at Caroline, but the kid goes off on another tangent before his mum can say a single word. "I'm taller than four steps now," he says, running to stand with his back to the side of the staircase. And he's not wrong – Patrick can see that Jack has indeed outgrown the height of the fourth step, which makes him a good bit taller than when Patrick last set eyes on him. His language skills have moved on quickly as well.

"I noticed you were sprouting up," says Patrick. "Sure, you'll be up to the fifth step soon."

Jack turns one-eighty degrees, and moves his hand in a line from the top of his head to the staircase. "Nearly," he agrees. "Maybe next week."

"The way he's growing," murmurs Caroline, "that isn't as overly ambitious as it sounds."

"I think you'll grow to be as tall as your da," says Patrick. "Which is a couple of inches taller than your Uncle Pat. Maybe not by next week, though."

Jack falls momentarily silent while seeming to think seriously about what Patrick's just said. Then Caroline says to the kid, "Jack, your Uncle Pat's going to put Daddy's clubs away, and Mummy's going to make some coffee. "Why don't you finish watching Histories by yourself, being as you're halfway through."

Jack seems to think about this suggestion just as seriously as he did Patrick's. Then, after a few seconds, with a couple of brisk nods, but without another word, he runs off back to his den.

Caroline watches him go with a wistful smile on her face. "He's so like Ricky," she says, almost to herself. "Always calculating – always thinking things through." Then she looks at Patrick directly. "Garage is unlocked. Meet me in the kitchen, yeah?"

By the time Patrick puts away the clubs and makes it to the kitchen, Caroline is grinding coffee beans and has the espresso machine switched on. The kitchen is pervaded by a scrubbed and lemony aroma, and most of its many surfaces and appendages appear almost surgically clean. Everything here is precision formed from either from chrome, steel, glass or granite, and Patrick can see precious little with any colour to it. That said, there are four bright red apples in a bowl on the breakfast bar, and a fifth apple on the work surface opposite – this apple half-eaten, with its flesh just starting to brown off. Splayed out next the apple it is an open booklet and some other paperwork.

"I was just looking out the guarantee on the microwave," says Caroline. "It's playing up at the minute, and you can't just go out and buy another one when the fucking thing is built into the wall."

"I'm sorry," Patrick replies. "Didn't realise I was interrupting anything."

"I told you before – you're not interrupting anything major. And I am glad of the company. Would you like one of the apples? They're good."

Forbidden fruit, thinks Patrick. "Thanks," he says, "but I'm fine."

"Or something different to eat? I can soon fix you lunch."

"Sure, that's nice of you, Caroline, but I'll be happy with a coffee."

"Wouldn't want you wasting away, now."

"Are you brewing that special blend of coffee?" he asks, seating himself at the breakfast bar and toying briefly with one of the apples, before setting it back down when it occurs to him that it's impolite to fool around with food he isn't planning to eat. "That blend from the emporium in town?"

"They're from the emporium, alright," she replies, pouring milk into a jug, and heating it with the steam wand on the side of the espresso machine. "God, we must have spent a fortune there since I discovered the place. But these beans are slightly different to last time. You must tell me what you think."

"I'm sure I'll like them. But if you want an expert opinion, sure, I'm no authority."

Caroline looks at him archly while she brews the espresso. "I'll teach you about coffee," she says. "One of these days."

"One of these days," he echoes, momentarily letting the idea linger, before he goes on to add, "Don't know what I could teach you in return, mind you. Not unless you want to hear about plumbing procedure and practice."

Caroline laughs. Her laugh is a thing of sweetness and wonder to him. "I'll get back to you on that," she says, setting their coffees down on the breakfast bar and sliding onto the stool next to his.

There follows a moment's brief silence – one long enough for Patrick to rub an imagined itch on the side of his neck, and in so doing to notice that his hands still feel clammy, despite the warmth of Caroline's welcome. "Four stairs," says Patrick, glancing at the apple he handled, guiltily wondering whether he left it shiny with sweat. "Sure, the kid's getting tall."

"He is," Caroline acknowledges, swinging her stool around for a better look at Patrick, but without elaborating upon the question of her son's height and rate of growth. Sensing Caroline doesn't want to discuss matters relating to Jack, Patrick sips his coffee and tries to come up with a different topic.

"Let's talk about Mr Patrick Mackey," Caroline says, beating him to the punch. "He must be – what? – eight stairs tall, at least, but has probably stopped growing by now. He and I don't have many proper conversations nowadays, and that seems sad. So tell me how you are, Pat."

"I'm fine. Sure, I'm… you know… "

"Just fine?"

"Just fine," he confirms, nodding for emphasis, and swivelling his stool in her direction, just as she previously turned towards him. He knows their knees are nearly touching, but won't look down for confirmation because Caroline is showing a lot of leg in those shorts, and he doesn't want to be seen to be leering. "I was going to ask you the same question," he finally adds.

"Well go on, then." She looks at him directly. "Go on and ask me."

"Alright… how are you?" he asks, conscious of her gaze and her immediate, physical proximity. He hopes his cheeks haven't coloured up, but suspects that they probably have.

Rather than answer his question, Caroline swivels slightly away, and then gets to her feet. "Back in a minute," she says, picking up her half-eaten apple from the nearby work surface, before walking unhurriedly from the room.

While she's absent, Patrick catches himself rocking backwards on the metal breakfast stool, trying to tilt it like he does his bar stool at The Lamb. But the centre of gravity on this stool feels all wrong, and it also has a circular base, meaning he can't keep it tilted for long without it rolling to one side or the other, however tenaciously he grips hold of the breakfast bar. Accordingly, he returns to an upright position, and tries to sit patiently while awaiting Caroline's return. He makes a mental note to see if he can buy cheaply – or even purloin entirely – one of the bar stools from The Lamb when the place closes down soon. It dawns on him abruptly that the council's decision is due next week, and he feels bad that The Lamb and

Musket's slide into non-existence is happening without very much resistance on his part. They (he and Ricky) have left it too much down to Gareth, that's for sure. Not that the two of them ever had much chance of preventing the closure, but Patrick feels they might at least have shown a little more *care* than they've managed of late.

Caroline returns within a minute or so, crunching noisily on the apple, and with her purse in one hand. She sits back down, opens her purse, and fishes around inside. He has a good idea what she's about to pull out, and, sure enough, there it is: his scorecard from the golf club, dating to the last time he played against Ricky. It's dog-eared and a little grimy, and as Caroline sets it down on the breakfast bar she reads aloud the words he wrote on it nearly three weeks previously.

"If you want to talk about anything (I mean anything at all) you have my number. We can talk in total confidence. It's okay."

Caroline swallows down one hunk of apple and bites off another. "Are you here to bring back Ricky's golf clubs?" she asks, crunching noisily on the apple, without bothering to observe any counsel she might ever have received that it's wrong talk with a mouthful of food. "And like a window salesman or religious zealot, you happened to be in the area? Or is it because I haven't phoned you, Pat, and you think there's something we should talk about?"

Those last couple of sentences came quickly, in a torrent, for all of her chewing on that apple (*forbidden fruit*), and Patrick senses an urgency – indeed, an *anger* – to her words.

"Sure, hang on," he replies, arms raised, palms open. "I'm really sorry, Caroline. I didn't mean to upset you by coming here. I can soon be back on my way."

He's actually getting to his feet when she forestalls him with a hand to his knee. Just the quickest touch from her feels electric to him – like a bolt of lightning from another, more magical world. "No," she says. "You're welcome here, you silly fucking idiot. Anytime. God knows, I wish we'd seen more of you since we moved to this place.

But you see, that's just it. Because you're not here often, I'd really like to know what made you come today, especially at a time of day when you know I'm likely to be here and the big baller isn't."

Patrick's certain his face is reddening now, and he knows there's nothing he can do to stop it.

"If it's really about timing and coincidence – if it's really about you having Ricky's clubs in your van, when you were doing a job round the corner – then that's fine. Look me in the eye and tell me again that that's all this is."

She affords him a moment to reply. When he doesn't, she pushed the handwritten note a further inch towards him and asks, "Or is it about this?"

Of course it's about the frickin note, but as Patrick reads it again and then looks at Caroline, he still can't find the right words.

"And what made you write it anyway, Pat?"

Patrick draws breath, but then angles his head off in the direction of Jack's den, which is across on the other side of the hallway. He scrunches his face a little, as if listening for the kid's approach.

"It's fine," says Caroline, flatly. "If his programme's finished, he'll have found another – cartoons and monsters, or some such. Tell me what made you write the note."

Frustrated, Patrick throws up his arms in an industrial-scale shrug. "Sure," he says. "I wrote you the note, Caroline, because I was concerned about you and Ricky. You said you'd phone and yet you haven't, and so I'm still concerned. That's why I'm here now. I'm sorry – maybe I should be minding my own business."

For a moment she just stares at him, her eyes wide with what he thinks is fury. Briefly, Patrick's sure she'll concur that he should, indeed, be minding his own business. But when Caroline finally replies, she does so quietly. "Oh, God," she murmurs, abandoning what's left of her apple, and getting up to go to the window. There, she stares out on a sunny afternoon, distractedly running a hand through her hair, pushing those sunglasses higher up her forehead. A hairclip falls away, and some of her hitherto piled-up tresses spool out to one side. When she next speaks, she sounds a dozen different kinds of sad.

"I'm the one who's sorry, Patrick. I shouldn't speak to you like that. It's just that… it's just… "

Patrick feels he should go to Caroline. He should get up from the breakfast bar and just hold her for a while. He should offer the woman some kind of comfort. But then he looks at her in those shorts, and knows that it's more than comfort he'd like to offer. *Fuck's sake*, he thinks. *This is Caroline. This is Ricky's wife.*

"It's just what?" Patrick asks quietly. He follows Caroline towards the window and stands off to her side. He's within touching distance of her; he's there if she wants to…

Wants to what?

"What do you actually know?" she asks, eyes fixed straight ahead. "What made you write the note?"

"I know you've been bickering, sure. I know you don't seem quite yourselves."

"What else do you know?"

Patrick doesn't reply. He hears someone sighing – sighing sadly, and with longing. Sighing as if badly conflicted. He realises it's him who's doing it.

"What else, Pat?" She turns towards him, her face a taut, tense mask of trepidation.

Patrick finds himself speaking at a pitch so low it's barely more than a whisper. "I know that when we're out having a drink, or sometimes a game of golf, Ricky gets messages on his phone – messages that are supposedly about work problems." Patrick pauses. He draws breath. He feels suddenly cold, as if his blood has iced over. "I know he often has to go and sort these problems out. Seems to me he gets a lot of messages, and he has to do a lot of sorting out, often at strange times of day or night."

Caroline turns away so that she's once more looking out at the sun-drenched garden – at its tended borders, its child's playhouse and its brick-built barbecue. Patrick doubts she's really seeing them at all. She folds her arms, and then raises one hand to brush a tear from the corner of here eye.

"Thank you," she says, after a silent moment.

Patrick, whose emotions have become an arcane mixture of heady relief and gut-wrenching guilt, tries to row back a little bit on what he's just implied. "But Caroline, sure, I don't actually *know* anything."

The noise which escapes Caroline's throat is part laugh and part sob. "Don't you?" she says, another tear forming and quickly brushed away, before she angrily flicks back the stray spool of hair which had become unpinned. "I think we both do."

This time it's Patrick's turn to look away and run hand through his hair. "Aww, Jesus, Caroline. Maybe."

"But why've you come round here, Pat? What made you write the note, and what made you come today? Who is this all about?"

The same questions he asked himself in the van. To whom doe he owe his greater loyalties? And what's his real motive for being here, in Caroline and Ricky's house?

"Aww, Jesus, Caroline," he says again, because he can, momentarily, think of nothing else to say.

Caroline lets out another of those choked noises which is part laugh and part sob. "All this, 'Aww, Jesus, Caroline,'" she says. "Esme picked you up about that kind of language in the pub. It's not what I'd expect from a good Catholic boy."

"Sure, we haven't practised that stuff for years."

"It's just as well," she replies. She moves closer to him, and there's a bitter little smile showing on her face. "If you don't mind me saying, you haven't made a very good job of not coveting your neighbour's wife."

"Aww, Jesus, Caroline. Has it really been so obvious?"

"To someone clever and wily like me, yeah. But I think you probably knew that, didn't you?"

"Alright, look," Patrick says. He feels as though he's going through a wringer, but there no longer seems a point to holding anything back. "You keep asking why I'm here, and what you seem to be asking is a question about my motives. Sure – my loyalties, if you like, because someone clever and wily like you has to know that my loyalties are divided in a situation like this. And when you ask me why I'm really here, I've got to be honest with you: I don't frickin know for certain."

Another sob/laugh combination. Caroline takes a sheet of kitchen towel from a roll on the wall, and after dabbing at her eyes, she uses it to blow her nose. "Thank you," she says to him.

"For what?"

"For at least being honest. I'm suffering an honesty deficit just lately. You don't know what it means to me to have someone speak the truth." She kisses her fingertips and then uses them to stroke his cheek. "This time, I must check on Jack," she says, and begins to brush past him to the door.

But unless Patrick imagines it, Caroline lingers slightly in the act of brushing past, and whether he imagined it or not, he can't be sure that a moment like this will ever come again. Therefore, casting both caution and all good sense aside, he reaches for her hand, pulls her close, and kisses her tentatively on the lips. Then he quickly backs off, half expecting an appalled reaction – a violent one, even – but finds the look on Caroline's face to be far from outraged. Her expression is a blend of amusement and mild surprise. And also desire, so he thinks. He therefore kisses her again. This time it's for longer, and this time she responds, gripping him tightly as her lips fandango with his.

Eventually, Caroline lets go of him and pulls back a little. "Maybe," she says, "you just did something to help resolve your uncertainties."

"Sure, maybe I did."

"Okay, Pat," she says, slightly breathily, her cheeks tinged with pink. "Stay right there. I really do have to go and check on Jack."

Caroline heads from the room then, leaving him alone with his thoughts, of which he has many. It seems that what just happened was crazy. Crazy, mad and stupid. Utterly insane, and completely wrong. Yet what he and Caroline did felt wonderful, too. Now Caroline's voice carries to him from Jack's play den, her tone warm, solicitous, and maternal, causing everything to feel right with Patrick's world – as if he's floating in a warm bubble of serenity and partially-suppressed excitement. Caroline may well come back and tell him to go home, cool off, and stop being such a moron. And if she does, well that will be perfectly okay. But Patrick doesn't think she will say that; he thinks she'll say something very different. And that, too, will be perfectly okay.

His instincts in the matter prove correct. When Caroline does return, she reaches for his hand. "Come with me," she says, and leads him from the kitchen. By the time they reach the stairs – *Jack is four steps tall, nearly five*, Patrick thinks – things are starting to feel all wrong. His sense is that Caroline is leading him to the bedroom she shares with his very best buddy, and Patrick doesn't think he can go there. That serenity bubble feels fit to pop.

Caroline has one foot on the second stair and another on the first when she pivots to face him, aware that he's holding back. As if reading his mind, she whispers, "It's okay. Come on. Spare room."

His pulse rapidly quickening, Patrick allows himself to be led.

+++++

The Renault's dashboard clock is illuminated and functioning, but the time is incorrectly set. Gareth, who's been gripping the wheel of this stationary car so tightly that it may as well have been the world's scariest rollercoaster, removes his left hand in order to check his watch.

Hell's bells – the others will be here any minute.

Knowing his nerve to be failing rapidly, Gareth realises that if he's going to back out of this at all, then he has to do so now. Once Bill and Ted and their cohorts arrive, they simply won't put up with Gareth having an attack of cold feet. In point of fact, he can barely put up with such queasiness himself. Illegal or not, he has made a commitment to play his part in this scheme, and he does need the money now that he has a legal bill to pay.

Yet the whole thing is surely an act of folly. Although he has read up on the internet just how many Cash for Crash scams are thought to take place, and how many people get away with it annually, Gareth also knows that every now and then the culprits do get caught. And when they caught, they go to jail. Directly to jail – without passing Go, and often without collecting even two-hundred pounds.

Something else he knows, intuitively, is this: whereas the likes of Bill and Ted are savvy enough to get away with their wrongdoing, it's people like him – the fodder in these squalid acts of fraud – who end up serving time at Her Majesty's pleasure.

Gareth imagines himself in jail. He further imagines one day being released, to a world where he has neither a home nor a job, and with nothing to show for his spell inside other than a drug habit and an enlarged rectal passage. He pictures himself living on the streets, sleeping in shop doorways between layers of damp cardboard, and begging the price of a cup of tea from whosoever is passing by. It's the realisation that he'd make a lousy beggar which causes Gareth's resolve to finally disintegrate. He fires up the Renault and accelerates away as quickly as he can – which is not quickly at all, given how the car struggles at low speed, but at least he's on the move. He only hopes that he can get clear of these ruinous badlands before the others all arrive.

He makes it out through the ramshackle gates, as far as the first of two small islands where the site's service road meets the main public highway. Obliged to give way at the first of these islands to a procession of cars coming from his right, he looks frantically at the drivers of each one in turn, willing them all to get a move on, and praying that a gap will materialise in the traffic before his partners in crime (or rather superiors in crime, he figures) finally arrive on the scene.

Twenty seconds go by while he sits there – twenty seconds which feel like twenty lifetimes – waiting for an opportunity to pull out. A big, white Ford goes by – some kind of people mover, he dimly registers – followed by a silver, sleek, shiny Mercedes. Then comes his chance. There's a gap – not a big gap, but still a gap. Enough of a gap, Gareth thinks, for him to slip into the flow of traffic without impeding the next car too much. It's an old, boxy Volvo, anyway, that next car. The kind of car driven by sensible people – the driver will surely slow down for him if necessary.

Gareth goes for it. He puts his foot down and releases the clutch. The little Renault starts to pull out, but then its known fault kicks in – namely its low-speed stutter – and he senses that the engine's about to stall. The car is only coasting now – coasting slowly, and the big Volvo is bearing down on it. Determinedly, Gareth puts his foot hard down. The power kicks back in, and the Renault shoots forward again.

Unfortunately, it shoots forward not very far – only into the nearside rear end of the sculptured Mercedes, which had slowed behind the big Ford, the Ford, in turn, having pulled up to give way at the second of the two islands.

It's a relatively low speed accident, yet to Gareth the impact feels immense. He hears a loud crump as metal and plastics collide, together with the harsh shatter of fragmenting glass, and a brisk whoosh as the airbag explodes hotly in his face – an experience he'll later rationalise as like being smacked in the mouth with a recently-filled hot water bottle. Meanwhile, thankfully, the seatbelt does its job, ratcheting tight so as to hold him in his seat.

Despite the shock and the sensory overload of the accident, Gareth's pretty sure that he hears a second, slightly distant crump only a split second after the first, and when his startled mind begins to compute this unfortunate turn of events, he suspects that having smashed into the rear of the Mercedes, he has also pushed it into the back end of the Ford.

This suspicion is confirmed when he sees the Ford disentangle itself slowly from the Mercedes with its rear bumper cracked and askew. The driver of the Ford then pulls up at the kerbside, just beyond the second island, where it's soon joined by the sleek German saloon. Gareth, whose hands are trembling, and who can feel in his ears the blood rush of a galloping heartrate, is quick to join them, climbing quickly from the Renault after parking up, finding himself unable to remain in his car a moment longer.

It doesn't help his peace of mind that of the two middle-aged men emerging from the Ford, the passenger is holding his neck and moaning, whereas the driver has decided on an all-out rant. "What the utter fuck were you playing at?" he rages as a man emerges from the passenger seat of the Mercedes. "You must've seen I'd stopped for traffic."

But he wasn't driving, thinks Gareth. *Don't yell at him. Can't you see he got out the passenger side? And besides, this is all down to me, anyway.*

The angry man from the Ford is broad-shouldered, stocky, and has the look of someone who'd be useful in a fight. The passenger from the Mercedes – an older man, who's tall and trim, and who looks very well groomed in a dark woollen suit – is swift and efficient in passing the parcel of blame. "Not our fault," he coldly replies. "The cretin behind ran into us."

As the Ford driver bustles towards him, Gareth studies the aggregate of damage caused to his Renault's front and the Mercedes' rear. The Renault's bumper is hanging more off the car than on, and one of the headlights is smashed in. The Mercedes has some equivalent tail-light damage, and there's a significant crease in its rear. Given that it's bent partly out of shape, Gareth finds his attention drawn to the Mercedes' number plate. 'GTT' read the last three letters. *Gareth The Twat*, he thinks desolately, as he awaits the Ford driver's wrath.

The man from the Ford gets face-to-face with him, and angrily repeats the question he asked of the Mercedes' passenger. "What the utter fuck were you playing at?" Close up, he has moustache as bushy and flourishing as Gareth's own – in different circumstances it might have been a talking point of social merit. "Tell me, eh? What the fuck were you fucking doing?"

"I'm sorry," says Gareth, who knows his insurers wouldn't want him admitting liability, but can't think of anything else to say. "I felt my engine cutting out, and so I gave it some extra gas. Then the car just seemed to shoot forward."

"Poxy old heap of yours," the Ford driver seethes. "Shouldn't be on the road if it's got a fucking fault like that."

"Excuse me," says a voice from behind Gareth. "I know you're upset, sir, but getting angry won't help the situation." When Gareth glances round, he sees that the voice belongs to a slightly older gent – one of similar age to the elegant-looking man from the Mercedes. Gareth sees that the big old Volvo is now parked up behind his Renault, and assumes that this man it its driver. Gareth feels pathetically grateful to him for stopping to help.

"That's alright for you to say," bridles the Ford driver to his Volvo counterpart. "You've not had your motor bent up by this fucking dickhead."

"He's right though, isn't he, mate? Accidents do happen." This latest intervention is from yet another driver, one who's pulled up behind the Volvo, presumably with the similar intention of helping out and making sure everyone's okay. "No one deliberately caused this, did they?"

With the three cars directly involved, plus the two driven by well-meaning witnesses, there are now five vehicles parked up by the kerb. Someone else is in the road, attempting to pick up debris, and there's a queue of traffic as other drivers slow down for a look at the goings-on. Meanwhile, a bit further back, at the entrance to the brownfield site from which Gareth has just fled, two other cars have arrived and their occupants disembarked. A couple of these individuals are clearly recognisable as Bill and Ted; they have cigarettes lit and are looking fixedly at the unfolding drama. Although the pair of them are too far away for him to study their faces, it doesn't take much effort for Gareth to picture their disdain. *Crash but no Cash*, he muses. *It takes an utter doofus like me to come up with that one.*

Meanwhile, the Volvo driver is on his phone, and the other witness is bickering with Mr Angry from the Ford. "Look mate," the would-be Samaritan is saying, "all this shouting isn't going to help. Why don't you try looking after your passenger? He looks like he might have whiplash or something."

"Eh? Well, if he has, yeah, we'll be taking this twat here to the cleaners." It occurs to Gareth, with bitter irony, that the driver of the Ford may as well be related to Bill or Ted, given his coarseness and absence of sympathy. "Him and his poxy fucking car – fucking hell, the fucking prick."

Then, a momentary distraction for them all. The driver's door of the Mercedes opens, and a young woman climbs out. A highly attractive young woman at that – a woman maybe half the age of her well-heeled passenger. Her long legs are showcased so well by a pair of high-heeled sandals and a short summery dress that Gareth can well imagine the sight of her causing a further accident before many minutes go by.

The road is uneven and potholed, necessitating that the woman moves cautiously in her heels. Like the second man from the Ford, she's rubbing the back of her neck, and although her older, male passenger – who had been standing off to one side of the quarrelling group, morosely smoking a cigarette – hurries around to her side of the car, his demeanour doesn't appear especially solicitous. The noise generated by the slow-moving-traffic prevents Gareth from hearing what he says to her, but by his gestures he appears to be protesting that the woman should get back into the car and stop drawing attention to herself.

The woman, though, is having none of it. She shakes her head hard at him – a movement which causes her to wince in even greater pain and clutch at her neck all the more. The passenger, in turn, throws up his arms in exasperation, before throwing his cigarette aside and hurrying over to where Gareth and Mr Angry from the Ford are cloistered with the two witnesses.

"Look," says the man from the Mercedes, "can we all just swap details and be on our separate ways?" He looks down his nose at Gareth's old Renault. "I think all the cars are just-about driveable, aren't they?"

"I'm afraid it's not that simple," says the Volvo driver, having just come off his phone. "The emergency services are on their way."

"The emergency services?" From the breast pocket of his suit jacket, the Mercedes' passenger produces a sleek, silver cigarette case, and pops a new cigarette between his lips. "Good God, man. What on Earth for?"

"What on Earth for? Well, sir, there are at least two people are rubbing their necks – one of whom I believe to be driving you. Then there's the matter of the debris that's all over the road. And I don't think it will hurt to have the police here given how tempers are rising a little."

"There's also this guy," says the other witness, gesturing at Gareth with his thumb. "Looks like he's out of it to me. Wouldn't be surprised to find out he's on something."

"On something, eh?" says the Ford driver, his moustache seeming to bristle at Gareth. "I'll bust the fucker up if he is."

Gareth briefly meets his aggressor's eye, before his gaze wanders to where the Mercedes' incredibly leggy driver is comparing injuries with the passenger from the Ford. Then he looks back down the road to where Bill, Ted, and their other accomplices are still just standing and staring in his direction. Finally, he turns to study the bent number plate on the creased rear bumper of the Mercedes. *GTT* he thinks again. *Gareth The Twat – Hell's almighty bells.*

+++++

Mid-afternoon in The Lamb and Musket. Mid-afternoon of a lovely summer's day, and Mel would like to be almost anywhere other than here. It isn't simply that she's bored, although bored she certainly is, what with there being no glasses unwashed, nor tables unwiped, and no empty bottles still to be gathered in and crated up for collection.

She's bored, also, because there are hardly any customers about. Ricky and Vince are propping up one end of the bar, while a handful of other regulars have drifted in and out. Derek has, as of yesterday, taken an old, boxy, twenty-four-inch TV, and set it up in one corner of the bar, apparently because the Open Golf Championship is taking place, and he reckons a good few of the regulars will want to watch it. So small is the picture that anyone wanting to watch the golf has to move within six feet of the set, and Mel hasn't so far seen a single customer take the trouble, never mind the numbers of people predicted by Derek.

But it's more than just her boring job in a dying pub which is causing Mel such frustration. It's that she's been unable, so far at least, to find a way of moving on from it.

Two weeks have gone by since her interview with Robert Hopwood of Hopwood and Partners Estate Agents. The interview went well enough – or at least so she thought at the time. Indeed, Robert Hopwood himself pronounced himself more than happy with her candidature. The only potential snag, if indeed it could be called a snag, came at the interview's end, when he said, "I just need to sit you in front of Harry, one of our other partners, for a final opinion. Give me a couple of days, and I'll let you know when he's free to see you."

Mel was reasonably happy with that, albeit a little baffled why the man with his name over the door wasn't the final arbiter on recruitment decisions. Perhaps such scepticism had shown on her face, because Robert Hopwood quickly added, "Harry's very shrewd, you see. He's been known to pick up on things I've missed, although I'm sure there'll be no problems in your case, Mel."

Whether there were problems or whether there weren't, four days went by before she heard from Hopwood again, when he sent an email apologising that Harry had been 'especially tied up', but that they'd be back in touch soon.

But as of now, more than a whole week later, that email remains her last communication received from Robert Hopwood or any of his partners, and Mel is beginning to feel deflated about the whole chain of events. From thinking she'd found herself a new job – and a better one than expected, come to that – it now feels as though the opportunity has gone cold, and she suspects she'll have to start the entire job search all over again. She will, of course, send Hopwood a polite email asking if Harry has become free, but even if Mel does remain under consideration for the role, it's disappointing to her that things are dragging out the way they are. She keeps thinking back to the posse of big kids clowning around when she first walked into Robert Hopwood's offices, and wonders how badly she really wants to work at a place such as that.

At the end of the bar, Ricky and Vince are finishing their first round of drinks. Ricky's had a pint of cold lager, Vince a glass of tap water with some ice. From the sportswear they both have on, and indeed from their talk of weights pushed, pulled and lifted, Mel knows they've been to the gym. She's aware that Ricky has resumed going there with Vince over the past couple of weeks, after a considerable period of abstention. Mel's also pretty sure that Ricky's reconnection with the free weights and the resistance machines has something to do with the moves he's been making on her colleague Yasmin, who looks in sensational shape herself – as Mel rather grudgingly admits – and is exactly the sort of shallow yet demanding bint who'll expect her men toned to perfection (*so good luck drinking lager, Ricky*).

Mel also has a pretty good idea why Ricky, now that he is exercising again, is doing so in the afternoons rather than the evenings. One of the other mums from school has both a job at the gym and a seriously loose tongue, and had previously made Mel aware of Ricky becoming more than friendly with one of the aerobics instructors. Now that he seemingly has a new girlfriend in Yasmin, Mel imagines that Ricky is pumping iron off-peak so he can avoid any awkward meet-ups with her predecessor. Unless Ricky can sustain more than one mistress at once, of course. Mel certainly wouldn't put it past the arrogant so-and-so.

Heading to Vince and Ricky's end of the bar, Mel asks them if they'd like a second round. They answer yes, and so she duly gets Vince another tap water. Given that Ricky has to drive afterwards, he requests a coffee, and she makes it for him while he goes for a cigarette. Mel reflects that it must be nice to be in Ricky's position – to have a senior enough job that he can slope off to the gym of an afternoon without having the boss on his case. It's a thought which brings back to mind her disappointment with the hold-up at Robert Hopwood and Partners, and her frustration in the matter must be showing because she catches Vince looking at her concernedly as she stirs milk into Ricky's mug.

She sets the coffee down, pats Vince's hand where it rests atop the bar, and gives him a little wink. "Are you alright, big fella?" she asks while willing her smile back into place.

It's a smile which Vince immediately mirrors, and then, after thinking about the question, he manages to articulate that he's fine, thanks, before going on to ask her how she is.

"Oh, I'm just great," she replies, hoping that by claiming as much she'll actually begin to feel that way.

Vince keeps on smiling at her, and she watches as one of his eyelids flutters half-closed a couple of times, before he finally succeeds in closing the eye entirely. He then opens it again a second or so later, and she realises that he has, with some effort, just returned the wink she flashed at him. The gesture makes her proud and sad in equal measure, as do many of Vince's efforts at the normal, everyday things which people whose brains haven't been bashed around manage to accomplish with scarcely a thought. Mel has noticed how pleased Vince is that Ricky has resumed going to the gym with him, but Mel also sees the glowering agitation on Vince's face when he spots Ricky chatting up Yasmin. It's probable that Vince, like Patrick, feels bad on behalf of Caroline, who Mel doesn't know well but who does seem perfectly lovely. Vince and Patrick clearly seem to adore her, and their endorsement of the woman is good enough for Mel, who thinks Ricky must be an arsehole and idiot to treat his wife this way, however high-powered a job he may have.

But these are thoughts which she is unable to dwell on for very long. That's because Bill and Ted walk in, and they stand brooding at the other end of the bar while Mel goes through the protracted process of exchanging money with Vince after he insists on paying for the round. Once she's seen that Vince has safely pocketed his change, she excuses herself and goes to serve Bill and Ted, neither of whom are very talkative to her, but have plenty to say to each other, most of it in tones which are low, belligerent, and condemnatory. The pair of them are clearly unhappy with someone, and at first, as she begins pulling their pints, Mel is shocked to think that it might be Vince they're upset with, for delaying their getting served. But then Ted mutters to Bill, "It's a simple enough job to get right, but the stupid fucker's gone and got it very wrong. I told you we shouldn't have trusted him. The bloke's an out-and-out shithouse."

"Easy for you to be wise," snaps Bill. "But we need new people constantly. The scheme doesn't work – does it? – with the same old faces all the time." He glances at Mel, as if to judge how much attention she's paying. "Too much suspicion, Ted, you know?"

A phone begins ringing – it's the phone on the wall, in the corridor behind the bar. From not having enough work to do, Mel suddenly finds herself wishing for a second pair of hands – ideally a pair fixed to mechanically extendable arms. For now, she keeps pulling pints and ignores the ringing, deciding that the phone will just have to wait a bloody minute. It's probably a wrong number or a cold call, anyway. Anyone wanting Derek will usually call his mobile.

"You're right, I suppose," Ted says to Bill, with a rueful shake of his head. Ted has a cigarette between his lips, and a lighter ready in one hand. His need to spark up is clearly acute this afternoon.

"But to be fair," replies Bill, "you are absolutely right about him. The bloke's a total fuck-up – a real weapons-grade muppet."

The phone has stopped ringing by the time Mel has served their drinks. Ricky, meantime, is back inside, sipping his coffee while jokingly comparing biceps with Vince. He also has his wallet out, but Mel soon clues him up. "No need," she says. "Vince paid while you were outside poisoning your lungs. Not only does he have the bigger muscles, but he's also quicker with his cash."

There follows a minor, friendly squabble between Ricky and Vince. Mel knows that neither Ricky nor Patrick like Vince to pay for anything, and have asked her more than once to refuse his money. But she also knows that Vince likes his own sense of independence – of being one of the guys. He's happy to pay his way, just like everyone else.

"An instant coffee and some water from the tap isn't an expensive round," Mel says to Ricky, laughing as Vince folds his arms tightly to avoid taking the fiver that Ricky is waving. "And it isn't as if Vince hasn't any money," she adds, knowing that Vince, indeed, has a part-time job at the timber yard she hears his dad was well liked and used to buy raw material for his workshop.

Ricky throws her an admonishing glance, as if to say: *just shut the fuck up*. She thinks he means it playfully – in part, at least – but she sees a darkness behind his eyes which reinforces a belief shared between her and many of the people who drink here that he'd be the wrong man to cross in any meaningful way. But as to this matey little spat between friends, Mel doesn't get to see how it concludes. The phone is ringing again, and she dashes off to answer it.

When she returns, some three or four minutes later, Bill and Ted have made it outside, and Ricky, having finished his coffee, is explaining to Vince that it's time he was on his way. Apparently, Ricky still has work to complete this afternoon – places to go to and deals to get done.

"This may sound strange coming from me," says Mel, "but how busy are you, exactly?"

"Reasonably," says Ricky, his eyebrows raised in enquiry. "Reasonably, but not desperately. Why? What's up?"

"Well, that was Gareth on the phone."

"Gareth?" he queries. "The moustache maestro? That Gareth?"

"The very same," she replies.

"Saviour of the pub Gareth?"

"You've got it. That's the Gareth I'm talking about."

"Okay. And, so what?"

Mel takes a deep breath. "Turns out he's got himself arrested."

"Arrested?" There's a tiny delay while Ricky absorbs this news. Then he begins laughing. "Have they got him for breaking copyright, finally? Recording too many episodes of Coronation Street?"

"No," says Mel, trying to remain patient, but struggling to make herself heard over Ricky's laughter.

"I bet Gareth still has VHS recorder," Ricky says to Vince, whose strenuous efforts at following the conversation are evidenced by the frown on his face. "You know, mate – videocassette?"

"Look, it's worse than that," says Mel. "He was very garbled on the phone, but so far as I can tell he's been involved in a road accident. One of the other drivers has had a go at him, and Gareth has punched him in the mouth."

"Punched him?" says Ricky, laughing some more, and with a glance at Vince to see how much of this his mate is taking in. "In the mouth? Who'd have fucking thought it?" Ricky slides down from his bar stool; he looks ready to go. "But anyway Mel, this is my problem how, exactly?"

"Well, he phoned asking for Derek," she replies, knowing that Derek happens to be thirty miles away, looking at another pub which the brewery have offered him. "But Derek's not here, and it seems his mobile is switched off."

Both of them are looking at her. Ricky looks torn between the options of getting on his way and sticking around for the next comedic bombshell. Vince looks much more serious, his brow furrowed and his eyes narrowed in concentration.

"Gareth sounds like he's at his wits' end," says Mel. "They've charged him and released him, but he's at the other end of town with no money, and he needs to get home. He's even got some idea in his head that the bloke he punched will be waiting outside for him with a score to settle. He was wanting Derek to come pick him up."

"Why Derek?" asks Ricky.

"Don't you see? Derek's the closest thing Gareth has to a friend."

"Seriously? The poor fucker if that's true. Anyway, I'm not picking him up, if that's what you're asking. Bloke needs a taxi, doesn't he?"

"Ricky! I just said he has no money."

"Well, he can get the taxi to swing by a cashpoint."

"Oh, piss off, then." Mel throws up her arms in exasperation. "Forget I ever asked. When I said Gareth has no money, I meant Gareth has no money, period. Not just no money on him, but no money anywhere. Certainly not in a cashpoint somewhere. I meant not in the world."

If Mel's outburst has shocked Ricky, or made him feel any more sympathetic to Gareth, it clearly doesn't show. "What a fucking doughnut," he sighs. "The bloke's how old, and hasn't got the price of a cab fare?"

But Vince, who's been looking and listening with the intensity of a laboratory scientist studying the progress of a ground-breaking experiment, appears to reach some kind of decision. He eases gingerly down from his stool, smiles beatifically at Mel, and then taps Ricky on the arm. "Come on," he says, heading for the door, moving quickly by his standards, his worst leg dragging badly behind him.

"What?" calls Ricky, still at the bar. "What do mean, 'come on'?"

"Ga-reth," replies Vince, without turning around, nor deviating from his relentless passage towards the door.

"Come on, Ricky," says Mel. "If you won't do this for me, do it because Vince is the one asking now. And think what Gareth has done for you in the past."

"For me? Like the fuck what?"

"Like the other week, when we had the quiz, and there'd have been a riot if it weren't for Gareth."

"Malachy and Patrick should thank him for that. It was their arses on the line."

"And yours," says Mel. "You sided with your friends at the time. And that's all I'm asking of you now."

Ricky draws breath. Mel's sure he's about to remind her that Gareth isn't his friend.

"Come on," Vince calls, impatiently from the doorway.

"Fuck's sake," mutters Ricky. He looks hard at Mel. "Which cop shop?" he asks.

She shrugs her shoulders. "Sorry – he just said the police station. At the other end of town. How many are there?"

"Jesus." Ricky looks towards where Vince is waiting in the doorway. Then he spends an apparently furious moment studying either his shoes or some other thing on the floor. After which he gives Mel a lingering, reproachful look, before finally following Vince towards the car park. "This will cost you, missus," he calls over his shoulder. "Fucking Vince as well. And Gareth – it will cost the lot of you."

Happy now, Mel watches them go. She has no doubt at all that Ricky's parting words were far from idle – sometime, somewhere, somehow, this favour will indeed cost her. But she's pleased for the moment at having done what she can for Gareth, and she laughs quietly at the image of Ricky driving around town, looking for the right police station, all the while grumbling at Vince, who, in turn, will be chuckling to himself about what a great adventure they're having.

Mel's mood cools, however, when Bill and Ted quickly finish their first beers and come back indoors for a second round. Mel feels uncomfortable being alone with them, and has felt that way since the unpleasantness outside, on the day the two of them got Gareth pissed. She doesn't like the way that Ted, in particular, is given to looking at her, especially when, like today, she's chosen to put her shorts on.

Thankfully, Bill and Ted seem distracted by other matters this afternoon. While waiting for their second round, they continue to berate the same luckless guy they were castigating earlier, to the point where Mel gets the idea that it's Gareth they're talking about. When she thinks back to the day that Gareth got so drunk, she remembers he rambled on about Bill getting him a 'money car', and it seems increasingly possible to her that Bill and Ted's bad afternoon is directly connected with Gareth getting himself arrested. There are some dots for Mel to join up here – much as she joined up the dots about why it was that Ricky had returned to the gym at off-peak hours – but join them she will, just as soon as she has a little more information. That information will have to come from Gareth, though. There's no way she wants to get talking with Bill and Ted if she can help it.

What with their ongoing need for nicotine, Bill and Ted head outside again once they've been served, leaving Mel to ponder the puzzle some more. Distraction soon arrives, though, when a handful of new customers appear, one of whom is Patrick. In that he's already changed out of his overalls, he appears to be working a short day.

But Patrick doesn't have much to say for himself. He's not merely less chatty than usual – he actually appears deeply distracted. Indeed, Mel thinks he seems spooked in some way, and it perturbs her that when she takes a pint glass and asks whether it's lager or Guinness that he wants, he shakes his head vigorously and asks for a whiskey. "Sure, Mel. A double, in fact." It seems to Mel that the hour is still early for any of the hard stuff, never mind a double.

"Irish, I take it?" she asks, receiving only a terse little nod by way of response.

Although he sits in his usual spot, Patrick makes no effort to rock back on his stool. Instead, he nurses his whiskey while hunched up against the bar, the two eyes in his head dulled over and the one in his mind staring goodness knows where. Mel tries to tell him about Gareth getting arrested, but Patrick appears inured to Gareth's misfortunes, and his only noticeable response to the entire story is to wince a little when Mel tells him that Ricky and Vince have undertaken a rescue mission.

Mel's so concerned about him just sitting there, apparently numb to the world, that she twice asks whether he's really okay. He smiles wanly and assures her that he's fine, and once, just briefly, seems all set to say something further, but then seems to think better of it and looks away again, presumably to resume staring into the mid-distance of his thoughts.

As he gets up to leave, Patrick rubs absentmindedly at the side of his neck, pushing back his shirt collar to reveal what is clearly a love bite. Aside from the mild envy she feels towards the biter – an envy she's reluctant even to admit, however mildly it is felt – Mel's other reaction is one of deep curiosity as to what has happened to Patrick, maybe as recently as this afternoon, to leave him so apparently overwhelmed by life. Mel tracks Patrick's weary-looking progress to the door, realising that there are a great many dots to join if she's to get to the bottom of this one.

2.2) Thursday Next

Ricky has a serious hankering for a cigarette, but decides to go without for now. That's because Patrick is queueing for their drinks, and given that this bar they've come to is so busy, they'll certainly lose their table if Ricky slopes off for a smoke. The kind of conversation Ricky wants to have with Patrick is one which requires Patrick to be in an open, friendly and tolerant mood, and Ricky knows that by forfeiting their table he wouldn't help matters in that regard. Patrick already seems a bit on edge, without Ricky doing anything to rattle him some more.

But having made the decision to hang tough, Ricky nevertheless finds himself toying with his cigarettes and lighter, and so he makes a deliberate effort to slide them away, simultaneously searching his pockets for some nicotine gum. He reflects, sourly, that he reached the age at which he could legally drink in pubs at pretty much the same time that it became illegal for him (or anyone else) to smoke in them. In retrospect, the timing of this inversion feels ironic to him, appearing to represent a classic case of his being unable to have everything he wants at any one point in time.

Another such example seems to be that he can't have a happy, healthy marriage while continuing to play the field with a succession of nubile young women. For the first time since he began being unfaithful to Caroline, Ricky feels cornered and exposed, as if he's on the verge, finally, of being asked to pay the price for his several infidelities. Becoming entangled with Yasmin before getting untangled from Lauren now feels like a mistake (what a fucking mistake, though – what a body Yasmin has), and Ricky has a strong sense of no longer being in control. He can foresee everything unravelling on him.

Ricky has felt this way for about a week by now. Mostly, it's Caroline's behaviour at home which has unsettled him. She's been different, somehow. As, indeed, have other things been different. The house, for example. The very house they live in seems to have undergone a change. It feels altered in a strange and insidious way, as if there's a new vibe about the place – one which he can't quite name or put his finger on.

Not that the change which has come over Caroline herself is one he can accurately name either. In recent days, she has, for the most part, been standoffish, cold, indifferent, and uncommunicative. But in contrast, on rare occasion, she's also appeared to be happy – privately, perversely, very guardedly happy. These mood swings are out of character. In the past, her long-ago post-natal depression notwithstanding, Caroline would have been constantly upbeat, whereas now she appears mildly depressed for the most part, with occasional peaks of seemingly furtive delirium. To Ricky, it's as if his wife has secretly left the building, to be replaced by some doppelganger merely playing her part, and certainly not playing it well enough to win any Golden Globes. Not playing it well enough, even, to win so much as a round of applause.

There have been a couple of occasions during the past week when she's overreacted to things – overreacted massively so far as Ricky's concerned. There was the dinnertime spat when Jack was playing up, for example, and then there was the evening when the garlic under Caroline's preparation fell from the chopping board to the kitchen floor. Neither episode, although annoying, merited the high temper she displayed, and Ricky was left with the idea that Caroline's anger was less about wasted garlic or Jack's tantrums than something else altogether.

Naturally, his first instinct had been to ask her what was really wrong. And just as naturally, he left the question entirely unasked, for the very simple reason that he badly feared the answer.

Ricky's obvious assumption is that Caroline has found out something about his extra-marital recreation. He can't be sure of exactly what she knows, how long she's known, nor how she ever found out, but Caroline must know something of what he's been up to. He can't think of any other reason for such a downturn in her mood.

And so here Ricky is, out and about for an early evening drink with Patrick. That's what blokes do, after all, when there's a shit-storm brewing. They go for a beer with their mates. They talk about stuff. They invite solutions to problems, and then kick the solution around for a while.

But they're not at The Lamb and Musket. The Lamb would be utterly the wrong place for a conversation as private as this one needs to be. He and Patrick are known too well known there – there'd be people listening in when the two of them tried to talk.

Ricky doesn't want people listening in.

Especially not Vince.

Vince may stand on a level footing with Patrick as Ricky's best mate – maybe, even, a footing slightly higher – but Vince just wouldn't get his head around any of what Ricky has to say. Vince would flip his spasticky lid – and please God, forgive Ricky for thinking that last thought, if God happens to be tuned in right now.

Patrick brings back two pints from the bar. "Sure, y'okay?" he asks, briefly meeting Ricky's eye, before glancing away, upwards towards the ceiling. Ricky can't swear to it, but he thinks Patrick's hands had the shakes just then. Certainly, he seemed very focused on not spilling the beers as he set them down on the table.

"They've had the ceiling whitewashed," says Patrick, "since I was here last and they had water leaking from the tank up above."

Patrick sounds his carefree self, but he's looking pale, and the hair on his forehead is damp with sweat. That said, it's another warm evening, and it must have been crowded at the bar. Still, though, Patrick hardly looks in tip-top form, and now that Ricky thinks about it, he was jittery and unsettled when they first met up tonight. "Mate, are you actually alright?" Ricky asks.

Patrick clears his throat and glances around the room. "I reckon I've a summer cold coming on. Might even miss golf at the weekend. But sure, I'm fine really. What about you?"

"I'm all good," Ricky lies, finally abandoning a fruitless search for nicotine gum. Then he too takes a look about the place. In particular, Ricky's on the lookout for anyone they happen to know, but can't help observing that it's a striking venue, this town-centre bar, The Beethoven Lounge – suggested by Patrick as the place they meet when Ricky asked for privacy. It has a strange and schizophrenic feel to it, being part high-end wine bar, and part Bohemian commune. Ricky's no expert, but the piano in the corner looks to be worth some serious money – and it's being roped off to stop people touching it tends to support his opinion – whereas some of the mosaics on the wall look pure Oxfam shop to him. And the customers also form quite a cross-section, from well-tailored blokes and skinny posh birds, to a cluster of off-beats in dungarees and kaftans – people who most likely wash their pants in the sink.

"So, what's this story," Patrick asks, "about you rescuing Gareth from the peelers?"

Ricky isn't here for small talk, but because he isn't sure quite where to start with the heavier narrative he has in mind, he doesn't mind indulging Patrick for a couple of minutes. A whole week has gone by since that dopey prick Gareth got himself arrested, and normally Ricky would have told the tale to Patrick within twenty-four hours, but in this instance that hasn't proved the case. Ricky has been preoccupied with Yasmin whenever he's been at The Lamb. And come to think of it, Patrick hasn't been there very much in any case.

"The stupid twat smashed up his car," says Ricky. "But not just his own car. He shunted fifty grand's worth of Merc' into twenty grand's worth of Ford, and then, when one of the other drivers got arsy with him, Gareth only went and gave him a slap. A decent one, too, so it would seem. Knocked the fella on his arse."

"Fuck's sake – that's unbelievable." Patrick reaches for his pint and takes a first sip. He certainly does have a touch of the shakes, and seems painfully aware of it, given how he lowers his head nearly as far as he raises the glass. Patrick's almost bending over to drink his beer.

"You sure you're alright?"

Dismissively, Patrick flicks out a hand, as if to swat the question away. "By that doesn't sound like Gareth," he says. "And I've seen his car the once since then – in the car park at The Lamb. Sure, it doesn't look any worse than usual."

"That's because he used his other car." A big grin forming on his lips, Ricky taps the side of his nose and winks at Patrick. In spite of everything, he finds himself warming to the subject.

"His other car?"

"His other car." Ricky finds his smile widening in proportion to Patrick's perplexity, and proceeds to recount the whole story as he knows it. He begins with Gareth's panicked phone call to The Lamb and how he, Ricky, was at first unwilling to help out. He goes on to describe how Vince and Mel cajoled him into getting involved, and how pathetically grateful Gareth was to see him and Vince when they arrived to pick him up from the police station.

Ricky goes on to tell Patrick that when he and Vince got Gareth home, they were puzzled to see Gareth's car still parked outside his house, and asked him what was going on – did he suddenly have two cars? That was when Gareth had cracked up entirely, and, in wretched, self-pitying tones, had told them a story about Bill and Ted, and about Cash for Crash, and how Gareth's nerve had broken and he'd fucked the whole scheme royally up the wall. Apparently, he'd felt so desolate after the accident – so nearly at the end of his tether – that he'd needed very little provocation to lash out at the driver of the Ford.

Ricky finds himself laughing by the time he's finished the story, and he sees that Patrick is as well. Whoever said laughter was the best medicine appears to have had a point – there's some colour back in Patrick's face, and his beer hand is looking steady enough.

"The poor, stupid fucker," says Patrick, shaking his head. "I'm amazed he'd get involved in anything like that. Sure, so he's ended up crashing after all, and causing a big insurance claim, but he won't make frickin penny."

"He'll also have those deadheads Bill and Ted on his case. They're nasty when they want to be. I wouldn't be surprised if they ask him to fork out to them for the failure of the scheme. I would, if it were me who'd set it up."

"Bloody hell. And he'll be prosecuted for assault as well?"

"He will. I doubt he'll go down for it – it's his first offence, and my old man committed a few before they ever banged him up – but they'll have Gareth over in court."

Patrick shakes his head again. "The poor, stupid fucker," he repeats.

A middle-aged couple get up from an adjacent table and head for the door. The Beethoven Lounge being so crowded, their table is quickly seized upon, in this instance by two punky-looking girls, both wearing Doc Marten boots, laddered tights – deliberately laddered, no doubt – and similarly distressed tops. Ricky doesn't care much for their dress sense, but one of them looks fit enough. But then inwardly he sighs – it's his weakness for fit enough birds that's at the heart of all his worries.

And while he's been busy eyeing up women, Ricky's missed something Patrick's just said. "Sorry, mate," he replies. "Say that again, would you?"

"I asked if you thought there was anything we could do for him. Gareth, I mean. Short of giving the dickhead some money, is there anything we could do to help him out?"

"Fuck all – short of giving him money, like you say. And I don't know about you, but there are limits to what I'll do for him, even if he did bale us out of a scrap the other week."

"Sure, we'd have battered those squaddies anyway," laughs Patrick. "Stinking Brit bastards."

"From the look on his face, I reckon your old man would have done the job himself."

Not that he's letting on to Patrick, but there is something Ricky could do for Gareth. He could put in a call to Chief Superintendent Stilgoe, a high-ranking local police officer, who, like a good few people locally, happens to owe Ricky a favour. Ricky could ask the Chief Super' to have the charges against Gareth dropped, and such is the magnitude of the favour owed, Gareth imagines his friend-in-the-force would make it happen.

But fuck it. This is only Gareth they're talking about, and Gareth simply doesn't matter enough for Ricky to burn up a rare favour from a senior copper. No, if Ricky's inclined to phone Stilgoe at all, it's to find out more about the prosperous-looking passenger in the Mercedes that Gareth crashed into – the car driven by the outrageously leggy blonde, who was wearing a surgical collar by the time Ricky picked Gareth up, but appeared to be moving okay. Both driver and passenger were leaving the police station at the same time as Gareth, and the bloke was in deep conversation with one of the uniformed sergeants. The thought which occurred to Ricky while driving Gareth home was this: given that the Mercedes' occupants were neither the victims nor perpetrators of the assault, why were they at the police station just as long as Gareth? And why was the bloke – who looked seriously wealthy, like a hedge-fund manager or an industry captain – as thick as thieves with the senior plod on duty? Back at Gareth's house, Ricky had asked Gareth for the woman's name and number, given that she'd swapped details with him for insurance purposes. But her name gave no clues, as it turned out she was called Vicky Smith – and there had to be a few thousand Vicky Smiths out there.

Patrick takes a swig of beer. He's also still musing about Gareth's predicament. "It's a shame for the bloke," he says, setting down his glass and glancing at his watch. "He'll have been at the town hall this afternoon, just as soon as he clocked off work. Sure, he'll have heard the verdict by now, and I don't suppose that will have been good for him either."

Realising that Patrick's talking about the council's decision as to whether The Lamb and Musket can be demolished, and a supermarket built in its place, Ricky feels a small twinge of guilt at having been so absorbed in his own problems that he completely forgot the verdict was due today. It will look bad, he realises, that he and Patrick were in town and not at The Lamb when the verdict came through. But hey… whatever. The two of them could have been on Jupiter, and it wouldn't have changed anything regarding the fate of The Lamb.

Besides which, there are other things to bother about right now. Those two punky girls on the adjacent table have taken out vaping pens and then set them down next to their drinks. So far as Ricky's concerned, they'd better go and vape outdoors given that he's not allowed to smoke in here. He'll be pissed off if they start vaping at the table.

But really, he realises, he shouldn't care about trivial stuff like this. He shouldn't give one single fuck as to how two grungy birds get their nicotine. Nor should he give any fucks at all about Gareth, Bill, Ted or Cash for Crash. And certainly no fucks concerning the council's verdict on the future of The Lamb. All of these are sideshows – mere distractions. Ricky had his reasons for coming here with Patrick, to a place where they won't be bothered by people. He wants to talk about the impending derailment of his life and marriage, and to see whether Patrick, just maybe, can help him prevent the carnage.

"Anyway, mate," says Ricky. "Like I said on the phone, there's something I need to discuss with you. It's not an easy subject, to be honest."

Patrick clears his throat. He swallows hard. "Sure, go on," he says.

Ricky also clears his throat. "Well, it's like this," he begins. Then his eye is caught by the fit-looking punk girl as she raises her vaping pen to lips adorned by purple lipstick. It's not that she's about to vape that bothers him – no, he's decided he can live with that. It's the inside elbow of her raised arm which grabs hold of Ricky's attention, absorbing it so thoroughly that his man-to-man pow-wow with Patrick is immediately aborted.

"Ricky?" queries Patrick when Ricky falls quiet.

But Ricky is thinking back to the confused and stricken description provided by his sister Esme of the woman who'd attacked her outside a nightclub. "Some tough little goth girl," Esme told him, the morning after the assault – a generalisation so vague as to mean very little in practical terms. Similarly, "dark hair and facial piercings" wasn't too helpful in narrowing down the aggressor's identity.

But Esme said something else as well. She said that when this girl had reached out and grabbed her by the hair, Esme had glimpsed a strawberry coloured mark on the inside of her elbow. "Not a tattoo," apparently. "Maybe a birthmark; maybe a bite."

Ricky can see that this punk girl, who's casually exhaling vapour into the air of a crowded bar, from a distance of less than two yards away, has a strawberry-coloured mark on the inside of her elbow. She catches Ricky staring at her, and flashes him a sneering, hard-faced look. *What's your fucking problem?* it seems to say.

Ricky leaps from his seat.

"Whoa!" yells Patrick, jumping up as well.

The punk girl has fast reflexes, and she's up from her seat like a cat. But she's certainly a cool one, and doesn't retreat very far as Ricky advances upon her. Instead, she stands staring scornfully as Patrick gets one arm across Ricky and tries to manoeuvre between them.

"I think you know my sister," seethes Ricky, surging forward some more as Patrick tries to hold him back.

"Ricky," pleads Patrick. "What the fuck? Try cooling it, fella?"

"Yeah, what the fuck, Ricky?" taunts the punk girl. "I know lots of people, don't I?"

"Course you do," says Ricky, dimly aware that his voice is starting to crack, so angry is he. "And now I know you as well. My sister was queueing at Browns nightclub a few weeks back."

The girl tilts her head aside and smirks at him. "Now I get it," she says. "Big mouth she had – a bit like yours. Little sis' recovering well? Tell her I'll go again, whenever she's ready."

"You can go with me this time." Ricky lunges forward again, despite Patrick's best efforts, and this time the girl does step back slightly. But her expression remains cool and insolent, maybe because she intuitively knows the same thing which Ricky has now figured out: he can't actually bring himself to hit her. Despite his righteous fury, he just can't do it. This is a woman after all – a young woman conceding him some five or six stone – and he's supposed to just stick it to the bitch in the middle of a crowded bar? For all his inner ruthlessness, Ricky knows he hasn't got it in him simply to lash out at her, however much he thinks she deserves it. He's grateful that by now there are others crowding in on the scene, warning him away from her, and getting between the two of them. If he could get to the bitch, he isn't sure what the fuck he could actually do to her.

"Ricky, come on," says Patrick, who himself is a good couple of stone lighter than Ricky, and who sounds out of breath from the rigours of holding him back. "Come on, mate. We'll sort it out some other way." In such close proximity, Ricky notices that Patrick didn't wash his hair when showering after work today. Ricky can smell on him that sulphury, coppery plumber's smell – the one he's heard Mel tease Patrick about when they've been drinking at The Lamb.

Among the people who've arrived on the scene are a man and woman, both short and slim, who look as though they're some sort of team. They're dressed similarly in dark slacks and white shirts, and something else they share in common is a panicked look on their faces. Ricky immediately supposes that they are Kris Cross and Chris Cross, the similarly-named and musically-minded proprietors who Patrick has mentioned previously. Ricky doesn't know whether the two of them have very much experience of confrontational situations, but from their tentative, inhibited body language, they don't look entirely equal to the task of defusing this one.

The woman who's probably Kris Cross casts Patrick a *what-the-fuck?* glance. Except that Ricky can't quite imagine her ever using the F word.

"I'm so sorry," Patrick says to her. "But this girl's a bad one, sure she is."

"Well, this isn't acceptable," the woman nervily replies. "We can't have fighting in our bar." Turning to the smirking, insolent punk girl, she adds, "And vaping isn't allowed in here. You'll have to leave, I'm afraid."

"You should be afraid," comes the immediate reply, "if you're going to try forcing me out."

Then the second punk girl gets involved. Her lips are pursed, and her face is pale – she isn't enjoying this in the same way as her friend, and seems less able to handle the situation. She steps forward and lays a hand on the other girl's forearm. "Come on," she says. "We should go."

The first girl's response is visceral and instant. She spins on the soles of her feet, and slaps the second girl hard across the face, sending her reeling away while clutching her cheek. The sharp, primeval sound of flesh striking flesh brings a collective gasp from those gathered round, one which hardly dies away before the first girl begins screaming at her supposed friend. "Fuck you!" she hollers. "You don't touch me, or tell me what to do." Then she snatches up her vaping device, and turns to re-confront Kris Cross. "You don't tell me, either," she says, exhaling another big cloud of vapour. "Or you'll get yours, into the fucking bargain."

Patrick, meanwhile, has loosened his grip around Ricky's midriff, and therefore Ricky steps forward again. He still can't bring himself to hit the girl, but given how she's behaved he doubts if anyone would think it unreasonable of him to put her in a headlock and throw her into the street. And if she happens to break a bone as she falls, well then, that's some kind of payback for Esme.

But he hadn't reckoned on Patrick acting ahead of him. "I'll tell you what to do," Patrick rages at the punk girl. He's clearly riled by her threats and aggression, because his face is darkly furious. "You've attacked my friends, and you've attacked your own. So now you're going to get the hell out of here, outside into the street. Or for the love of God, I'll tear your frickin head off."

"Course you will," the girl mocks. "And then what? Make it suck your dick?"

Suddenly it's Ricky's turn to hold Patrick back, clamping both big hands on Patrick's upper arm. Patrick may be a couple of stone lighter than him, but he's taut and wound and ready to go.

"Sure, you listen to me," says Patrick, jabbing at her with one finger of his free arm. "I wouldn't want your diseased mouth anywhere near my dick. But I'll tell you this: I reckon the only thing preventing my friend here from burying you is you being female. But where I come from, a combatant is a combatant. I don't make gender distinctions, and you're on your last frickin warning. Get the fuck of here – right now."

A couple or so seconds pass, a couple or so seconds of tense, charged silence, while Patrick and the punk girl stare each other down. It's a silence broken when Christopher Cross lets out an embarrassed cough and says, "Same goes for me, young lady. It won't stand – you coming in here and threatening my wife."

The punk girl doesn't respond directly to Chris Cross; nor does she acknowledge his intervention in any other way. Instead, she continues staring coolly and disdainfully at Patrick. Then she breaks into a malevolent grin. "Big tough Irishman?" she says, finally retreating a pace or two. "We'll see just how big and tough when the time comes, you miserable paddy fuck."

Snatching up her phone from the table, and with a "Come on, you," to her friend, the punk girl struts away to the early-evening streets.

+++++

It's approaching half-nine at night when Patrick arrives home from The Beethoven Lounge. Leaving the Audi parked in the street – for his van takes up the whole of his driveway – he sets off on the short walk to The Lamb and Musket. The heat has gone out of the day, and he's grateful for a cooling breeze which has begun to pick up. He still feels hot and sticky. He feels, above all, mixed up. Patrick's head is swirling.

What a frickin night so far. He arrived for his and Ricky's man chat half expecting Ricky to confront him with both a baseball bat and the knowledge that Patrick had slept with Caroline. Then there was the mad-crazy episode with that lousy skank who'd beaten up Esme. After which, when they eventually got round to talking – and it did take some time, given that they first had to mollify Christopher and Kristina Cross – an emotional Ricky owned up to cheating on Caroline, confessed that he thought she'd rumbled him, and then asked Patrick what the fuck he should do next.

In the matter of which, Patrick found himself burdened with a massive conflict of interest, albeit not one which he dared admit to Ricky.

One of the few things of which he feels certain is that he needs a drink. After an initial couple of pints, his and Ricky's serious talk became fuelled by coffee – an awful lot of coffee, even by Patrick's relentless standards of consumption. He's had so much that his brain feels to be saturated by caffeine, in addition to its being overwhelmed by dilemma, conflict, and the utmost sense of guilt.

The car park at The Lamb is all but empty, and there's no one at the tables outside. Indoors, it's a similar picture. Mel is serving the other parties to Gareth's idiotic crime caper – the pair of jokers Patrick now has fixed as Bill and Ted, although he neither knows nor cares which is which – and no doubt the pair of them be off outside with their cigarettes in a moment. Bill and Ted apart, the place is empty except for a couple of other locals: the perpetually pissed Dave Isherwood and his daft loon of a mate, Robbie Something-or-Other. (It's Robbie the Jobbie, according to Rudi and some of the fellas from the car dealership, after Robbie worked there for a while but got the boot after less than a month.) Dave and Robbie are gathered around the crappy old TV which Derek supposedly installed for the golf, and are chuckling in time with the canned laughter accompanying whatever comedy it is that they're watching.

Desultory.

That's how The Lamb feels tonight – desultory. That's how Patrick would sum the whole place up.

Except for Mel. Mel looks great.

But then Mel always looks great. Why could he not have asked her out instead of getting entwined, quite literally so, with Caroline?

Fuck's sake. He can't rewrite history. And anyway, given the chance of a rewrite, would he really do anything different anyway?

"You alright?" asks Mel.

"Sure, I'm fine," he replies, nodding in emphasis. "And you?"

"I'm fine, too," she says, although now he's standing up close, leaning on the bar, he'd say her eyes look tired. "What are you having?" she asks.

"Whiskey, please. Irish and large. And whatever you'd like."

Mel takes down the whiskey bottle and studies the label. "Thanks," she says. "Maybe I'll have one of these too."

Another time, Patrick might have queried her choice. He might have sought an explanation for her choosing a tough, feisty drink. But tonight all he says is, "I recommend it, sure. Drink a double measure with one ice cube."

Mel pours both drinks. She says, "I suppose you've heard?"

He nearly says: 'heard what?' But then he stops himself, remembering that the council's verdict on the future of The Lamb was due this afternoon. Just as Ricky had forgotten about it earlier this evening, the matter had subsequently slipped Patrick's mind as well.

"I haven't heard," Patrick says. He makes a point of glancing around the near-empty pub. "But I'm not seeing any victory parties."

"You're right," says Mel. "We lost." She takes a cautious sip of whiskey, screws up her face, and adds a second ice cube. She sets the drink aside, presumably giving the ice a chance to dilute it.

"Mel, I'm sorry," says Patrick.

"I'm sure we all are." Her tone, while civil enough, isn't altogether friendly.

"And you're sure you're alright – about it all, I mean?"

"I'm fine."

"And Derek? Gareth?"

"Derek's fine as well," she replies. "He's got another pub to go to – in fact, he's got a choice of pubs."

She pauses, and catches his eye. Patrick asks, "Gareth, though?"

Mel lets out a little sigh. "Gareth's absolutely in bits. Not just because we lost and because he takes it personally. Apparently, the council members officially recorded their disgust with him for using those profile sheets to lobby them. And it was also mentioned in the minutes that he – the leader of our cause, if you like – is facing a day in court to answer charges of common assault. It seems they really had it in for him down there."

Patrick slides into a bar stool, rocks it backwards, and hooks his toes under the foot rail, just as he's done a thousand times or more. He closes his eyes, and thinks back to the laugh he and Ricky shared at Gareth's expense while they were drinking in The Beethoven Lounge. He wills himself not to laugh any more – not even to smile, in fact – because he's sure he'd piss Mel off by doing so, and yet he can't help finding funny the idea of Gareth getting censured by the council. Maybe it's the idea of one set of busybodies rounding on another which amuses him.

And yet, Patrick thinks, *Gareth's fundamentally a good man, who did his best to try keeping the pub open. Which must make me a bad man for laughing at the silly fucker.*

"Vince was here," he hears Mel say, keeping his eyes closed while listening to her. "So was your dad. Your… da. Vince waited around for you and Ricky, but in the end Malachy made sure he got home okay."

A properly bad man, then.

"Although, to be fair," she quietly adds, "Vince is more than capable of getting himself home. You're all overprotective of him, sometimes."

So, Patrick wasn't there at the pub when the announcement came through. And he wasn't around to talk do his da, either. Nor did he make himself available to walk his disabled friend home, although he's actually being over-solicitous on the nights when he does fulfil that particular duty.

The little accusations – both implicit and explicit – just keep on coming. And they all serve to augment the big, cumbersome burden of guilt under which he's labouring, a burden which has grown steadily over the past week, what with his having shagged Caroline on three days of the preceding seven.

Although his eyes remain closed, Patrick can nevertheless picture the disapproval on Mel's face. It's not like her to throw these brickbats his way, and in spite of her twice claiming she's alright, it doesn't sound to him as though she really is.

"Mel," he says, opening one eye and then the other, all the while remaining rocked back on his stool, "how are things with you at the minute? How are you getting on looking for a job?"

"I've been offered one," she sighs. "Just this morning, coincidentally enough."

"You have? Great news. Sure, that's fantastic."

"Well it is, and it isn't."

"Alright, so tell me about it," he replies, rocking himself upright, leaning on the bar, and figuring she might lay off him if she gets around to talking about her own frickin problems.

Mel sighs again. "Well okay, it's like this. I left my CV with an estate agent a few weeks ago – it was the morning you gave me a lift back from town, when I was wearing a suit…"

"Aha, sure."

"Well, the chief partner got in touch pretty quickly. Actually, he even came here to scope me out."

"Here?"

"Yes, here. I'd have found it creepy, only he had his wife with him, and that made it okay I suppose. After that he invited me for an interview at his offices – I should mention that this is for a manager's job, by the way, someone in charge of a branch – and anyway the interview went well enough, and I'm like, 'When can I start, then?' But he says it's not quite so simple as he wants me to meet another partner first."

Mel pauses for breath. Patrick nods and makes affirmative noises, but in truth his mind is already wandering away, back to the problems looming large in his own life.

"There was quite a delay after that, and I thought the whole thing had probably gone cold, but then the call came through to come and meet the other partner. Which is what I did – just this morning, as it happens. He only met me for ten minutes before he confirmed that the job was mine, and I ought to be happy about that, except I didn't like him very much. In fact, this guy I really do find weird."

Ricky started all this shit, thinks Patrick, by now listening to Mel on only a distant level. *Ricky started this by shagging other women.*

But then Patrick asks himself who he's trying to kid. Ricky shagging other women can hardly excuse Patrick shagging Caroline, and certainly not in Ricky and Caroline's house while Jack – who's four steps tall – plays downstairs. Truth is, there's no moral high ground left for any of them to stand on.

"You see, I'd seen this other partner before. He's a clammy-looking fat guy, and I caught him ogling me in a coffee shop on the day I started job hunting. Later that morning, I saw him in a different estate agent's – I thought he might have been a guy called Hugo Albrighton – and I was surprised to find out this morning that he was really in business with Robert Hopwood. And he just… well, he freaks me out a bit. I remember he looked really odd, staring out of Hugo Albrighton's window, just before that big bloody meathead pushed me into the glass."

Patrick's phone hums with an incoming text, and when he checks he sees it's from Caroline. She asks: *How did it go?*

She means the chat with Ricky – how did the chat with Ricky go?

Jesus, he thinks, staring at the screen. *Where do I frickin start?*

It's when he looks up from the phone that he realises Mel's not there anymore. And as he recces the pub, he can't see her collecting any glasses. She must have gone through the doorway at the back of bar, he supposes. Maybe she's taking empties outside, but it could just be that she's pissed off with him for inviting her to tell him a story and then not really bothering to listen.

He tries to remember what she was just saying. Something about her being offered a job, but not being sure about it because the guy's a weirdo pervert.

And something else…

Fuck's sake – did she just say a big bloody meathead pushed her into some glass? Or is Patrick hallucinating stuff by now, so bonkers is the evening he's just had?

"Mel?" he calls out, towards the doorway at the back of bar.

But he receives no reply. And it's now so quiet in The Lamb that he can hear voices from the comedy show playing at low volume on the television, together with the laugh-along, drunken chuckling of Dave Isherwood and Robbie the Jobbie.

Patrick knocks back his whiskey, plonks his elbows on the bar, and rests his head in his hands. He actually stopped short of giving Ricky any practical advice when they met up tonight, but what he could have said was: 'Sure, Ricky, give the other women up, go and see Caroline, confess everything, and beg her to forgive you.'

Having told Ricky to do that, Patrick could then have gone to see Caroline and said, 'Thanks for a sweet time, but you and I should call it quits. Ricky's going to ask your forgiveness, and I believe you should try to be kind to him, for the sake of all that you have together.'

And then things might have returned to how they were before.

Except that they wouldn't have. Things can never return to how they were before, because such an outcome relies on too many genies going back into too many bottles. It's also a scenario which totally ignores quite how Patrick feels about Caroline.

Patrick is nuts about Caroline. Crazy about Caroline. Yet it feels so wrong to feel so crazy.

If only there were two of her: one for him to keep, and another for Ricky to make up with.

"Oh, Christ above," Patrick mutters to himself. He takes his head out of his hands and looks up to see that Mel's back behind the bar. He's about to ask for clarification of her story – a recap of that bit about the meathead and the glass, if that's what she actually said – but Mel has an implacable, affronted look about her, and Patrick senses that she won't want to revisit any of her narrative. Wordlessly, she takes his glass and pours him another whiskey. Large, Irish, and with one ice cube.

Regarding the whole situation with him, Caroline and Ricky, Patrick isn't sure of very much, but one thing he knows is this: things can never be the same again, and there's going to be plenty of heartache for everyone concerned, whatever does happen from here on in. People are going to get hurt. And Vince, who would no doubt die for any of the three of them – well, Vince will be destroyed by it all.

And on top of these major problems, here are some minor griefs on top: his local boozer is closing down, and he's done something to irritate his favourite barmaid in the world. Maybe Mel has sussed out his sexual maladventures just as he sussed out Ricky's, or maybe it's simply that he isn't paying her enough attention to keep their friendship bubbling over. Either way, even more troubling than The

Lamb closing, or Mel being pissed off with him, is the realisation that he hasn't the emotional bandwidth or nervous energy to give very much of a shit about either, what with the bigger, more complicated devilments festooning his fuck-up of a life.

Patrick takes a large sip of his second whiskey, while managing to reflect that, actually, things could be even worse than this. His family might have remained in Belfast, for one thing. As such, he could have ended up active in the republican cause – and in a paramilitary way, not merely political. He might have ended up in prison for his actions. Or dead, for the matter that.

But by the time he's drained his glass, and is calling Mel for another refill, Patrick is no longer sure that the paramilitary option would have been very much worse at all. At least he'd have felt some sense of honour as a freedom fighter for his community. He feels none whatsoever in the role of someone sleeping with his best mate's wife. Even if he loves her. And even if his best mate did invite the situation.

Against the tides of sense and reason, some part of Patrick still clings to the hope that there'll be a good and practical way around or through all of these agonies. But if the solution is there at all, he can't frickin see it right now.

Sure, what an almighty mess.

3) September Fortnight

3.1) Closure, Minus 2 Days

Patrick is sure they'll get caught out soon – he's never been more certain of anything. There's no way that he and Caroline can carry on like this and realistically hope to keep getting away with it. Lying on his back, staring at the rose-patterned coving on the wall of Caroline and Ricky's spare room, Patrick is fully aware that he and Caroline are perpetuating this affair entirely on borrowed time. It's purely a question of when they'll get caught, not one of if.

Unless he does something pre-emptive, of course. Or unless Caroline does. Something to tell the world – or more specifically Ricky – about this ongoing liaison of theirs. Something to render redundant the question of when it is that they will be discovered.

Caroline turns towards him. Lying on her side, propped up on one elbow, she runs a hand through the hairs on his chest. She smiles at him; it's a gentle smile – gentle and melancholic. "Listen to the rain," she says. Patrick takes her hand and he listens.

He likes the rain for many different reasons.

Patrick likes the rain because it evokes memories of his early childhood in Belfast – a city of many downpours, even when the sun was shining. He also likes the rain for its debilitating effect on many a golfing opponent. It seems to him that the golf swings of other players fall apart in rainfall, whereas he, in comparison, is pretty good at keeping his game together. It may be the case, he supposes, that his rainy Belfast childhood is partly the cause of his wet-weather golfing prowess. When you get used to the rain as a kid, maybe you mind it less as an adult.

Another thing Patrick likes about rainfall, heavy rainfall especially, is its rhythmic spatter against the window when he's lying snug and secure in bed. Trouble is, the bed he's lying in needs to be his own if he's to feel snug and secure, not the one in Caroline and Ricky's guest room. Not when he's lying here with Caroline, one ear cocked for the sound of a car on the drive or the slam of a door, either of which would herald Ricky's early and unexpected return. In these circumstances, the noise made by the rain on the window is an impediment to his picking up such important audible clues. As such, the rain's a frickin bastard today. Bollocks to the rain. It can go fuck itself.

Patrick turns on to his side, so that he's facing Caroline across the bed. He rubs a foot down her calf and marvels at the smoothness of her skin. "I love the rain," he says. "It reminds me of so many things."

Seven weeks have gone by since Caroline first led him up the stairs and into this room – seven weeks in which summer has conceded to autumn and sunny skies have given way to rain-drenched vistas like this morning's. Patrick's been here fifteen or twenty times since that first occasion, and each visit which passes without their getting caught only adds to his suspicion that next time is when they will.

A big concern in the early days was that Jack would grow restless in his den, and would either come looking for them upstairs, or instead head for the kitchen and cause himself some kind of injury on a hotplate or with cutlery. And so Patrick and Caroline's initial, frenzied lovemaking took place with ears attuned not only for Ricky's unexpected arrival, but also for Jack taking such measures as might equally spoil the party.

But Jack started at school three weeks ago – a rite of passage which made Caroline sad and yet happy at one and the same time – and an undoubted bonus of this development was that Patrick and Caroline became free to carry on their illicit affair without harbouring the additional guilt of leaving Jack unsupervised, or the worry he might start asking awkward questions as to why Uncle Patrick was coming round the house so often. Questions he might, indeed, have asked in front of his dad.

Actually, Patrick realises, Jack may well be asking such questions anyway, for all of Patrick's precautions when visiting here. These precautions include, but aren't limited to, parking his Audi in an adjacent street, and then walking the rest of the way. But although this seems more sensible, and less likely to arouse neighbourly suspicion, than repeatedly leaving his car immediately outside the house, Patrick does wonder what would happen were Ricky to make an impromptu return home, during the course of a working day, and find Patrick on foot, a hundred yards or so down the road. What would Patrick answer in reply to the question, "Hello, mate. 'Fuck are you doing here?"

That both he and Caroline are mindful of such considerations makes it all the more remarkable that they choose to keep meeting here rather than someplace else. Once Jack began school, and was off Caroline's hands for a few hours most days, they could have picked a safer rendezvous. Patrick understood that she didn't want to come to his place, given that there were too many prying eyes in a neighbourhood where she and Ricky grew up, but nor did Caroline prove keen on the suggestion that they take a room in some town-centre hotel, citing cost and inconvenience as reasons not to do so.

"Well, the cost is all mine," Patrick replied. "And sure, it can't be so very inconvenient, can it? I'd say less inconvenient than Ricky coming home at exactly the wrong time and getting to wonder why the two of us are naked and sweaty upstairs."

"But Ricky's office is in town, Pat. We'd be more likely to bump into him there than here."

"Alright, then. Let's make it a hotel outside of town."

"But he knows people everywhere."

"They don't know us, though. Nor our relationship to him."

"Look, let me think about it, sweetheart. We'll talk again, next time."

Only they never do talk about it. At least not conclusively. Patrick continues to sneak in and out of the house, and given the degree of prevarication he meets whenever he talks about rooms in hotels, he's almost stopped raising the subject at all.

"Penny for your distant Irish thoughts?" Caroline asks, wriggling her foot out and away from their dying game of footsie, and laying her leg across his waist.

"I'm thinking," he replies, "that I'm running late for a big job I have on at midday. And that I could do with the rain letting up, or I'll get soaked moving stuff to and from the van."

"Must you go?" she asks. "You could put them off a day. It's forecast dry tomorrow."

"I didn't build my reputation by putting people off a day." He kisses Caroline's forehead, eases out from under her leg, and swings his feet out of bed and onto the floor. "Besides, I'll feel bad if I don't go. Nearly as bad as I'll feel when I'm actually there, having left the world's most desirable woman alone in a warm bed."

Truth to tell, Patrick's done more than his share of putting people off in recent times. Not only has he eased up on accepting new bookings, but he's made a minor art-form of juggling his current ones around. All in the cause of coming here, to his best mate's house, in order to fuck the bejesus out of his best mate's wife.

But today's job is one which simply won't wait. Just as predicted, albeit a little ahead of schedule, the call from Kristina Cross came in three days ago. "Patrick, help," she said. The Beethoven Lounge needed a new boiler, and it needed one in a hurry. And not only in a hurry, it needed one for the best possible price he could manage, given the money Kris said they'd spent up upgrading their security following the "spat" involving Patrick and his "pals".

Patrick doesn't want to let the two of them down. He likes both Kris Cross and Chris Cross. And he does feel bad about the commotion between him and Ricky and the prickly bitch who'd apparently beaten up Esme. And so he needs to go. He needs to go right now.

But after planting his feet on the floor, he delays a few seconds before actually standing up from the bed. And that's time enough for Caroline to sidle up behind him and slip an arm over his shoulder. "Do you have to go just yet?" she murmurs, her breath warm on his ear. "After today, you won't be back before next week."

"Fuck's sake, woman," he replies. "Do you have any idea how long it takes to fit someone a new boiler?"

"Mmmm, not as such." She slides her other hand around and begins toying with his penis. "But I do know something of heat and pressure."

Patrick succumbs, and he twists around so that his lips can meet hers and their dance begin anew. But forty minutes later, when he finally leaves for work, actually grateful to the rain for the excuse it gives him to pull up the hood on his parka, thereby becoming less recognisable, he gets to wondering once again about where all this is going, and why Caroline won't meet him anywhere other than at home.

The thought occurs to Patrick that maybe she actually wants the two of them to get caught in sexual congress. Doubtless she'd dispute any such claim on his part, and on any rational, conscious level she'd most likely believe her own denials. But maybe Caroline's guided by her subconscious in this matter. Maybe some part of her wants Ricky to find out about hers and Patrick's affair, so as to bring all of this out into the open without her having to take the initiative. Maybe, just maybe, that's the answer. Caroline might want Ricky to know what's going on without taking the excruciating step of actually telling him.

But if on some level Caroline does want to get caught out, then to what end? Is it about saying: "Anything you can do..." to Ricky, partly as a means first of getting even, and then of getting back together, leaving Patrick cast aside? Or does she want a clean break with the man who's her husband and the father of her child, without being the one to call it quits, at least not unilaterally?

Patrick returns to where he left the Audi, in a quiet cul-de-sac a five minute walk from Ricky and Caroline's executive home. Five minutes today is a long enough walk to get thoroughly soaked by the rain, and he might have removed his sodden parka before climbing into his car were it not that he likes the anonymity of keeping his hood up. He thinks, as he slides into the driver's seat, that he glimpses a disapproving face through the front window of the house opposite – probably that of someone pissed off that he keeps parking at the end of their garden – but he averts his gaze, avoiding eye contact so as to sidestep the prospect of confrontation.

As he starts the engine, it seems to Patrick that confrontation is what all three of them are trying to sidestep – he, Caroline, and Ricky – whether that's direct confrontation with each other, or simply with the big, tough issues rising ever to the surface in their lives. He, himself, is totally nuts about Caroline. Yet he's frightened to push for more than he has with her – namely a snatched couple of hours, two or three times a week – in the event that by doing so he loses the small prize already won. Regarding Caroline's own needs, wants and desires, he isn't sure what they are, and doubts she's certain of them herself. And as for Ricky, well fucking hell, where does Patrick even start?

It's clear that Ricky has attempted to change since his confessional with Patrick at The Beethoven Lounge. He's genuinely tried to see less of other women, and Patrick suspects that Ricky has managed to end his affair with the instructor from the health club. According to Caroline, her husband is certainly spending more evenings at home, which must mean he's spending fewer with Yasmin from The Lamb – a state of affairs in keeping with the bragging Ricky sometimes does about his about his abstinence from adultery on the relatively rare occasions when Patrick sees him for a pint just lately. But fewer evenings with Yasmin isn't the same as no evenings with Yasmin, and Patrick infers from the times when Ricky doesn't boast of having behaved himself – together with the sly looks and furtive smiles still exchanged by Ricky and Yasmin across the bar – that there remain occasions when Ricky has a supposed 'work problem' to sort out late at night. And for this, Patrick is actually grateful. He'd feel even guiltier about carrying on his affair with Caroline if Ricky had, in contrast, managed to mend his ways in their entirety.

Patrick soon has his car clear of Ricky and Caroline's exclusive little neighbourhood, back out onto the main road. The rain is really teeming down, but the Audi's wipers move like the clappers when called to action, and so visibility is good, especially now that Patrick has finally pulled back the hood on his parka. How great it would be if the future were as clearly defined as the road ahead.

There are some things he's certain of, however. Among them is this chunk of reality: in not much more than forty-eight hours from now, The Lamb and Musket will close its doors for the very last time, and soon after the bulldozers will move in and level the place to dust. Patrick only wishes he had time and attention enough to genuinely give a damn.

+++++

Mel sits at her desk in the corner office of Robert Hopwood and Partners' local branch. It's the desk previously occupied by Robert Hopwood himself, following his dismissal of Mel's predecessor – the desk, no less, on which Mel once left her CV, so igniting a chain of events which sees her sitting behind it today. She's been in the job for four weeks, and it took Robert Hopwood no more than the first fortnight to conclude she was doing well enough that he could move out and base himself at a different branch more in need of his attention. Mel was grateful for such an early vote of confidence, albeit a little surprised.

She's also pleased, and again surprised, at how quickly she was able to get some of the staff to shape up. Take Jimmy, for instance. As part of some juvenile tomfoolery, he spent most of her first visit here face down on the floor, but the turnaround in his attitude has been remarkable. This morning, he's courteous and presentable as he sets down two coffees on one corner of the desk, before enquiring whether Mel and her guest require anything else. When Mel tells him no thanks, he smiles and nods politely, before leaving the office. Mel's confident that once back at his own desk, Jimmy will go industriously about his job, and that Gemma, who nowadays wears her name badge the right way up, will be doing likewise. The two of them have responded well to Mel's no-nonsense style of management, and will have noted the speed with which she manged to dispense with the carroty-headed Philip when his reaction to her appointment wasn't quite so encouraging.

Mel reaches for the two coffees. She takes hold of her own, and then pushes her visitor's cup and saucer closer to where he's sitting. "Here you are, Harry," she says. "Hopefully this will warm you up a bit."

The man Mel has come to know as Harry Adkins smiles his gratitude and takes a sip of coffee. He arrived five minutes since, drenched by heavy rain, and carrying an umbrella blown inside-out by the wind, all the while complaining loudly and theatrically about the demise of summer. Having abandoned his sodden mac to a spare hook on her coat-stand, he then sank into a chair across the desk from her, mopping his face with a red silk handkerchief from the beast pocket of his suit.

Harry Adkins is the same man Mel once thought might be Hugo Albrighton, and whilst they do, at least, have the same initials, she was as wrong about his name as she was about his character. Having thought of him as creepy and leering, Mel now feels ashamed at having jumped to such a conclusion on the basis of his having a weight problem and what turns out to be an eye defect. Surprised as she is to find herself sitting at this desk, and equally taken aback by the transformed attitudes of Gemma and Jimmy, Mel's even more nonplussed to find herself with an affectionate liking for the larger-than-life, politically incorrect, and hysterically snobbish Harry Adkins – a man who's bearing is, in truth, much more that of an Etonian Hugo than an east-end Harry.

A week-and-a-half into her new job, she'd plucked up the courage to mention to him that she "thought" she'd seen him in Hugo Albrighton's shop. "Darling, I'm sure you did," he immediately replied. "I go there all the time – and to everyone else's offices too. Didn't you know that I'm the company's spymaster-in-chief?" Mel didn't trouble to ask whether he'd noticed her, or spotted the big lout pushing her into the window, instead preferring to grant him such benefit of the doubt as his dodgy eyesight justified. "It's such an incestuous industry we're working in," Harry further replied to her enquiry. "Everyone knows everyone else, and we all know what each other are up to – or at least we did before this God-awful plethora of online companies came to market. And old habits die hard, you see – I like to keep my ear to the ground."

This morning, Mel sits at her desk and sips coffee with the man she now thinks of as a favourite colleague. He continues dabbing his face, and entertains her with talk of a poor meal served at an overpriced restaurant the previous evening – "I sent the lamb back with my compliments, and challenged the chef to box three rounds with my nephew's favourite chauffeur." Mel laughs along, and concentrates on getting some coffee down her throat. She needs the caffeine because she's desperately tired, having been burning the candle at both ends, although not in a manner which would give Harry Adkins any scandalous gossip to go spreading around.

Mel can trace her tiredness to the day she resigned from The Lamb, giving Derek two weeks' notice that she'd be leaving for newer pastures. Looking back, she should have been firm about the two weeks, but when Derek pleaded that she stay on – maybe on reduced hours – until The Lamb actually closed down, she found herself readily agreeing. It seemed a reasonable request on Derek's part, give that he'd struggle to recruit anyone new when he could offer them only a few weeks' work. And yet it wasn't really because of Derek that she agreed. She stayed on for the sake of the regulars – her friends – thinking that they might create some good memories to share of The Lamb's final few weeks.

Well, so bloody much for that. Here she is, working a day job to build for the future, and a night job in order to give the past a proper burial, but few of her supposed friends who share that past appear to give a damn for it.

Both Ricky and Patrick appear at The Lamb far less often than once they did, and seem very distracted when they do manage to get there. Gareth, meanwhile, so far as Mel knows, has called in only once during the whole seven weeks which have passed since the council called time on the old pub, the councillors delivering their verdict while excoriating Gareth's character into the bargain. Mel has thought of going round to Gareth's house and giving him a good shake, telling him that life goes on in spite of both the council's actions and Gareth's impending prosecution for assault. Yet she's held back from making any such visit, figuring that her turning up on his doorstep might give him the wrong idea entirely.

Bill and Ted, meanwhile, appear as frequently as ever, but their presence is of no comfort to her given that they're such a pair of arseholes. Dave Isherwood and his mini crew of numpties are other regular customers, but although she finds them less menacing than Bill or Ted, they are always drunk, and what conversation they do bring tends to be the utmost load of old cobblers.

Of course, there are other locals who come and go, but she knows them less well. There aren't really any others she thinks of as friends, certainly not to the extent that she'd have extended her notice period for them. Except for Patrick's dad, Malachy, of course, who's always up for what he calls 'the craic'; and then there's Vince, too, when Mel can spare the time to focus on his halting, truncated line in conversation. Vince talks to Malachy often enough, but it's plain to Mel that Vince is downcast of late, and she's sure that's down to Ricky and Patrick being around less frequently than before.

But such is life. And Mel can't dictate how others live theirs. As for The Lamb and Musket, it will shut up shop on Saturday night, and those who want to say a proper goodbye will be there to do so. Those who can't be bothered will stay away. Afterwards, Mel will be moving on, in more than one sense of the word. She's certainly banished any thoughts of romantic involvement with Patrick, about whom she has pretty strong suspicions as to why his head seems all over the place.

No, on Saturday night she'll say her goodbyes, and help Derek lock up one final time. Then she'll head home, maybe have a cocoa with Gabby if the girl's still up, and then take a long hot bath. She will, quite literally, wash the pub trade out of her hair, before resting up over the remainder of the weekend. If she does anything at all on Sunday, then –

Oh shit.

Harry Adkins just said something to her, but she was away with the bloody fairies. She failed to take in a word he said, and now he's squinting at her over his coffee cup while awaiting an answer.

"Erm, I'm really sorry, Harry," she bashfully replies. "I just had a moment there. Got myself side-tracked. Would you mind saying that again?"

Harry Adkins allows himself a low chuckle as he sets down his cup. "My dear," he says, "you had more than a moment. Is everything alright with you? Boyfriend trouble, possibly?"

"I don't actually have a boyfriend."

"Hmmm, you've said as much before, and I remain confounded now as then. Still, there's hope for you. You can move in with me once I've had Amanda melted down and auctioned off by the litre."

"I'm sure she'll be thrilled to know you won't be lonely in her absence."

"She does care deeply about me – yes. But look, now that I do have your attention, I was trying to talk to you about this drinking den you're so unreasonably attached to."

"The Lamb and Musket?"

"The very same." Harry Adkins' good eye narrows as he asks, "Incidentally, you're not still working there, are you, Mel?"

"I, err, I…" Taken aback by the question, Mel averts her gaze, neither wanting to lie nor admit the truth.

"Aha. Now I know why you look so tired."

"I'm sorry," she says, feeling a blush of embarrassment colour her cheeks. "I haven't been working there very much. It's just that they can hardly recruit when they're shutting up shop. I said I'd do a shift or two to help out. But on reflection, I shouldn't have. I can see that now."

Although Harry Adkins shakes his head in reproach, there's a smile not far from his lips. "I won't tell Robert," he says, "just so long as the moonlighting does end tout de suite."

"I said I'd help out tonight, and then again on Saturday, after which The Lamb closes for good. But if by tout de suite you mean now, then I'll phone them this minute. I'll tell them I can't get in tonight – that I need my beauty sleep for my proper job."

"I know you don't like to let people down, my dear. So I won't get hideous with you over two more shifts. But you won't be taking on any further bar work, will you?"

"Cross my heart; hope to die."

"Now don't go doing that. And you will move in with me, won't you, once I've found a buyer for Amanda?"

Mel laughs. "Much more of this, Harry Adkins, and I'll be finding a buyer for you. And be warned, I'm getting good at finding buyers."

"Indeed." He nods his head in appreciation of the increased sales levels Mel's branch is achieving. "But you can't blame a man for trying, can you now? Maybe you'd agree to one debauched night with me if I told you what I've managed to find out about The Lamb and Musket."

"Or maybe I'd ask Jimmy to make you another cup of coffee."

Harry Adkins shakes his head in what she trusts is only faux disappointment. "Not even the crumbs from the table, then. But alright, here's what you wanted to know: the sale of the public house known as The Lamb and Musket from The Hippy Hops Pub Company to Shop City Supermarkets hasn't quite been finalised. George Timkin's people are yet to exchange contracts with Shop City's in-house property directorate."

Mel finds herself perking up. "Really? That's interesting."

But interesting though the news is, Mel isn't sure of its relevance. All she knows is that Ricky asked her a question five nights since. "Hey, Mel, do you happen to know whether Shop City has actually bought The Lamb from George Timkin's company yet?"

Given that Ricky had been visiting The Lamb and Musket only rarely, and hadn't proved especially talkative when he did show his face, it was surprising that he asked her a question at all, never mind one as intriguing as this. "I've no idea," she replied, "but I'd assume so. I mean, we close down a week from now."

"I'd assume so, too. But you know what they say about assumptions. Have you any way of finding out for sure? Does Derek know? Has he said?"

"He hardly says anything; his head's all full of his next pub. But what's your interest, Ricky?"

Ricky grinned. Irritatingly, he tapped the side of his nose. "Can't really say yet."

"In which case, nor can I help yet."

"Come on, Mel. You owe me, remember?"

"For what?"

Ricky raised a hand to his lips, and caressed an imaginary moustache. "From the time I agreed to wet nurse soppy-bollocks Zorro, after he smashed up those cars and then another bloke's face."

Mel felt like smashing up Ricky's face. But what would have been the point? And anyway, she was curious to find out where all this might lead. "Alright," she sighed. "Let me see what I can find out."

"By Friday if you can, yeah? Sooner ideally, but by Friday if you can."

And so Mel asked Derek. But the outgoing licensee had, quite predictably, neither known nor cared. Which was when her mind turned to Harry Adkins, the commercial property specialist within Robert Hopwood and Partners – a man with extensive contacts and an ear to the ground.

"Is there anything to suggest," she now asks him, "that the deal may be off?"

"Just because they haven't exchanged contracts on the sale? No, not really. Although the details of a deal may have long since been agreed, Shop City wouldn't have made a final, legal commitment before permission was given for the pub to be bulldozed and the site to be granted a change of use. And given that said approval occurred just a few weeks back, then finalisation of the deal is probably just a question of internal procedure – of getting in-house paperwork signed off by both parties before the sale can go ahead."

"I see."

"So far as I can tell, from asking around, no one knows of any snags on either side to prevent everything from going through."

"Okay, thanks. That's understood."

"Is your friend thinking of jumping in?" asks Harry Adkins. "Making a counter offer, perhaps?"

Mel doesn't know, and admits as much. But why else would Ricky be interested? She remembers that he wanted answers by Friday, and already it's mid-day on Thursday. She isn't sure that she even has Ricky's phone number.

"My advice, for what it's worth," says Harry Adkins, "is that your friend ought not to get into a bidding war with Shop City Supermarkets. Doubtless they've got deeper pockets than he has, and the financials will work out better for them in the long run. This hostelry, The Lamb and Musket, may well be a profitable pub, but it will be a much more profitable supermarket – trust me on that. QED, Shop City can afford to spend more buying it than your friend can."

All of which makes sense to Mel. And she imagines it will also make sense to Ricky, who seems very savvy when it comes to business, despite some fundamental failings as a functioning human being. "Thank you, Harry," she says to her visitor. "And now I'll get you that other cup of coffee."

Mel heads into the main office to order up more hot drinks. Talking on the phone to a prospective buyer, Jimmy is standing at his desk. He has his head up and his shoulders back; his stomach is pulled in, and he has his thumb hooked into a belt loop on his trousers. "I'll advance your offer to our clients," he says, sounding quite the hot-shot, "although I should tell you that they have already turned down higher bids than yours, and interest in this property is high."

He's showing off, thinks Mel. Jimmy is putting on an act for Gemma, who's sitting at her own desk and typing on her keypad. Mel and Gemma swap wry smiles. "Would you mind," Mel asks her, "getting us more coffee, please? Being as Gordon Gekko there is so busy."

Probably clueless about who Gordon Gekko was, but giggling sufficiently to suggest she gets the gist, Gemma agrees to get the kettle on. Mel takes another glance at Jimmy as she heads back to her own office. He definitely is trying to show off, bless him.

Which is surely what Ricky is doing with his enquiries about The Lamb. He must be showing off to Yasmin by putting an alternative bid together. It wouldn't be the first time a normally level-headed businessman has overreached himself trying to impress an attractive young woman, and, on that basis, it would be a kindness on Mel's part if she avoided passing on the information received from Harry Adkins. She could claim that she was unable to get an answer to Ricky's question, or she could even propagate a far bigger lie: she could tell him that the deal between Hippy Hops and Shop City is signed and sealed already.

But Mel is curious about Ricky's plans, and would like to see where he's going with this. Besides which, he was right when he said she owed him, and this is hardly the worst way she can imagine having to return the favour. And so, while she and Harry Adkins await their second round of coffees, Mel begs Harry's indulgence while she gets out her phone and looks to see if she can find Ricky's number.

+++++

Rain has poured all afternoon, and the outside temperature is falling as dusk draws in. It's the time of day when many town centre workers are shutting up shop and heading home, perhaps tarrying for a drink at one the bars nearby their place of work. It is Thursday evening, after all. Nearly the weekend.

The Beethoven Lounge is just the kind of bar which people go to upon leaving the office. As such, business is brisk, and Patrick is glad about that because the combined body heat of all these customers helps offset the heating not being switched on.

The reason it isn't switched on is that Patrick hasn't finished installing the new boiler.

And although he's now very close to completion, Patrick nevertheless feels bad about how late he's running on a job he originally planned to have done and dusted by mid-afternoon.

A combination of events has caused the delay. The first of these was, of course, Caroline's detention of Patrick in her bed for longer than he had planned. The second snag arose at Brian Baxter's plumbing supply business, where an unholy trinity of a new manager, a botched upgrade to the accounting software, and a trainee assistant on the front counter all combined to cost Patrick even more time. The fledgling manager, who looked barely older than the front-counter trainee, initially refused to release the boiler Patrick had ordered, allegedly due to Patrick not having paid his bills. It took an hour of arguments and verifications to resolve the issue, and Patrick had to reconcile his online bank statements with the merchant's paper invoices before the boiler was finally released. Even then, a phone call to Brian Baxter himself was required, and they were apparently lucky to catch him, given that he was about to play golf. Patrick cursed the man for having time to play.

After that, the niggles just kept on coming. Upon arrival at The Beethoven Lounge, it wasn't immediately obvious where to switch off the gas, and then, once Patrick had put paid to that particular problem, he found the old boiler to be so heavily corroded at the back that he spent ages simply removing it from the wall. A further complication was that the network of pipes leading to and from the boiler were so arcane and convoluted that he used up a chunk of time reconfiguring them – cutting and then welding on new sections – before he was finally able to offer up the new boiler itself.

And while Patrick laboured away, his mind cogitated obsessively about the situation between himself, Caroline and Ricky – so much so that his attention regarding professional matters became disturbed. From time to time, therefore, Patrick had to pause and force himself to focus more intently on his work, reasoning that this was, after all, the gas supply he was working with, and that all the registrations and safety certificates in the world counted for absolutely nothing if he couldn't manage to concentrate properly. Many years on from the era when Irish republicans regularly sent bombers into England, it occurred to Patrick that he could easily blow up a pub full of Brits through nothing more than professional tardiness.

For that reason, he forced himself to double check, and then triple check, everything he did, thereby only adding to the total of time taken.

But now the job is nearly done. The new boiler is mounted up and plumbed in. The gas is reconnected. Earlier, he flushed out the radiators. He now just needs to switch the heating back on, and then stick around for long enough to make sure everything is working okay. That, and clear up his God-forsaken mess. Patrick rates himself a good plumber, but admits he's never been a tidy one.

The other thing he should do, because his checks will take half-an-hour or so, is move his van. Kris and Chris Cross have kept an eye on it thus far, in order to guard against traffic wardens giving him a ticket. But the Beethoven Lounge is busy now, and the proprietors will be too busy to play at being lookout. Patrick decides he'll load the old boiler and the heavier of his tools into the van, and then remove it to a proper parking space where it can remain until he finishes his work.

Accordingly, he brings the broken, aged boiler out from the back kitchen where he's been working, and begins carrying it through the bar, towards the front door. His eyes are soon drawn to a group of six or seven fellas at a table near the entrance. They look like trouble to him. It could be their heavy leather jackets and facial tattoos which make him wary, although it might equally be their extreme haircuts – shaven heads for most of them, with a couple of long, greasy pigtails among the remainder. Or maybe it's just the arrogance with which they sit there – arms folded, legs apart – that sets Patrick on edge. His wariness is clearly shared by the contracted doorman who's part of Chris and Kris Cross's new security detail, and who hovers close by with a pinched look of caution on his face. Patrick is curious as to whether the guard has any backup nearby, and how quickly it would arrive if needed. One fella on his own would certainly have trouble if anything were to kick off, because –

There! Fuck's sake!

He's late, almost too late, but Patrick suddenly spots that one of the men in the group isn't actually a man at all. Rather, it's the punky young woman whom Ricky confronted when he and Patrick came here, back in the summer. Patrick vividly remembers that he too lost his temper with her, after she first admitted attacking Esme, and then assaulted the girl accompanying her at the time. Given the heightened security measures subsequently adopted at The Beethoven Lounge – measures put in place as a specific response to that incident – Patrick is surprised that the evil bitch hasn't been barred by now.

Before she can recognise him, or at least before he thinks she can, Patrick hoists the old boiler up to head height, and carries it out through the door on his shoulder, so that it blocks off the woman's view of his face. He doesn't hear raised voices, and nor does anyone follow him out onto the street – and so it appears he's currently in the clear, thank goodness. The rain is still falling hard outside, and Patrick hurriedly stows the old boiler in the back of his van before jumping behind the wheel and driving to a nearby car park. He buys a ticket from the machine, and then returns to the driver's seat, where he sits quietly for few minutes, getting his thoughts together and giving his nerves a chance to settle.

It's a walk of more than five minutes from the car park to The Beethoven Lounge – time enough for Patrick to get soaked through. But he's grateful for the wet weather, just as he was when leaving Caroline and Ricky's house this morning, and for exactly the same reason: the rainfall makes it okay for him to pull up the big hood on his parka, hiding his face into the bargain. He forces himself to look straight ahead when he walks back through the door of The Beethoven Lounge, deliberately not glancing at the little group of likely troublemakers sat off to one side. Again, nobody calls out, and nor does he hear anyone getting up to follow him. Once more, he appears to have got away unrecognised by the punky woman.

But there is trouble lurking at the far end of the bar.

One member of the gang has moved away from his friends, and after stepping over the rope cordon encircling the piano, has proceeded to sit down at the ivories. To say he's now playing the piano would be an ugly distortion of the truth, for he's simply bashing the keys in a ham-fingered way, creating a noise no more akin to music than that made by a jackhammer in the hands of a hungover navvy.

"Lah-lah-lah-lah-lah," the man chants loudly, and surely drunkenly. "Lah-lah-lah-lah-lah."

As Kris and Chris Cross look on anxiously, their security guard tries to persuade the man away from the piano. The guard is a similar age to Patrick, and he's a biggish man in apparently good shape. Doubtless he's equal to the task of knocking heads among groups of boisterous young lads who've had a shandy too many. Patrick also supposes the guy could have dealt with the nasty, skanky woman were she on her own.

But the man in at the piano is a different proposition. He's simply enormous, for one thing, and the muscles of his arms stand out even through the sleeves of his quilted black bomber jacket. "Lah-lah-lah," he chants some more, still pounding the keys, clearly indifferent to the guard's attempts at talking him away from the piano. "Lah-lah-lah-lah-lah." For now at least, he seems in a cheery frame of mind, and isn't currently hurting anyone. But from his shaven head, his bovver boots, and the tattoo on his neck of an evil-looking snake, Patrick can imagine him entirely at home kicking the fuck out of somebody as they lie curled up on the floor.

I should walk straight past all of this, Patrick reasons. *I should walk past, and into the kitchen, where I should finish my tests on the boiler. I should concentrate on my job, and let the man in the security tabard concentrate on his.*

Trouble is, the man in the security tabard won't get his job done if left to do it by himself. Quite obviously, he is out of his depth. "Come on, big man," he says to Snake Neck as Patrick draws near. "Just get away from the piano, and back to your friends, yeah?"

"Or else what, you silly streak of piss?" asks Snake Neck, jocularly. "I've shit better security than you before now, and on an empty stomach as well."

Patrick catches a look in the eye of Kristina Cross – a look that begs his help. Exactly what help he's supposed to offer, Patrick isn't entirely sure. Really, he thinks, either Kristina or Chris should call the cops – although he can understand why they wouldn't. It can be bad for a bar's reputation, and therefore for its turnover, if the police have to be called in. Besides which, how quickly would the peelers actually get here? Patrick suspects not quickly enough, given how the situation is threatening to escalate. The big bastard and his mates could do some serious damage, both to property and people, long before help were to arrive.

"I'm trying to be reasonable about this," says the guard, attempting to assert himself, but sounding, unmistakeably, as though he's shitting his pants. "You should know that I've got colleagues covering other bars nearby. I just need to page them, and they'll be here."

"Oh, page them, will you? Big fucking deal." Snake Neck reaches out and grabs the security guy by his tabard. In a moment of nonchalant, apparently effortless strength, he pulls the guard down and towards him, so that their faces are merely inches apart. "How good are you at paging people with your fingers all in pieces?"

"Call the coppers now," says Patrick, quietly, to Kris Cross. "I'll do what I can until they're here."

"You think your pissy guys are a match for mine," Snake Neck is taunting the hapless guard. "We're all lethal fuckers – even the bird. My mate with long hair – we call him KGB. He's got a knife hidden in his shoe, and he'd chop your balls off before you knew what was happening. Then there's Cyanide Steve – he needs no fucking knife. And nor do I, if you were thinking of asking."

Patrick steps inside the piano's rope barrier. He squats down on his haunches, and without removing the hood of his parka altogether, he pulls it back a little, so that Snake Neck can better see his face. He has in mind to play a part he's seen his da play very well – that of the lunatic Irishman, daft-as-a-brush and superficially friendly, but maybe more dangerous than he initially appears.

"So get this straight, you sad slap of shit," says Snake Neck to guard, "if I want to play the piano, I'll play the fucking piano."

Despite any constraints to his peripheral vision occasioned by the hood of his parka, Patrick is vaguely aware, mostly from the cheering and the catcalls, that Snake Neck's friends have noticed the altercation and are egging the big man on. Patrick also realises that if they all come over here, then there'll be big trouble. That hellish woman will recognise him from their previous encounter, and events will take a turn very much for the worse. Still, though, it's a bit late for him to be changing his mind. He's here, on the participants' side of the rope cordon, and from the way the big man's eyes have swivelled towards him, it's clear that Snake Neck is aware of his presence. And so, speaking at a brisk tempo while exaggerating the Irishness in his accent, Patrick says to Snake Neck, "Ah well, now, I wouldn't be playin' the fookin' piano if I were in yer position, like."

Still keeping hold of the guard by his tabard, Snake Neck turns his head fully towards Patrick, who remains squatted down at the big man's eye level. "And what's this?" Snake Neck asks quietly, his voice honeyed with sarcasm. "Dara O'Briain meets Obi Wan?"

"Ah, yer a funny man to be sure," replies Patrick, attempting to keep his delivery rapid and his tone just about cordial. "But seriously, ya wanna be fookin' careful takin' liberties in here. Ya don't know who owns the bar, and ya don't know who owns the fookin' piano."

"And who fucking does?" Snake Neck laughs. "The fucking IRA?"

Patrick winces deliberately, and then shakes his head in a way he hopes will convey well-meaning admonishment. "Mister," he says, "ya want to keep yer fookin' voice down, mentionin' the republican army in here. Let's just say that the interested parties won't be worried about a long-haired man with a knife in his shoe. They'll shoot his kneecaps through while he's bendin' down to reach it. Same goes for the rest of ya, so it does. A lethal fooker in English suburbia is a lot less lethal from than a lethal fooker from west Belfast – no disrespect, like."

Snake Neck doesn't immediately answer, and Patrick thinks he sees a flicker of doubt in the man's cold, pitiless eyes. Also, although Snake Neck still has hold of the guard by his tabard, it might just be that the big fella's grip is loosening. Patrick presses on. "Why d'ya think someone puts a big-money piano in downtown bar, anyway? You never heard of fencin' money? And where does money come from these days?" Patrick puts a finger over one nostril and sniffs expansively up the other. "Seriously, these are heavy fookin' people yer in danger of crossin'. You see me carryin' a big old boiler out? What the fook d'ya think might've been hidin' in it?"

Kristina Cross materialises at Patrick's side. "They're on their way," she says.

Patrick stands up – setting aside any dramatic effect of his doing so, his haunches are killing him anyway – and pulling his hood a fraction further back, he leans in closer to Snake Neck – close enough to whisper in his ear. "Sure, ya should get out now. Outside and gone – yer self, yer friends, yer knives. Yer playin' in a far bigger league than ya realise – no fookin' disrespect, like I said before."

Patrick steps back slightly, lets Snake Neck see the fear in his face, and hopes the huge fella will interpret it as fear for him rather than fear of him. Worried that he's over-egging the pudding, but helpless to resist the impulse, Patrick blinks repeatedly and rapidly with one eye, as if to show to the kind of nervous twitch typical of a pumped-up madman.

Snake Neck stares furiously at him for what feels like half a lifetime. Then he pushes the guard onto his arse, and after getting up off the stool, he kicks it furiously over. Finally, he turns and forges a path back through the crowd – a crowd which has thinned somewhat since this whole confrontation commenced. "You lot, come on," says Snake Neck to his friends, barely breaking stride, but nearly breaking the door as he barges his way outside.

After a moment of quiet incredulity, the others get up and follow him out. Several of them turn a wary, resentful eye towards Patrick as they traipse after their leader. They'll have seen Patrick's face to some extent, he realises, despite the hood of his coat. At first he hopes that the punky woman hasn't recognised him from their previous encounter, but maybe, on reflection, it would be no bad thing if she did. He acted like a mad bastard back then, and maybe her recollection of the episode would only add to his cover.

+++++

There's a whole lot of grey going on.

Gareth stares at his reflection in the bathroom mirror. His four-weekly haircut is two weeks overdue. His moustache is untrimmed and straggly. He has a three-day growth of beard.

It's the greyness which really gets to him. He has so much grey hair. It's everywhere, Hell's bells.

He takes a trimmer from the pocket of his dressing gown and attends carefully to his moustache. He then washes his face in the sink and lathers up with shaving foam, before taking a razor to his neck, cheeks and chin. Next, he takes a hot shower and washes his hair thoroughly, waxing it neatly into place once he's dried himself off. He may be overdue a haircut, but he can look smart nevertheless.

And Gareth certainly wants to look smart. Two nights before it closes, he's off to The Lamb and Musket for the first time in perhaps four weeks. Maybe five weeks, even. And it will be only his second visit in approximately two months.

According to Derek, with whom he's swapped a text or three, the regulars believe he's stayed away because of the council's verdict. People think he's taken the closure decision personally, especially as certain members of the planning committee singled him out for criticism. Also, according to Derek, word is out concerning Gareth's arrest for common assault in the aftermath of a road accident, and The Lamb's patrons imagine that his shame and embarrassment are further reasons for his ongoing absence from their pub.

These people are correct in their assumptions. But only up to a point.

Yes, Gareth does take the closure decision personally. And he is mortified to be facing a criminal prosecution for punching the loud-mouth from the Ford in his runaway mouth.

But these aren't the only reasons Gareth has gone missing from The Lamb.

Barely solvent at the best of times, he's been sitting on a demand from Bill and Ted for four-hundred pounds – this being the amount of money Bill claims to have spent on buying the Renault which Gareth subsequently wrote off in entirely the wrong crash. Gareth hopes that his insurance policy will eventually pay out, but as of now the insurers are dragging their feet. He's hardly surprised about such a delay, and imagines that there are loss adjusters investigating the circumstances of his claim. When a man acquires and insures a cheap, old car, and then, almost immediately, has an accident with two other vehicles, both far more expensive than his, the circumstances certainly appear dubious. His insurers are probably trying to decide exactly how dubious, in which context his arrest for assault will certainly have muddied the waters. Probably, and deeply ironically, the people at the insurance company probably suspect some sort of Cash for Crash scam.

As much as for any other reason, this is why Gareth hasn't been to The Lamb and Musket in recent times. Unable to pay his debts, he would feel awkward to be drinking in a pub frequented by his debtors.

The story gets worse for Gareth, too. Although willing to show a degree of patience as regards his getting the money together, Bill has also indicated that four-hundred pounds isn't the full extent of Gareth's liability. Bill, apparently, has other out-of-pocket expenses regarding the aborted scam, and did mention, during Gareth's one visit to The Lamb since the day of the crash, the necessity for Gareth to compensate him for the cost of the insurance premium itself, and also for loss of profits arising. And it's not as if Gareth can completely duck the problem merely by staying away from The Lamb: Bill has subsequently phoned him to issue a further 'friendly' reminder.

Bill's intimations of punitive liabilities have cost Gareth a great deal of sleep in recent weeks, adversely affecting his performance at work. "We 'preciate you coming clean about your arrest," his team leader recently said, "and as long as you don't end up in clink it shouldn't cost you your job, not when you've worked 'ere 'slong as you 'ave. But when you're packin' the wrong stuff in the right boxes, or the right stuff but not 'nough of it, that's a differen' story. You need to sort your shit, Mr Gareth. Or else, you know?"

Gareth takes another look in the bathroom mirror. He does need to sort his shit. He's been going grey for quite a while, but it seems his greyness is burgeoning with the worry of recent weeks. Also, Saturday night is the last night ever at The Lamb. He'd dearly like to be there, and he'd like, equally, to be able to enjoy a drink with at least some of his anxiety abated.

That's why he's off to The Lamb tonight – shaved, showered, and wearing clean clothes. He wants to have this out with Bill and Ted.

They're welcome to the four-hundred pounds if and when his insurer pays out. But that will have to be the end of it, as he has no other money left to give. And if those two are going to hassle him, he's fully prepared to go to the police and make a clean breast of everything. He wants Bill and Ted to fully understand this.

Still looking in the mirror, Gareth strokes his moustache, and then practices staring down both Bill and Ted. Not entirely convinced, he nevertheless switches off the light, goes downstairs, puts on his coat, and heads out through the front door.

+++++

It took half-an-hour before any police got to The Beethoven Lounge. Even then, their response was far from overwhelming. Only two of them came – one woman, one man – and they arrived on foot. Patrick cynically observed that the male peeler had spectacles and a weight problem, whereas the female appeared red-faced and breathless purely from the exertions of showing up.

Patrick wasn't alone in doubting the capabilities of the attending officers. Later on, after the police had left, Kris Cross opined that they'd arrived too late to have helped, and that the pair of them appeared physically inadequate anyway. "Thank God you were here, Patrick," Kris sighed, while looking at her hired security guard in a way suggestive that she felt equally short-changed by both the private and public sectors alike.

Patrick told her it was nothing – "part of the service, at no extra charge" – and in his statement to the police he'd certainly be keen to downplay his role. But in truth, modesty apart, now that matters have calmed down, Patrick is feeling pleased with himself. What he did feels like a brave thing to have done – far braver, for example, than scurrying around shagging Caroline while, at the same time, never finding the courage to properly discuss with her where the relationship may be going.

Although modest about his own involvement, Patrick tried in his statement to emphasise just what a brutal bunch Snake Neck and his gang clearly were. He spoke of Snake Neck's sheer size, of the man's callous, casual threats – threats augmented by his easy manhandling of the security guard. Patrick spoke also of the big man's cohorts: of the one alleged to have a concealed knife, and of others supposedly so formidable as not to need one. And he told the police that there was a woman in the gang's midst – young and pretty, but hard-faced – one with whom he and Ricky had argued before while drinking in here. He stopped just short of telling the peelers about the woman's assault on Esme, partly because he didn't actually witness that fight, and partly because he wasn't certain that either Esme or Ricky would necessarily want the matter raking up again.

Ultimately, however, despite his best efforts, Patrick concluded his statement believing he had failed to adequately explain just how dangerous Snake Neck and his supporting act truly were. Patrick had looked into the big man's eyes and seen not only a ruthless lack of human empathy, but also a vengeful, predatory instinct which Patrick found no less chilling than any of his da's worst tales of the troubles. The local constabulary, however, saw nothing more than an undamaged pub – one without so much as a scratch on the piano – and a security guard also undamaged beyond a shattered sense of pride and a tabard stretched into misshape. The police said they'd keep a look out for a big man with a snake insignia on his neck, while suggesting to Kris and Chris Cross that they take greater care about their entry policy in the future. The two officers took their leave after that, leaving Kris Cross visibly fuming and Patrick with the Laurel and Hardy theme playing in his head.

Once the police had gone, Patrick realised he felt exhausted. He hung around for a short while, making sure that the heating did indeed work, and sipping a large whiskey eagerly bestowed upon him by a grateful Chris Cross. Finally, after making an agreement that he'd pick up the remainder of his tools in the morning, he headed outside for the short walk to his van. Although the rain had finally stopped, the streets were still wet and beginning to grow dark.

He walks those sodden streets now, retracing his steps to where he previously parked his van. The night is autumnally chilly, and the air feels fresh after a day's worth of rain. It's that time of year when people will be switching on their heating after the summer, and many householders will find faults with their system upon doing so. Patrick expects the call from The Beethoven Lounge to be the first of many he'll receive, resulting in bookings which he will this year have to juggle around the desultory, shameful, and yet glorious affair he's conducting with his best mate's wife.

Yet when he checks his phone for messages, he finds none other than the text Caroline sent him just after five – a text in which she enquired how the job was going. It was such a mundane thing for her to ask, he realises – both it and his reply being the kind of texts sent between people easy in each other's company and familiar with the other's foibles. Already his relationship with her, while illicit and forbidden, has elements to it which are beginning to feel commonplace and everyday.

Back at his van, in a three-quarters empty car park, he opens the rear doors and spends a couple of minutes strapping down the old boiler so that it doesn't clatter around on his way home. So focused on the task is he, and so absorbed is his residual attention on matters regarding Caroline, and so numbed are his senses by the whiskey he drank earlier, Patrick either doesn't notice the nearby murmur of voices, or doesn't assign any importance to them. It's only when he steps out of the van and slams shut the doors that he becomes aware that there are two or three people talking, somewhere close by. Their tones are low, mocking and spiteful.

Urgently, with a rising sense of panic, Patrick looks around. This end of the car park is bordered, in part, by a high wire fence. The fence's other side marks the termination point of a short, stubby cul-de-sac – one with a rough-looking pub located no more than a stone's throw from where Patrick's van is parked. Presumably having spilled out of the pub, there are three men observing Patrick from the other side of the fence. Their faces are pressed up close to it, in order to best see him through the hexagonal pattern of the wire.

"Cooey!" says the man in the middle of the three.

It's getting seriously dark by now, but the car park's lighting is good enough for Patrick to see the three men clearly. The huge one in the middle is his new acquaintance, Snake Neck. And for good measure, the big man is flanked on each side by a drinking buddy from earlier. If Patrick has it correct, the one on Snake Neck's right is Cyanide Steve – a man alleged to need no knife in order to do his worst.

Once Patrick focuses on them, all three start laughing. "Hello Paddy," says Snake Neck. "How's your evening, now? We didn't see any of your so-called associates turning up at the other place. Just a couple of spastic rozzers."

Patrick urgently scans the rest of the car park. That fence is too high to climb, and he could be in his van and gone by the time any of these three men managed to run the long way round. But Patrick is concerned that more of the gang may be lurking on this side of the fence, either in the shadows or crouched behind cars.

"Oh, you're safe enough for now," mocks Snake Neck. "But I'll be coming for you soon. You're not really the heavily-connected badass you claim to be, are you?"

Patrick tries reverting to the mad Irishman of earlier. "Mister, yer readin' too much," he says, "into the peelers arrivin' at that bar before my friends got there."

But the spell is broken. The three scumbags laugh some more, and Snake Neck shakes his head to indicate that he's sussed out Patrick's act. He then takes out his phone and moves off to one side, so as to create a better angle for photographing the side of

Patrick's van. "You're Patrick-Fucking-Mackey," he says, as the flash on his camera phone flares. "Plumbing and heating engineer, apparently. And I don't think there were any drugs in that old boiler you carried out. Only dust and cobwebs."

Patrick gives up on his gangster intimations, and on the exaggerated Belfast patois. After closing the van's rear doors, he moves to the driver's side and makes a show of studying the signage. "It's funny," he says, "but I can't see the bit where it says 'fucking'."

"Oh, you're a funny man," says Snake Neck, examining the image he's just captured on his phone. "The fucking part is what I'm going to do to you next. I've got your phone number, Paddy, and your fucking email. It won't take long to find where you actually live."

Opening the door, Patrick climbs behind the wheel. "Maybe longer than you think," he says, trying to sound brave. He feels relieved, and partly reassured, that he has a policy of not advertising his home address.

"Not that long," says one of Snake Neck's mates, just before Patrick slams shut the door and fires the ignition. "I've seen this van before now – it's parked up a lot at The Lamb and Musket."

+++++

Yasmin walks into The Lamb barely ten minutes after Mel's penultimate shift there has begun. Mel has to concede that the girl looks stunning, albeit slightly slutty. Yasmin has on a tight black top and even tighter jeans – jeans which boast a zip on the reverse side. A big, bold zip which runs provocatively up the middle of her near-perfect arse.

It turns out that Yasmin is also there to work, or at least to perform what passes for work according to her way of thinking. Her attendance pisses Mel off, because The Lamb isn't busy enough for them both to be on shift. Of the regulars, Mackey Senior is here with one of his golfing buddies, and Vince, in the absence of Patrick or Ricky, is coat-tailing Malachy's conversation, doing his best to keep up, and contributing here and there. That piss-head Dave Isherwood, his regular mates being elsewhere, is also hanging around Malachy's group, although Mel notes that his contribution to the conversation seems less intelligent than Vince's. (*Vince is actually a bright guy*, thinks Mel, not for the first time. *Yes, he's slow, and sometimes there are big gaps in his awareness, but eight times out of ten he's on the money. Just a little bit behind everyone else.*)

It seems to Mel that The Lamb has become less busy since the closure announcement, although she does expect it to get livelier again tomorrow – which is a Friday, after all – and trusts it will be rammed to the rafters for Saturday night's big closing-down party. But as of now, there's one whole member of staff for every two customers, and Mel thinks it's only sensible for either her or Yasmin to go home. But weary as Mel feels after a day spent in charge of an estate agency, she recognises that if either of them is to leave then it will have to be Yasmin. Derek went out for the night just as soon as Mel arrived, and Mel knows that Yasmin doesn't have the wherewithal to run the place on her own.

But just as Mel's about to ask her colleague if she fancies an evening off, three more customers come walking in. Inevitably, two of the newcomers are Bill and Ted. The third, not so inevitably nowadays, is Ricky, who's still in his work suit even though the evening's getting old. Mel would preferably deal with Ricky, leaving Yasmin to serve Bill and Ted. That way, Mel would not only avoid her least favourite customers, but she'd have chance to quiz Ricky further regarding his interest in the information she phoned through earlier – namely that the sale of The Lamb is not fully finalised.

But things don't go as she'd have preferred. After punching Vince's arm and shaking Malachy's hand, Ricky asks Mel if he can please borrow Yasmin for five minutes. Scarcely before Mel can reply,

Ricky leads a bemused-looking Yasmin outside, pausing halfway to the door, and calling out, as some kind of afterthought, "Thanks, Mel, for your help this morning."

All of which leaves Mel none the wiser, and with Bill and Ted requiring beer. She serves them quickly and without ceremony, given that she's still communicating with them on a bare-minimum basis. Bill informs Ted that he's going to the toilet. Ted says he'll wait indoors for him, as it's "fucking parky" outside. Grateful for any excuse not to have to talk to Ted, Mel heads to the other end of the bar, where Malachy's group look in need of their next round.

For whatever reason, Mackey Senior and friends are talking about the actor Tom Cruise. Malachy's golfing buddy, who's probably Malachy's own age, but is jowlier and with thinner hair, says that Cruise still does his own stunt work, even though he's some way beyond the first flush of youth. Malachy agrees that this is impressive. Vince doesn't comment, but does look thoughtful, and Mel wonders whether he might be reflecting that life can turn horribly pear-shaped when the taking of such risks – driving very fast, specifically – happens to go wrong.

Dave Isherwood, though, does have something to say. He slurps the last of his old pint, before offering the view that Tom Cruise is looking older in his most recent films – an observation Mel classes as reasonable enough, albeit a little bit obvious. But then Isherwood, who's seen in female company less often than Her Majesty the Queen is spotted in McDonalds, adds that the famous Hollywood actor is "probably struggling to pull any birds these days."

There follows a brief silence during which the others first wait for a punchline, and then study Isherwood's face for traces of irony, or to see whether his tongue may, perhaps, be lodged in a cheek. When they finally conclude that Dave Isherwood was talking on the level, Malachy and his mate break out in incredulous grins. Vince is slower to cotton on, but does begin smirking a few seconds later when Malachy says, "Sure, and you'd know all about pulling birds then, David?"

"I'm just saying, that's all," replies Isherwood, looking mildly flustered. "Time catches up with everyone in the end."

"True enough, son. But it caught up with you at puberty, didn't it?"

It's a line which raises a chuckle, and then, once the laughter subsides, Malachy's jowly golfing buddy asks Mel what she thinks – is Tom Cruise still capable of pulling the birds?

"I'm getting on a bit myself," she dryly replies, "and I'm not sure you can still call me a bird. But my daughter's away tonight, and if Tom were to knock my door then I may let him show me some stunt work."

Another line, another laugh. As Mel gets the group their drinks, she notices from the corner of her eye that Bill is back from the toilet, and that he and Ted are heading for the exit. The two of them, as ever, have cigarettes and lighters at the ready, although their summer-wear has given way to body-warmers and tracksuits now that the cooler weather is here. Setting down Malachy's fresh Guinness, Mel also spots Gareth arriving at exactly the moment that Bill and Ted are walking out the door. For a fleeting moment, all three of them stand just inside The Lamb and Musket and look at wordlessly at each other. Then Bill and Ted quickly huddle around Gareth. Words are spoken – they're spoken urgently, and in raised voices. Finally, Gareth breaks away and resumes his course to the bar. "Hell's bells," he calls back to them, "I've only just got here. But I'll come and talk to you outside, once I've got myself a drink."

"I think you've met Gareth, haven't you?" Malachy murmurs to his golfing buddy. Malachy keeps his voice low, but not so low that Mel's unable to hear him while she continues serving their drinks. "He's another one with no clue about the female of the species. If he were to stumble upon a woman who found him attractive, it would be like his finding a briefcase full of military secrets in an empty train compartment."

The golfing buddy smiles in anticipation of Malachy's punchline.

"Having no idea how to proceed, he would hand her on to someone in authority."

Gareth has made it to the bar. He stands near its centre, not making himself part of Malachy's group, but hovering close enough to it for civility. Greetings are exchanged. People tell Gareth it's good to see him, and that it's been a while. He agrees that it has, and asks how everyone is.

Yasmin isn't yet back from her outdoor expedition with Ricky, and so, having finished serving Malachy's group, Mel moves across to pull Gareth a pint. Gareth has arrived clean shaven, and in the overhead bar lights he has a scrubbed look to him. But his hair is longer than previously, and he appears to have used some sort of product to jounce it backwards into a corny eighties mullet. As well as being longer, his hair also looks to have greyed rapidly, although maybe the effect is an illusory one caused by whatever styling agent he has used. But then again, Gareth surely wouldn't have rubbed hair gel into his moustache – would he? – and that too seems more salt 'n' peppery than before.

"How've you been?" Mel asks Gareth, cascading real ale into a glass without troubling to ask what he's having. They haven't sold much beer of this sort during Gareth's absence, and Mel hopes the stuff has kept okay. "Seriously – how've you've been?"

Gareth smiles wanly, and caresses his moustache. "I won't tell you lies, Melanie: I've been struggling a bit." He takes a handful of coins from the pocket of his jeans, and begins arranging them into little stacks on the bar – fifties, twenties, two tens and some copper. Then, quite palpably, he puffs out his chest and straightens his shoulders. "But I'm better now," he says. "Oh yes – much better, thanks." He sounds like he's trying to convince himself as much as her.

Mel sets down Gareth's beer. It's very frothy, and she tells him she'll top it up in a moment. Then she gets her fingers behind his assemblage of coins, and slides the whole array towards his edge of the bar. "On the house," she says.

"No," he replies.

"Yes," she insists. "On the bloody house, be told."

"Really, Melanie. You're very kind, but just because I said I'd been struggling, that doesn't –"

"I said be told, Mister. This isn't about you struggling. It's about you being a good friend of The Lamb and Musket – one who did more than anyone else to try keeping it open. You're owed, Gareth. You get that? Owed."

Gareth looks pained, but he removes his coins from the bar and puts them back in his pocket. "Thank you," he says. "Like I said, you're very kind."

"And you'll still be owed on Saturday night. Derek will understand that, and if he doesn't then I'll make sure he does. I take it you'll be here? Last night at The Lamb?"

"Nobody will owe me anything. But I do hope to come along."

"You'd better, Gareth. You're a big man round these parts."

He smiles at her, but it's such a forlorn smile that Mel's certain Gareth doesn't feel like a big man – round these parts or anywhere else. "Since you put it like that," he says, "I'll be sure to put in an appearance. And thank you again. But for now, there's a conversation I need to have with Bill and Ted, even though I'd far rather talk to you. I'm sorry, Melanie – please excuse me."

"That sounds ominous. Is everything okay with you and them?"

"Everything is fine." He offers up that forlorn little smile again. "But there are things that need to be said – things that should have been said some while back."

Gareth puffs out his chest again, and heads away from the bar. He carries with him his beer, despite it not having been topped up as promised. "Kick ass," Mel calls after him, trying to boost his confidence for the tough talking she supposes will follow. "Don't take any shit from them, Gareth."

Gareth doesn't reply and doesn't look back, but he gives her a thumbs-up as he goes. Mel watches him to the door, pondering that he's lost as much weight as he's gained grey hair. Her mind casts back, replaying scenes of a sunny day when Gareth was drunk outside with Bill and Ted. Further remembrances follow – those of her walking Gareth home while he talked, barely lucidly, of 'money cars' or some such. Then there was Gareth's frantic phone call to this place, on the day of his car crash and arrest. Since when he's hardly set foot through the door.

Abruptly, Mel arrives at a decision. She returns to Malachy's end of the bar.

"So, I'm there in Billy Pearson's plunge pool," Dave Isherwood is saying. "There's me, Billy himself, and three seriously fit birds. Two of 'em are completely starkers and the other has just –"

"Shut up a minute, Dave," says Mel. "Malachy, I think Gareth's in some sort of trouble with Bill and Ted. And I don't think he knows how to handle it."

Mackey Senior appears to be studying the lettering on his beer glass – intently so, almost as if it's some kind of ancient scripture, or a secret recipe for health, wealth and happiness. "Sure," he says absently, "that'll be Gareth. He could get into trouble with Sooty and Sweep and be unable to handle it."

"That's not fair," she replies. "He calmed things down for you in the summer, when you were going to fight those soldiers." Mel immediately feels a sense of déjà vu, remembering she leveraged the same episode in persuading Ricky to rescue Gareth from the police station just a few weeks ago. Vince, who was here with Ricky on that earlier occasion, breaks into a grin. He gives her a look which suggests he's cottoned on quicker than he sometimes does. It's a look which maybe says: *Seriously? You're running this one again?* In spite of the urgency of the circumstances, Mel finds herself smiling conspiratorially back at him.

She has time enough to absorb Vince's reaction only because Malachy takes so long to reply. When the Ulsterman finally looks up from his glass, his face is missing the spark of vitality which made him look younger than his jowly golfing friend. Mackey Senior suddenly appears very senior indeed – older even than his years. He could actually be Patrick's grandad, or maybe granda – whatever those daft paddies call it. "Gareth did help me," he slowly concedes. "He helped us all. And I feel a bit responsible, sure, for the trouble he's in as of now."

"Responsible?"

"Well you see now, Gareth once asked me how I thought our friends, William and Edward out there, managed to come by their money. I suggested he use some initiative by asking them himself. And in so doing, I may have set Gareth off on an unfortunate adventure – the latest chapter of which is most likely a very awkward conversation currently taking place outside."

"What kind of unfortunate adventure?"

"A criminal caper gone wrong. Such details as I know have come to me third hand, based on something Gareth said to Richard and Vincent, and which then reached me via Patrick. I do have reason to suspect that William and Edward believe that Gareth owes them money. I doubt that Vincent here would disagree."

Everyone looks to Vince while he computes Mackey Senior's rather meandering explanation. After quite a few seconds, he purses his lips and shakes his head. He might mean 'no' – he has no reason to doubt the truth of the story. Or he might equally mean 'no' – he can't work out what the fuck Malachy just said.

"Bloody hell," says Mel, intuiting that the gist of Malachy's report is correct, given that it seems to tie in with what she already knew. "Do you suppose we should do something to help him?"

"Gareth, you mean?" asks Malachy.

"Of course, Gareth I mean," she replies. "Did you think I meant Elvis Presley or someone? Why are men so flaming thick?"

But before Mackey Senior can respond, the stage is stolen by Yasmin as she returns from outside. She returns alone, without Ricky, and her gait is brisk and furious – at least to the extent that briskness and fury are possible in heels so high. Yasmin keeps her head up and her eyes forward, without offering a glance to anyone as she comes back behind the bar, from where she storms through the doorway leading to the back corridor and kitchen. Momentarily, while close up and under bright lights, she appeared to be fighting back tears, but Mel imagines that the men will more likely remember their fleeting view of her rear as she flounced out of sight, a view accentuated by that big, bold zipper running up the middle of her behind.

"That's Richard for you," sighs Malachy, once Yasmin has gone. "Another one bites the dust."

"I'd say she's bitten it quite hard," replies Mel.

"Indeed." Malachy lets out another sigh. "Alright, Melanie. Tell you what. You go and patch up the pouty princess before she has some sort of spasm. I'll do this helping out of Gareth which you asked me about. I'll just nip outside and have a word."

"Nip outside? Right now? You're sure?"

Malachy rolls his eyes, and then sighs for a third time. "Will you make up your mind what you want?" he says. "One of the reasons why men are – as you say – so thick, is that our brains have been pulverised in our ceaseless consideration of women's ever-changing whims."

"Sorry," says Mel, momentarily wrong-footed. "Look, of course I want us to help Gareth, but you need to be careful of Bill and Ted – they can be nasty when the mood takes them. Ricky could help you if he's still around outside. Who knows – Patrick may soon be here as well."

This time, Malachy doesn't sigh. But he gives Mel a withering look. "I'm from Turf Lodge," he says.

Mel holds up her hands. "I know," she replies. "You've said before."

"I don't need back-up to talk to a pair of spunks like William and Edward."

"Okay, okay. I get your point."

"I certainly don't need Patrick or Richard."

"Alright, Malachy. I understand what you're saying."

Malachy sets down his glass. He rolls his shoulders, readying himself for the walk outside. "Besides," he says. "I've got Vincent, if needed."

Vince? Mel thinks. *He's fucking disabled, in case you hadn't noticed.* She gives Malachy a severe look, just out of Vince's eye line. But Mackey Senior responds with nothing more than a nod, a wink and the darkest of grins. Surprisingly, it's Vince himself who replies to her a couple of seconds later.

"I'll be fine," he says.

"Anyway," adds Malachy, looking first to his golfing buddy and then to Dave Isherwood, "we've also got Roy and David here. So there's safety in numbers. Sure, we'll be fine."

"Bloody make sure you are," says Mel, briefly fixing Malachy with another glare, before nodding pointedly at Vince. "And I'll be out there myself in a minute."

She makes towards the doorway at the back of the bar, her intention to go and find Yasmin. But before she can leave, Vince says, "Mel?" and when Mel turns back, Vince beckons to her with his good arm. She moves close, leaning on the bar so that he can whisper in her ear.

"Go easy… on her?" he says.

"I will, sweetie," she replies, and then turns away, believing that to be all Vince has to say. But he hasn't finished – he reaches for her arm, and pulls her gently back towards him, before taking a moment longer to sequence his next passage of words.

"Go easy… on her," he finally repeats, before adding, "She's… a bit dim. She has… her jeans on… the wrong way round."

Mel laughs, but then abruptly checks herself, uncertain whether Vince was trying to be funny or not. Then she sees that he's laughing, and allows herself to join in. Subsequently, she finds it hard, thirty seconds later, to keep a straight face when she finds Yasmin sitting on the back stairs with her head bowed. Yasmin looks up as Mel draws near, her distress are shown in stark relief by the bare lightbulb overhead.

Initially at least, Yasmin glowers angrily, possibly assuming that her colleague is there to gloat. But then Mel digs a tissue from her pocket, and hands it to Yasmin while doing her utmost to appear sympathetic. "How about I get you a drink?" she asks.

Yasmin dabs her eyes. She sniffs, and shakes her head. Momentarily, she appears incapable of speech. If Mel were her friend, she'd squeeze in next to Yasmin on the stairs. Then, after wrapping an arm around the girl, she would tell her that this is Ricky's loss – that the bloke is totally not worth it. She'd assure Yasmin that everything's going to be fine, and then suggest they go out together at the weekend.

But Mel doesn't think of Yasmin as a friend, and so she continues to stand a pace or two away, still trying hard not to laugh at the notion that the girl has her jeans on back-to-front.

Yasmin blows her nose hard into the tissue. It's the most inelegant thing Mel's seen her ever do – an action which makes it all the harder for Mel to keep a straight face. Then Yasmin says, "No one dumps me. Not ever."

Someone just has, thinks Mel, but chooses not to say so. *And stunning though you look, Yasmin, someone will again. Or they'll cheat on you behind your back – and that's even worse. Ricky will have done his share of that before now.*

Mel says, "I think Derek made a mistake rostering both of us on tonight. Before Ricky walked in, I was going to ask if you wanted the night off. How about it, Yasmin? Why not get yourself home?" Uncharitably, she thinks: *You're even less use here than you usually are.*

Yasmin just sits there, staring straight ahead, her forearms resting on the tops of her legs, and her fingers toying distractedly with that snotty used tissue. The girl takes so long to reply that Mel pops back into the bar to see if anyone needs serving. The place is deserted – Malachy, Vince and the others clearly having gone outside. Mel dashes a big slug of brandy into a glass, before hurrying back to where Yasmin still sits near-catatonically on the stairs. "Here," says Mel. "Drink this."

Yasmin looks up at the glass. The mistrust has gone from her eyes, but her upset is clearer than ever. "He's going back to his wife," she says, sounding increasingly embittered. "Can you believe it? Back to his fucking wife?"

Mel finally does sit down next to Yasmin, just about squeezing in on the staircase. She doesn't quite put an arm around her, but does rest one hand on Yasmin's nearest shoulder, at the same time pushing the brandy glass into her grasp. "Come on," she says. "Drink up like I said."

"What is it?"

"Brandy. It will help."

"I don't even know if I like it."

"Just drink the fucking brandy, Yasmin."

Yasmin swivels towards Mel. Her eyes flare fiercely; their message is clear.

Mel stares implacably back. "Don't you tell me to fuck off," she says.

Yasmin looks away. Then she knocks back half the brandy in one quick gulp. She splutters a little, pulls a face, and sets down the glass on a lower stair. "Shit," she says. "I don't like the taste, but it makes me feel warm."

"They say brandy's good for when you've had a shock."

Yasmin uses what's left of the tissue to blow her nose again. "A shock? I've sure had one of those."

This time, Mel does put an arm around Yasmin's shoulders, and then pulls the younger woman closer. "Listen to me," she says. "You'll keep getting shocks if you involve yourself with men like Ricky. Men who'll betray their wives will betray you too, as beautiful as you are, and as hot as your sweet ass happens to look in jeans like those. Even you, Yasmin, will get dumped if you keep the wrong company – not as often as some women, but get dumped you will. And it's not nice when it happens. There are people who'll enjoy your downfall, and you'll have to eat a lot of humble pie."

"Like now," Yasmin says.

"Like now. Humble pie, washed down with cheap brandy from a clapped-out old pub."

Yasmin manages the smallest of laughs, and Mel goes so far as to stroke her hair before getting up from the stairs. "Finish your drink," she says, "while I check up on something outside. But make sure you finish it – have another if you want – and then tidy up that pretty face of yours. Whenever you're ready, we'll get you a taxi. High heels and brandy aren't a good mix when it comes to walking home."

Another small laugh. Mel begins to walk away. Yasmin says, "Mel?"

Mel turns around in the doorway to the bar.

"Thanks," says Yasmin. "For being nice, I mean. And your face is pretty, too."

"You're welcome," says Mel. "And yeah, thanks. I've seen sights worse than the one in the mirror."

At that, Mel leaves Yasmin sitting on the stairs. Leaves her in a hurry. Because not only is the bar still deserted, but Mel can hear raised voices from outside. She rushes to the door, pushes it open, and hurries on through.

It's fully dark by now, and the air feels damp and soggy after all that rain. But paradoxically, though, there's a real tinderbox atmosphere just outside the door.

Bill is sitting at the smokers' table which he usually shares with his younger sidekick, Ted. But right now he's sharing it Mackey Senior, who is seated directly opposite, wearing an expression which Mel has heard Patrick describe as Malachy's Mad-Dog-Irish face. Indeed, to Mel, Malachy's expression looks like the devil's wrath, and Bill is clearly moved by it, because his face is white and his usually cocksure tone of voice is suffused with a frightened little tremor.

"It's fine, Malachy," says Bill. "Everything is fine. I'm more than happy to agree."

"I'm Mr Mackey to you, William. Now and forever. Do we agree on that as well?"

"Of course we agree – Mr Mackey it is."

"And for the avoidance of doubt, you accept that Gareth owes nothing whatsoever to you pair of arse-wipes? Absolute diddly squat?"

"Yes, yes, yes," says Bill, hurriedly. "We totally, totally agree on that."

Gareth, who's standing off to one side, with both Malachy's golfing buddy and a goggle-eyed Dave Isherwood, decides to say his piece. "In fairness, Malachy, I'm happy to pay the four hundred. I told Bill as much, before you intervened."

Still with his eyes on Bill, Malachy says, "God love you, Gareth, but you should keep your potty mouth firmly closed."

"We're all good, Gareth," Bill is quick to confirm. "The slate is clean."

"I'm so glad we've got that settled," says Malachy.

"Thank fuck," moans Ted. "Can this one let me up now, please."

Although Malachy's golfing buddy and Dave Isherwood both seem content to spectate, it's clear that Vince, in comparison, has become more actively involved in events. Perhaps Ted cut up rough during Bill's negotiations with Malachy, because Vince has twisted Ted's arm up his back and pinned him face down on the table. Actually, on closer inspection, Mel can see that things are even worse than that for Ted, because Vince has pushed his face down not only onto the table, but also into an ashtray. Mel is both impressed and taken aback by the spectacle. She knew that Vince was strong – in one arm, at least – but had always thought of him as slow. Well, perhaps it's time she revised her appraisal, as it's clear there are parts of him, at least, which can move quickly when required. Vince now looks at her, and repeats that other trick he did recently – firing off a series of rapid little blinks, leading up to a fully-fledged wink.

"Erm, this isn't my fight," Mel says tentatively to Vince, "but I think it's okay to let him up."

"I think so, too," adds Gareth, seemingly embarrassed to be the cause of a fracas. He briefly looks all set to say something more, but then, perhaps remembering that Malachy told him to stay quiet, he closes his mouth and toys nervously with his moustache.

"Vincent," says Malachy, in tones gentler than those he reserved for Bill, or even for Gareth, "it's all okay. Melanie is correct – you can let Edward go."

Mel isn't sure whether Vince is slow to compute Malachy's request, or whether he's only feigning slowness. That said, she suspects his delay in releasing Ted may have reasons rooted more in badness than miscomprehension. It's the look on Vince's face which suggests as much. For once there's real malice showing – a delighted little look at having bested someone he clearly doesn't care for. It's a look Mel's seen on Ricky's face before now, and on Patrick's from time to time. But not on Vince's, she thinks – not before today.

"Come on now, Vincent," says Mackey Senior, trying to coax a response. "You can let the lad up."

"You hear that?" whines Ted, tapping the table with his free hand. "You can let go my arm."

Vince grins some more at Mel. It occurs to her, now, that he may be doing this for her. Vince has probably noticed the recent rancour she's shown towards Bill and Ted, and sees this as payback for whatever grievance she may have had with them. "It's okay, Vince," says Mel. "It really is okay to let him go."

Vince lets go of Ted's arm, and stands slightly away while a spluttering Ted straightens up, wipes fag ash from around his mouth, and begins massaging his shoulder. Still with some wickedness to his smile, Vince shrugs languidly at Mel. It's a lopsided shrug, the shoulder of his good arm rising that bit higher than the other.

"Fuck me," moans Ted, to no one in particular. "I think my arm's –"

Vince steps in close again, places one hand on Ted's chest, and gives him an almighty shove. Ted freewheels a few paces backwards, before landing on his backside in the car park.

Meanwhile, his eyes still fixed on Bill, Malachy says, "You won't be reneging on what you just said, will you? About the slate wiped clean?"

Bill glances at his mate, scrabbling to get up in the dark and the dirt and the wet. "No," he says solemnly. "We won't."

"That's good," says Vince, slurring slightly as he utters the first words he's spoken since Mel walked out here to the car park. All eyes turn to him, as the direction of his own gaze moves up and away, towards the sign above The Lamb's front door, and he takes a few seconds to form his next sentence. "We should... all... have a drink."

And then Vince leads everyone – Bill and Ted apart – back indoors.

Where he insists on buying the next round.

Gareth, briefly, protests that idea. He's suddenly a few hundred quid better off than he expected to be, and in recognising a debt of gratitude to Mackey Senior and Vince, he wants to pay for the round himself.

"Buy the next one," says Malachy, with a little wink for Gareth. "But let Vincent get these. Or you too could end up outside on your arse, perhaps with your arm hanging out of its socket."

Gareth accordingly relents, and Vince buys drinks for them all, Mel included. Yasmin emerges with her face made up, and insists on serving the drinks while Mel remains with her friends on the customers' side of the bar. Yasmin returns Vince's wide smile when he says, "Have one... yourself... lady," and she replies that she'll have another of those brandies, if that's okay.

Mel warms to their exchange. *Vince can't remember Yasmin's name*, she thinks, *any more than I can remember what Malachy's golfing buddy is called.*

The goings-on outside have perked everyone up, and both the beer and conversation flow easily. Malachy foots the bill for the round following Vince's, waving away Gareth's renewed protestations, and telling him to enjoy his "lucky night." They all reminisce about old times, and speculate about those to come. Mindful of the conviviality and goodwill, Dave Isherwood winds his neck in a little, telling a tale or two not quite so implausible as his usual big whoppers. And all at once, this begins to feel like the real Last Night at The Lamb – certainly it does to Mel, and, she suspects, to the others as well. Yes, the place is open tomorrow, and then on Saturday there'll be the big closing-down party. But somehow this night feels like the last.

It's also the night on which Yasmin, somewhat belatedly, begins to look like a competent member of the fraternity of bar staff. Seared by Ricky's rejection of her, soothed by Mel's ministrations, and mellowed by a large brandy or three, she operates smoothly behind the bar, not only serving the drinks, but doing a fair job of tidying up, washing glasses, emptying drip trays, and – shock, horror! – taking a crate of empty bottles out to the back yard. She moves so smoothly behind the bar that she appears unencumbered by her high heels, and at one point, while Yasmin is distracted, Mel stands on the foot rail and cranes her neck in order to confirm her suspicion that Yasmin is, indeed, working barefoot.

Her pretty feet will be filthy, thinks Mel, *and she'll be lucky not to end up with cuts.* But what the hell! Mel, too, is feeling mellower after a good slug of booze, and is in no mind to give Yasmin a hard time, not when the girl's had a rough enough evening already.

Talking of rough, Patrick walks in when they're halfway through Malachy's round. He looks utterly worn out. "You alright?" asks Mel. In the bright lights above the bar, Patrick's sexy Irish eyes look sleepless and bloodshot. And they look wary as well. Wary and guarded – like the eyes of a vulnerable little vole when there are large predators stirring in the woods.

"I'm fine," Patrick replies, mustering a smile of sorts.

Vince reaches out with the same strong hand which he used to put Ted so emphatically in his place. He grips the sleeve of the damp parka Patrick has on. "Sure?" he asks.

"Sure, I'm sure," Patrick feebly quips. Then, "Has anyone asked after me during the evening?"

His enquiry provokes an exchange of glances among the group, followed by a collective shake of heads. "Such as who?" asks Malachy. Although the look on his face is shrewd and sharp, his tone of voice is gentler, reflecting a clear measure of concern for his exhausted-looking son.

"Sure, just some people from another bar in town," replies Patrick, shrugging as if to say the matter is of little consequence. "I was fitting a boiler at The Beethoven Lounge, and a couple of customers there said they might want some work doing."

"Nobody's asked after you here," says Mel. "Yasmin, could you get Patrick a drink, please? Whiskey, I think – the Irish one there. Large, with one ice cube."

Mel studies Patrick closely. In an age of super-smart phones and permanent connectivity to social media, the idea that Patrick's customers might leave messages for him at his local boozer – as if this were the seventies, or some other time-warped era – seems somewhat far-fetched. And from the sceptical look on Mackey Senior's face, he appears to be having much the same thought.

"Anyway," pipes up Dave Isherwood to Patrick, "we might have missed it if any messages did come in for you. What with all the arguing and scrapping going on."

"Scrapping?" queries Patrick, his expression, if anything, turning even more ashen than before.

"Yeah, scrapping," enthuses Isherwood. "I'll tell you what, Patrick, it's been absolutely boss." He then spends a couple of minutes relating an aggrandised version of Malachy and Vince's conflagration with Bill and Ted, one in which Isherwood himself claims to have taken an active part in laying down the law to Gareth's tormentors. Mel doubts there's very much truth, if indeed any, to Isherwood's claims of involvement, and her suspicion appears borne out by the bemused smile among the others gathered round.

Patrick seems to relax as Dave Isherwood gets further into his story. Halfway through, he sits down on a bar stool and performs his usual shtick – tilting the stool back and hooking his instep under the foot rail. When Isherwood finally wraps up, Patrick gives a little low whistle, and then looks to both Vince and his dad. "Well done, gentlemen," he says. "Frickin well done."

Vince ponders Patrick's words and then performs another of those lopsided shrugs, perhaps as if to say, 'shucks – it was nothing'.

"Sure, I've left the van at home," says Patrick, "but I'll walk back you after, in case either of those scrotes are still hanging around."

"I'm not… worried," replies Vince, pulling a scornful face.

"I think they'd be more worried about Vincent than vice-versa," adds Malachy, "and I expect the two of them are long away home. But look, there is safety in numbers, and so it wouldn't hurt if we went home accompanied. Maybe I'll walk with you as well."

"Me too," adds Gareth. "And being as this was all for my benefit, I ought to explain quite how I got myself into such a mess."

"We're all cool, Gareth," says Malachy. "Explanations really aren't necessary."

"But I feel I owe it to you all," Gareth replies, and then takes his turn to launch a narrative – one of how he became embroiled with Bill and Ted, and not only failed to make money, but found himself facing a demand for recompense from Bill in particular. Mel already knows parts of the story, and suspects that Malachy and Patrick know even more, probably having heard Ricky's take on earlier events. And then there's Vince, of course. He was there when Ricky brought back Gareth from the police station, and will have heard much of this before now. Mel wonders how much of it Vince understood then, or how much he remembers now, given how fixedly he concentrates on Gareth's confessionary, his eyes focused and his brow creased.

"And so you see," Gareth wistfully concludes, some minutes later – after a couple of diversionary questions from Dave Isherwood about whether Gareth will be going to prison, and how much he'd have made from Bill's scheme if he hadn't cocked it all up – "I came here tonight to have it out with Bill, but Malachy did my talking for me. Admirably assisted by Vince, of course."

Who'd have thought it? thinks Mel. For an intelligent man, Gareth often seems a big daft prat, but even so, she wouldn't have imagined him getting mixed up in a criminal scam like the one he's just described.

"What would you have done with the cash?" asks Dave Isherwood. "Upgraded that old motor of yours?"

Gareth, who has laid bare his soul over these past few minutes – and shown much self-control and minimal embarrassment while doing so – finally blushes a deep, dark red. He begins to stroke his moustache quite feverishly, as if by doing so he might somehow dampen down the colour in his cheeks. "No," he finally says. "I wouldn't have risked getting involved for anything quite so trivial – Hell's bells, no. You see, I had this idea about hiring a solicitor, to try keeping this place open. But I didn't have the money myself, and the fighting fund was depleted. Also, I felt we'd reached the point where people were getting fed up with collection buckets getting passed around. And so, well... you know what happened."

"Ah, Gareth, no," groans Patrick. "It was all for the pub?"

"You're a silly wee sod," adds Malachy.

And Vince has apparently kept a good track of things, because he moves closer to Gareth and gives him a comradely slap on the shoulder.

"I remember looking at this bent up number plate," mulls Gareth. "It was from the Mercedes I hit, and half of it was angled towards me. 'GTT' – that's what the letters were. And all I could think was that they must stand for 'Gareth The Twat' – pardon my language, Melanie. They were the only words I could put to those initials."

Malachy tells Gareth that it's time to get a grip of things. Vince slaps him on the shoulder for a second time. Patrick adds that Gareth should stop being so hard on himself, adding the muttered aside that they should all peer into his (Patrick's) life if they really want to see how an idiot really carries on.

Although she's curious as to that last remark of Patrick's, Mel feels compelled to join in with the consoling of Gareth. "Your motives were really sweet," she says to him. "So stop beating yourself up over it. It was bloody foolish, mate, but still incredibly sweet."

It's also been sweet of Yasmin to stay on and serve drinks after the shock that Ricky sprung on her earlier tonight. But she's looking tired now. Mel turns to her and says, "You've done great, but it's time you got home. I'll arrange you that taxi."

Yasmin says thanks, and offers an appreciative smile.

"It's also time I was going," says Malachy's golfing buddy. "I'll give you a lift, young lady, if you'd like."

Yasmin looks uncertain about the idea, but Malachy is quick to reassure her. "You'll be fine with Roy," he says. "He's okay to drive because he's been on tonic water, and Mrs Beresford would castrate him with something rusty from the shed were he to think of trying his luck with you."

"And we'd send Vince round to do his arms," says Patrick. "Sure, that should be warning enough, given what I hear has gone on tonight."

"True," says Malachy. "Not that any such impediment would adversely affect Roy's golf game. It couldn't get worse than it already is."

"Insolent paddy fuckwits," muses Roy, setting down his empty glass.

Three minutes later, Roy is driving away in a people mover of some indeterminate make. Yasmin is in his passenger seat with her shoes back on, having exchanged a hug in the car park with Mel. Mel watches them a short way down the road, and then returns inside, goes back behind the bar, and surveys proceedings on the other side. Dave Isherwood is telling Patrick and Malachy about a girlfriend he once had who looked just like Yasmin, "'cept with a bigger rack"; Gareth is desperate to pay for a round, and is leaning across the bar with his wallet at the ready; Vince, meanwhile, has a knowing little smile on his face, and seems to be drinking the whole scene in. He's studying the others carefully, apparently with amusement. .

"What's everyone having?" asks Gareth.

"Lager top," calls Dave Isherwood.

Malachy looks at his watch. "I should be getting home," he says, "or I'll be in a degree of trouble with Patrick's mother."

"You've got to have a drink with me," replies Gareth. "I let Vince buy a round because you said I could get the next, and then you went and paid for it yourself."

"He's saving up the favour," Patrick tells Gareth, "for when he needs a bomb planting somewhere."

But rather than laugh, Gareth still looks pained, and so Malachy says, "Sure, get me one of those whiskies which my son's so very fond of lately. I can put it away sharpish, and it'll warm me for the walk home."

"I'll have one as well, please," says Patrick, "being as I'm so very fond of them lately."

"Melanie," says Gareth, "make sure you have whatever you're having, too. Vince? More tomato juice, young sir?"

Vince stirs in his seat. "No juice… thanks," he says. "I'll have… a… whiskey too." He turns his smile directly towards Mel. "No ice… for me… thank-you."

Mel and Gareth exchange fleeting looks of minor panic, as each queries of the other whether Vince should be drinking whiskey. But then Malachy calls, "Well done, Vincent. Make it a large one, Melanie, being as Gareth is paying."

To hell with it, thinks Mel, pouring Vince a generous measure while wincing commiseratively at Gareth regarding the price of the round. Gareth, though, doesn't seem to mind. He merely smiles, shrugs, pulls a second note from his wallet, and says he'll have a large whiskey too.

Once everyone has their drinks, Gareth proposes a toast – "to good friends, very good friends indeed" – after which Mel starts clearing up behind the bar, and the others splinter off into two separate discussions. Gareth begins educating Vince about the differences between Irish whiskey and scotch, a lecture to which Vince seems happy to listen, judging by the furtive little smile still playing about his face. Dave Isherwood, meanwhile, his imagination doubtless fired by Patrick's bomb-planting quip, starts to regale Malachy with a highly fanciful tale concerning some supposed local bomb-makers – "friends of big Simon's, from the flats" – who are willing and capable, Isherwood claims, of improvising any explosive device to order.

"Any explosive device?" asks Malachy, the look on his face suggesting he's had his fill of Isherwood's yarns for one night. "How about thermonuclear?"

"Not sure about that," replies Dave Isherwood, tilting his head meditatively to one side, as if giving the query some genuinely serious thought.

Mel's on the point of intervening – of winding Dave Isherwood in for his own good – when Patrick catches her eye. After a couple of whiskies, Patrick finally has some colour back in his cheeks, but he still looks profoundly tired – so tired that Mel worries he's finally going to fall off his stool with it rocked back like that. She's about to tell him as much when he says, "Yasmin seemed different tonight."

"Different?"

"Definitely. Less full of herself. And the two of you seemed friendlier than before."

"We're almost best mates now," says Mel, with a laugh. "Let's say I was a source of comfort to her earlier, after she received some disappointing news."

"Sure, what news was that, then?"

"Aha. I take it from you having to ask that he hasn't told you?"

Patrick rocks his bar stool back to an upright position. "Who hasn't told me what?"

"A certain person has given her the elbow."

"Serious?" Patrick suddenly looks very alert.

"Serious," Mel replies.

She pauses then, unsure whether to say what she's thinking of saying next. It's news which, if Mel's suspicions are correct, would surely hurt Patrick, and he doesn't look like a man who could deal with much hurt right now. But then Mel finds herself saying it anyway. Maybe it's important to her – more important than sparing Patrick's feelings – that she has those suspicions confirmed.

"Apparently, that same certain person told her he's getting back with his wife."

Patrick doesn't reply, and he doesn't even stir in his chair. But unless Mel is imagining things, a look of baffled hurt appears briefly on his face, although it's very quickly gone again. "Sure," he says, "bully for that same certain person, eh?"

But any conversation on the subject ends there. Malachy's clearly had enough of Dave Isherwood, because he drains his glass, plonks it down on the bar, and announces, "Time to go. Patrick, drink up."

Patrick knocks back his whiskey and sets down his glass. "You too, Vincent," says Malachy. "Gareth, are you walking with us as well?"

Nodding in acknowledgment, Gareth raises his glass. Having elected to join in drinking whiskey with the others, and having waxed lyrical to Vince about the differences in blends, he doesn't seem to be finding the stuff very much to his taste. But he makes the effort, anyway, finishing off his drink in two large sips.

Vince, however, is in no such hurry. "I'm not… ready yet," he says to Malachy and Patrick. "I'll stay… a while… for now."

Whatever other woes Patrick has on his mind, he's clearly bothered about the idea of Vince walking back by himself. "Sure, my da was right," he says, "when he said we should all go home together."

"He said we… should be………acco………accom………accom…panied," Vince replies, grinning in apparent self-congratulation upon getting that last word out. "Same goes… for Mel. So I will…… accom…pany…… Mel after… she locks up." He then turns to Mel and dials his endearing smile right up to the max. "If that is… okay… with you… Mel?"

Mel is totally unsure what she's supposed to make of that.

Then she meets Vince's eye, and the mystery only deepens. She thinks she sees mischief within him, and that may be a clue as to what he means by 'accompany', but Mel's still far from certain whether Vince intends merely to walk her home, or whether he has something more in mind. Come to that, she realises she has no idea whether Vince is actually capable of such a something more. From the gob-struck looks on the faces of the others, and from the way those two bonkers Irishmen are, for once, lost for words, she suspects no one else has much of an idea, either.

But then again, these various uncertainties about Vince's intentions don't feel like worries. Whether Vince is or isn't capable of what he may or may not have in mind is a matter of intrigue to her – of excitement, even. It's a question to quicken her pulse. And even if it turns out that all he wants to do is see her to her door, well then, there's something very nice about that.

Albeit anticlimactic.

And it would be anticlimactic, Mel realises, for she does find herself hoping that Vince has more in mind than a walk back to her place and then a simple goodbye.

Mel returns the big guy's smile. She hopes she isn't blushing too obviously, but rather suspects that she is. "Thank you," Vince, she replies. "That would be lovely of you."

3.2) They're Closing The Lamb and Musket

It's a cold, damp morning – one to suggest that autumn is truly ensconced. Nevertheless, the leaves in the trees have a few weeks of green remaining, and they cling doggedly to their branches despite the best efforts of the stiff breeze blowing through them. In a corner of the park given over to soft landscaping and children's rides, Jack clings just as tenaciously to his end of the seesaw, imploring his dad to make it go faster and faster. Caroline hovers close by, ready to catch Jack if he falls, a measure of anxiety forming on her face as the seesaw reaches ever greater speeds. "That's fast enough for now," she says, but Ricky proceeds as if she doesn't really mean that, pushing down hard on the seesaw's opposite end – so hard that Jack begins to fly upwards from his seat at the point of maximum elevation, his bobble hat threatening to take leave of his head. Squealing happily, the kid tightens his two fists around the handle, but although his mum laughs along with him, the look she gives Ricky says this far and no further – or else, Mister. Ricky grins an acknowledgment, lights a cigarette with his free hand, and tries, mentally, to dampen down the fire which is burning in his mind.

He keeps thinking back to a summer's day when Caroline sent him a photo of Jack from this self-same park – a photo in which Jack is smiling so adorably that Ricky has taken to keeping it as the desktop on his phone. He remembers that the summer's day in question was one on which he spent the morning playing golf with Patrick, and the afternoon sweet talking Yasmin in the pub. He feels like awful about Yasmin. Awful for beginning an affair with her. Awful for ending it.

"Faster, dad," yells Jack, holding onto the seesaw's handle like a mariner holds onto anything that floats when his ship has gone down. "Faster, faster, faster."

But Caroline is shaking her head. And even if Jack doesn't fall off, he's going to end up with a severely sore arse from all this crashing back down whenever he flies up from his seat. Ricky meets

Caroline's stern look with a cheeky smile, but he does slow the seesaw down a little. "How about the roundabout?" he calls.

"Swings next," comes the reply.

"I liked the roundabout when I was a kid."

"Swings next."

"Only not too high," says Caroline.

Ricky loves his wife. He loves his son, too. Simple as, and end of. But Caroline has scared him in recent weeks. Scared Ricky by becoming remote – by seeming to sever connections from him, while creating emotional distance between them. These are connections he's now trying to repair, and distance he's trying to close. He's attempting to repair their relationship by being around his family more than before. And by jettisoning his other women – Lauren first, and now Yasmin as well.

He's smoked his cigarette quickly – very bloody quickly. It's nearly down to the stub. He takes a last drag, and then crushes the cigarette underfoot, fighting the urge to immediately light another. Jack runs to the swings, and Caroline pushes him a few times, before stepping back to allow Ricky a turn. "Not too high," she repeats, casting him a look of such suspicion that he thinks it must reflect mistrust about weightier matters than how hard he's going to push his son on a playground ride.

Has he left it too late, he wonders, to come back to her? Is the span of emotional distance too great for him to close? And if he is to make good to Caroline, can he actually do so without owning up to his several infidelities?

In response to the last of those questions, he suspects the answer is no. This psychological estrangement he feels from her, if it is ever to be healed, will require him, he thinks, to be totally upfront and honest.

Yet Ricky doesn't know how or where to start with that. He doesn't know how to tell Caroline about Yasmin or Lauren, or any of the others. It would help, he thinks, to know just how much she's already learnt, but even then he'd still find it hard figuring out just where to begin.

"Faster," Jack calls, and after a glance at Caroline to okay the request, Ricky gives the swing a firmer push.

In the matter of confessing all to his wife, Ricky can see a sizeable problem looming near and large. Tonight's the last night at The Lamb and Musket. And although Caroline's hardly a regular there nowadays – and hasn't been since giving birth to Jack – The Lamb was her local pub when she and Ricky were growing up. They have many great memories of the place, and Caroline has indicated a wish to attend The Lamb's last night. The trouble, of course, is that Yasmin will surely be working there. Which means that Ricky either has to do his coming clean in an awfully big hurry, or devise a world-class piece of chicanery to prevent Caroline hearing directly from Yasmin the crushing news that Yasmin was Ricky's bit on the side until forty-eight hours ago.

On reflection, he should have waited until after The Lamb closed down before he dumped Yasmin. But then again, he felt an urgent need to act, given how he seemed to be losing Caroline so suddenly and so rapidly. Panic was taking a hold, he realises. And it still has a hold on him, despite these recent efforts.

The phone in his pocket begins ringing, and so Ricky casts his wife an apologetic shrug while stepping away to let her push Jack's swing while he takes the call. He stands and smokes while listening to the caller. It turns out that he's required at a meeting this afternoon, and he reflects, with some irony, that he'll have to leave Caroline to look after Jack while he attends to what, on this occasion, really is a business issue. It's not the everyday business of staffing and recruitment, however – he'd have told the caller to stuff it had the call been about such mundane matters. No, this is a piece of business which may mean that tonight's big party won't, after all, herald the end of life at The Lamb and Musket. But time is short if he's going to make something happen. And making something happen has become important to him – he sees it as part of his reinventing himself. Part of his coming back to Caroline.

Ricky stamps out his cigarette, puts his phone away, and hurries to make the necessary excuses to his sceptical-looking wife.

+++++

Having pushed his drive into the thick stuff on the right, Patrick plays a good second shot, hitting a crisp wedge from the long grass – one which clears some bushes and easily finds the fairway. Having recovered well, however, he then makes a hash of his approach to the green, catching an eight-iron thin, so that his ball scuttles across the putting surface and finishes through the back. He chips back on and takes two putts, recording six shots on a hole where he'd expect to need only four when on form, or five on days when things aren't going quite so well.

His playing partners this morning are the Maxwell brothers, with whom he isn't paired often, but who know his game well enough to realise he's playing short of his abilities. They commiserate awkwardly with Patrick over his six, and the elder Maxwell says he's sure Patrick will do better on the next hole.

But as they walk from green to tee, Patrick finds himself at odds with that view. The six he just carded was pretty representative of his form over the eight holes played so far, and he has no great hopes for the ninth.

Patrick's heart isn't in this. He has too many distractions to be playing good golf. There are too many things bothering him.

Bothering him more than anything else is the state of his relationship with Caroline. Or maybe, he fears, his *former* relationship with Caroline. Since Ricky dumped Yasmin on Thursday evening – telling her, according to Mel at least, that he was getting back with his wife – Patrick has found Caroline to be evasive. Her answers to his texts have been short, summary, and lacking in depth.

Can't talk right now.

Ricky's here. Awkward.

Get back to you. (Without, so far, getting back to him).

Faced with a choice between he (Patrick) and a version of Ricky who's mended his ways, Patrick doesn't know who Caroline would choose. And nor is he confident that Caroline herself knows. Nor, even, does he know who he would want her to choose. Sure, he's crazy about the woman, but she happens to be wife to Ricky and mother to Jack.

This, Patrick is sure of: he and Caroline would not have got together if Ricky had remained faithful to her. And if Ricky wants her back, and if Ricky – damn the fucker! – is going to make amends, shouldn't Patrick do the right thing and stand aside?

Yes, he should. But he doesn't frickin well want to.

Small wonder he can't hit a drive down the middle, or strike an approach shot cleanly.

Patrick selects a three-wood for his tee shot on the ninth. Having greater loft than his driver, the club is more forgiving of an off-centre strike, and allows him a better chance of finding the fairway, albeit at a cost of some distance off the tee. After struggling to get really comfortable at address, he does manage a straighter shot than before – albeit, sure enough, a shorter one – but even with a three-wood in his hand, he isn't quite straight enough, and his ball finds the first cut of rough. It's far from being a calamitous drive, however, and he imagines he'll have both a reasonable lie and a good line in for his second shot.

Shouldering his golf bag, Patrick walks after his ball. It's a measure, he supposes, of how badly he's been bitten by the Caroline bug that he's given so little thought to the other big problem in his life. That problem being the abuse, threats, and all-round hard time he's received over past day-and-a-half via text and email. The threats come via a phone number he doesn't know, and from an email account in the name of Nightmare_Bastard, but Patrick is in no doubt that such missives as 'Coming 4 U Paddy' and 'Day Of Rekkoning At Hand' have surely come from the big, big man with the snake tattoo on his neck.

He really ought to have reported matters to the police. But it isn't only because the coppers were so lank and ineffective the other night at The Beethoven Lounge that he hasn't yet done so. His Irish republican roots also weigh heavily with Patrick, the west Belfast community of his birth being generally mistrustful of the official state police force. Patrick's da has never sought recourse to the peelers, and notwithstanding the kind of clear and present danger found two nights ago in The Beethoven Lounge, nor will Patrick himself.

All of which leaves the question as to what should be done about Snake Neck and his hangers on. For now, there seems little Patrick can do other than watch his back. That in mind, he asks himself whether it's sensible for him to attend The Lamb's last night, given that one of the gang has spotted his van there in the past, making The Lamb a logical place to try tracking him down. But on the other hand, he's been drinking at The Lamb for pretty much half his life, and doesn't want to miss its farewell evening simply because some arse-wipes are out to get him.

Patrick finds his ball in just the kind of lie he expected. It's nestling down a little in the first cut of rough, and when he swings he'll get wet grass between clubface and ball, making control of the shot difficult, particularly if he takes a long enough iron to go for the green from here. But it's far from the worst lie he's ever found after missing a fairway, and he does, just as he thought, have a good line to the flag. And there's an added a bonus: he has a bit of wind in his face which will hold his ball up in the absence of any backspin.

Sure, the safe shot is a short little punch with his wedge, before trying for the green with his third. But if he was playing well, he wouldn't worry about safe shots – they wouldn't merit his consideration. He'd aim a three or four-iron at the flag. Patrick would go for it.

Despite not wanting to slow his playing partners down, Patrick takes a good thirty seconds to think about the shot. Then he reaches a decision. He decides he'll go to The Lamb tonight. He'll go early in the evening, because if any of his newly-made enemies come looking for him, he thinks they'll arrive later, for the reason that they'll expect him to be there during peak hours. Patrick will go early and he'll leave early – the other advantage of which is that the early evening is when he's most likely to see Caroline and Ricky, given that that's when they'll find it easiest to get a sitter for Jack. And Patrick does so want to see Caroline and Ricky – not necessarily for any kind of confrontation, but to see how the land is lying between the two of them, and also how it's lying between the two of them and him. He supposes it may make up his mind, and maybe Caroline's as well, about just how the future is supposed to work out.

Decision made, Patrick takes his three-iron and addresses the ball. He swings back smoothly, and connects superbly on the downswing – it's the best shot he's hit all morning. He watches, with a smile on his face, as his ball zings towards the flag, and from thirty yards away he can hear the Maxwell brothers begin their applause for a tough shot well played.

+++++

Ricky's afternoon meeting lasts a good long while – far longer than he expected beforehand. There's hostility, at the outset, from the man across the table – a man whom Ricky thought he'd won round to his way of thinking the previous afternoon, but who arrives for this meeting re-entrenched in his original position.

And so Ricky has to win him round again, which he does in the ruthless manner he's developed over the years, making sure the man realises not only that Ricky has the whip hand, but is willing to use the whip unsparingly.

Only when the man across the table realises there's no way back is he willing to discuss the way ahead. And when the three of them – Ricky, the man across the table, and the man across the table's adviser – begin to discuss the way forward, it soon becomes clear that there's a lot of detail to cover.

But they get there in the end. They reach the basis of an agreement, and when they're finally leaving the hotel suite which had been booked for the meeting, the man delays no more than a second when Ricky offers a handshake.

Ricky has an hour's drive home. Evening will be falling by the time he gets back. Indeed, his journey would normally be longer than an hour, but he canes the BMW at high speeds along motorways and A-roads which are far quieter on a Saturday afternoon than they would be during the week. He keeps his eyes peeled and his radar detector on; his mood, meanwhile, in the wake of a successful meeting, is ebullient. Twice, he allows himself something he normally forbids: the smoking of a cigarette in the car. He's always happy after striking a deal, of course, but this deal feels especially good because it isn't just about him. Or at least in one sense it isn't just about him. In another sense, he realises, the deal is totally about him, because no one else would have had the balls or the chutzpah or the pure animal cunning to do what he's just done. In self-congratulation of his achievement, he pushes the accelerator ever harder – "Faster, dad, faster," he remembers Jack calling out this morning – surging past the other cars as though the gods were pushing him forward while pulling all of them back.

Tiredness and reality hit home when he finally pulls in alongside Caroline's car on the drive. Ricky thinks back to that school-day in the early summer of 2002, when everyone came early to watch the bloody football. He recalls that from his perspective the game was most memorable for Caroline allowing him to get touchy-feely with her arse in front of everyone gathered in the assembly hall. He remembers, also, that it was just a few days later that he began bragging to some of his classmates – kids such as Vince, and their new friend, Patrick, plus a few others as well – that he and Caroline had begun having sex. Truth was they'd been doing no such thing, and in reality a few more months would go by before Caroline would consent to that particular rite of passage. Among all Ricky's memories of those times, none are more vivid than how furiously Caroline set about him when she heard of his lies, tracking him down to where he was smoking behind the science labs, and then screaming her contempt into his face – screaming it loudly enough to be heard at the far end of the sports' field.

Yet Ricky expects Caroline's anger back then will prove small potatoes alongside her reaction a couple of minutes from now, when he heads indoors and tells her about his other women.

Ricky has made up his mind that he is going to tell her, and that he's going to do so this evening. He realises he can't avoid the issue. Whatever Caroline may have found out already, Ricky has to find sufficient courage to tell her the rest, rather than leave open the risk that she'll find out anyway, of her own volition at some future point, either tonight at The Lamb, or maybe several months on from now.

He climbs from his car into the deepening chill of late afternoon. After brushing cigarette ash from his suit trousers, Ricky removes his jacket from the BMW's rear seat. Yes, he has to confess all to Caroline, and he has to do so tonight – but God, he feels tired all of a sudden. Tired, and scared of what he has to do. He's hungry, also. When did he last eat, for fuck's sake? Tired, and scared, and hungry – yet he has to do this thing.

Inside the hallway of his house, the temperature is much warmer. The radiator is on. It may or may not be on for the first time this autumn, but it's certainly the first time he's noticed.

Tired, and scared, and hungry. All that chutzpah evaporated.

Jack emerges from his den, a big, beautiful smile on his face, like the one in the photo on Ricky's phone. "We've been playing Skeleton Homestead," he yells.

Ricky draws him close, pulling Jack's head against his hip and ruffling his hair. "I'll bet your mum's been winning," he replies.

"Not always. Sometimes I won."

"Sometimes you did," says Caroline, following Jack's path from play-den to hallway. She's changed out of this morning's designer jeans, and has on some old tracksuit bottoms and a well-worn jumper. "You're definitely a clever boy."

"He gets that from his mum," says Ricky.

"And his cunning from his dad."

Ricky picks Jack up and steps closer to Caroline. But she turns her face away, and his attempted kiss lands chastely on her cheek. "Smoking in the car?" she asks, stepping aside. "The smell really clings when you do that."

"It stinks!" blurts Jack.

"I'm sorry," says Ricky, gently setting down the kid, who subsequently loses little time returning to his den. "I was pumped up after my meeting, and needed a cigarette. But I also wanted to get home quickly, so I was smoking on the move. Sorry – we can take your car tonight if mine smells. I don't mind driving."

He sees that her eyes are searching him appraisingly. "To The Lamb, I mean. I take it you still want to go?"

"Sure," she replies, but without particular enthusiasm. "Mum and Dad are happy to have Jack for a while."

Tired, and scared, and hungry. He's especially scared that Caroline's once again acting so distantly, when only this morning it seemed he was thawing some ice. She must definitely have her suspicions, Ricky tells himself. In which case, she probably thinks he's spent the afternoon playing away.

"Right then," Ricky says. "The Lamb it is. But do you think, before we go, after we've dropped off Jack, we could go somewhere else beforehand. Somewhere quiet – just the two of us."

"I should think so." Her expression grows ever more interrogative. "Mind telling me why?"

"There's something I need to tell you about. Once we're alone."

"I see."

"It doesn't have to be a big deal, this thing. We can get a takeout coffee and sit in the car awhile. I just need to talk to you privately."

By now, Caroline looks scared as well. Less scared than Ricky feels, but scared nonetheless. She stalks away, towards Jack's den, and after sticking her head round the door, presumably to make sure that her son is fully occupied, she comes back to the hallway and faces her husband. "Ricky, is there something I should be worried about?"

"God, no." He runs a hand through his hair. "Everything's good. Really good." *Just so long as you'll forgive me.*

"What, then?"

He reaches for her hand, and she doesn't resist. "I'd rather we talk properly, without the risk of getting interrupted. But Caz, it's nothing to worry about. I mostly need to talk about the future," – *if and when you have forgiven me* – "and it involves the meeting I had today, among other things."

Her eyes search his face some more. "Okay, we'll talk," she says. Then letting go his hand, she moves towards the stairs as she adds, "I need to get showered. So do you, after smoking in the car."

Momentarily, he thinks she's asking him to join her. But then she says, "You can go after me. Or use the guest bathroom, but I won't be long."

"I'll go after you," Ricky replies. "Rather than mess up the guest shower."

"Cool."

Tired, and scared. And hungry. "Is there anything to eat?" he calls after her.

"Last night's lasagne." She's halfway up the stairs by now. "Keep an eye on Jack, won't you?"

"Will do, Caz."

Ricky goes to the kitchen. Dusk is falling outside, and he flicks on the spotlights, thereby bathing the kitchen in a warm, bright glow. He throws his jacket over one of the high stools at the breakfast bar, and then digs out the lasagne from the fridge. He removes the foil cover and puts the dish in their new microwave – the one Caroline had fitted a few weeks back, after the old one packed up under warranty. Of course, he's used this microwave before, but not that many times, and because he's so tired he finds his brain fogging up, and he can't remember the correct sequence in which he's supposed to press the bloody buttons.

Absentmindedly lighting a cigarette – if he were to think about it, he'd remember that smoking indoors is a no-no – Ricky goes to the drawer where he believes the microwave's instruction manual is kept in a folder. If he remembers correctly, the manual is stored in the folder along with the warranty card and some other gubbins. He takes out the folder, spills its contents onto the work surface, and picks up the manual. But beneath it, he notices another piece of paper – one which looks out of place among all the kitchen-related stuff. He peers intently at the rogue document, and then picks it up for even closer inspection. Strictly speaking, it isn't a piece of paper. Rather, it's a piece of card.

It's a scorecard from the golf club.

Curious as to how the card made its way to where it did, Ricky draws deeply on his cigarette, and then studies the sequence of recorded scores, wondering whether by doing so he might recall the round in question. But the scores are marked in Patrick's handwriting, a curiosity even more peculiar than the card being there at all, and when Ricky turns the card over he reads something more peculiar still.

If you want to talk about anything (I mean anything at all) you have my number. We can talk in total confidence. It's okay.

Even then, Ricky's so tired that he doesn't immediately grasp the note's implications in their entirety. He reads the note twice, and then a third time, while he stands there with his cigarette burning down. *Patrick's been a shoulder to cry on for Caroline*, he thinks. *Bit bloody snarky of him – he's supposed to be my mate. And what the fuck has he told her, anyway?*

"I've just remembered –" he hears Caroline say, but then silence intervenes as she breaks off abruptly. When Ricky looks round, he sees her framed in the doorway and wearing her bathrobe. More than anything, he absorbs the look of horror on her face as she stares mortified at the scorecard, and that's when he begins to fully realise what's been going on behind his back.

Patrick has been much more to Caroline than a shoulder to cry on.

Connections begin tumbling into place. They tumble quickly, despite Ricky feeling so tired. He remembers an evening in the summer when he and Patrick met up at that bar – The Beethoven Lounge – because he, Ricky, need a serious talk, and Patrick turned up pale-faced and sweaty, claiming he had a summer cold. But it was no summer cold – Patrick was shitting his fucking self because he thought Ricky had found them out.

This has been going on since the summer, then, at least.

Another thing... setting aside Caroline's coldness, Ricky has felt there to be a different vibe about the house – something intangible which he couldn't quite define. He realises, suddenly, that he can define it, and that it's more than merely a vibe. It's a smell, just the faintest of aromas, something he picks up only occasionally. His mind once more flashes back to that evening at The Beethoven Lounge; he recalls Patrick holding him back as he confronted that bitch who'd attacked Esme, and he remembers thinking that Patrick hadn't showered because he had that coppery plumber's smell about him. The same coppery smell Ricky now knows he's detected around the house.

Not just anywhere around the house, either. He detects it most often on the stairs, now that he thinks about it.

Wide-eyed, horror-struck, still framed in the doorway, Caroline opens her mouth to speak. But no words come out, and Ricky gets in first.

"Caz?" he queries, initially. And when she still can't find any words, Ricky loses his shit.

"You bitch," he spits. "You total fucking bitch."

"Ricky, I, hang on –"

Tired and scared and hungry. And vengeful, now. Vengeful and furious.

"You filthy, disgusting, skanky little bitch."

"Ricky, keep it down. You'll upset Jack."

"Well, he'll have to fucking deal with it." Ricky throws what's left of his cigarette into the sink. "How fucking long has this been going on?"

Caroline has stepped in from the doorway, closing the door behind her so as to contain the noise in this room. By now her wide-eyed fear has given way to cold anger, and although her hands are partially hidden by the capacious arms of her robe, a closer looks reveals they have bunched into fists. Caroline, too, is losing her shit. "How long?" she hisses back. Not as long as it's been going on with you, I'm willing to fucking bet."

Ricky's mind scrambles to regain the high ground. "But here?" he rages. "With fucking Patrick?"

"So, what are you saying? If I'd gone to a cheap motel with that bloke you pay to mow the lawn, everything would have been fine?"

"Oh, fuck you, Caz." Ricky snatches up his jacket from the stool at the breakfast bar, and hurriedly throws it on.

"Where are you going?"

"To find that slimy paddy fuck-face." He pushes past her and reopens the door to the hall. "I'm going to take his eyes out and make him fucking eat them."

"Ricky, no," Caroline yells, scurrying behind.

"Then I'll bury the wanker where they'll never fucking find him."

"You can't." She's pleading now. "You mustn't."

Ricky's at the front door, with Caroline pulling at his jacket, when he hears Jack call out.

"Mum! Dad!"

Ricky takes a hand off the door latch and turns around. The kid's standing just outside his den, his eyes as wide with horror as his mum's just were when she caught Ricky reading Patrick's note.

"Jack, go back to your den," Caroline begs. "Mum and Dad are just playing a game."

But Jack doesn't move and his expression doesn't change.

"I'm just going out, son," says Ricky. "But I won't be long, and everything's going to be fine. Be a big boy, and look after your mum. She's a little bit upset."

Ricky suddenly isn't tired. Nor is he scared or hungry. He's switched on, focused, and hell-fucking-bent on revenge. He takes Caroline's bag, which is hanging on a peg near the door, and slides her car keys into his pocket, so as to stop her following him. Then he opens the front door and begins to step outside.

"No," begs Caroline, still trying to hold him back by his jacket.

But Ricky's far too strong for her. He gets hold of Caroline's wrists and pushes her backwards until she's sitting on the stairs. Her robe has worked loose around one shoulder, and he can't help feeling aroused as he stands over her. That he feels turned on by his wife after she's been with Patrick disgusts him. And his disgust only serves to make him all the angrier.

Ricky leans in close – close enough to whisper in Caroline's ear. "The last thing I want is to leather you in front of our kid, but I swear to you, Caz, that if you get up from these stairs before I'm out the door, then I'll knock you the fuck into next week."

He stands up sharply. He again reassures Jack that he'll be back soon. And he leaves Caroline sobbing quietly on the staircase as he steps outside and locks the front door.

Very soon, Ricky is smoking in his car again, even before he's reached the end of the street.

+++++

The Lamb and Musket is filling up nicely for its final night of business. It's still early evening, not fully dark, and there's a good crowd in already. But other than the place being busier than usual, this could be just another night. No one, it seems, has taken the initiative to do anything out of the ordinary. Derek has neither laid on food nor reduced the price of his beer. He hasn't pinned up any old photos of his regulars, who, for their part, haven't made any particular effort other than to turn up with their wallets open. And there doesn't appear to be anyone here from the papers, unlike on some of those nights when the campaign group met with the purpose of keeping the place open. Nights which seem like a long, long time ago.

No, there's seemingly nothing out of the ordinary. Just a big crowd of people getting through a great deal of booze, and an ancient jukebox doing brisk business on its final night of service.

On reflection, Mel prefers it that there's nothing special happening. She's happy that there's no food, no gimmicks, no posters. And no fancy dress, either, although it has to be said that Yasmin has certainly dressed to catch the eye, even by her own provocative standards. She's wearing a breathtakingly short denim dress – one which buttons up at the front, except that she's left the top three buttons undone, possibly as much out of necessity as choice, given that it looks to be at least one size too small. And she's paired the dress with some thigh-length boots in black suede, which are surely going to chafe with all the bending and lifting required to be done, given that she's brought to this shift the same improved work ethic she finally discovered on Thursday last. So far, at least, Yasmin doesn't seem to mind that the blokes all want to be served by her, and Mel certainly isn't bothered either, in that by being comparatively less busy she does get a moment or two to chat with Vince, who sits dutifully at the end of the bar, wearing his omnipresent smile.

Vince, as things turned out, certainly had more in mind than a walk home the other night, and did, once a couple of coordination issues were resolved, prove perfectly equal to the task of making good on his intentions. And so Mel not only has a new job, but also a new love interest. That Vince can be slow and childlike will no doubt test their relationship in many ways – some of which Mel's sure she's yet to even imagine – but Vince's disabilities are part-and-parcel of his attraction. And anyway, Mel has come to understand that Vince certainly has his compensating qualities – there's no doubt about that.

Sitting next to Vince is Patrick, his stool tilted customarily backwards, and his foot hooked under the rail. But although his posture is as per normal, he's unusually quiet and very much on edge, even by his withdrawn standards of recent weeks. His answers are short and snappy whenever anyone speaks to him, and Mel is concerned about how much he's drinking. He arrived very early, and has already put away several pints of Guinness and a good amount of whiskey. Combining her strong suspicion that Patrick's been carrying on with Ricky's wife, and Ricky's assertion to Yasmin that he was returning to said wife, Mel can well understand that Patrick is feeling angsty. She worries about what will happen when Ricky arrives – maybe with Caroline – and is concerned that Patrick will cause some kind of scene. She hopes his dad's here by that time, as he has a better chance than anyone of controlling an intemperate Patrick, but there's no sign of Malachy as yet. For that matter, there's no Gareth either, but of course it's still early in the evening. There's plenty of time for all the old faces and, who knows, even some new ones. Mel's definitely pleased to see Ricky's sister, Esme, here, with some of the girls whose friendship she renewed on quiz-night a couple of months back. A shame, though, that Patrick was offhand with her when she came over earlier, in order to say hello to him and Vince.

Vince signals to Mel that he's off to the gents. It's the second time this evening that he's done so, and she has to force back a giggle at the idea that having shared her bed a couple of nights back, Vince now feels it necessary to let her know when he's going to the toilet. She offers up a silent prayer of thanks that tonight is the last occasion on which she'll work behind this bar, as she isn't sure how many of his notifications she can take.

While Vince is gone, Patrick rocks his stool upright and signals to her. "Ya havin' a good time?" he asks, sounding more like someone from Belfast than he does when sober. It's a phenomenon Mel's encountered before – Patrick's accent thickening when he's either dead drunk or well on his way.

"About as good as a girl can have when she's working, Patrick. It's good to see some old faces, and say a proper goodbye."

Patrick laughs, finding something funny in either her reply or whatever he'll say next. "Even better," he retorts, "to have a proper drink. Guinness, please. And a whiskey chaser."

Mel takes his beer glass and reluctantly begins to refill it. Patrick is beginning to slur his words, and at this rate there's no way he'll last until closing time. She doesn't want to refuse him a drink on The Lamb's last night, and in fairness he isn't quite at the point where she'd do so. But he isn't far from that stage, and Mel finds herself hoping, again, that Malachy will arrive soon. Until then, she decides to drop Patrick the friendliest of hints. "Do you fancy chasing it with a coffee?" she asks. "We might run out of whiskey the way you're going."

Patrick laughs some more. "Sure, I'll just have the scotch pish when yer out of Irish."

Mel bites her lip and begins getting him a whiskey. Patrick pats Vince's temporarily vacated seat. "Don't forget," he teases, "a tomato juice for lover boy in the toilet."

Mel completes the round, takes Patrick's money, and then returns his change with a cold look which she hopes will penetrate his thick head with an understanding of her displeasure at how much of a cock he's acting. Vince isn't back yet, and it's getting even busier around the bar, and so she gives Yasmin a hand with some other customers.

"This isn't how I thought it would be," says Yasmin, as they stand alongside each other while pulling pints of lager.

"Let me guess," replies Mel. "You expected a prize draw, some look-down-Memory-Lane graphics, and then a bonfire of furniture, outside in the car park."

"Maybe not the bonfire," says Yasmin, taking money from a middle-aged man who then stares rapaciously at her legs while she goes to the till. "Maybe not even the other stuff. Maybe, just, I don't know…"

"Maybe something a little bit more than a big rowdy crowd drinking the old place dry?" Mel glances across to where Patrick has his stool rocked back again, and Vince is yet to return from the gents'. Patrick has his phone out, and is staring at it in the way that drunks sometimes do – as if trying, with very great difficulty, to focus on the screen.

"Exactly," says Yasmin. "Something more than a load of people getting off their faces. You must think I'm being really naïve."

"Maybe you are," muses Mel. "But then I was thinking exactly the same thing just a few minutes ago. I was thinking that –"

But the last part of her sentence – the words 'nothing's really happening' – dry up in her throat when she sees that, actually, something really is happening.

What's happening is that Ricky, wearing the kind of smart suit he'd normally wear on a weekday, has walked through the front door of The Lamb and Musket, and is zeroing rapidly in on Patrick, shouldering aside anyone who happens to be in his way. As he moves ever closer to Patrick, he raises his fist and gets ready to let fly.

Mel looks on in appalled yet fascinated desperation. It's as if events are happening in slow motion, and every conceivable contingency which might save Patrick from his fate is a second or two behind play. Patrick's just setting down his phone, but doing so too late to spot what's coming in sufficient time to dodge it. Vince has now returned from the toilet, but he's still a couple of yards from his seat, and that's a couple of yards too far for him to get in the way of

Ricky's haymaker. His face wears a look of horror, one which Mel later supposes must have mirrored her own.

In the end, it's Dave Isherwood, a hitherto useless, bullshit-infested drunk, who makes things not quite as bad as they might otherwise have been. Either he sees what's coming slightly before everyone else, or he simply manages to react the fastest. Either way, he throws himself at Ricky, and rugby tackles him around the waist, thereby stalling Ricky's progress just a fraction as he begins to throw his punch.

Had Ricky's momentum not been checked – had he managed to take an extra half step – he'd probably have landed a blow fit to take Patrick's head off his shoulders. Even without that missing half step, the outcome is not ineffective. Ricky's fist crunches Patrick square in the mouth, and would probably have knocked him over even had his bar stool been vertical. As things are, absorbing the impact with his seat tilted backwards, Patrick has absolutely no chance of remaining upright. Mel thinks she sees a tooth go flying as Patrick crashes heavily to the floor.

The next couple of minutes are brutal and frantic. They're bloody noisy too – noisy enough to drown out the jukebox, with seemingly everyone, Mel included, screaming and shouting. Having knocked Patrick to the floor, Ricky shakes free of Dave Isherwood's grip and begins kicking Patrick in the ribs. Vince and Dave Isherwood get in each other's way trying to stop him, before Ricky's sister, Esme, come running over from her table and shouts at him to stop. She succeeds in distracting Ricky long enough for Patrick to uncoil from a foetal position on the floor and kick out at Ricky's shin. Ricky's response is to pick up Patrick's bar stool and lift it to head height, with the clear intention of crashing it down on his one-time best mate. That's when Esme, bravely, stands over Patrick and dares Ricky to throw the stool. As he screams at her to get out of the way, Vince and Dave Isherwood jump on him, Isherwood grappling with Ricky for the stool, while Vince, with his one good arm, gets behind Ricky and wrestles him a yard or two from the fray. But Vince wrestles Ricky only into a new fray, as luck would have it. Malachy has finally arrived – along with Gareth – and upon finding Ricky being hauled away from a beaten-down Patrick, the Ulsterman reacts instinctively, leaping into the air and butting Ricky in the face. He butts him so hard that Ricky falls back with his nose burst open, taking Vince with him as he falls to the floor.

Thereafter, Malachy becomes the focal point of attention, putting the boot into Ricky while Gareth tries to hold him back and Esme screams at him to stop. In the midst of the mayhem, Patrick hauls himself to his feet, snatches up his phone, and makes hurriedly for the door. He runs drunkenly, in a line no straighter than the S-bend on any of the sinks he's ever unblocked.

Mel watches him go. Time was when he'd have been her primary concern. That honour now goes to Vince. Mel's spent the last minute or so stunned into immobility, but now she dashes from behind the bar to where Ricky is half-sitting, half-lying on the floor, with his hands over his face and blood gushing from his nose like oil from a well. A near hysterical Esme is nevertheless tending to him, while Vince is half-knelt nearby, offering himself as a shield between Malachy and Ricky, rather as Esme had between Ricky and Patrick.

Derek, who's hardly been the most dutiful of landlords in recent weeks, has at least emerged from wherever he was skulking, and has joined both Gareth and Dave Isherwood in surrounding Malachy and trying to talk him down.

Mel squats down beside Vince and lays a hand on his arm. She's concerned about how much of this he has or hasn't understood. She's worried as to how bewildered he might be. How frightened.

"Are you okay?" Mel asks.

To her great surprise, Vince responds with a laugh. "Better than… Ricky," he replies. "Or Patrick… Hurt my… elbow… is all." He lifts his weaker arm and tries to take hold of her arm, but he can't quite coordinate properly, and after he twice grasps at thin air, she takes his wrist and guides his hand for him. "You okay?" he asks Mel, once he has a grip of her sleeve.

"I'm fine."

"You should… go… check… Patrick inside."

"He'll be fine." *Outside*, she thinks. *You meant outside, Vince, not inside.* "I'm more worried about you, sweetheart."

"I'm fine… Please… check Patrick… Too much… to drink."

Esme has helped a moaning, cursing Ricky to sit up further. Yasmin appears with a roll of kitchen towel and some ice – a gesture Mel thinks is supremely magnanimous given that barely forty-eight hours have passed since Ricky walked in here and dumped her.

Meanwhile, the triumvirate of Derek, Gareth, and Dave Isherwood have calmed Malachy down to the point where he's no longer trying to get at Ricky. "Where's my son gone?" he says, looking around for Patrick.

"Go on," says Vince to Mel. "Go… and… check."

"Come on, Malachy," says Mel. "Come with me. Patrick ran outside."

She leads Mackey Senior outdoors, where darkness is descending fast. There are a small handful of smokers – notably not Bill or Ted – and a couple of people who, for curiosity's sake, must have followed Patrick to the door. But The Lamb's final-night patrons are mostly still inside. There's no sign of Patrick, and the crowd out here is sparse enough that it's impossible not to notice the four newcomers who have arrived on the scene.

Mel's new boss, Robert Hopwood, is one of them, along with Mrs Hopwood, whose name Mel forgets but whose face she remembers from quiz night a while back. They're accompanied by Harry Adkins and a tall, handsome woman who Mel supposes is Harry's wife, Amanda. All four of them look dressed more appropriately for the opera than the bloody Lamb and Musket.

It's been a surreal couple of minutes. Mel just stands there, dimly aware that her mouth is hanging open. She finds nothing at all to say.

"Hi Mel," beams Robert Hopwood. "Alison and I had such a blast last time we came. And we knew you'd be here for closing night, so we thought we'd say hello."

"Oh, right. So… you knew I'd be working?" She casts what she hopes is a subtle look of enquiry in Harry Adkins' direction.

"I mentioned to Robert you were helping out tonight," he says. "For one night only, of course, it being the big closing down event, and all hands needed on the pump – maybe quite literally, as it were."

"I see," says Mel.

"It seems pretty wild again," says Robert Hopwood.

"Um, it is, rather," she replies.

"Sounds as though someone's getting rousted in there," says the woman who's probably Amanda Adkins.

Mel isn't sure what 'rousted' means, but concurs that the woman is probably right.

While they've been talking, Malachy has made a hurried circuit of the car park, and spent some time peering both ways down the road. Now he hurries over to where everyone is standing, and interjects summarily on the conversation. He asks the four new arrivals: "Did any of you see someone come running out?"

"Tall, slim, swarthy fellow?" queries Harry Adkins. "More than somewhat arseholed, and with a bloody mouth to boot?"

"Your, son, I think," adds Robert Hopwood to Malachy, "if I remember correctly from quiz night."

"My boy Patrick, yes. Did you see where he went?"

"He jumped into our taxi," says Harry Adkins. "Scarcely before we were out of it."

"I thought he had the hounds of hell on his tail," adds the woman who's most likely Harry's wife. She looks Malachy up and down. "It appears I wasn't far wrong."

"Did he say where he was going?" asks Malachy.

"Sorry," replies Robert Hopwood, "not that we heard." Hopwood points in the direction of town. "The taxi went that way, though."

"Towards the bright lights," mulls Malachy, grimly.

Towards Caroline and Ricky's house, thinks Mel. Taking out her phone, she says to Malachy, "I'll try phoning him."

Then Yasmin comes outside. "How are we doing?" she asks, as Mel stands listening to a ring tone while willing Patrick to pick up.

"We seem to have misplaced Patrick," Mel replies. "Sorry, Malachy, he's just not answering."

"He doesn't always," grumbles Mackey Senior. "Mind you, he could have dropped his phone back there."

"I saw him pick it up. Maybe it's on silent."

"Or he just doesn't want to talk. He's like that when he gets the mood on him."

"At least we know he's in a cab," says Mel. "Not staggering around the streets somewhere."

Yasmin lets out a little shiver. Whether that's because she's come outside scantily dressed, or because Harry Adkins is eyeing her over, Mel isn't entirely sure. But if Harry feels any remorse for ogling a half-naked, staggeringly attractive young woman while in the company of his wife, he puts on a bloody good show of not giving a damn.

"Do you work here, too?" Harry asks Yasmin. "For tonight, at least?"

"For now, like you say," she replies. "Mostly, I'm a student."

"Tell me, my dear, have you considered a career in property?" Of Robert Hopwood, Harry then enquires, "Do we have any further vacancies?"

"There are worse careers," Mel says to a confused-looking Yasmin. Then she looks down and away, and concentrates hard on redialling Patrick's phone. So absurd are the circumstances, she's finding it hard to resist a fit of the giggles.

+++++

Alone at a small corner table in The Beethoven Lounge, Patrick checks his watch. It has scratches and scrapes too numerous to count, some of which he supposes may be recently acquired from earlier events at The Lamb – all that rolling around on the floor. New scratches are of no consequence, however. Cheap at the time of purchase, his watch is valueless nowadays. Not like Ricky's Breitling.

Fucking Ricky. Fucking Breitling.

It's the first time he's come to The Beethoven Lounge on a Saturday, and his friends Kris and Chris Cross are doing good business. There's a decent crowd in. All around Patrick there's the bubble and bluster of the young and affluent enjoying their night out and getting slowly oiled.

Though ancient and battered, his cheap old watch can nevertheless tell the time of day. It can tell the time of night, too. It's ten-twenty p.m, and since Patrick set off for The Lamb and Musket far earlier this evening, a good many hours have gone by. Most of them drunkenly.

Fuck – what a mess.

He checks his phone for messages, but there's nothing new since last he looked. His phone was dead busy earlier on. There were about a zillion missed calls from Caroline – calls he simply didn't hear because he was pissed and The Lamb was noisy – along with two voicemails and one text message as she tried in vain to warn him that Ricky was on his way and wanting blood. A bit later on, there were further calls and messages from both Mel and his da, in the aftermath of his fleeing from the pub. Given that the messages were mostly querying whether he was alright, he feels guilty, now, about not having answered them sooner than he did. It's just that when he was escaping The Lamb and Musket in that very convenient taxi, he had other priorities in mind.

Those other priorities were the reason why he had the taxi take him to Caroline and Ricky's house. At first Caroline was unable to even open the door, but even after finding a key was so horrified that she didn't want to let him in. Patrick was drunk and half-deranged, and if his manner wasn't enough to frighten Jack – who Caroline claimed was already traumatised by the row she'd had with Ricky – then Patrick's bloodied appearance would surely do the trick. Besides which, she imagined Ricky would be back at any minute, and who knew what might happen then?

In the end, though, Caroline relented, perhaps realising that Patrick wasn't going anywhere until he'd said his piece. She allowed him into the hallway and listened to him beg for five or maybe ten minutes, her face growing increasingly forlorn. By the end, they were both crying, albeit quietly in an effort not to disturb Jack any further. Once Patrick had no more left to say, they sat on the floor for some time, she holding him, and he just feeling empty. Caroline eventually said he'd better go, but when his next taxi arrived he realised he wasn't in the mood for home, and so he had the driver take him into town. Specifically to The Beethoven Lounge, his rationale being that although he was in such a disreputable state that many bar owners would deny him entry, Kris Cross and Chris

Cross owed him a favour, at least to his way of thinking. They'd let him in and serve him a drink, so he thought.

And they did. Sure, they glanced concernedly at each other, but they sat him down at a corner table and got him a whiskey. And then a few more, along with a coffee or two along the way, the caffeine maybe intended to stop him collapsing in a stupor. As Saturday night's revelry went on around him, Patrick texted back Mel and he texted back his da. He was fine, he told them. He was in town, having a drink, straightening a few things in his head, and thanks for their concern. Sorry he hadn't replied earlier.

With that job done, he sat there and continued to drink. He drank and seethed and stewed and despaired. Contrary to what he'd said in his text messages, he didn't spend very much time straightening his thoughts. Instead, he allowed those thoughts to gang up on him, to the point where he felt like crying again, just as he had at Caroline's. Actually, maybe he did cry again. It could even be that he still is, judging by the looks he's getting from some of the people gathered around.

Kris Cross appears, smiling sympathetically. She puts another whiskey before him, and another coffee as well. She sits down in an adjacent chair, and swaps a friendly word with the people at the next table. Confirmation that Patrick really is crying arrives when she pushes across a cluster of tissues and tells him, not unkindly, to dry his eyes.

While Patrick does as she suggests, Kris Cross informs him, still not unkindly, that these are his last drinks of the night – "I should have stopped you an hour ago" – and that she has called him a taxi.

Patrick laughs at that, except that his laughter seems to bring on even more tears. "It's like Groundhog Day," he slurs, dabbing at his eyes. "I keep ridin' taxis tonight, Kris – sure I do."

She gives his hand a squeeze. "You're welcome back anytime," she says. "And if you want to come tell us what's so wrong in your life, we're good listeners, Mr Cross and I. But not right now, Patrick my sweetheart. You need to be home – tucked up in your bed."

Patrick nods, and sips his whiskey. "Yer a good woman, Kris Cross," he says. "Sure, have I paid ya for my drinks?"

"Many times over," she laughs, getting up from his table. "Just not tonight, though."

They're the last words the two of them exchange this night, for it's Chris Cross who comes over and tell him when his cab arrives, even escorting him outside and making sure he gets in. Patrick knows that Kris Cross was right – he does need to be home, tucked up in his bed. Yet he simply doesn't feel ready for it yet. There are things to be said and sorted – if the right people are still around. And so he asks the driver to take him to The Lamb and Musket. First job, once he gets there, is to take a leak. None of that coffee has sobered him up very much, but it's left his bladder fit to burst.

+++++

There are twenty minutes until theoretical last orders, and The Lamb remains seriously busy. The crowd has thinned only a little, whereas the stocks of alcohol are very much reduced: two of the beers are now off sale, and Mel can see that there's neither Bacardi nor vodka left on the shelf. She imagines Derek will keep the place open later than usual. He hasn't mentioned doing so, nor said anything about an extended licence, but she doesn't suppose he'll be kicking everyone out exactly on time.

Mel can hardly believe it's already so late. Time has flown, even if the night has passed relatively uneventfully since the manic events of much earlier on. She doubts if Ricky would have been welcome had he chosen to stick around, but he was off home not long after Yasmin and Esme had manged to staunch the flow of blood from his nose. Malachy hung around for a short while, seething and brooding, and drinking another couple of pints, before heading off not long after Patrick texted to say he was okay. Likewise her new colleagues, Robert Hopwood, Harry Adkins and their wives, were here for a similar length of time, departing after a couple of rounds, seemingly enlivened at having roughed it for a while. Esme, Ricky's sister, who'd obviously been upset by events, surprised Mel by staying on after Ricky's departure. Esme's still here now, with her little group of friends, and Mel is pleased that Vince has gone over to talk to them, allaying some of Mel's earlier fears that Vince ran the risk of becoming too clingy.

Derek, meanwhile, rather than help Yasmin and Mel behind the bar, is sitting at a corner table with Gareth, who's just bought a round for the two of them. 'Bought' is hardly the operative word, however, given that Mel winked at Gareth and told him it was on the house, freeing him up to put a few coins in the jukebox, and so ushering in a Beatles medley. It does piss Mel off that Derek simply sits there when they're this busy, especially as she did him a favour by extending her notice period. But not to worry – this will all be over in an hour or so, by the time they've sent everyone home and got the place cleaned up.

"How're you doing, chick?" Mel asks Yasmin as the two of them converge on the alcopop fridge.

"Oh, I'm fine," Yasmin replies. "Except that I'm tired – tired and fed up with having to stoop down here in this dress while trying not to show off too much flesh."

Before Mel can reply, Yasmin adds, "I know, I know. I dressed myself, it's true. I guess there was an element of wanting to show Ricky what he was missing."

"Move on, Yasmin," warns Mel, as they both stand up to serve their respective customers. "No good will come of you chasing after him."

"Yeah," she sighs. "I know. You said."

"And I was right. Find someone else."

"Maybe not Patrick, though," says Yasmin, gesturing with her eyes. "Not when he's so bloody wasted."

Startled, Mel follows Yasmin's line of sight to where Patrick, looking haggard and insensible, has lurched into the pub and is beating a path towards the toilets – a path just as unsteady as the one he took out of here three of four hours since. Mel looks across the bar, trying to catch the attention of Derek, Vince or Gareth, or just about anyone else who's male and not totally shit-faced. Someone to go and make sure that Patrick is okay.

"Are you okay, sweetheart?" says the man in front of her. "Only I thought you were getting my beers?" Realising she's pushed her personal pause button halfway through serving a round, Mel apologises, sorts out the rest of the man's drinks, takes his money, and gives him his change. Then she looks up again, once more searching for a helpful face,

But she sees only the stuff of nightmares. Specifically, she sees the big, brutal bastard with the snake tattooed on his neck – the very same big, brutal bastard who pushed her into Hugo Albrighton's window on the morning she went job hunting. He too has entered the pub, and is also heading for the toilets. He isn't lurching or swaying, and he's flanked by two other creatures of the night, all of them dressed in black.

Watch the fuck where you're going, you festering little bitch.

Mel goes weak at the knees, and has to grab the bar edge to steady herself as her bad memories of that morning come hurtling back.

+++++

Patrick zips up his jeans and turns away from the urinal. He turns slowly and mindfully, as drunks often will, so as to keep his balance and ensure he remains upright. Then, acting on a post-piss afterthought, he stops, turns carefully back, and spits against the porcelain. His phlegm is tinged with pink. Not the vivid red of earlier this evening, but there's definitely some pinkness there – just enough to let him know that his gums are still bleeding, even if only a little.

When, finally, he gets around to washing his hands, he happens to glance at his reflection in the mirror over the sink. The mirror, which is chipped and old, and flaunts the logo of a long-defunct brewery in one lower corner, has, like most things in the pub, only an hour or so remaining of its serviceable life. Drunk and melancholic, Patrick takes a moment to study his reflection carefully and with intent, as if seeing himself properly for the first time in goodness knows how long. It's a handsome face which stares back at him, dark-eyed and a little bit swarthy – prototypically Irish. Patrick raises a hand to his swollen lip and winces slightly. His mouth will be sore in the morning, an additional discomfort to the storm-force hangover he knows is coming to him – a hangover he could no longer avert even were he to draw an immediate line under the night's drinking and go home right away. Patrick glowers at his reflection and breathes a deep, drunken sigh of regret. He's had his share of hangovers, and this is hardly the first time he's been smacked in the mouth, but tomorrow will be made more difficult by the remembrance that it's Ricky he's been fighting with.

Still moving slowly and deliberately, Patrick turns away from the sink and the mirror and the reflection of his bashed-up face. While he stands swaying at the asthmatic-sounding hand dryer, the door opens from the connecting passageway to the bar, and two more drunks come tottering in. Before the door can swing closed again, Patrick briefly absorbs the hullabaloo of several dozen conversations, a sudden torrent of casual laughter, and the playing on the jukebox of what he thinks is *Back in the USSR,* by the Beatles. Again thinking back to events of earlier this evening, Patrick heaves out another drunken sigh. The last night at The Lamb, and things had to end up like this – scrapping with his best frickin mate in the world. Meantime, that jukebox will soon fall silent for the very final time.

Of the two other men who've come into the washroom, one is bloody Dave Bickerstaff – a harmless enough loon for sure, albeit one who can drive a man to distraction with his ceaseless bullshit about the many racy cars and even racier women which he insists have adorned his life. Bickerstaff hastens into one of the two cubicles against the far wall, where he immediately begins the undignified process of throwing up the excesses of booze which he must have put away tonight. The other newcomer is basically still a kid – he's tall and skinny, without much facial hair, but sporting an egregious outbreak of acne on his chin and forehead.

Although Patrick doesn't know the kid, the kid appears to know him. "Alright, Pat?" the kid slurs, weaving his way to the urinals. Although most certainly drunk, the kid's probably less drunk than Patrick, and clearly in a better state than Dave Bickerstaff, who sounds to be throwing up so violently that Patrick wonders whether the lining of Bickerstaff's stomach will egress along with all that puke.

Patrick isn't in a sociable mood. And he objects to the excessive familiarity shown by the kid, whose casual use of use of 'Alright, Pat?' has served to wind him up far more than it ever should have done. Briefly, Patrick considers having a harsh word to set the young sprog straight – he tries out several replies in his head, each more belligerent than the last. But in the end, the only harsh word he has is with himself, and before saying anything aloud he resolves not to be quite such a pompous twat. "Sure, what's yer name, kiddo?" he finally asks by way of response.

"Darren," comes the reply, the youngster glancing over his shoulder as he stands at the porcelain. "Or Daz, if you like."

"Well, Darren, I'm alright then. And I hope yer alright too."

Patrick pivots away, puts one foot in front of the other, and aims his drunken self towards the door. He realises that in talking to the kid he still managed to sound up his own arse, but he hopes he spoke in a way which wasn't unfriendly. It seems important, right now, to avoid being unfriendly, for the simple reason that he's had enough trouble for one evening, and surely doesn't want any more. But then, as he reaches out to pull open the door, someone else begins pushing from the other side, and when Patrick takes a step back to see who's coming in, he realises, with a sinking sensation in his stomach, that he will be getting more trouble tonight, whether he happens to want it or not.

In walks the huge, shaven-headed fella who Patrick knew would come for him eventually, but whom he'd largely forgotten about during the drunken travails of the evening so far. The man is again wearing his quilted bomber jacket, with the collar worn low so as to show off the image of the snake tattooed upon his neck. Following him through the door, and then fanning out on either flank, are two of his inhospitable-looking friends. The first, Patrick thinks, is the one they call KGB – the wiry-looking bloke who, ridiculous as it sounds, is alleged to keep a knife in his shoe. The other accomplice is female. It's the same attractive but hard-faced brunette from The Beethoven Lounge, the girl believed to have beaten up Ricky's sister while she was queuing for a nightclub. In addition to a sleeveless leather jacket, the brunette has on a tiny mini-skirt and whale-net tights. Her confident manner suggests she's in no way uneasy about walking into the gents' toilet of a crowded pub while wearing very little, and she smiles almost lewdly at Patrick while her accomplice does the talking.

"My, oh my," says Snake Neck, shaking his head in mock regret and making a show of cracking his knuckles. "Looks like you've been fighting with your silly mates already. But you're in the big boys' playground now, and we hit so much harder than your friends do."

Snake Neck takes a step forward, and Patrick instinctively takes one back. The sudden imminence of danger has taken the edge off his drunkenness, and his mind feels sharp as he frantically considers his options. The hard-faced brunette and KGB have advanced either side of Snake Neck, leaving Patrick no room to try wriggling around the sides. And he also has to rule out any thoughts of locking himself in the second cubicle when the pimply kid, Darren ('or Daz, if you like'), chooses that particular sanctuary for himself. It seems, then, that there are no credible means of escape, and Patrick seriously considers shouting for help as the three hard-nuts back him further into the room. But he soon dismisses that idea too. The Lamb is packed out for its final night of trading, and it's way too noisy out there for anyone to hear some hapless dickhead hollering in the shitter.

And so, other than curling up and taking his beating, Patrick considers himself to have only one option left. He can take the fight to these three Brit bastards – yeah, that's what he can frickin well do. His uncle and the others back home would certainly approve of the idea, as would his da, for sure. And even Patrick's ma would have to agree that he was only trying to defend himself.

But if he is going to fight, then he needs to fight soon. He's been backed up to the wall by now, the old wrought-iron radiator pressing into the small of his back. He can feel the radiator's gurgling hotness even through his coat, and despite his precarious circumstances he takes a moment to reflect that the radiator will soon fall cold and silent, its working life over, just like those of the jukebox, the mirror over the sink, and all the other hardware to be found around the pub. It's a big beast, that old radiator, and Patrick knows it will be worth a few quid to whoever weighs it in at the scrapyard.

"Nowhere left to run, asshole," says Snake Neck, less nonchalantly this time, from only three paces away. "You're gonna get such a slapping you'll wish you'd stayed in the old country with the rest of your paddy filth."

Now it's the brunette's turn to make an elaborate display of cracking her knuckles. Then she examines her nails and says to Snake Neck, "Let me have first hit."

Snake Neck glances first at her, and then at KGB. He smiles cruelly, but doesn't immediately reply. In fact, for a brief couple of seconds, no one has anything further to say, neither Patrick nor anyone from among his trio of would-be assailants. The only sound to be heard is the dry retching of Dave Bickerstaff, who has emptied his stomach but seemingly can't abate the need to vomit. Patrick cocks an ear towards Bickerstaff's cubicle, and then summons the courage to take a long hard look at the three people who are here to kick his face in.

"That man being sick," says Patrick to Snake Neck. "The only reason he's so ill is he saw yer fuck-ugly face in town tonight."

Snake Neck, who possibly hadn't expected defiance, looks momentarily taken aback, his mouth falling open just enough for Patrick to imagine the big bastard's teeth clacking together from a good hard smack to the jaw.

"I mean, come on," continues Patrick, by now feeling sharp of mind as the adrenal mechanism of fight-or-flight kicks in. "Ya look hideous enough the way God made ya, but even worse with such a shite tattoo as that." Patrick gauges the distance between himself and Snake Neck, and then shuffles minutely to adjust his footing, getting onto the balls of his feet and bunching his fists. "Seriously," he adds, "just take a look at yerself, will ya? Small frickin wonder yer mates are so gruesome as well."

Now all three of them look momentarily surprised. But Patrick knows that 'momentarily' is the operative word in this instance. They will all tear into him in a minute, unless he can launch his own attack while they're still registering his unexpected insolence. It's now or never for Patrick, and he certainly doesn't want it to be never. And so, with surpluses of adrenalin and whiskey coursing their way through him,

Patrick puts a foot on the radiator and pushes off hard, launching himself forward with his fists clenched and ready to swing.

+++++

"Mel, are you okay? Mel?"

Still gripping the edge of the bar, Mel turns her head towards the originator of that enquiry. It's Yasmin, pulling a pint and looking at her with an expression of concern, if not worry. And now that Mel notices, a couple of people queueing for drinks are staring at her with similar looks on their faces. It's no wonder, really – not when she's just seen a ghost.

"Are you okay?" Yasmin asks again. "What's the matter? You look like I did the other night."

Watch the fuck where you're going, you festering little bitch.

"I'm not, no. I'm not okay, Yasmin."

Yasmin aborts the pulling of her customer's pint. She moves closer to Mel. "What is it?" she asks, laying a hand on Mel's arm. "Is it Patrick?"

Maybe it's the touch of Yasmin's hand on her arm, or maybe it's the younger woman mentioning Patrick's name. Either way, Mel is suddenly galvanised into action. She takes Yasmin by both hands and speaks to her urgently. "Look, sorry, I know we're busy, chick, but hold the fort, will you? There's something I need to deal with."

Without waiting for a reply, she ducks under the hatch, and heads across the room to the corner table where Derek and Gareth are talking. Derek appears to be telling Gareth about his next pub. "I'll shake it up a bit," he's saying. "Get some guest beers in."

"You've got some guests in here," says Mel. "Unwelcome guests."

Derek, despite his various faults, is rarely unmindful of security issues. And he's known Mel long enough to take her seriously regarding such matters. He sits up now, straight and alert, brushing back his thinning hair with one hand. "Who and where?" he asks.

"There's this guy," replies Mel. "He's big and violent – really bad news. It doesn't matter how I know – he just is. And he's just gone in the gents with two of his mates."

"Drugs?"

"Don't know. I just know about the violence." Without thinking about it, Mel finds herself feeling the side of her head, where the bump she sustained that summer morning has long since gone down.

"Well, we'll give them one minute to come out," says Derek, "then, I'll go take a look."

"We might not have that long. Patrick's also gone in there, and I've got a feeling they're after him."

"Patrick?" says Derek.

"Patrick?" echoes Gareth.

"Patrick," she replies. "He just staggered in and made straight for the toilets. They came in seconds later, heading exactly the same way."

"Fuck's sake," groans Derek.

"Hell's bells," says Gareth, rubbing his moustache between finger and thumb. "He should've stayed away after everything that happened earlier."

"Look," says Mel, exasperated that neither of them have got up off their arses, "never mind what he should have done. He's here; he's in trouble."

Mel feels a hand on her arm. Not Yasmin's this time. It's Vince who has taken a gentle hold of her. "What's wrong?" he asks. He's backed up by Esme; both are looking concerned.

Mel feels she scarcely has time left over to explain, never mind wait while Vince comprehends. "Patrick," she says simply. "I have to help him."

She turns away from them all, and begins hurrying towards the toilets. One of the customers who'd been queueing at the bar, a loud, boorish man whose name she forgets, manages to step across her path. "Come on, woman," he says, "are you serving us beer or chewing a brick?"

"Fuck off, you turd," she replies, nimbly sidestepping the bloke, just about resisting the urge to knee him hard in the balls.

But she feels a hand on her shoulder before she gets very much further. "Not so fast," says Derek. "I'll go first. And if I'm not out in two minutes, call the cops, would you?"

+++++

Clatter-clatter-clatter.

Clatter-clatter-clatter.

The cause of the clatter is the old radiator reverberating against its mountings after Patrick used it as a launch pad to commence his attack. The noise seems to fill his ears during the single second which passes between his take-off and landing.

Clatter-clatter-clatter. The sound seems to last an age – far longer than the leap which precipitated it. Patrick can still hear the radiator clattering away as he lands on one foot and pitches forward again, channelling everything he's got into a fast, furious, full-blooded punch.

A punch which meets its target hard and square on.

Namely the chin of the fit-looking but loathsome bird who, seconds earlier, had said, "Let me have first hit." The clatter-clatter-clatter of the radiator is finally drowned out by the crunch of fist against jaw – bone against bone – and then the woman's eyes turn vacant as she crashes backwards to the floor. Patrick's momentum carries him forward, and he ends up standing over her.

Which means he's now on the right side of his remaining adversaries to make good his escape. The door to the corridor beckons.

Yet Patrick doesn't immediately rush towards it.

Possibly because he's still pissed as a fart, or possibly because one of the few things more despicable than hitting a woman is hitting a woman and then running away, Patrick turns to face Snake Neck and KGB.

For a moment, no one speaks. It's as if they're all too stunned by what just happened. The only sounds are the much diminished clattering of the radiator, which has returned nearly to rest, and the low retching of Dave Isherwood in his cubicle.

Then Snake Neck says, "The fuck? You just fucking hit her?"

As if in confirmation, the woman begins moaning on the floor.

"So what?" says Patrick. "The bitch was owed."

"Well now it's your turn, you snivelling paddy cunt."

His face contorted, Snake Neck takes a step towards Patrick. But one step is all Snake Neck gets to take, because he's soon compelled to turn, in surprise, towards the dual sounds of a cubicle door opening and of footsteps rushing his way. Given that Snake

Neck is standing between him and the cubicle in question, Patrick's view of what happens next is partially obscured, but he does see the young kid, Darren, dashing out from the cubicle, with something flat and white held high above his head.

Patrick has just enough time to register that the flat, white thing is actually the lid from the toilet cistern – a lid made of porcelain, and therefore heavy – before Darren swings it down towards Snake Neck's head. Although the huge man raises a hand in defence, and tries to duck away from the blow, the lid nevertheless catches him a solid blow to the face, and he too crashes to the floor – landing partially and comically on top of the punky woman – with blood pouring from his nose in the same copious manner as blood poured from Ricky's nose earlier in the evening. Scarcely has Snake Neck gone down before a mixed group of people burst through the door. Patrick's instinctive reaction is to fear that more of the enemy have arrived, but then he sees that Derek's at the head of the line. Behind him are Mel, Vince, Gareth and Esme. And behind them, there appear to be others waiting in the corridor. With the door open, Patrick can once again hear the jukebox playing in the bar. Dimly, he registers that The Beatles are now singing *Help*.

Meanwhile, the man they call KGB has backed up to where Patrick had previously been standing against the radiator. He has his hands raised in surrender. If he does have a knife in his shoe, he looks ill-inclined to make a move for it.

Shrugging apologetically at an incredulous looking Derek, Patrick says, "Bit of a turn for yer last night, eh?" To the kid, Darren, who's still holding the cistern lid, he adds, "Sure, that was nice of ya. Thanks very much, by the way."

Then the toilet flushes in the other cubicle, and the door opens to reveal Dave Isherwood, pale and pasty and with vomit dripping from his chin. Everyone who's just burst in laughs at him as he stands and blinks at them, as if he's awakening from a dream.

"Bless ya, David," says Patrick, leaning heavily on the sink because he suddenly feels as though he may pass out. "Sure, this could've been yer best story ever, if only ya'd had yer head out the pan to see events unfold. Not sure ya'd have got laid this time, though."

3.3) Closure, Plus 3 Days

Ricky gets out of his BMW in the car park of The Lamb and Musket. It's a grey, gloomy Tuesday afternoon, not one week on from Saturday's closing night, and already The Lamb has a derelict feel to it. The cheap outside tables, which clearly weren't taken indoors or otherwise disposed of, have been pushed onto their sides and dragged haphazardly into one corner of the car park, like cadavers hauled from the scene of battle. Someone – maybe the same someone who displaced the tables – has sprayed graffiti onto the peeling paintwork of the barred double door. Meanwhile, a decrepit, door-less washing machine has been fly-tipped into a different corner, along with two sacks of rubbish and what may be a roll of linoleum. It would be easy, Ricky knows, to blame the toe rags from the flats and the council housing, but there are toe rags aplenty on the property owning side of the main thoroughfare. Patrick Mackey is certainly a toe-rag. Patrick Mackey – the fucking, fucking bastard.

Ricky lights a cigarette, and grimaces at his reflection in the darkened window of his car's rear door. Yes, he'll learn to live with – and maybe even come to like – the crooked asymmetry of his recently broken nose, but the black eyes do him no favours at all, and the sooner they heal up the better he'll feel. It will probably take a week, so the doctor says, before he's back to looking normal, and in the meantime he should apply plenty of ice to his nose, and try to avoid activities considered strenuous.

Fuck's sake – the living of Ricky's life is an activity considered strenuous.

He isn't sure why he has come here – not entirely sure, anyway. Yes, The Lamb is not far from where Vince and his mum live, and Ricky is early for a meet-up he's arranged with Vince in order to apologise for his behaviour on closing night. And so in that sense The Lamb is a perfectly reasonable place to come and kill five minutes with a smoke and a think about old times.

But Ricky has never been one for nostalgia, except, perhaps, as a means to an end – the buttering up, perhaps, via a few hoary war stories of someone from whom he wants a favour. But there's no buttering up to be done today, and no favours to be asked of anyone, because Ricky's pretty much on his own at the moment. Caroline has fled to her parents' house – taking Jack with her – from where she currently refuses to see him. In turn, Ricky has ostracised Patrick. That leaves Vince, who he's off to see now, so that he can set matters straight after unwittingly involving his longest-standing mate in Saturday night's unseemly round of aggro.

Ricky inhales quickly, and then exhales slowly, a big lungful of smoke. Saturday was three days ago, and three days seems too long a passage of time to let slide when required to make good with a badly-wronged friend. And therein lays an important point about pubs like The Lamb. Previously, if Ricky had inconvenienced Vince – and it certainly is inconvenient to be knocked to the floor while breaking up a fight among more able-bodied people – Ricky would have caught up with him the next day. He'd have done so at the pub. He'd have bought him a pint, or more likely a tomato juice, and been sure to clear the air.

Only there's no longer a pub at which to catch up. There isn't a neutral, companionable territory – the kind of place where a bloke can call by and expect the friend in question to be around, or leave word for that friend if they're not. Instead, Ricky finds himself brokering catch-ups at people's houses – doing so by phone and by text.

And yet, looking to the future, it doesn't always have to be this way.

That's because Ricky has it in his gift to change the situation. He could have The Lamb reopened in a couple of weeks, give or take a few days. By dumb luck, a half-chance to do so began to emerge on the evening that he and Vince collected Gareth from the police station, in the aftermath of the silly mug's arrest. Ricky's been probing at that half-chance in recent days and weeks, eventually turning it into a full-blown opportunity – an opportunity resulting in the agreement he reached on Saturday afternoon just gone.

But then he came home and learnt that one of his two best mates had been shagging his one best wife – a discovery which overshadowed and soured any plans he had for The Lamb and Musket, not least because said plans involved both Caroline and Patrick.

Ricky crushes his cigarette underfoot, and climbs back behind the wheel of his car. Patrick Mackey – the fucking, fucking bastard.

A bastard who Ricky will nevertheless have to talk to in the near future. Setting aside any ideas about reopening The Lamb, there's the matter of their jointly held bank account containing the funds amassed for Vince's future benefit. How will they administer that when they're no longer good buddies with each other?

The houses in the street where Vince lives have either very small driveways or no driveway at all, and so the road is clogged with parked cars, even on a weekday afternoon. Ricky squeezes the BMW into a tight space, gets out, and walks up Vince's front path. Vince's mum's tiny hatchback is missing from the short, gravelled driveway, and Ricky supposes she'll be out at work. But any ideas he has that he and Vince will be alone in the house duly evaporate when the door is opened by Mel, the barmaid from The Lamb. Ricky is nonplussed that she's here, and instantly feels embarrassed, both by his panda-eyed appearance and for the trouble he caused her, among many others, on Saturday night just gone. Momentarily, and unusually, he's at a loss for words, but Mel seems keen to put him at his ease. "Come on in," she says brightly, showing him the same welcoming smile he's seen in The Lamb over the years.

"Thanks," he says, stepping past her, into the narrow hallway. "Surprised to see you here, Mel."

"I'm sure Vince will explain," she says, sounding determinedly upbeat. If Ricky offended Mel by querying her presence here, it doesn't show in her tone. "Go on through. They're in the kitchen."

Ricky had been looking at the hallway's faded, flowery wallpaper, remembering that he and Patrick told Vince's mum – many months ago – that they'd redecorate for her. That the two of them have failed to deliver on that particular promise is something else to feel guilty about – guilty enough that he doesn't query who or what Mel means when she says "*They're* in the kitchen."

It's when he walks through from the hallway that he realises what she meant.

Vince is, as expected, sitting at the small pinewood table. But next to him is Patrick Mackey. Patrick Mackey – the fucking, fucking bastard.

Vince gives Ricky a frank look. "Alright?" he says, and motions with his good hand for Ricky to sit down.

Patrick, on the other hand, looks much more tentative. Just as he fucking ought.

"No way," says Ricky.

"Ricky," says Patrick, spreading his arms in supplication, "we're going to have to talk."

"Not a fucking chance," replies Ricky, turning tail, brushing past Mel, and marching back through the hall. Yes, he and Patrick will eventually have to talk, as Ricky admitted to himself only five minutes since. But just at the moment, Ricky can't stand sharing Planet Earth with the fucker, never mind Vince's mum's kitchen. Especially since Patrick's facial bruising looks nowhere near as bad as his own.

"Ricky, please," says Mel, after he has swept past her.

"Not your business," he replies.

Ricky opens the front door. He hears the scrape of a chair being drawn back in the kitchen. "Ricky!" he hears Vince yell. Vince doesn't normally do yelling – it seems to require too big an effort on his part.

"Bollocks!" Ricky calls back, stepping outside and closing the front door behind him. He closes it firmly, but he thinks not so firmly that an impartial person would call it a slam. Under the circumstances, it seems to him that he's showing considerable restraint.

But restraint notwithstanding, he's actually fucking furious, and it doesn't calm his temper that he has to reverse twice and drive forwards three times in order to prise the BMW out of the tight space into which he squeezed it. While he's halfway through the manoeuvre, his phone starts ringing, and 'Vince' flashes up on the in-car display.

He does answer, but only after he's escaped from the parking space, has lit a smoke, and is driving away faster than he normally would in a built-up residential area. "Just fuck off," he shouts in the general direction of the microphone, hanging up again before any of them have chance to reply.

3.4) Closure, Plus 5 Days

"Not your business."

That's what he said to her. That's what Ricky said to Mel when she asked him not to walk out on Vince and Patrick.

And he was right, Mel thinks. This isn't her business. This is the business of Patrick, Ricky, and Ricky's wife, Caroline – the three people comprising this rancorous love triangle. Arguably, it's Vince's business too, in that he's been close friends with the three of them for half their lives or longer. Yes, Vince has a legitimate role, so it would appear, as a mediator and an arbitrator – a healer of wounds.

But Mel feels awkward about being made a part of it all. She didn't go to school with these people. She isn't even from the same part of town. Mel's only known Ricky, Patrick and Vince since she started serving at their regular pub, less than six years ago. As to Ricky's wife, Caroline, Mel doubts that the woman has been to The Lamb on more than fifty occasions in all of that time. Although Caroline seems pleasant enough, what Mel knows about her she knows second-hand, from listening to the boys talking at the bar.

And yet Vince wants Mel here at these meetings – the short-lived one with Ricky on Tuesday, and now, two days later, at an imminent face-to-face with Caroline. The venue is the same: Vince's mum's kitchen, where in the absence of a time display on the oven, a large, pine-framed wall clock – with a pendulum, no less – ticks away the seconds to Caroline's arrival.

Mel casts a glance at Vince. Asks him if he's okay. He says he is, and manages a tight little smile. But there's strain showing on his face this afternoon, the kind of strain she hasn't seen there before. His friends are his world, Mel recognises, and right now he's doing what he can to keep his world together, while worrying that it won't prove enough.

Mel reaches across and squeezes Vince's hand. "Things are going to be fine," she says, determined that things are, indeed, going to be fine, even if Vince can't keep his world together. She'll help him build a new one if needs be.

The doorbell rings – bang on time. Vince looks out, through the hallway, towards the sound of the bell. Then he casts a skittish glance at Mel. He's clearly more nervous about meeting Caroline than he ever was about Ricky. "It's okay," Mel says, squeezing his hand again while getting to her feet. "I'll let her in for you."

Mel goes to the hallway and opens the front door. Their visitor stands there, her hands thrust deep into the pockets of a long leather coat. Mel hadn't been sure whether Caroline would appear nervous, just as Vince does, or whether she'd stand there all angry and defiant. But what Mel certainly hadn't banked upon was Caroline's blue eyes sparkling with quite so much mischief. It's almost as if she's arrived accompanied by the invisible man, and he just quipped something funny in the seconds before Mel answered the door.

"Hi there," says Caroline brightly.

"Hi," says Mel, stepping aside to let Caroline through, mentally discarding the battery of small-talk she'd rehearsed in order to coax Caroline indoors, should any coaxing have proved necessary. *Come on in. Vince is through the back. I'm Mel from the pub, as you may possibly remember. Hope you don't mind my being here. Say so if you do.*

"Well done on your new job," says Caroline, with no let-up in enthusiasm. "Bet you're glad to be out of that pub. Vince in the kitchen, is he?"

"Thanks, I am. And yes, he is. Please go on through."

This is Patrick's doing, Mel tells herself as she follows Caroline towards the kitchen. *Patrick told Caroline about me and Vince. She knew to expect me here.*

Caroline breezes into the kitchen, Mel one pace behind. Vince's face lights up when he sees the sparkle in his visitor's eyes, and Mel finds herself feeling ever so slightly jealous. They're all suckers for Caroline – Ricky, Vince and Patrick. Mel knows that the guys all adore her, and supposes that in her different ways, Caroline adores them all back. Come to think of it, some ways not so different to others.

Vince starts to get up, but Caroline bustles forward and wraps him in a big hug before he's halfway out of his seat. "My sweet," she says. "I'm sorry. I'm so, so sorry about everything that's happened." She keeps hold of Vince for an age, and then, when she does let him go, she slides cosily into the chair immediately alongside.

It makes Mel smile to see that Vince is blushing. Better bashful, she thinks, than downright nervous. He offers Mel an embarrassed, almost apologetic look. Then he turns to face Caroline. "Not your fault," he has two attempts at saying.

"Not all of it," Caroline replies softly. "But some of it certainly is my fault. Quite a lot, actually." She appears to catch herself holding one of Vince's hands tightly in her own, and she also throws Mel an awkward, guilty glance, but without actually letting go.

Mel is filling the kettle at the sink. She shrugs at Caroline as if to say everything's cool, and asks her if she'd like coffee. Caroline says she would, please, and while Mel busies herself making drinks, Vince explains to Caroline that he has a girlfriend these days. "I've heard, my sweet," Caroline replies. "It was high time you found yourself a nice girl, and I hope Mel doesn't feel patronised when I say you've found a really nice one."

Mel has her back to them. She's spooning coffee into mugs. "Thanks," she says, "I'm blushing, but not patronised."

She is, however, impatient, and would like one or the other of Vince and Caroline to cut to the chase. These peace meeting are all very well, but this is the second time in a week that Mel has had to scrounge time away from the office. Bloody good job her sales numbers are still riding high. She puts the coffee jar away, and gets milk from the fridge.

As if on cue, Vince begins getting to the point. "I was… looking… forward to… going out," he says to Caroline. "You know… four of us… You, me, Mel… Ricky."

"With Patrick sitting Jack for us, maybe," replies Caroline, exaggeratedly brightly, as if to point up the improbability of the situation. Then, no doubt realising her response to be unkind, she bites her lip in contrition, and gives her head the tiniest of shakes.

"Now listen, Vince", Caroline goes on to say, still holding his hand. "I appreciate you and Ricky will always be mates, and I want you to know that I'll never try to split you up. And I'll always be your mate, too. I'll always be a friend for you, Vince, my sweet." Caroline comes to a halt, and swallows hard. He voice breaks a little when she adds, "I'll always be here for you, and we can go out for beers. But I can't promise you that Ricky and I will be a couple anymore."

For a moment, there's silence in the poky little kitchen – a silence broken only by the ticking of the wall clock and by Mel setting down their coffees on the table. Pulling out a chair, she sits down and crosses one leg over the other. But she doesn't pull the chair in again, because she doesn't want to get too close. This is one of those moments when she's conscious of the history that the others share but from which she's excluded.

Not your business.

Vince looks close to tears. And, clearly, he's finding it harder than ever to get his words out. "Caz…you have… you… have… to try."

Caroline tightens her grip on his hand. "Don't get upset," she says, her own voice not very much more than a whisper. "I'm not saying we definitely won't be a couple; I'm saying I can't promise that we will – not right now. It's just too soon to say that, Vince."

Which is, Mel supposes, as good a response as Vince is going to get – at least for today. Vince has questions to which Caroline simply doesn't yet have the answers.

"But you… have to… talk," Vince is saying to Caroline. "You can't… just… shut… Ricky out."

Not your business.

All at once, Mel feels especially uncomfortable about sitting here. Vince, so it seems to her, is pushing his luck, and though she hates herself for thinking this thought, she wonders whether Caroline would be so indulgent of his questions if it weren't for his disabilities. Mel uncrosses her legs, and with both feet planted firmly on the floor is about to make her excuses and get up from the table.

But then Caroline says, "Please don't go."

Mel draws breath. "Alright," she says, pulling her chair closer to the table, and taking a first sip of coffee. "I'll hang around, if you insist."

"Thanks," says Caroline, by now sounding simply weary. "I'm in no position to insist, but I am really grateful." She lets go of Vince's hand, pats his arm as if to say she intends no withdrawal of affection, and then leans back a little, so as to better address them both. "Ricky's been unkind to me," she says, after composing her thoughts, "and I've been unkind to him. I don't think I'm telling either of you anything you don't know, but I do think it's a situation we can recover from, assuming we're both willing. And we should both be willing. We've got Jack in common, and many happy years behind us."

Caroline pauses, looking at Vince to see if he's following. After a few seconds he begins nodding, as if in encouragement. "Go on," says Mel, sipping at her coffee and sensing that there's more to come.

"But on Saturday night," says Caroline, "when he found out I'd cheated on him as he'd cheated on me, he was catastrophically angry. Hurtfully angry, spitefully angry. Venomously, and frighteningly… yes, frighteningly angry." She pauses then. Lets her words sink in. "That's why I'm questioning whether we really can get back together."

Vince listens to that last part, and then sits there with his brow furrowed, maybe replaying Caroline's words in his mind, as if to make sure he has it all right. He looks to be struggling to deal with it all.

Then Caroline asks, "What do you think, Mel?"

Mel takes her time answering. She understands that it can be good to have a viewpoint from someone who isn't directly involved, but Mel also feels that she simply doesn't know enough to speak with very much authority. Finally, she asks, "When you say 'frighteningly', do you mean he threatened you physically?"

Caroline clears her throat. She answers Mel's question indirectly. "Ricky's dad has spent his life in and out of prison," she says. "He has convictions for petty assault. And Ricky has a dark side as well – there's no doubting that – but I've never felt personally scared of him until last Saturday. That's when things were said. Heat of the moment stuff, I know, but still they were said. And they made me wonder – that's all I'm saying."

"Is that why you've moved out?" asks Mel. When Caroline doesn't immediately reply, she adds, "Sorry to be so direct, but you did want me here."

"I did – that's true. And well, alright, let's say it was part of the reason."

"Ricky wouldn't… hit you," says Vince. "He always… says… he won't… end up… like… his dad."

"But can you be sure about that?" asks Mel, deciding she may as well give free rein to her opinions. "Let's not forget that Patrick, of all the bloody people, knocked a woman out last Saturday night. I know the circumstances were different, but it just goes to show. You can't be sure how someone will react when you put them under stress."

"But you're right to say the circumstances were different," replies Caroline. "The girl was there to do him over. And she'd already beaten up Esme. The little bitch had it coming."

"I suppose."

"And anyway, it'll teach her not to hang around in gents' toilets."

The two women share a small laugh, and then Vince says, "Ricky... couldn't... hit her."

"Couldn't hit who, my sweet?" asks Caroline. "Who're we talking about now?"

"The woman that... Patrick hit." There follows a pause while Vince marshals his thoughts. "Ricky... and Patrick... saw her. Weeks ago... in the... Beet-hoven Lounge. Ricky was... really angry... but could not... ... ... make him... self... hit her."

"I didn't know that," replies Caroline, looking and sounding surprised. "Ricky always said he'd get even with the woman."

"I didn't know, either," adds Mel.

"Patrick... told me," says Vince. "Ricky... could not... hit her."

A brief silence falls around the table; everyone, so it seems, has their thinking caps on. Mel wonders whether Ricky could ever act violently towards Caroline, given that he couldn't hit the woman who'd beaten up his own sister. Then again, if you're married to someone, and they sleep with your best mate...

"Look, Caroline" Mel says eventually. "I don't whether you and Ricky have a future or not, but Vince is right – you will have to talk to him. In fact, it's the only way you'll get to find out."

"Yeah, you're right," Caroline sighs. "I'll have to – I know."

"You will. You'll have to talk to Ricky, and so you may as well make a start. But I don't want to sit here and tell you to do this, and then read about your murder next week. Don't look at me like that, you two – go and check out how many women do get killed by their partners. So look, yes you should meet him, but you should do so in a public place. You should have some kind of chaperone, too. I'd do that for you, if that's what you wanted."

"You would?"

"As I say, if that is what you wanted, then yes, of course." Mel casts a glance at Vince to make sure he has no objection. "I don't really know you, Caroline, but I'll do what I can to help."

Mel can see that Vince has a bit of hope back in his lovely big face. And Caroline looks relieved, as if she's made some kind of decision.

"Alright," says Caroline. "I will talk to him. And you're right – I'll do it somewhere public. Can I please get back to you about the chaperone idea?"

"No problem," replies Mel.

"Tell Ricky" Vince says suddenly says to Caroline, "if he… ever… raises… a hand… to you… I will… chop his… fucking balls off."

Just as on Saturday at The Lamb, Mel finds herself wanting to giggle in highly inappropriate circumstances. But Caroline herself is beginning to laugh, and her doing so makes Mel's amusement okay.

"I mean it," says Vince, with sudden clarity, and no little anger. "Clean fucking off."

The more vehement he sounds, the funnier Mel finds it. She reaches for Caroline's arm and laughs along with her. If Vince has ever previously sworn during the few years she's known him, Mel certainly can't remember the occasion.

3.5) Closure, Plus 7 Days

It's a wet and windy Saturday, and Patrick gets drenched during five hours of golf. The skies do begin to clear, however, while he walks the sixteenth fairway, and the sun is trying to shine as he leaves the eighteenth green.

He doesn't hang around after his game, not stopping for even a very quick pint at the clubhouse bar. Instead, after the briefest of chats with his da, he drives home and parks up outside his house. Then, before opening the driver's door, he takes a careful look around the street, at what's happening beyond the Audi's windows. He remains wary of reprisals from Snake Neck and his gang, although he's heard nothing from them since last Saturday's showdown in the inelegant setting of The Lamb and Musket's toilets. Maybe the gang will offer no more trouble. But for now at least, Patrick needs to watch his back.

Happy that the coast is clear, he gets his golf bag from the Audi's boot, and once indoors he leaves it to dry by the kitchen radiator. He flicks on the kettle, and considers showering before Ricky arrives, but decides against it as time will be tight if Ricky proves to be punctual. He makes himself a coffee, and sits down with it at the kitchen table, still in his damp golf clothes, and with the radio switched on. Phil Lynott is singing the attack mantra from *Yellow Pearl*, causing Patrick to give a little shiver as he remembers the ferocity with which Ricky attacked him a week ago this evening. That in mind, he heads into his utility room, where he takes down a claw hammer and hefts it in his hands. He taps the head of the hammer into the palm of his left hand, imagining its impact against a human skull if propelled with the force equivalent to, say, a golf swing. Patrick lets out an even bigger shiver than the one he gave while unarmed, and after hanging the hammer back up he returns to the kitchen empty handed. Ricky's terse text of yesterday – the one which presaged this meeting – simply stated: 'Okay, we need to talk.' Patrick will just have to hope that talking is all Ricky has in mind.

After sitting back down, Patrick finishes his coffee. As he's getting up to make another one, there's a knock at the door. He refills the kettle, sets it to boil, and then switches off the radio. Conscious that the next few minutes may comprise a key moment in his life, he goes to answer the door, on the way making a mental comparison between his claw hammer and a kettle full of boiling water as effective weapons against unwanted intruders. Then he catches himself on – he tells himself to stop it with these eejit thoughts. When he's finished with the self-talk, he takes a deep breath and opens the door.

Patrick supposes that some part of him – the naïve part no doubt, the one clutching a tourists' guide to The Land of Wishful Thinking – had been hoping, or even expecting, that Ricky would bring a peace offering with him. Maybe a bottle of whiskey. Irish, of course.

And in the absence of any such gift, a nice consolation prize would have been for Ricky to stand on the doorstep with a little half-smile playing on his lips – a little half-smile dipped in irony. A little half-smile proclaiming: 'Well, old mate, this is a fine fucking pickle, isn't it?'

But there's no gift of whiskey, and there's no little half smile, dipped in irony or otherwise. Ricky's wearing an overcoat suited to a funeral director, and has the look on his face of a man who's here to hold his nose with one hand while unblocking a drain with another – and God help anyone who tries to stop him.

Fuck's sake, Patrick. You shagged the man's wife. Repeatedly so, over the course of two months, thereby betraying nearly two decade's worth of friendship which began when Ricky saved your ass in a fight at school. And you thought he'd bring fucking whiskey?

"Sure," says Patrick, trying to mirror Ricky's solemnity. "Come on in." He leads Ricky through to the back for the latest of several meetings to have taken place over recent days, each meeting having featured two or more participants from a cast list numbering him, Ricky, Vince, Caroline and Mel. This meeting, though, is to be the first at which he and Ricky will finally sit down together. "I'm making coffee," Patrick says. "Would you like one?" He nearly says, 'Would you like one, *mate*?' but that last word is stillborn in his throat.

Ricky takes a second to think about it. "Alright, "he says, easing into a chair at the table. "Why not?"

"Coming right up."

Nothing more is said for a further thirty seconds – thirty seconds which feel like thirty minutes. Then Ricky thaws the atmosphere minutely while Patrick is opening the milk. "Did you win today?" he asks.

"You know how good I am in the rain." Patrick leaves the milk on a countertop while fishes for the two twenties he took from his playing partners. He places the money on the table, and then resumes making coffee. "It's hardly my biggest win ever, but I'll get it paid into Vince's account."

"Nice one," says Ricky, a thimbleful of acid in his tone, "but I didn't mean it like that."

"I know you didn't," says Patrick, softly and with exaggerated patience. He brings the coffees to the table, sets them down, and then pulls out a chair. But because a thought pops into his head before he can take a seat, he heads off to the utility room, where he empties out a miscellany of washers from an old sweet tin, before bringing the tin back to the kitchen. After opening a window wide, he places the tin next to Ricky's coffee. "Best ashtray I've got," he says. "And sorry about the draught. I don't mind you lighting up, but the smoke detector might have something to say."

"You're sure?" queries Ricky, as Patrick finally sits down.

"Sure, I'm sure. As you know, I ask smokers to go outside normally. But the circumstances are some way from normal."

"Agreed." Ricky conjures some cigarettes and a lighter. Patrick watches him spark up. There's more sunlight in the kitchen than at the front door, and under close scrutiny an aurora of bruising remains around Ricky's eyes. Sure, and his nose is also bent all to fuck, but its crookedness actually seems to suit him.

"Yep," says Ricky, exhaling smoke through his nostrils and apparently reading Patrick's mind. "Your old man's a fucker, right enough." He places his cigarette packet on the table, with the lighter on top. Then he meets Patrick's eye with a steely look. "Being a fucker must run in families, I reckon."

Patrick sighs. He rubs the back of his neck. "I don't know your da all that well. But sure, I know enough to know that he's a fucker, too."

Ricky takes another drag on his smoke. He grins a grin at Patrick. It isn't a nice grin. "Guess you're right about that."

Patrick hunkers forward in his seat. He lifts his coffee mug, pleased to note that his hand isn't shaking. "Ricky," he says evenly, "I'm thankful you wanted to meet, because I've got stuff I need to say. But I'm sure you have as well. So which of us is going to go first?"

Ricky's eyes don't leave him. "You, I reckon," he replies.

"Alright then," says Patrick. He sets down his mug, and uses the index finger of one hand to begin numbering off the points he wants to make on the fingers of the other. "Firstly, thanks for saving me from a hiding the day England played Brazil. And thanks for being my best mate from that point up until last weekend."

"Yeah, right – very touching."

"I'm going to hear you out when you say your piece," replies Patrick. "How about you do the same for me?"

Ricky takes a deep, deep drag on his cigarette. He gestures with his hand for Patrick to carry on. Patrick continues counting off points on his fingers.

"Second, as good a mate as you've been, I resent how you've made me complicit in your cheating on Caroline so many times over however long it's been. All this bollocks about having to go off and resolve a labour shortfall somewhere, without ever having the good grace to front up about what's really been going on. You've completely pissed me off at times. And you've pissed Vince off too. He can read the lie of the land equally well as me."

Patrick pauses then. He looks to Ricky for a reaction. He gets one of sorts when Ricky briefly averts his eyes.

"Which is another thing," continues Patrick, his tallying-up finger hovering stationary in mid-air. "Vince has got more about him than you and I credit him for. He's pulled a bird for fuck's sake."

"Yeah – a fit one, come to that."

Momentarily, a chance opens up. Ricky and Patrick break into grins. They exchange a look of mutual pride in Vince. There's a brief, fleeting opportunity to swap some banter – to joke a little bit about Vince and his bird.

An opportunity to be mates.

But then the grins fade, and the shutters come down.

"Have you finished yet?" asks Ricky. He draws down another deep lungful of smoke before mashing out his cigarette in Patrick's old sweet tin.

Patrick's given up counting on his fingers, and he has his hands splayed across the table. "Sure, I could leave it there," he says. "But there is something else."

"Go on then."

"Alright, well it's this: I love your wife." He pauses for effect, and to take a deep breath. "I love your wife deeply. I think she's the most adorable woman in the world. And anyone, feeling as I do, would act on those feelings when you show every sign of not loving her as once you did."

"I've never stopped loving Caz," Ricky snaps back.

"I'm not saying you have. But you showed some signs. Because shagging other birds is showing some signs, yeah?"

To his credit, Ricky does hang his head.

"What I did wasn't right," says Patrick. "But it was definitely natural, given how I feel about Caroline. And yet sure, all of that said, she is your wife, you have got a son, and I have grown up with both of you – and Vince – as my very best mates. So if you are trying to repair your marriage, I won't be hindering your efforts. Good luck with it – sincerely. I'll stay well away.

"But remember to treat her well, Ricky. Or you'll have me to answer to – one fucker to another."

Ricky already has another cigarette out. He pauses on the verge of lighting it, seemingly ready to reply. But Patrick isn't done yet. "Something else," he says. "We may not be mates anymore. But we do have Vince in common. And quite a lot of money in a fund for him – we have that in common, too." Patrick picks up his latest winnings between two fingers and a thumb. "Quite a lot of money, with a little bit more to come. At some future point, when these wounds have begun to heal a bit, we are going to have to discuss the money properly."

Ricky nods a perfunctory agreement while lighting his cigarette.

"And that's me done," says Patrick. "If you came here for an apology, sure you can have one, but the fact I haven't said sorry so far should tell you how sincerely I'd mean it."

Ricky pushes his chair a short distance back. He crosses his left leg so that the ankle rests on top of his right knee. He leans an arm on the chair back, and cups the side of his face in the palm of one hand. For a short while, he just sits and smokes thoughtfully. Ash falls onto his funereal overcoat, and he makes no effort to brush bit off.

"I'm glad you haven't apologised," he finally says. "Caz told me you were noble – she said you were nobler than me. I thought it was a strange word to use – it's the sort of word Gareth would come out with – but I knew what she meant and I suppose that she was right. Caz is usually right."

Patrick shrugs. "I've no argument with that."

"She said the reason you were noble is that you came round to our house after we fought in the pub, and that you begged her to take me back."

"I've no argument with that either. Knowing as I did, that you were finishing with your other women, I did tell her she should take you back – as long as you were going to stay faithful this time."

Ricky blows smoke through partially clenched teeth. "I suppose I should be grateful for that."

Patrick only nods in reply.

"But the fact remains. You had sex with my wife."

And it was fucking great, thinks Patrick, trying to keep a smile off his lips. "Yes, I did," he says. "That fact will always remain. Sure, I can't frickin change it."

"No, you can't. You had sex with my wife, and I hate you for it. Two facts, then; and both will always remain."

Patrick doesn't answer; he merely nods some more, to say to Ricky that he gets it.

Ricky sighs, and stubs out his cigarette before it's fully smoked. "I came here," he says, "because I'm trying to make up with Caroline, and she said before I could make up with her, I had to make peace with you. And so that's what I came here to do, even though I thought we'd end up fighting.

"But I don't want to fight, Patrick, even though I hate you – and yes, I do hate you; I can't fucking help it. And despite you not wanting to say sorry to me, I do want to say sorry to you. I want to say sorry for punching you like that, when the way you'd behaved was no worse than the way I had."

"Apology accepted."

"And I hear you knocked out that evil bitch – the one who attacked Esme. I should thank you for that."

"Sure, but I was fighting my way out of a corner. Honestly, Ricky, I'm ashamed of myself for hitting a woman, even if she did deserve it."

Ricky's playing one-handed with his lighter, but shows no sign of lighting a third cigarette. "I should be more ashamed," he says. "I didn't hit Caroline last weekend, but I did threaten her, and one thing she certainly didn't deserve was that. Even though I hate you, I hate myself more for some of the things I said to her that night. If I could change one thing, I'd take back those words."

"Then we're both fuckers – just as we agreed earlier. We've both got bad shit we have to live with. But we're fuckers with twenty grand on account for Vince – our mutual best mate, who happens to have a few disadvantages in life. We're not all bad, Ricky, you and me. Even if we have fallen out."

Ricky continues toying with his lighter. He does so absentmindedly, while apparently thinking something over. Then, to Patrick's utmost surprise, Ricky steers the conversation down an entirely tangential route. "Anyway, I heard you got some help when you were scrapping in the shitter at The Lamb?"

Patrick utters a short laugh. "Did I ever," he replies. "Darren, the kid was called. Sure, I hadn't seen him before. Haven't seen him since. It's a weird one."

Ricky sparks up his lighter, but his cigarettes remain in their packet. He sits and stares at the flame, apparently transfixed by it, just as a caveman might be. "Surprising how many people come to The Lamb," he finally observes. "The place has more potential than you think."

"Came and had," replies Patrick.

"Say again?"

"Came to The Lamb. Had potential. Came and had, not come and has. The place has closed, remember?"

"Of course, you're right," says Ricky, snapping shut the lighter, as if to break some kind of spell. He gets to his feet, and actually claps Patrick on the shoulder. "Thanks for relaxing the smoking rules," he says. "And you're right – we will talk about Vince. Vince and his twenty grand. Once a few wounds have healed."

"Twenty grand, plus forty sheets," replies Patrick, idly gesturing once more at this morning's winnings. "Like I said, not a bad tally for a pair of fuckers like us."

"Maybe not," replies Ricky, a sad smile rising briefly to his lips and then dying again. "I'll see myself out," he adds, clapping Patrick on the shoulder for a second time as he walks on by.

Patrick searches for a reply. 'Bye' or 'See you' don't seem to cut it, given that he senses an era ending right here and now. But as to what he might say in response, he doesn't exactly know. And then, almost before Patrick realises, Ricky has gone. Patrick hastens to his front room window in time to see his one-time best mate sidle up to that big BMW like a Wild West bounty hunter sidles up to his horse. When Ricky climbs into the car without a backward glance, Patrick suddenly feels tearful and hollow. He has a sense of being old and used up, and it's more the case that he staggers back to his kitchen than he walks there. He quickly finishes off his coffee, before pouring a generous slug of whiskey into the empty mug. He knocks back half of it in one go, and doesn't wait long before raising the mug again.

The mug is at his lips when he hears a knock at the door. It's a distinctive knock – the same rat-a-tat-tat with which Ricky knocked previously. Patrick checks the table, thinking that maybe Ricky left his cigarettes behind, but of them he can see no sign.

When Patrick goes to the hall and opens the door, he finds Ricky standing there for the second time in twenty minutes. But Ricky looks different this time. This time he has a little half-smile on his lips – a little half-smile dipped in irony.

"Now look," says Ricky. "Do you fancy going for a pint? Maybe at that place with the piano – the place where they like you so much?"

"A pint? At The Beethoven Lounge?"

"Exactly, Patrick. I want to tell you about a plan I've hatched. A plan to keep The Lamb open."

And suddenly, it's as if Ricky bleeds back into full-colour reality. He still has on that oppressively dark undertaker's coat, but his face is alive with a story he wants to tell. Patrick suspects that Ricky has wanted to tell it for quite a little while. The silly bastard must have pulled off one of his coups.

This doesn't help, thinks Patrick. *We can't turn back the clock. Our being friends is damn' near impossible, and going for a pint won't help the situation with Caroline.*

But then he remembers how empty he felt just now, when Ricky walked out of his house and out of his life.

Patrick responds to Ricky's ever-broadening smile with one of his own. "Hang on, mate," he says. "Hang on while I just get my coat."

3.6) Closure, Plus 13 Days

Quite late on Friday morning, the bosses at the warehouse come looking for volunteers to work overtime that same afternoon. Gareth's supervisor asks him to put in two more hours on top of his regular eight-hour shift. Having clocked on at six, Gareth wouldn't finish, were he to agree the request, until four in the afternoon.

Normally, the overtime wouldn't be a problem. Gareth would be more than happy to agree. He needs the hours because he needs the money – as ever. And not only that, but in the two weeks which have passed since The Lamb and Musket closed down, he has nothing else to do. He goes out to work, and then he comes home again. The warehouse of his employment apart, Gareth doesn't go anywhere, and he doesn't meet people. Even his coaching of junior football has died a death nowadays, given that most of the parents didn't want to entrust their kids to a man facing charges of assault.

When he asks himself what the others from The Lamb are up to – how they're filling their evenings and weekends – Gareth reaches the depressing conclusion that they have, as a collective, moved on without him. They all talk to each other via the monstrosity of social media – he's sure that they do. Everyone is an online friend of everybody else. One of them will have chosen a new pub, and word will have got about online.

But nobody's thought to get in touch with Gareth. Clearly, the 'big man round these parts' – Mel's words – isn't so big that he can't be forgotten pretty quickly.

Or at least that's what he thought until midweek just gone, when he received a text from Ricky – of all the people – saying there was something they should talk about, and could Gareth meet up with him on Friday afternoon?

Gareth replied that they could, and then asked where.

'lamb & musket' Ricky replied, with a disregard for capitalisation which made Gareth wince. 'you must know the place. 3 o clock'

Which leaves the small matter of the eleventh-hour overtime requirement he's now being asked to fulfil.

"It's disappointing, Mr Gareth," says his supervisor, when Gareth politely declines to remain behind. "You're gettin' not so reliable as you used to be."

Gareth really shouldn't rise to such bait. And normally he wouldn't do so. But for whatever reason — maybe because his life at the moment is an even bigger drudge than before — he finds himself biting back. "Not so reliable. Hell's bells. When was the last time I turned down any overtime?"

"I'd have to check back."

"You'd have to check back a long way."

Gareth's supervisor flashes him a look of considerable irritation. The supervisor is a busy man, and he too shouldn't be bothered with petty arguments. But just like Gareth, he chooses to prolong the debate. "It's not only the overtime," he snipes. "You should have more consideration when we're givin' you time off for your court case next week."

"Oh, really? So, you're giving me time off? Is that what it's called when I legitimately book part of my holiday entitlement? Entitlement I haven't fully claimed in either of the past two years, I might add."

The supervisor's irritated look morphs into one of outright anger. But whatever reply he may have in mind will have to wait. Seeing a cluster of guys from C-Cell (Priority Pack Beta) heading off for their cigarette break, he begins chasing after them, no doubt hoping there's a volunteer or two among their ranks. He leaves Gareth with nothing more than a half-snarled, "We'll talk about this later."

They never do talk about it later, and Gareth clocks off just after two, aware that he may have moved higher on the list of people who'll be out the door in the event of downsizing or cutbacks.

Yet right now, he doesn't care too much about any such eventuality. Instead, he's thrilled to be meeting Ricky at The Lamb and Musket, and finds himself deeply intrigued by the prospect of reconnecting with his old life, which, deeply unsatisfactory though it was, was eminently more satisfactory than the one he's led for the past fortnight. And although he partially loathes himself for getting so excited about a meeting whose purpose Ricky refused to reveal by text, the loathing doesn't diminish his excitement by even the slightest degree.

When Ricky set The Lamb as a meeting place, Gareth assumed he meant the car park. But now, upon arrival, Gareth spots that the front doors are ajar. Ricky's car is parked up, and Patrick's van as well – which is an interesting development, especially since one of them was hell bent on killing the other just two weeks ago, on the night The Lamb closed down. A skip has been dropped in one corner of the car park, and Gareth notices that the outside plastic furniture has been thrown in, along with the other rubbish which had been accumulating here over the past couple of weeks.

Feeling utterly fascinated, but also harbouring no small measure of trepidation, Gareth parks his car and walks into the pub.

The lights are on, but the heating isn't. The shelves behind the bar are all but empty. Most of the tables and chairs have been pushed away to one corner, allowing the carpet to fully show its very considerable age. The place would feel totally desolate were it not that Patrick, Ricky, Vince and Malachy are sitting at the bar on four of the five stools which haven't been stacked with the rest of the furniture. The fifth barstool stands empty next to them.

Patrick, of course, has his stool tilted back, and a foot tucked under the rail. Ricky is wearing a smart suit. The others are in casuals. On the bar itself is a sleek, silver, push-button coffee machine. Malachy is examining it closely, pushing its buttons as if experimentally.

"Hello, Gareth," says Patrick. "He's here," he adds, unnecessarily, to the others.

"Great," says Vince.

"Just in time for coffee," adds Malachy.

Ricky walks towards him, shakes his hand, thanks him for coming, and then guides him to the remaining stool. "You'll like the coffee," he says. "It's good stuff – the kind we'll be serving here. I get great beans from an emporium in town."

"Serving here?" queries Gareth, as he sits himself down. Ricky responds with a sly wink, but no words.

"You're getting ahead of yourself, Richard," says Malachy. "You've been doing so all your life."

"Agreed," chimes Patrick.

"You haven't known me all my life," Ricky responds, quick as a flash. "And anyway, getting ahead of myself is still getting ahead – whatever you may think."

"Fair point," says Patrick, agreeably.

"And you are right about the coffee," says Malachy, pushing a steaming mug into Gareth's hand. "It is very good."

"Bloody right," says Ricky.

By way of getting the others' attention, Vince rattles a spoon against the side of his mug. "We need to… talk… properly… to Gareth," he says, once all eyes are upon him. "There are things… we need… to say."

"Clearly there are," Gareth replies, feeling bewildered, albeit in a good way. The mood among these guys is evidently more convivial than when they were punching and kicking and butting each other.

"You're correct, mate" says Ricky to Vince. "There are things we need to say. Alright Gareth, you'll remember we had an altercation among ourselves back on closing night."

"I could scarcely forget."

"Well, we'd like to thank you," chips in Malachy, "for helping keep such peace as was able to be kept."

"You're welcome. And – what? – you're all friends again, now?"

A grin breaking out on his face, Ricky lights up a cigarette. "I've wanted to smoke in here for years," he says, "so I'd better take the opportunity while I still can." Then his face clouds over a little. "It's too soon to say we're all friends again, but I've forgiven Mackey Senior for busting open my face. Meantime, Vince has persuaded Mackey Junior and me to work on resolving our differences."

"And we won't lie to you," adds Patrick. "When Ricky says work on our differences, work is what he means. Our differences were, and remain, considerable."

"But maybe less considerable than they were," replies Ricky, taking a deep drag on his cigarette.

"Sure, that's agreed," says Patrick.

"I think I understand," says Gareth, proceeding with caution. "There were a lot of rumours flying around, post-fight on closing night, about what your differences might be."

"Indeed," says Malachy, with a withering glance for the pair of them. "But Richard and Patrick are, as they say, working on it."

"The other thing I shouldn't let pass without mention," says Patrick, "is the further rumpus I got into at the end of the night. I know you all arrived after the fireworks, but it's noted that you were among the group of people who came to my assistance in the shitter. So thank you for that, as well."

"It was no trouble." Gareth takes a first sip from the coffee Malachy passed him. It's okay, but he finds it bitter. He'd rather have tea, like he has at home, and like Melanie used to make him when he came here and didn't want too much beer because he was chairing a campaign meeting. He sets the mug down and asks, "Did any of you land in trouble with the police."

Three of them – Patrick, Ricky, Malachy – immediately burst out laughing. And after a few seconds, Vince joins in. "No, Gareth, sorry" Malachy chuckles eventually. "We were only talking about this before you arrived. We've all had our fights and aggro, sure we have, but you're the only one who has to answer for yours – to the official authorities at any rate."

To Gareth, it seems deeply unfair that it's he alone who's facing punishment for hitting out at someone. "Sure, Gareth, we are really sorry," says Patrick, without looking sorry at all. "How is your coffee, by the way?"

"It's great," he lies.

"Ricky," says Vince. "You… get it… now… To show Gareth."

"Sure will," says Ricky, heading behind the bar, where he stamps out his cigarette on the linoleum floor before rummaging around on a low shelf where some glasses were previously kept.

"Show me what?" asks Gareth, with a look first at Malachy, and then at Patrick, both of whom respond only with innocent smiles.

"Here you are," says Ricky, coming towards him with something which is smooth and shiny, and not entirely flat. "You must recognise this beauty."

Ricky holds up the object for Gareth to see clearly. It's a bent-up number-plate. It's *the* bent-up number plate – the one from the crash. Gareth remembers, very clearly, the second sequence of letters: GTT.

Gareth The Twat, he thinks, staring with dismay at this new reminder of the day he embarked on Cash for Crash and fulfilled only the Crash part of the concept.

"Okay, and what?" he asks, getting to his feet. "You've got me here for a joke at my expense?"

"Please," says Vince, sensing his upset.

"Sure, we're cool," says Patrick.

"Everything's okay, Gareth," says Malachy. "But it is time the boys put you out of your misery."

"You see," says Ricky, wearing the world's biggest grin, "what do you suppose GTT stands for?"

"Well, I had a few ideas."

"You did, I know. You told us all about them. But rather than 'Gareth The Twat', the letters actually stand for George Tiberius Timkin." Ricky swaps delighted looks with the others, while giving Gareth a moment to let the news sink in. "Just think, Gareth, you crashed that poxy old heap into a car belonging to George Timkin, owner and chief executive of the Hippy Hops Pub Company."

Another pause. Another moment for Gareth to figure things out – to make a few connections.

"And not only did you crash into George's car, but you did so when he was being chauffeured by a leggy blonde who I couldn't help notice looked less than half his age. You'll remember, won't you, that they were both at the cop shop when me and Vince picked you up? Well, it turns out that the woman is George's girlfriend, Gareth, and George was deep in conflab with the local plod because he was trying to secure their discretion about it all. So, have a think about this for a moment. George Timkin has a fit-as-fuck girlfriend whose existence he wants to keep a secret. It's a revelation which would prove very grave news to George's wife – as I've been at pains to point out to him in recent days."

"Very grave news, I'm sure," adds Patrick, shaking his head in mock solemnity. "Very grave news, indeed."

"And as you'll appreciate," continues Ricky, "our learning that George has a secret girlfriend does give us a certain degree of leverage over him. Which is why he's agreed to abort the sale of this pub – so beloved by us all – to the Shop City group of supermarkets."

"It's also why The Lamb is therefore staying open," says Patrick. "All thanks to your clumsy act of genius, Gareth, and Ricky's conniving brilliance."

"All of that pissing about with campaign groups and posters," says Malachy. "And then you went and smashed up the fella's Mercedes while he was in compromising company. The long arm of coincidence has reached out, Gareth, and given you an almighty hug."

"Boom," says Vince, and the others all laugh.

"Okay, then," replies Gareth, noting the absence of Derek from these proceedings. "Who's going to be running the place?"

"Us," answers Ricky.

"Us?"

"Me and Vince and Patrick. You see, at first, I thought I could simply take over the leasehold and the licence from Derek. I thought I'd run the place with Caz – that's Caroline, my wife – believing that the idea would bring us closer together. But then later, when I was feeling less deluded, I realised there were better ways of shoring up my marriage – and my marriage certainly does need shoring up, as I'm sure you'll know from those rumours you say you heard. It also occurred to me that in a year or two, when George Timkin has either shored up or terminated his own marriage, we'll be in a less powerful position to stop him reinstating his plans to sell this place.

Ricky places the bent-up number plate down on the bar. He lights another cigarette before he continues.

"So, while my bargaining power with Mr Timkin remains high, I've persuaded him to sell the Lamb and Musket to us. The whole thing – the building and the land – to me, Vince and Patrick. We've got a bit of money set aside between us, and we'll be taking out a small mortgage into the bargain. We'll get the place properly done up, we'll get the old crowd back in, and we'll attract a new crowd too. We'll soon have business booming."

"I'm sure you will," replies Gareth, trying to come to terms with events.

"Only we will need a good manager. Patrick and I both have other business interests which are too lucrative simply to give up – at least for the moment. Vince will play an active part day-to-day at The Lamb, but his head turns to popcorn at times, and he can't do it all by himself."

"And we will be honest, Gareth," says Patrick, taking his turn to explain matters. "You weren't our first choice for this."

"Me... what?"

"Sure, our first choice was Mel. But as she and Vince now have a scene going on – a romantic scene, as it were – she thinks it's better the two of them have separate careers. You know – not be in each other's pockets all the time."

"Not that she's averse," adds Ricky, "to nipping in and giving you a few pointers."

Gareth picks his coffee back up. He takes a sip. He'd definitely prefer tea. "Let me get this absolutely straight," he says. "You're buying The Lamb and Musket, and you want me to be manager."

Vince lets out a big sigh, and when the others look to him he says, "I thought... I was the... slow one."

Patrick and Malachy burst out laughing. Nor can Ricky keep a smile off his face, but he retains enough self-control to add, "Look at it this way, Gareth: you're currently under-employed, relative to your intelligence. As well as being smart, you're honest and reliable. Also, you know a bit about accounting, and you're interested in beer. The locals all like you, and you're in with the real ale crowd. There are courses we can send you on to learn specifically about the licensed trade. Besides which, Mel will help when she can, she says.

Gareth looks at the faces of the three men – each a decade younger than he – who are suggesting he manages their pub. Given how desolate his life has been these past couple of weeks, the idea certainly has some appeal. Yet Gareth freely admits to having made some bad career choices, and wonders whether he's on the verge of yet another. He suspects that Ricky's main motive in buying The Lamb is to show everyone – once again – just how clever he is. And maybe Patrick and Vince are in it only to keep together a friendship which has looked close to breaking point of late. Also, as to this idea of Vince being involved day-to-day, how will that work if Vince is part owner and Gareth is manager? Hell's bells – who will actually be running the pub?

But on the other hand, Ricky and Patrick both have a head for business. They seem to have money. They have nice cars. Who's to say that they're ideas about The Lamb won't work out?

In his confusion, Gareth casts a glance at Mackey Senior. "Are you part of the operation?" he asks.

"Not formally," Malachy replies, giving Gareth a shrewd look back. "I'm going to be involved, short term, as unofficial security detail. It transpires that my son here isn't the only member of The Lamb's wider community to have experienced conflict with the three characters who got their comeuppance in the toilets a fortnight since. And sometimes, when the long arm of coincidence reaches out, you have to snap the fucking thing off at the wrist. I'm taking on that job, should the need arise and those characters come back for more."

"I see," replies Gareth.

"It's a good arrangement," adds Ricky, his hand feeling for his misshapen nose, "Malachy's handy on the security side."

"But sure, Richard, you can hold your own just as well," replies Malachy, before turning his attention back to Gareth. "There is another reason why I'm here today. If you are interested in this job, then there's going to be a conversation about money – about wages and benefits. I'm here to represent you in any such conversation, Gareth – to ensure fair play. Because if there's one thing you're bad at, it's acting in your own best interests. And you need someone who will act in your own best interests when you're talking to the three fuckers here."

Gareth looks again at the trio of younger men. They all look intent and focused. Not just Ricky and Patrick; Vince also. Vince especially, come to that.

"And going forward," adds Malachy, "there may be other times when you require me to mediate, informally of course. They're a devilish jumble of personalities, these boys. But we can make this work for the good of everyone involved."

Gareth's beginning to think that just maybe they can. Hell's bells.

"How about it?" asks Patrick. "Are you interested, Gareth? Do you want to talk turkey with my da in your corner?"

Gareth picks up the bent-up piece of number plate. He turns it over in his hands, and looks at it for a few seconds with no small sense of wonder.

"By the way," says Ricky, "a friend of mine – a senior officer from the local police force– will be putting in a word for you at your court appearance next week. That applies whether you take our job or not – he'll use his influence just the same. He doesn't reckon your punishment will be all that heavy."

Gareth puts the number plate back down. He looks at the three faces again, and at Malachy's as well. He takes both a pause and a deep breath while he gets ready to assert himself – to show the others that he can act in his own best interests. Then he jumps in at the deep end. "I'd be happy to talk about your job," he says. "But as your prospective new manager, is there any chance of some tea? I'm no fan of the coffee, sorry to say, wherever it is that the beans are from."

THE END

Other Books by Richard Cunliffe

All These Nearly Fights

Fault on Both Sides (The sequel to *All These Nearly Fights*)

How to Buy a Car (Non-fiction)

Printed in Great
Britain
by Amazon